Mercy of a Rude Stream

Volume I

A STAR SHINES OVER MT. MORRIS PARK

HENRY ROTH

Picador USA | New York

Picador® is a U.S. registered trademark and is used by St. Martin's Press under license from Pan Books Limited.

Design by Jaye Zimet

Library of Congress Cataloging-in-Publication Data

Roth, Henry.
        Mercy of a rude stream / Henry Roth.
                p.   cm.
        ISBN 0-312-11929-1
        1. Immigrants—United States—Fiction.   2. Boys—United States—
Fiction.   I. Title.
PS3535.0787M47   1994
813'.52—dc20   93-37270
                                                                      CIP

First published in the United States by St. Martin's Press

First Picador USA Edition: January 1995
10   9   8   7   6   5   4   3   2   1

To Larry Fox
''So here's a hand my
trusty friend.''

THE FAMILY OF IRA STIGMAN
Ira's Mother's Family Tree

married)
children ⊤

Nathan (Ira's granduncle)

Zaida (Ben Zion Farb) — Baba
11 children: 9 survived
5 daughters, 4 sons

Leah (Mom) — Chaim (Pop)

Ira

Mamie — Jonas

Stella   Pola

Genya (died in concentration camp) — Leibel

Son

daughter (died in concentration camp)

Saul

Moische/ Morris/ Moe (Ira's "other" favorite uncle) — Ida Link

Ella — Meyer D

Max F   Harry

Sadie — Max S

Ira's Father's Family Tree

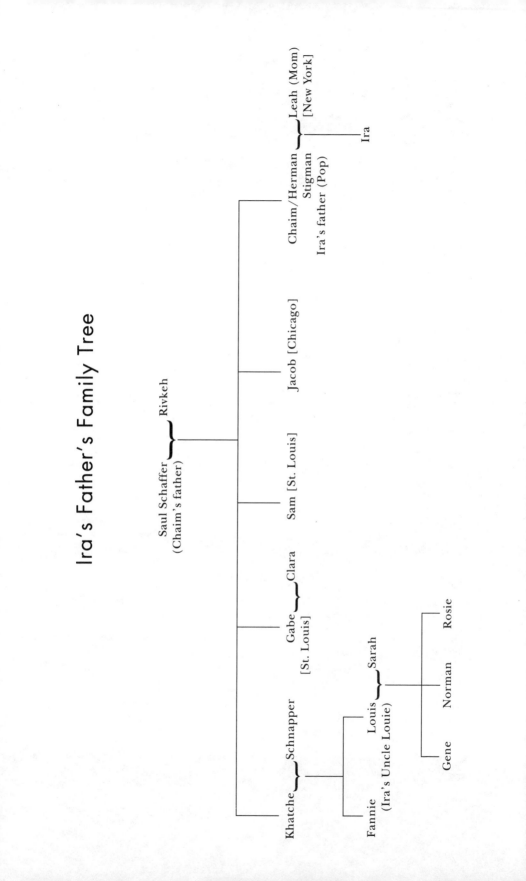

I have ventur'd,
Like little wanton boys that swim on bladders,
This many summers in a sea of glory,
But far beyond my depth. My high-blown pride
At length broke under me, and now has left me,
Weary and old with service, to the mercy
Of a rude stream that must for ever hide me.
Henry VIII, III.ii

Not to dare quibble with peerless Will, I still question how 'tis that his little wanton boys on bladders are first descried swimming in a sea of glory, and lastly being swept away by a rude stream—which suggests a torrent, not a sea, unless of course an ocean stream, like the Gulf Stream, but that's scarcely rude. Tide, the alternate word, might have been more exact, but not nearly so felicitous.

Also I would like to observe that while his use of the word mercy is ironic, mine is not. It is literal. The rude stream did show me Mercy.

CONTENTS

P A R T   O N E

I

Midsummer. The three incidents would always be associated in his mind, more durably, more prominently than anything else during that summer of 1914, his first summer in Harlem. How remarkable, too, that the coming of Mom's kin, the move to Harlem, and the ominous summer of 1914 should all have coincided—as if all his being and ways were undermined by the force of history disguised in the simple fact of the accession of new relatives. A thousand times he would think vainly: If it had only happened a few years later. Everything else could be the same, the war, the new relatives; if only he could have had, could have lived a few more years on the Lower East Side, say, until his Bar Mitzvah. Well . . .

It was in August [Ecclesias, or *m'aivtate*], the pair of newspaper hawkers charged into 115th Street bawling headlines in Yiddish, dissonant and confused. Each vendor toted a portentous accordion of Yiddish newspapers slung from a leather strap across his shoulders. "Wuxtra! Wuxtra!" each bellowed: "*Malkhumah!*" followed by a garble of Yiddish. The eight-year-old Ira had just come into the front room where his grandparents were seated next to the windows in the shade of the awnings, enjoying a breath of fresh air. Like them, his attention was drawn to the shouting below, and he looked down into the street for the cause. Beneath the window, the sun glared on the torrid sidewalk, shimmered on the black macadam. And the street, so lethargic and quiet until a minute ago, was now disturbed by two men flushed crimson roaring a hoarse gibberish of which only one word was intelligible—and repeated and repeated: "*Malkhumah! Malkhumah!*" War! Out of neighboring doorways of houses and stores came a scattering of buyers, some hurrying after the yammering pair of vendors, others waiting for them. The buyers frowned at the headlines, displayed them to one another, spoke, gesticulated, called up to people leaning out of windows.

"He cries war," said Zaida.

And, "Woe is me," said Baba.

"What is that coin I see them paying for the newspaper?" Zaida asked.

"I think it's a nickel, Zaida," Ira answered. "Five cents."

"This kind?"

"Yeh."

"Run, child. Fetch me one." He handed the nickel to Ira, who with coin in hand sped down the two flights of stairs to the scorching street, pursued the vendors, still bawling their wares. He proffered the nickel; the newspaper was whipped out in exchange. And with the hectic cry still pursuing him, Ira raced back to the house, mounted the stairs with eager haste, and came panting into the front room.

"Indeed, war," said Zaida after a glance at the lowering Yiddish headlines. "They're slaughtering one another again."

"Who?" Baba said.

"Austria and Serbia."

"*Oy, gewald!*" Baba groaned. "My poor daughter. My poor Genya, and with child again in the midst of that peril. The Lord protect them. The Lord have mercy on them!"

"Madmen! Destroy! Destroy! Nothing else will suffice," Zaida fumed. "Fortunate, we escaped in time from that charnel house. Praise His Holy Name."

Thus the Great War came to Harlem: roaring news vendors hawking warm newsprint in the hot street; the diffident youngster offering a nickel to the sweating, red-faced herald of disaster. . . .

II

It was July of that year, still one month before the outbreak of war. Mom's immediate kin were due to arrive in America in another few days. From the little hamlet of Veljish in Austria-Hungary, whence they had set forth, they would soon take up residence in Harlem. Their apartment, a large one with six rooms, only two flights up, and supplied with steam heat, electricity and hot running water—and even striped awnings above the two front-room windows—was located in the middle of the block—in the middle of 115th Street, between Park and Madison Avenues. It was called in Yinglish a *shaineh b'tveen,* meaning—literally—a lovely between. It was not only a thoroughly Jewish and congenial block, but one most conveniently located to shopping as well. Just east of it was the Jewish pushcart district that found shelter under the wide steel overpass of the New York Central Railway on Park Avenue. There the immigrants could haggle freely in Yiddish with the peddlers. The apartment also had the additional advantage of being across the street from the apartment of Tanta Mamie and her family (undoubtedly that was another reason why Ira's two Americanized uncles, Moe and Saul, had chosen the place). Mamie could speak to Baba or Zaida, or one of her immigrant siblings—and they to her—from window to window, without anyone leaving the house.

Meanwhile, Mom, in anticipation of the joy that being near her family would bring, and Pop, in anticipation of the rewards that becoming an independent milkman might bring (made possible by moving close to the milk-shed, the freight yards on West 125th Street), abandoned their breezy East Side eyrie four flights up on the corner of Avenue D and 9th Street, and with their eight-year-old son, Ira, moved, united in hope, to Harlem. In her eagerness to be near her kin, and still stay within her husband's limited means, Mom had resigned herself to living in three rooms "in the back," the cheapest she could find in "Jewish Harlem," three sweltering little rooms, on 114th Street, just east of Park Avenue. Into this cramped, airless little flat, the Stigman family moved as soon as school was over and summer vacation began.

The immigrants arrived: Mom's father and mother; Zaida, bearded, orthodox Jew, already a patriarch in his mid-fifties, discontented and irascible; Baba, his patient and shrunken wife (she had loved her spouse greatly once, Mom said, but his all-consuming selfishness had drained her of affection). She had borne him a progeny of eleven children. The last two, twins, would have been Ira's age, Mom told him, had they survived, but they died in infancy. Of the nine remaining, five were daughters and four were sons. All had now emigrated to America, except Genya, second child, Mom's younger sister. Most attractive, according to Mom, of all of Zaida's brood, Genya had married a man earning a fine income as an expert appraiser of lumber. They both decided to stay on in Austria-Hungary with their infant son.

Oh, the things that happen, Ecclesias, the things that happen, to me, to us, to my beloved wife and me, this 14th of January 1985, to our heirs, to our country, to Israel, the things that happen. My good friend, the writer Clarence G, was wont to storm at generational novels (he had Thomas Mann's work in mind). "I hate generational novels, don't you? They drive me crazy!" he would exclaim. I think I agree with him, but this is different, Ecclesias; how different I have yet to discover myself. . . .

Nine surviving offspring, five daughters and four sons, and all but Genya in America (Genya and daughter later vanished in a Nazi death camp. Husband and son, because of their shared expertise, were allowed to live—and to watch the two women herded into a lorry, and to hear the young girl cry: "Papa, I'm too young to die!"). All but Genya were in America. Mom came over first, brought here by Pop, who, in common with other immigrant husbands already in the new land, scrimped and saved, and in his case, stinted to the point of alimentary collapse, until he had accumulated enough to buy steerage passage for his wife and infant son. "We saw leviathans, great sea-creatures following the ship," Mom tried vainly to awaken Ira's memory. "You don't remember? And you cried for milk, for which we had to pay extra: milk, the only word you could say in Polish."

After Mom came to America, Mamie followed, Baba's third child and Mom's second younger sister, mettlesome and assertive Tanta Mamie. Once here, she boarded with Zaida's brother, Grand-uncle Nathan, a thriving diamond merchant of somewhat flawed scruples. The poor girl was virtually indentured in his household as a domestic—until she found work in the garment industry, and thus earned enough to rent a room of her own in Manhattan. Almost at the same time she met her future husband, Jonas, an immigrant of equal acculturation as herself, a gnome of a man who worked in the adjacent building as a cloak's operator, "by clucks." At first, he courted her at lunchtime, then after-hours, when he would escort her to her room, and at length, to show serious intent, took her to the Yiddish theater on Second Avenue on Saturday night to hear the famous Yiddish thespian, Tomash-evsky. They married, set up housekeeping, not on the East Side, where Mom and Pop already lived, but in a small apartment in Jewish Harlem, in the same *b'tveen* where Baba and Zaida and their unmarried children were later to reside.

Next in order of birth, and next to emigrate to the United States, was Moe, Baba's fourth child and first-born son. Unlike his sister Mamie before him, Moe boarded with Ira's family, by now living on 9th Street, high above the horse-car trolley tracks on Avenue D. Moe eschewed the needle trades; he preferred to work in heavy industry: he applied to steel fabricating shops, to a storage battery plant, but was turned away because he was a Jew. He found work in a café, and there toiled inordinate hours as a busboy, regarded in those years as the necessary apprenticeship to becom-ing a waiter. Of above-average height, for the epoch, though not tall, Moe was solid and robust in build (he had worked in logging camps in the Carpathian forests). Blue-eyed, fair, anything but the "typical" East European Jew in appearance, Moe was the guileless, outspoken country bumpkin. Endowed with Mom's kindliness, her

open-handedness, her lenience and her ready laughter, Moe was
unaffectedly fond of his first-born nephew, first-born grandchild
of Ben Zion Farb, the patriarch. Moe, or Morris, the name he
preferred, would return from the sawdust-strewn café where he
worked, trudging home on a summer night, to the big corner house
on Avenue D; and with his nephew hanging on to his hand, make
for the candy store at the foot of the house. There he would buy
five or six or more penny Hershey chocolate bars, and bestowing
one of these on his clamorous nephew, strip the wrappers off the
others, and crowd the dainties one after another into his mouth,
until for a minute he radiated chocolate spokes, like misplaced rays
of the Statue of Liberty.

Moe was the second of Mom's immediate kin to make the
crossing (Utter rustic! In Hamburg, where the young simpleton
had to stay in a lodging house overnight before boarding ship the
next morning, he blew out the gaslight ere he went to bed, and
had it not been for the timely arrival of a bed-fellow, Moe's journey
to America would have ended then and there).

Next came Saul, devious, surreptitious, hysteric Saul, who also
became a busboy like his brother, but unlike his brother, as soon
as he reached the status of waiter, he spurned working in Jewish
restaurants. The best hotels, the most exclusive dining rooms—
where the "white slaves" worked, as Pop called the German waiters,
when he himself became a waiter, too—were the only places Saul
would deign to wait at table.

The sun reflected off the windshield of a passing car. The light burst into
lurid spectrum, shattering the darkness of Ira's half-closed eyes focused
on the computer screen. Ira mused on the meaning of the Syrian-controlled
PLO hit squads reported by radio to be slipping into other countries for
the purpose of assassinating Arafat's henchmen. And the mind with its
involuntary shorthand signaled: Arafat was cozying up to Hussein, and
he to Iraq, while Syria was to Iran. Did that mean Arafat was becoming mollified, resigned to reaching a compromise with Israel? Doubtful.
Highly.

Saul strove after all things American: "Especially loose *shiksas*," Mom murmured to her young son in embarrassment. "It's not seemly." Among the scanty images of his uncle, incubated over the years since childhood, two were preserved intact: Saul's vindictive swatting, with a rolled-up copy of the *Journal American,* of a couple of copulating horseflies on the sunny granite rocks of Mt. Morris Park. By some chance Ira had accompanied Saul, and the younger, lately arrived uncle, Max, to the park. . . . Another time, of an evening, as Ira stood by, listening: In reply to Pop's proposal that he and Saul both pool a couple of hundred dollars each, and as partners invest in a certain luncheonette, Saul bragged, lifting a reckless, yet Semitic, face to the light of the street lamp: "I've spent more than that on a whore for a night."

"Shah!" Pop exclaimed, shocked—and cautionary of the young ears heeding.

These four siblings, Mom and Mamie, Moe and Saul, were already in the New World. Some time in the spring of 1914, Zaida sold his little *gesheft* in Veljish, his little general store, and used the proceeds to defray the cost of second-class passage to America. Second-class passage was much more expensive than third-class, and the expense of transporting six adult passengers practically exhausted Zaida's resources. But since only thus could he assure himself and his family a kosher diet during the crossing, the six arrived second-class. They came to America in style, though almost penniless. Zaida would rely on his two sons in America to take care of him—and of Baba—until his immigrating offspring could help shoulder the burden, which they did, unquestioningly.

Two parents and their four children arriving in the new world: two sons, two daughters, all four unmarried.

At one stroke the number of Zaida's and Baba's offspring in America was doubled; at one stroke Ira acquired not only two grandparents, but four new uncles and aunts. Six close relatives all at once. It was a little bewildering at first.

Ella was the oldest of these four new siblings. Quiet, plain, self-effacing, she was extraordinarily gifted in needlework. (Years later, Ira would muse on what these, like millions of other immigrants, might have achieved in the new world, given the least guidance,

the least assistance.) Products of Ella's handiwork were the delightful Hebrew samplers on the walls of the new apartment, the only
adornments other than savings bank calendars. Ella's were the
traditional lions of Judah rampant over the tablets of the Law
embroidered on the sapphire velvet of the bag in which Zaida
stored his phylacteries and prayer shawl; hers the charming gold-
threaded designs on the scarlet velvet *matzah* caddy that graced the
table on the Passover.

Next in age, and quite unlike her older sister temperamentally
and in many other respects, was Sadie. She was very homely; she
was rambunctious; she was rashly impulsive and willful. She was
illiterate as well. Perhaps due to her extremely defective vision,
which, in the hamlet where the family dwelled, had gone uncor-
rected for lack of an oculist, Sadie was the only illiterate one of
Zaida and Baba's brood of nine surviving children. So myopic was
she that twice she poked her head through the panes of closed
windows in the Harlem apartment. Taken by Mom to be fitted for
glasses, when Sadie was asked to read the eye chart, she began a
pathetic alphabetic chant of "Ah, beh, tseh, deh . . ." Commented
Mom dryly: "The oculist understood what he had to do." Later,
when she was engaged to be married to Max S, a waiter, from
whom her illiteracy was concealed, Sadie, by now fitted with eyeglasses, gave herself over to an earnest attempt to learn to read a
little English under her juvenile nephew's tutelage. The effort was
vain. Fitful, spasmodic, she seemed unable to focus on print—and
after awhile, the adolescent Ira was unable to focus on teaching
her. Her twitchings, her flutterings of helplessness aroused him—
which she noticed—and sessions were suspended.

After her vision was corrected, Sadie too displayed exceptional
manual aptitude. Following her initiation into the ways of the
American shop (and the ways of getting there and home), she
became highly adept in the making of feather ornaments for ladies'
hats, earning by piecework higher wages than Ella did with her
fancy embroidery. Her very good wages, after deductions for room
and board to the common household fund, left her a tidy surplus;
part of this, of course, she deposited in the savings bank, and part

of it she spent on finery and cosmetics. It was the cosmetics that drove her older brother Saul beside himself. Not only long since Americanized, but well acquainted with the subdued elegance of the suave patrons he waited on in the high-toned hotel dining rooms—and the high-tone harlots he pined for—he objected violently to the strong perfumes, the thick shingles of face powder, the lurid rouge with which his sister bedizened her features. A frenetic he was, and his sister, in her willfulness, a match for him: fierce spats broke out between them, in which "whore" and "whore-monger" were bandied about, until such a vortex of acrimony was reached, especially on a Sunday, when all were still in bed, that the other siblings were drawn in, egging on or protesting. The apartment became a *babel*, an uproarious *babel* in Polish, Yiddish, Slavic and broken English, a *babel* only Zaida could quell. And quell it he did, wading in with cane and *yarmulka* and flailing adversaries and adherents right and left without distinction. Two or three of these hideous squabbles Ira witnessed: Impecunious little *shnorer* that he was, Sunday mornings were the best times for him to visit Zaida and Baba's house, to collect a few coins, the small gratuities of kinship. Once, he entered the house just as his uncle Saul leaped out of bed, and rushing over to Sadie's bed, slapped her; she retaliated in kind. Instantly the apartment became bedlam. Poor, patient, wrinkled Baba retreated to the kitchen murmuring to herself unhappily; and Zaida, uttering towering imprecations, restored order in customary fashion: with cane and *yarmulka*.

So there was Ella, there was Sadie, and what hatred she and Pop harbored for each other! *Die blindeh,* he dubbed her: the blind one—because she stood her ground, refused to be intimidated by his wrath, as Mom so often was in those early years. Not in the least cowed, Sadie would fling back at her brother-in-law: *Meshuggener hint!* Mad dog! (And too often, alas, Ira secretly agreed with her.) "Why didn't I learn to read?" she confided bitterly to her young instructor during those fruitless and now ambiguous sessions, when it was becoming all too evident that his flighty, twitching pupil couldn't curb her restlessness, nor Ira his carnal hopes. "I didn't learn to read," Sadie said, "because I was sent to be a little serving-maid in your parents' home in Tysmenitz where they lived with your father's father—on *his* bounty. At a time when I should have received some schooling I was there instead, tending to you, an infant." Her brown eyes behind thick glasses trained an angry gaze at her nephew; whose own glance wavered between distraction of her thick, plastery powdered nose and fierily rouged cheeks, and distraction of his guilty desires. "And do you know what your father would do to me, when your mother was heavy with you, when your mother was in labor, and I took care of the housework? He would fart in my face."

"Yeah?" Ira projected sympathy. Strings were a single strand; ropes were twined: ambivalence about the genuine: What if Baba's twins had lived, the boy and the girl, the girl, the girl his age to teach English to? Maybe . . .

There were Ella and Sadie. The former married Meyer D, owner of the then-thriving kosher butcher shop across the street, where Baba traded, and continued to trade when she realized Meyer was an eligible bachelor. He was a heavyset man, taciturn, quite middle-aged, his sole diversion apparently a game of pinochle played in a café on 116th Street. So Ella was married first, and then Sadie. She married the tall, slender Max S—who discovered too late, so well dissembled was it, that his bride was an illiterate (*Ut azoi und ut azoi*, ran the Yiddish ditty, *nahrt m'n uhp a khoosin*. "This way and that way the groom is duped." Max S made light of the revelation. He had found what he sought, a compatible, faithful and diligent Jewish wife.

Ira's two new uncles were the youngest members of his grandparents' family. Of the two, Max F was older than his brother Harry—and far more beguiling, whimsical and humorous. Average in height (for those times), Max was close-knit and well-proportioned; his eyes blue, his nose snub, Slavic, like Baba's—and like Mamie's too. His hair was chestnut in hue, and surpassingly thick and wavy. In addition to being ingenious, inventive, a great "fixer," Max was a self-styled Hero (It was one of the first English words that Max learned; his use of it puzzled Ira at first, who associated the word with a warrior of great daring. Only afterward

Ira realized that Max meant "*ein Heldt*," which in Yiddish didn't nec-
essarily signify a person of great valor, but a stalwart person, or
even one who was merely hale and hearty.). Max actually undertook
to prove he was a Hero—and an ingenious one as well: With a
contraption of hooks connected by cords to a heavy comb, he sank
the teeth of the comb into his dense locks, and engaging the hooks
at the other end under a weighty bureau, he lifted the bureau
from the floor. Could Samson himself brag of more heroic hair?

An hour after the new arrivals had installed themselves in the
apartment—it was to be Ira's earliest, earliest recollection of his
uncle Max—the young immigrant invited his boy-nephew to guide
him to the pushcart mart under the railroad overpass on Park
Avenue. There, he asked Ira to inquire as to the price of two small
carrots. They cost one cent. Max produced the copper, and Ira
made the purchase. How neatly, how deftly Max scraped the carrots clean with his penknife—and then proffered his nephew the
smaller of the two roots:

"But it's raw!" Ira drew back. "Nobody eats a raw carrot,
Uncle."

"*Ess, ess,*" Max urged (in Yiddish). "Taste. It's sweet." And to
Ira's surprise, so it was: sweet and crunchy. The memory, the
fading composite of the vaguely smiling Max, the produce on the
pushcarts, the penknife peeling a carrot, the warmth of summer,
and the contrast between the shadow under the huge steel canopy
of the railroad trestle and the bright sunlight on the sidewalk,
would condense for Ira into the first inference he was ever conscious of *as* inference: From that summery composite, he could
deduce the kind of life that was lived by Mom and her family, by
Zaida, Baba and the rest in the lethargic, *Galitzianer* hamlet named
Veljish. The moist, orangy, peeled carrot at the core of recollection
substantiated all that Mom had told him: about the meagerness of
rations, about the larder kept under lock and key, about Zaida's
autocratic sway, his precedence in being served, in being served
the choicest—and to satiety. As to his progeny, "The child who is
given good bread and butter ought not look for more." That was
Zaida's maxim.

III

And now would follow one of those episodes, the first of many Ira was ashamed of, that seemed to indicate the beginning of attrition of his identity, an episode that Ira always connected with his removal from the East Side to Harlem.

Shake your head in reproach, my friend; let your fingertips join in a cage, and ponder: You brought home for the first time in your public school career a report card marked C C C, unsatisfactory in deportment, in effort and in proficiency. It was so disgraceful a report card, you tried to inveigle Mom into signing it without Pop's seeing it, but she refused . . .

Harry, Ira's youngest uncle, was sixteen years old. Still regarded as a child by Baba—and his earnings not required toward the support of the prosperous household, to which five wage earners contributed, for Max too had found work—Baba was eager to have her youngest son enrolled in an American public school, and given the advantages of an American education—like those enjoyed by her oldest grandchild. Moreover, enrolled in the same school as Ira, the uncle could learn the routines and protocols of classroom attendance from his nephew.

Unfortunately for Harry, and for Ira too, by the time school opened in September, Mom and Pop had decided to move from 114th Street, east of Park Avenue, to 119th Street, east of Park Avenue. A difference of five blocks, yet the move was a fateful one. Not only were they relocating to a much less desirable *b'tveen*, a *goyisher b'tveen* instead of a Jewish *b'tveen;* but the school nearest Ira's house was an elementary school: P.S. 103 on the corner of 119th Street and Madison Avenue. It accepted children up to the sixth grade *only*, which meant that the oldest children in P.S. 103 averaged about twelve years of age—while Harry was already sixteen!

Why did this unfortunate situation come to pass? Because Mom had become unhappy with their first choice of rooms in Harlem. Not only were they small and sweltering. That could be endured. After all, the rooms did have hot running water, and would have steam heat in the winter, like Mamie's and Baba's. No, Mom had become unhappy because the rooms were "in the back." The view out of the windows was lifeless and unchanging; the same back-yards met the eye day after day. It reminded her too much of her old home in Veljish: dormant. Inanimate. She became despondent. She craved a window to lean out of and contemplate the changing scene below. She craved a dwelling with windows "in the front." Such had been their home on 9th Street. All the windows looked out on the front: On one side, Avenue D, full of movement of old and young, of people waiting on corners for horse-drawn trolley cars. Why, Woodrow Wilson himself had appeared on Avenue D doffing his stovepipe hat to the public on either hand. Only four flights down, you could see the light glint on his *zvicker*, the pince-nez eyeglasses the presidential candidate wore. You could see 9th Street out of the other windows. You could see the East River. Ah, a wonderful thing was a five-room flat on the corner. "I lacked only one thing," said Mom. "What nonsense: *lyupka*."

But front-room dwellings in Jewish Harlem were exorbitant—by Pop's standards. Everything Jewish was dear, dear because Jew-ish and dear in dollars and cents. Outside of Jewish Harlem, how-ever, rents dropped sharply, especially rents for cold-water flats. And Pop, intent on saving every nickel for his project as milkman-entrepreneur, decided to sacrifice a Jewish milieu for a cheaper rent. So outside of Jewish Harlem they moved: to a four-room cold-water flat, a flight up, "in the front." Their new residence was the five-story, dingy, gray and brown brick tenement that occupied the lot at 108 East 119th Street.

It was here, even if they had to give up certain amenities—hot running water, electricity, steam heat, private bathroom—it was here that their needs most nearly dovetailed: Mom had a window on the street to lean out of, Pop had to pay only $12 per month for rent. And miraculously, a block away on Lexington Avenue, there was a stable where he could put up his newly purchased old horse and milk-wagon. What a convenience, what an auspicious omen! What if their new home was on the borderline between Jewish and *goyish* Harlem? Jews would be sure to move there in the not-too-distant future. What if they had to use gas light for illumination, and not electricity? They were used to that on the East Side. What if the bathroom-toilet was not in the house, not intramural, but in the hall, and the bathtub looked like an immense green-painted tin trough set in a wooden coffin of matched boards, and the paint came off and stuck to your bottom in hot water? They had no hot running water anyway, and bathed in warm water from the kettle rarely. Rent was only $12 per month; that was the important thing. Mom had immediate access to a window on the street, Pop a convenient stable for his horse and milk-wagon.

But for all the satisfied needs and auspicious omens, only misfortune ensued. For Ira, misfortune was long lasting. It altered his entire life for the worse. For Harry it was short-term—painful, but brief. Had Baba not been so persuaded by her acculturated American son, Saul—with Pop to confirm him—that Harry would fare best under Ira's guidance, and instead of enrolling her youngest living offspring in P.S. 103, enrolled him in the large and conveniently located school on 116th Street west of Fifth Avenue, P.S. 86, a combined elementary and grammar school that went all the way to the eighth grade, the lanky stripling Harry might have passed relatively unnoticed among the fourteen- and fifteen-year-olds attending the school. And of much greater importance: He would have been in a school that was largely Jewish in composition, and at the very least, tolerant of the new immigrant. In P.S. 103 he became at once, from the moment of his appearance, the object of derision, of Irish derision (and what derision had a sharper edge?). He became the object of taunts and Jew-baiting: target of spitballs, rubberbands, blackboard erasers and pieces of chalk. That was inside the school. Outside the school, the target of bolts of horse manure and stones, and later on, in cold weather, of ice-filled or gravel-filled snowballs. Over and over again, in full view of his cringing, craven nephew (whose final recourse was to disown his kin, slink into a bystander role, even appear to participate in the hounding), his uncle would stand at bay attempting to drive off a swarm of maddening Irish gamins.

Apparently in despair of ever resolving the situation, Miss Flaherty, the principal, relieved Harry of regular classroom attendance, and gave him private lessons in English within the sanctuary of the "Principal's Office." In between times he was dispatched on errands: to buy bananas at the fruit stand on the corner, to deliver messages to individual teachers, to carry stacks of textbooks or supplies from repository to classroom. The apparition of the lanky, glum greenhorn coming through the door in the midst of a lesson was something Ira would never forget: the snickering, the suppressed catcalls, the taunts, despite the general reprimand of the teacher, would remain clearly in memory all the rest of his life— ineffaceable emblem of his first repudiation of his own kith and kin, cruelly assailed. After many decades, Ira would speculate on what would have been the result had Harry been enrolled in an East Side school, with its myriad of recent immigrants providing the very latest ones with a kind of protective matrix. How much happier that outcome for both himself and his adolescent uncle would have been. As it was, not only was Ira's first report card marked C C C, failure in all three categories of performance, but his second and his third report card as well. Not till his fourth would the marks improve to B B B, and whether Harry's quitting school in favor of getting a job had anything to do with the improvement, Ira would never know. He doubted it.

He doubted it because this was not the only instance of rejection of his own kind. The seed of rejection had already been sown— before his abandonment of his youthful uncle—sown weeks and weeks before, before school opened, sown at the first sight of his new kinfolk. At the moment of their entering their new apartment in Harlem, rejection inherent in the chagrin and disenchantment he felt at his first encounter with them. It was then, at that very instant, that irrevocable disappointment made its corrosive inroad: When the two taxicabs drew up to the curb in front of the apartment house, the two taxicabs bearing the six immigrants and their baggage—and their two shepherding sons, Moe in the one cab, Saul in the other—and the newcomers alighted in the sunlit street, Mamie, ever volatile in emotion, and close to fainting with rapture, screamed from the window: *"Mominyoo! Mominyoo! Tata! Tata!"*

And Mom, though more self-controlled, carried away by excitement, and tears of joy welling from her eyes, and everyone, even little Stella, Mamie's child, all crowding into the two front-room windows, screaming down at the uplifted faces screaming upward to mingle in joyful Yiddish cacophony that brought people to the windows of neighboring houses, it was then and there the desolate breach opened between himself and himself that was never to close.

For during the days and weeks preceding their arrival, as Mom's anticipation grew, her longing, perhaps entangled in the nostalgias of her own girlhood, transmuted itself within Ira into fantasies as remote from the actuality he was soon to encounter as dream: into noble images of uncles and aunts, kindly, munificent, affectionate and indulgent. He imagined, in childish fancy, that the newcomers would be like "Uncle Louie"—Pop's nephew, though older—Americanized, a government employee, a letter carrier in postman blue; who had served in the United States Army, could reminisce entrancingly about Indians and buffalo, about mountain and desert; and above all, was boundlessly generous with his pretend-nephew, fond and generous, never leaving after a visit, whether to the house on 114th Street, or the one on 119th, without first bestowing on Ira a handful of small change, an entire handful to a child who otherwise could rarely boast of possessing an entire nickel. Though Pop might cry, "*Beloy! Beloy!*" Desist! Desist!, Uncle Louis would override him with his square, gold-dentured smile, his brown eyes arch behind his gold-rimmed glasses. "*Beloy! Beloy!*" was to no avail with Americanized Uncle Louie! What jingling, silvery rich coins were Ira's. . . .

He thought the new relatives would be just like Uncle Louie, bountiful, endowed with a store of beguiling anecdotes, with rare knowledge of customs and places which they were only too happy to impart on their doting little kinsman. In short, they would be somehow charmingly, magically, bountifully pre-Americanized. Instead—they were greenhorns! Greenhorns with uncouth, lopsided and outlandish gestures, greenhorns who, once they cried out how big Leah's infant had grown since they last saw him, paid no more attention to him, greenhorns engaged in all manner of talk too incomprehensible for him to understand, speaking "thick" Yiddish, without any English to leaven it, about the ways of the New World, the kosher shopping nearby and the work to be found here, and about relatives and friends and affairs in the little hamlet they had left behind: dull, colorless, greenhorn affairs.

Once again—Ira would reflect later—had their advent into the New World taken place in the ambience of the East Side, their outcry, their foreignness, their *Yiddishkeit* would not have seemed so garish. But here, already translated from that broader, homogeneous Jewish world, already glimpsing, perceiving on every hand, in every cautious exploration of the surrounding neighborhoods, how vast and predominant was the *goyish* world that surrounded the little Jewish enclave in which he lived, almost at once, a potential for contrast was instilled, a potential for contrast that waxed with every passing day on 114th Street. From erstwhile unawareness, awareness became insupportable; contrast became too much to bear: The newcomers' crudity and grimace, their green and carious teeth, the sense of oppressive orthodoxy under Zaida's sway—how they rushed to the sink at his behest to rinse their mouths in salt water—their totally alien behavior combined to produce in Ira a sense of unutterable chagrin and disappointment.

After he returned from his excursion with Max in the pushcart district, a feeling of isolation, of such intense disenchantment pervaded Ira, that to escape from his disconsolateness, he asked Mom if he could go downstairs. She consented, and in token of her joy, gave him a nickel to spend on anything he fancied. He descended the two flights of stairs, came out of the hallway into vacant, bright and comfortless 114th Street; and finding no one there his own age to strike up an acquaintance with, he trudged aimlessly west toward Fifth Avenue, then into the first candy store he came to, and bought a cheery box of Cracker Jacks. Munching the sweet, molasses-covered popcorn, he turned south toward the 110th Street corner of Central Park.

The Cracker Jacks did little to relieve him of his dejection. After he had consumed half a box, they afforded no comfort at all, rather an obligation to eat all he had paid for, despite his becoming cloyed with them. He felt inconsolable; he had been tricked somehow by the perversity of reality, a wayward reality that flouted all his cravings, his needs, his hopes. Greenhorns, crude, embarrassing uncouth greenhorns, of no avail against the vacancy gaping ever wider within him since moving to 114th Street. How homely they were, what impenetrable Yiddish they spoke, with what contortions they accompanied speech. They were here to learn about America themselves, to learn American ways, to earn their living in America, not to treasure him, or slip coins into his hand.

No, no, no. They had no money themselves: Max and his two carrots for a penny, Max splurging a whole penny to buy a treat. He had come here to find work, because you couldn't make a living in that hamlet, Veljish, and his two aunts to find work *and* husbands. Otherwise they'd become old maids, as Mom had told him. Nahh. You'd have to wait until they got jobs before you could hope for a nickel . . . He veered toward the curb. Always the same cloying sweetness, molasses sweetness, covered each cluster of popcorn. It made you thirsty. The happy picture on the box of frolicking kids at a baseball game promised way, way more than was inside. Nah. He wished he had his nickel back. He dropped the empty box into a small puddle at the curb. Never again.

Prosperous Fifth Avenue . . . He trudged south. This part of Fifth Avenue always seemed fat to him, fat and prosperous: like chicken *schmaltz*. Full of "all-rightnicks," complacent, well-fed, contented Jewish people. Fat couples in summer wear with their kids licking ice cream cones. Even the stores and the restaurants looked prosperous, looked fat. Only he, mopey he, threaded among the self-satisfied strollers, discontented. So . . . that . . . anh . . . that yearned-for passage, passage from himself to them, Mom's relatives, was barred, utterly untenable. The longed-for communion, lost sense of belonging that gnawed at him, almost without his knowing, ever since leaving 9th Street, that he hoped they would provide, the way Uncle Louie did, so briefly, with his sympathy and understanding, his largesse and laughter, they never would, they never could provide. Ludicrous to think so. The new kind of loneliness that he had begun to feel ever since coming to Harlem deepened. Grotesque greenhorns his delightful envisagings had become. What a dope.

He entered the park: sunny, restless ripples on the lake, rowboats floating on spangles of water, troubling the smother of reflected brilliance. Shifting pedestrians, noisy kids running about, infants in prams, mothers seated on the green benches, admonishing, gossiping, couples sauntering. Two paths opened before him as soon as he entered the park, two paved walks diverged. He could take the one that skirted the lake west toward the boathouse. He could take the other that skirted the lake toward the south. To walk west was to walk parallel to 110th Street, parallel to the car tracks on which the electric "dinky" ran, the little, lurching, battery-powered crosstown trolley that everybody made fun of. To walk south was to walk "downtown." To Ira, 110th Street was a kind of subjective southern border of Harlem. The sprawling Harlem Casino, used for Jewish marriages, fancy Bar Mitzvahs, and other special occasions, that stood on the corner of Fifth Avenue and 110th seemed the anchor of the solid rows of choice elevator apartments that stretched from Fifth Avenue west, imposing elevator apartments of eight or ten stories, in a solid front toward Lenox Avenue and Seventh Avenue, all the way to the imaginary west boundary of Harlem, the lofty El curving in charcoal sweep around the northwest corner of the park. Beyond that, affluent Central Park West became workaday Eighth Avenue.

Ira already had determined these boundaries, determined his own boundaries, because he had no one to ask, because he had scouted the precincts alone. Alone; that was altogether different from the way he had reconnoitered the environs of 9th Street when they first moved in, always, always in company of other kids, Izzy or Moish or Ziggy or Hersh or Yussie. With one or another or all, almost in awe they had stood in the shadow of the dark, brooding Fulton Street Fish Market under the bridge to Brooklyn, the looming gas tanks on East 14th Street, like huge drums by the drumstick smokestacks. Or the other docks on the East River, where you could watch scows with all kinds of cargo aboard, lumber or coal or cobblestones, shepherded by different tugboats to their moorings, see the great hemp hausers looped around the iron stanchions. Or hie westward to Avenue A, and the Free Baths with the slippery tile floors. Ah. But now solitary.

In whichever direction one chose to go after entering the park, west or south, one walked alongside the iron-pipe fence that bounded the small lake. On the other side of the lake, a bosom of stone swelled up from the water, a granite bosom, surmounted by shrubs and trees that grew thicker and thicker until they met the sky at the top in a high, shady grove. The grove seemed to beckon, offering seclusion in keeping with his own sense of isolation. He walked south, skirting the lake, until he came to a paved walk leading upward. . . . Stone steps and paved walk and stone steps once more, until he reached the summit. From there, narrow wooded trails led down toward the lake, patches of whose glittering water he could glimpse from above. From the summit too he could see the facades and windows of apartment houses on 110th, and even a "dinky" trolley jigging along its tracks. It had rained the day before, and near at hand, rills still ran through channels over bits of twigs and last year's brown leaves.

He was thirsty. And yet, not so thirsty he couldn't easily have waited until he got back to the faucets in the kitchen of Zaida and Baba's new house. But his thirst seemed bound up with vague new longing spawned by disenchantment, as if intense disappointment distilled its own anodyne to assuage it. Fancy suddenly imbued him. Fancy suddenly buoyed him up, lifted him high above despond, scattered disgruntlement: He was a Scout, lone explorer in trackless America, self-sufficient, resourceful and intrepid, roving through the visionary land, and arrived at this rivulet in the primeval forest. For a moment the countervailing thought crossed his mind that the rill at his feet might have been peed in; though it looked clear, maybe wasn't safe to drink. But he had to be resolute—he was a bold, buckskin-clad Scout, the wide-ranging explorer, slipping silent as a shadow through the trackless wild: He had pledged himself to a new resolve, to a new "pledge allegiance," a new covenant he couldn't name, an American covenant; he had to drink to confirm it: Kneeling, he bent facedown to streamlet, sipped a few mouthfuls. . . .

IV

It was still vacation time, a few days before school, P.S. 103, opened. So persistently had Ira nagged Mom to revisit 9th Street, to revisit the East Side—out of a longing grown all the more intense now that he found himself in Irish-dominated 119th—that she finally consented. Truth was she too wanted to meet old neighbors and acquaintances in the old surroundings. On a morning before Labor Day, he and Mom made ready to go.

Spruced up, in fresh blouse, best knee-pants, he skipped along beside Mom in happy jaunt as the two walked east along 116th Street all the way to the Second Avenue El station, where Pop had directed them to go. There they boarded the almost-empty train, rode downtown on clacking wheels, stopping at countless local stations, while Ira, jubilant, kneeled on the straw-colored train seat and gazed out of the open window at the roofs and rusting metal eaves of the rows and rows of low, dull brick houses that lined the El route.

They came at last to the 8th Street station! Scarcely heeding her admonitions to be careful, Ira skipped down the El stairs to the street, beyond the farthest boundary of his and his friends' wanderings, Second Avenue; still, even from there he could already descry to the east familiar landmarks: First Avenue, the green corner of the little park on Avenue A, where the Free Baths were, where he and Izzy and Heshy and Mutke and the other East Side kids dowsed under showers during the summer, slid on their pink butts for a sleigh ride over the slippery tiles.

They walked on; and soon he was in his old haunts, Avenue C, with its lines of pushcarts and stir and gabble of haggling and cry of wares—in Yiddish—and flow of crowd of shoppers, Jewish crowd, hands waggling and whiskers prominent. Already he could see the tall red-brick house—his!—on the corner of Avenue D . . . the windows up there near the edge, high, his, and a little patch of the river, the cool East River always at beck, beyond the junkyards with the carrion stink of dead cats, where they played follow-the-

leader over old boilers and scrap machinery, past the blacksmith
shop reeking of seared hooves, and that little wooden house where
the sandy-haired Polish janitor's kid had called him a sheeny; and
Ira's, "Wait, till I get you downstairs." How bold he had been then,
a good fighter, the other kids said; and he had posed for his tintype
with fists outstretched in approved boxer's stance: had to hide
under the bed and listen to Mom lie that he wasn't home, when
some irate mother of a kid whose nose Ira had bloodied came
storming up to the house. And now he had become apprehensive,
he had become uneasy.

"Oh, I wanna go back," he suddenly cried out in English—he
was sure Mom would understand. "I wanna go back to 9th Street.
I wanna come back here. I don't wanna live in Harlem."

"*Bist Meshugge?*" Mom said startled. "Are you mad?"

"It's full of Irishers. They always wanna fight."

"And you can't? Since when?"

"Yeah, but everybody! Everybody is Irish. They're all on their
side."

"*Nu,* you'll have to learn to avoid a quarrel—with a good word,
a jest. How can I help you? This is an ancient story of Jews among
the *goyim.* You got a Jewish head. You'll have to learn to fend for
yourself."

"Yeah, but even 114th Street was better!"

"I'll sit there looking out at brick walls? And what? If your
father is a lunatic and seeks only *dreck? Twelve shmoolyaris* a month.
Pay another dollar or two, and rent something with electricity, with
hot water—No! A twisted head. And every penny he had to save
to buy milk from the farmers, to buy oats, to buy hay. And he
works day and night. Another would be satisfied to work for a
boss. What can I do?"

"Ahh!"

"Go, don't be a fool. I have there my sisters, my mother, a little
happiness. He has his stable nearby. You'll have to make the best
of it."

Ira was silent. It was useless. They passed the *cheder*-entrance
across the street, passed the weathered wooden platform in front
of Levi's Dairy for whom Pop had once worked, the platform where

Ira had sat with other kids a summer afternoon, and still remembered Mutke saying, "So if there was a Silver War, when was the Golden War?" They reached the candy store where his uncle Morris had been so generous, even saved up enough purchase-tickets to take Ira and Mom to the premium store and buy his nephew a tricycle, which was stolen from him the first day. How he wept! It was his street, his world, his life. Here. Where were the kids?

"I'm going upstairs to see Mrs. Dvorshkin. Do you want to come?"

"No, I'll go around the block. Maybe they're around that furniture factory. They make bows and arrows from the thin pieces the factory throws away."

She didn't understand. "*Nu.* Be careful." She climbed the low stoop. "Don't wander too far." She went inside the hall.

A minute longer he tarried in front of the house. In that hallway he had tried to kiss pretty, dark Annie. She had scratched his face. And across the street lived Izzy with whom Ira had gone into partnership, devising a try-your-luck you-never-lose machine, an arrow over a board with sectors divided on it, and a stick of chewing gum in each sector, and an entire package in one. By the carbide lights of the pushcarts on Avenue C, they had set up shop, tempted passersby to wager a penny. The two had made a profit, divided it up and come home—late: It was after nine o'clock, Pop's milkman's bedtime hour. And what a thrashing Pop gave him! But he could have been a businessman, a Jewish businessman. It was fun, it was exciting to be with the Saturday night crowds, after the Sabbath was over, to yell: "Try your luck, you never lose!" But now on 119th Street, among all the *goyim* jeering at Jews: "Mockies: Make money, *oy.*" Some even had learned how to say it in Yiddish: *Makh geldt,* waggling hands under chin— He hated it.

Ah, the East River—he walked toward the corner—the only time, or nearly the only time Pop seemed friendly, at ease with Ira, as he with him, was when the two went out on the big wooden dock at the end of the cobblestone street, and sat there on a bulky beam above the water, in torrid summer, when the river breeze was like the river's gift, a benison cool and encompassing.

No. Nobody around the block. He turned back. Maybe he'd

better go upstairs to Mrs. Dvorshkin's, where Mom was; maybe Heshy was there: the top floor, five flights up, one floor above the floor the Stigmans had lived on; go all the way up there, one flight below the roof. Oh, the time Pop laughed, when he and Ira both went up to the roof on a cold day: Pop hung two calves' feet in a smoking chimney, just as they did in his own country far away across the ocean in Galitzia.

Was that Izzy's shout? Ira stopped at the threshold. Lucky! He was about to go in, but they had spied him, before he had seen them. And look: They had a wagon, Heshy and Izzy, coming toward him from Avenue C, the one pushing, the other steering with ropes tied on the front axle, and Heshy picking up speed, now that they had seen him. Ira ran out into the gutter to meet them. "Izzy! Heshy!"

Oh, it was as if he still lived there, the way Izzy pulled the wagon over to the curb in front of a pile that a horse had left, and all three pranced for joy at meeting again: swarthy, quick Izzy, with his thick eyebrows and flat, spreading nose. Heshy with his likable smile and sandy hair that had a slightly rancid odor as if it had been buttered with old butter. They jabbered about the past and the times spent together, and who lived in his "house" now, and how they had gotten the baby-carriage wheels—in exchange for roller skates "wit liddle windows in de steel w'eels a'ready." They were now partners in the "Try-your-luck machine."

"You gettin' fat," Heshy said. "You like it where you live?"

"No, it's lousy. It's no good!" Ira could almost have wept. "It's full of lousy Irish *goyim*. They call me Jew bestit all the time, an' they wanna fight."

"You're a good fighdah," Izzy reminded him. "So give 'em."

"Not there," Ira hung his head sullenly. "Everybody cheers on their side."

"Nobody's Jewish?" Heshy asked incredulously.

"Nearly nobody."

"So why did you move dere?" Izzy asked.

Ira tried to explain.

"Where do you go to *cheder*?" they asked.

"I didn't go once yet."

"O-o-h! You don't go to *cheder?* Dere's no *cheder?*"

"Yeah, but my fodder wanted the money for a milk wagon."

It took them a few seconds to absorb the sobering import of Ira's answer. "Wanna ride?" Heshy invited.

"Nah, it's your wagon. Lemme push."

"Nah, you get on."

"No. I'm suppose to push first."

"Get on," they insisted.

In vain he protested. That was not the custom, not proper: It was their wagon. He was supposed to push first; that was the code. It was only after he had pushed them around the block to their entire satisfaction, then and then only did he earn a claim to the driver's seat, to hold the steering ropes. Everybody knew that was the accepted order of things. But the other two wouldn't hear of it. He was their guest. And look how clean he was! A clean shirt, clean knee-pants. He could right away get dirty pushing.

In the end, it was they who prevailed; it was they who pushed him! Unhappy in the driver's seat, and protesting his unmerited privilege, he let them take turns pushing him from Avenue D half the way to Avenue C, and back. "Now let me push," he importuned. No one could any longer deny it was his turn to push. Instead, they excused him. No, he didn't have to. It was all right. His mother might come down; she wouldn't know where he was. He better stay here. They could coast down together on the slope in front of the "ice house" across the trolley tracks on 10th Street. They only had to push the empty wagon up. And with Izzy steering, and Heshy bent over providing traction, they left him on the corner of Avenue D.

His throat thickened with unaccountable sorrow; latent tears pressed against his brow. He was a guest now among his own kind. He, who had been so undifferentiated from the rest until only two months ago, was now excluded from belonging. Intuition divined it all: His special treatment was a sign that he was banned from return.

Mom noticed how quiet he was on the long ride home. "*Nu,* did you enjoy yourself?" she asked.

"Yeh."

"You have so little to say about it? You were so eager to go."
She looked at him more closely. "Why have you become so sulky?"

"I'm not sulky. I don't wanna talk Yiddish in the train."

"Who is listening to us?"

"I don't wanna talk."

"Foolish child. Until 116th Street?"

Ira made no reply.

"Do you need to relieve yourself? Is that the trouble?"

"No. I went in the street."

"Are you hungry?"

"No," he replied irritably. "Leave me alone."

"Then I won't speak—until we reach home." She leaned over,
whispered teasingly. "Afterward I may?"

"I'm gonna take off my good clothes an' go to the liberry."

"Aha. Another story with a bear. Will it be open still?"

"Till six o'clock they let you in."

V

How swiftly the changes had taken place within him, in these few
months, from the time they first moved into the house on 119th
Street to the time his Uncle Harry quit school. He was different
now, different from that very first day, after he had helped Mom
unpack the sugar barrel in which the crockery came packed,
wrapped in Yiddish newspapers. When he grew bored, he had left
the kitchen, and descended the linoleum-covered stairs warily, like
a young animal appraising new surroundings—and stepped quietly through the long, shadowy hallway between the janitor's flat
and the one occupied by the cigar makers. He had seen them sitting
next to the open window on the ground floor rolling cigars. Daylight shone on the battered brass letter boxes in the foyer. Just
outside, on the stone steps of the stoop, three kids were sitting,
three kids his own age, the backs of their heads bleached to tow

by the summer sun. He had stood on the top stone step just outside
the door, waiting—while they talked, talked in hard, clear, Gentile
voices—waiting for some sign of recognition, some acknowledgment of his presence. The one who sat in the middle—Heffernan—Ira would learn the kid's name later—turned his head: "You
livin' here?"

"Yeh," Ira offered eagerly. "We just moved in."

"We don't want no goddamn Jews livin' here."

"No?"

"No." The boy was blue-eyed, with winning countenance, fair
of skin and with upturned nose: "You lousy Jew bastards, why
dontcha stay where you belong?"

Stabbed, Ira retreated into the hall, climbed up the stairs again,
and stormed into the kitchen.

"What is it?" Mom asked.

"They're sitting on the stoop, the Irishers."

"So. Let them sit."

"They don't like me. They called me a dirty name. They called
me a Jew bestit."

"That's news indeed," Mom said. "What better to expect from
goyim? Don't play with them. Go somewhere else. Go to Baba's. Go
to 114th Street, where we lived. I'll look out of the window until
you leave the corner."

"I don't wanna go there."

"Then stay here and help me unpack the Passover dishes."

"I don't wanna stay here, I wanna go downstairs."

"Then what do you want of me?"

"We shouldn't have moved here."

"Again?"

"Yeah."

"I'm more concerned that I still haven't found my red coral
beads, my wedding present from my Aunt Rachel in Lemberg."
Mom tore the Yiddish newspaper from around the silver Passover
salt cellar. "Such heartless thieves, these movers. I haven't come
across it anywhere. The lovely coral. *Gewald.* Where is it?" And to
Ira, in vexed tones: "Don't be like your father. Don't quail so before
a *goy.*"

"I'm not quailing!" Ira flared. "There's three kids down there on the stoop."

"Then what can I do? Do you want me to contend with them?"

Full of rancor, he left the kitchen, passed through the two freshly painted, intervening bedrooms to the front room, with its furnishings still in disarray, and leaned out of the open window on the street. He leaned out of the unobstructed window; the other opened on the fire escape, on the black iron balcony shared with the neighbors next door. On the stone steps of the stoop below sat the same three kids, the same blond-haired kid in the middle, the lousy Irish bestit who'd called him a dirty Jew. He'd show him.

Hiding his fierce spite from Mom, acquiescing with a noncommittal, "Yeh," to her preoccupied behest that a soft word would keep him out of trouble, he went back through the kitchen and down the stairs again. Sunlight shining on their fair hair, their backs were turned toward him. With fist doubled, he sneaked out of the doorway behind Heffernan—and struck him as hard a wallop on the cheek as he could. The kid rocked with the impact. Then Ira fled back into the hall, and upstairs.

He said nothing to Mom. Once more at the window, he could see them below, still sitting on the stoop. And then one of the trio left. Ira went downstairs again, came out of the hall onto the stoop. Fists clenched, prepared for fray, he descended to the street, eyes fixed vindictively on Heffernan: The kid smiled back, deprecating, amiable, in sign of truce.

It was what he should have done, Ira would tell himself over and over again years later: fought, fair or foul, but fought. He would remember "Greeny," a few years older than himself, but a total greenhorn, a young Jewish immigrant from Russia whose family came to America only a few months before Ira's relatives. Greeny had fought his Irish tormentors on 119th Street. He had been licked, nose bloodied, both his eyes blackened, but he fought again—and again. He reached the point where the Irish accepted him; they took him to the parochial school gym to learn to box, seconded him when he was matched in a bout—and played a dirty Irish trick on him by telling him to stuff himself with food, and guzzle all the beer he could, because that would make him strong:

He retched all over the ring—to the boundless hilarity of the spectators. Still, they accepted him: long nose and Jewish accent and all. He became a member in good standing with the gang on 119th Street.

It was what he should have done, Ira told himself, and recalled that even then, that first day on 119th Street, the lesson wasn't lost on him—though it did him no good either. He lacked the moral courage—so it would seem to him—the pluck, the persistence, to cope against such odds. He grew flabby, too. Shortly after the second term began, the spring term, 3B, he brought home a note from the school nurse advising his parents that he suffered from "malnutrition"—poor nourishment, his teacher explained—at which Mom scoffed: "I don't give you enough *bulkies* and butter to eat, and *lotkehs* and sour cream, or what?" Flabby, overweight, he lost agility and stamina. And in that fateful street-fight in late winter, the recent snowfall treacherous underfoot, he was being bested by his skinny, wiry Irish adversary, on whose large two front teeth the saliva glistened distractingly—when of a sudden Mom came rushing into the circle of hostile partisans. *"Gerara!"* She raised a threatening arm against Ira's opponent.

"Aw, g'wan yuh lousy Jew!" His adversary defied her. Still, he retreated before the menace of Mom's upraised arm; he jeered and retreated.

And Ira—Ira burst into tears. He would never live down the humiliation. What more woeful stigma of ignominy than to be rescued from defeat by your pale and agitated Jewish mother, by your taunted and frantic Jewish mother, wading in to your defense. Weeping, Ira ran from his exulting opponent, ran through the circle of jeering kids, ran for the house. He felt as if his spirit were crushed forever.

And, alas, so it was. His East Side cockiness was gone. Though he fought other Irish kids in the street thereafter, it was always in the hope that some adult would intervene, or someone warn of an approaching cop, or any other pretext would crop up as an excuse for disengagement. Never did self-assurance return, never did he win, never expected to. Oh, this was grievous, this plummeting of self-assurance—he could tell it was happening to him—this erosion of self-assertiveness in the kid once so pugnacious. He could feel the undoing of self, the atrophy of the one he was on the East Side.

And when to this, in earliest spring, a little pack of Irish kids, mostly younger than himself, followed him home after school from the corner of Park Avenue on the way to the stoop, chanting: "Fat, fat, the water rat, fifty bullets in your hat!" he turned once or twice to scare them off. And away they scampered, pell-mell in elated flight. He climbed upstairs, entered the kitchen, where he found Pop alone reading his Yiddish newspaper. Ira got out a library book, and lost himself in a fairy tale. . . .

Suddenly a sharp knock at the door startled them. Opening it, Ira stood face to face with Mrs. True, the young Irish matron from upstairs on the fourth floor. And surrounding her, some of those same Irish gamins who had baited him only minutes ago: He had thrown her little five-year-old Danny to the sidewalk, she accused Ira, and the child had suffered a deep gash on his head. She was a pretty brunette, Mrs. True, and the wrathful flash of her brown eyes set off her pert, rosy features. In vain, Ira denied responsibility. He never pushed her little Danny, or anyone: The kids called him names, and he just turned around to scare them, so they ran away, they shoved each other—No, they didn't! the other kids clamored: Ira had knocked down little Danny.

And all at once, Mrs. True drew back her hand and slapped Ira in the face. As if the blow were an incitement, it released in Pop all his terrified fury. Ira never could recall afterward with what rod he was chastised, whether with a stick or a stove poker. He was being sacrificed to avert more disastrous reprisal. He could only recall that he groveled, screaming, "Don't, Papa, please, Papa! No more!" He screamed and moaned without bringing a stay to Pop's ferocious blows. And had it not been for Mrs. Shapiro, new tenant in the "back," dumpy, shapeless Litvak Mrs. Shapiro, there was no telling where the scourging might have ended. Pop had lost all control, and was already treading his son underfoot, stamping on him, so that even Mrs. True's look of satisfaction had turned into one of aversion. Mrs. Shapiro interposed herself between the howling child on the floor and his insensate father, interposed herself stolidly, stubbornly.

"What, you'll destroy your own son for a *goya's* sake?" she said in Yiddish. And she refused to move, or be moved by Pop's raving curses, but obdurately stood her ground, and even withstood his savage thrust. And now, Mom, apprised by her son's screaming as soon as she entered the lower hallway of the house, rushed up the stairs and into the kitchen.

"Mama!" Never had her face seemed more heaven-sent than now, furious in his defense.

"Lunatic!" she screamed hoarsely at Pop. "Wild beast! Mad dog! What you've done to the child! Be cloven in two!" Formidable in wrath, she confronted Pop with outthrust face, and arms spread ready to come to blows. He retreated. And the next second, Mom turned fiercely on Mrs. True. "Vot you vant?" she demanded.

Mrs. True and her entourage of kids silently withdrew.

He would remember that fearsome afternoon, as a kind of atonement for all he had been, a kind of extinction of all that he once felt was right and commendable about himself—but no longer was. He would have to learn other ways; he would have to try to . . . stay out of fights, stay out of trouble, disputes, learn to say yes, slur over differences, smooth over gritty places with a soft word, as Mom advised. Or with a noncommittal, conciliatory: "Yeah? I didn't know that." He could almost feel the once self-assured East Side kid shriveling within himself, leaving behind . . . a kind of void.

VI

Eddie Ferry became his fast friend, little Eddie Ferry, son of the widowed janitress who moved in on the ground floor. Together, the two friends constructed tin-can telephones, stretched the connecting string from ground floor a flight up the tenement stairs, from flat to flat. Together, they hiked west along Gentile, fancy 125th Street, sampling show-window displays as they went, their goal always the same: the rewarding, well-stocked hardware store far to the west, just short of the Eighth Avenue El. There they clung, slid squeaky, streaky fingers along the plate glass of the double show windows—from street to entrance on one side, and back on the other side, from entrance to street: Ah, the ravishing display of brass telegraph sets, and coils of copper wire to go with them, and dry batteries and electric bells and camping gear, fishing rods and lustrous Daisy air rifles—if only they had the money!

Eddie taught his friend how everything worked. He knew all about electricity; he knew how to make homemade batteries out of the zinc and carbon rods of discarded ones and ten cents' worth of sal ammonia, which you could buy in the drugstore. He didn't mind that Ira was Jewish; he said Ira wasn't like the other Jews, dirty Jews: like Davey Baer, and his younger brother Maxie, who moved into the red-brick tenement across the street, and always beat Eddie tossing picture cards of baseball players, or flipping checkers or matching pennies. Only rarely, a very few times, flaring up at something Ira said or did that displeased him—"Yuh lousy Jew!" Eddie flung at Ira.

But it seemed only natural; he didn't mean anything by it, just grabbed the nearest handle to twist in show of disapproval. Ira learned to buffer the epithet with a deprecating grin—covering slight embarrassment, the same way that Eddie grinned when his harassed mother fumed about the tenants, saying: "I don't give a fart what they think." (Did the poor woman really say, "I don't give a fart," Ira would wonder years later. Or did she say, "I don't give a farthing." It would be awhile before he learned that a farthing was a coin.) It was with Eddie, in the lee of his Irish boldness, that Ira first began those explorations into the reaches of other parts of the city, westward to Riverside Drive, all the way to Grant's Tomb, to the freight tracks beside the awesome, broad Hudson River; or eastward, on 125th Street, past glamorous vaudeville theater marquees, by chophouses with *treife*, alluring T-bone steaks on the cracked ice in the show window—and those strange, repulsive, green, mottled creatures with great claws, moving sluggishly on their icy bed. "Them's good; them's lobsters," Eddie assured the doubting Ira.

"Good? Them? With all those green legs?" Ira screwed up his face in revulsion. "How c'n you eat them?"

"What d'yuh mean how c'n you eat it? Jesus, you Jews must be dumb. Yuh cook 'em an' break the shell with a nutcracker. Them two big things in front ain't legs. Them's claws."

"Like that?" Ira conciliated.

Eddie's was the world Ira now yearned for, to be allowed to share, allowed access to. He was only too ready to gloss over differences, lull the felt sense of strangeness the East Side had implanted in him, in the sanctity of kosher food, in custom, in observance. They were all impediments to entering Eddie's world, world of rooftops and flying kites, of journeys to the marvelous turning bridges over the Harlem River like the one at the end of Madison Avenue, where a whole bridge swiveled slowly around to allow a ship to pass, and the bewildering network of tracks in the huge freight yards on the other side of the river, in alien Bronx. Or way over east, past little Italy, where people spoke a strange language, haggled over produce in long, sometimes strident syllables, gesturing violently all the time, strange produce on pushcarts and in stores, that even Eddie didn't know the names of—"Aw, dem's for wops"—to the floating swimming pool in the East River, where, under Eddie's tutelage, Ira finally learned to float in the water, and—miraculously—to dog-paddle. Amid the naked, splashing, shrieking kids—"Everybody pisses in de water; so don't swallow even a mout'ful," Eddie advised, "or it'll make ye puke." Together they climbed the foecally malodorous rocks to the summit of the Mt. Morris Park . . .

Something had been preying on his mind, something that demanded to be taken into account, demanded a retracing of steps for the sake of authenticity. Its omission awoke in him a sense of panic, an irrational fear, akin to the catastrophe long ago that arrested normal progress, and now unforeseen stretched tentacles into his psyche in the present. Never mind, he tried to reassure himself—append the omitted material, and go on; the substance is trifling. And yet, without it, the narrative would remain defective, the portrayal incomplete: Ira and his parents were *not* the first Jews living on 119th Street. He was not, in short, without alternative of Jewish kids to hobnob with, enticing to the writer as that sort of extreme predicament might be.

Another Jewish family lived in his own house, Mrs. Schneider across the corridor, though there were no boys his age. Jewish families may already have lived in the landlord Jake's hulking tenement, on the corner of Park Avenue, though none of the kids played in the block. A scattering of Jews already lived in the six-story apartment house on the other corner of Park Avenue (apartment house because it boasted hot and cold running water—and steam heat), comfortable enough for the family of the Jewish pharmacist to occupy, Biolov, whose pharmacy—drugstore—was on the corner also, and whose plump, condescending wife wheeled the fanciest baby carriage in the neighborhood. But none of the kids of the corner apartment house, if they were big enough, played in 119th Street. Only the kids of the appallingly destitute Jewish family living in the red-brick, six-story, cold-water tenement across the street played on the block: scrawny, dark-skinned Davey, and his equally scrawny, dark-skinned younger brother, Maxie. They had a sister, Dora, between them in age, and in complexion like them, shrinking and fugitive as a mouse; also an infant brother with a frightful rash. A thin, dark-skinned mother, and a short, affable father were their parents.

They lived in such bleak destitution that even Ira, grown accustomed to squalor, and not too observant of it either, was taken aback on entering their home. Would he ever forget the scabby baby in his scarred, smeared, old high chair catching a cockroach in his splotched fist, and offering to throw the insect into his doting and gently reproving papa's glass of tea. Mr. Baer was a gambler, Mom said: He refused to do anything, except spend his time at the card tables. And wizened Davey and Maxie too were expert gamblers. Whatever the game they played, always they played with the same ruthless concentration, clawing and squalling for advantage. It was too much for Ira to withstand. He learned early to shun gambling with them.

They met, perhaps that very first afternoon, when he so treacherously struck Heffernan. The brothers were newcomers to the street like himself. Their common Jewishness confirmed, and encouraged because they now numbered three, they set out on a ramble. They entered Mt. Morris Park at the corner of 120th and Madison, stared in wonder at the lofty, rocky, tree-grown hill rising in the midst of the park, and lifted perplexed eyes to the wooden bell tower rearing up on top of the hill. They came out at the uptown end of the park, at 124th Street, where they turned west, passed the hushed, sedate brownstones, and marked the staid, gray · public library set in the midst of the brownstones. They crossed bustling Lenox Avenue, and still forging westward through a rich, subdued neighborhood of dignified townhouses, they reached prosperous Seventh Avenue. Elegant stores at the foot of tall, exclusive apartment buildings lined the way; Pierce Arrows and Packards were parked along the curb. The three stood and gazed; at the 125th Street corner of the wide and prosperous avenue the tall, impressive Hotel Theresa dominated its well-to-do neighbors. And at the very corner where they stood, on 124th Street itself, how sumptuous, how decorous, tubs and tubs, a whole row of wooden tubs with short evergreen trees in them, all closely aligned, so that the branches of the trees interlocked, were set out on the sidewalk. They formed a green hedge in front of a restaurant; they formed an outdoor café.

The three crept up to the dense front of leaves and boughs, and peeped through: On the other side stood neat round tables covered with blue-and-white checkered cloth, and in the midst of each round table stood a trim, creamy vase with flowers in it. The blond, bow-tied waiter, in his plum-striped jacket, lifted his head from the cutlery he was setting out on one of the tables, and his eyes came to rest on the other side of the hedge where they stood. He gave no sign of having caught sight of the trio of Jewish gamins.

He picked up a napkin, appeared to flick a crumb from a table, and still intent on his duties, stepped toward the sidewalk entrance of the café. But Davey had already divined the waiter's purpose, and signaled the others to poise for flight. And fortunately they did, for they dashed past him as he came out running. And pell-mell east they fled through 124th Street, as fast as they could, and he after them. But he chased them only a short distance. For when they looked over their shoulders, they saw he had given up pursuit—or had only feigned it. So they also stopped running, stopped in the middle of the secluded street, and Davey and Maxie, with hands cupped around mouths, uttered a defiant, half-scared bray of deliverance.

VII

The summer came and went, and he still hadn't attended *cheder,* excused by the upheaval of moving from the East Side to 114th Street in Harlem—and then to 119th Street. Attendance also entailed a twenty-five-cent tuition fee to consider, which for the time being Mom was only too relieved not to defray: Pop was at the lowest ebb of his fortune, when his shining delusion of obtaining bulk milk directly from farmers at the West Side milk-shed faded, and with it his dream of becoming an entrepreneur. The big companies—so a word here and a word there picked up from his parents' conversation interlaced into meaning—the big companies prevented Pop from carrying out his scheme; they foiled his plans; they warned farmers not to sell him milk. In pitying or in derisive tones, sometimes Mom, sometimes Zaida, or Ira's uncles would say:

"Of course, the big companies will let him establish his own milk route? Borden and Sheffield will play with him? Go."

For a short while, Pop's nondescript milk-wagon stood at the curb in front of the house, and for a while, between the shafts, the poor old nag—of which Ira felt ashamed among all these *goyim*—tossed her feed bag upward to catch the last of the oats in it, stamped at the flies on her legs above the manure—stamped when the Irish kids pulled long hairs from her tail with which to plait rings— And then horse and wagon disappeared: to Ira's relief. But only to be replaced by another horse and wagon, much like the first only this time with the words HARLEM WET WASH stenciled on the sides in large white letters—and inside the wagon, gray bulging bags full of soiled laundry to wash, or still dripping to be returned. . . . That too disappeared, and Pop was jobless, frantic and jobless. Mom's gold wedding band, and the diamond ring she had bought on installments from Ira's Granduncle Nathan, when they still lived on the East Side, the Passover silverware and Pop's gold watch went into pawn—and Ira was excused from *cheder* attendance.

He was excused from *cheder,* and yet, despite his failure to attend, he still retained his glibness at reading Hebrew. Piety still held sway during those first months of their removal from 9th Street to Harlem. He even accompanied Zaida on his Saturday morning worship in the dingy, cheerless little synagogue on the ground floor of a house on East 115th Street, with its few rows of hard benches, its musty prayer books, whose dog-eared pages bearded Jews like Zaida turned with moistened thumb in their peculiar way. *Davening,* they hawked up rheum and voided it on the bare wooden floor, smearing the gob underfoot, *davening, davening,* swaying irregularly and resolutely in worship. Those first weeks, Ira even returned with Zaida at dusk for vesper services on Saturday, the *havdallah,* led by Schloimeh F., Zaida's uncle, imperial on the Sabbath in his black silk top hat as he walked to *shul.* With forked white beard only inches above the scroll on the lectern, he prayed, clearing his throat luxuriously. Ira, dutiful grandson, trying to win praise, waited out the *havdallah* in the bleary little ground-floor synagogue. And after the Sabbath was over, and the bare electric lamps on the ceiling were lit, he too shared in the post-Sabbath snack: the small bumper of wine given him by one or another of the beaming and more affluent congregants, a chunk of pickled herring, slice of rye bread, and—the astounding, the transfixing, fat, jet-black Greek olives that one suddenly relished despite revulsion.

So those first weeks were spent, Harlem continually displacing the East Side, plying new impressions into old memories, like those raffia braids he would weave in school to make mats out of, new bunches of raffia plaited into the old. After Saturday morning services he followed Zaida upstairs into the kitchen—or was invited upstairs to light the gas stove, since he was too young to sin—and stood there awhile afterwards talking to meek Baba, while her husband's dinner warmed. Served, Zaida fell to voraciously— halted in mid-mouthful: "Here, my child, before you go, relish this." He picked up a boiled chicken foot from his plate, bit out the one meaty bubble at the base of the toes, and handed his grandson the yellow shank and skimpy talons.

"Thanks, Zaida."

Before the end of the summer Pop's fortunes mended. At his brother-in-law Moe's urging, Pop became a busboy in the same res- taurant where Moe worked as a waiter, Karg and Zinz. Forthright, muscular, kind-hearted Moe, striving to help out his poverty-stricken sister. But before Pop quit—or was fired—he created a scene of ter- rible proportion—only years later did Ira learn, from Pop himself, laughing at the farce of his own creating (he did have that aptitude, in common with his son, of perceiving the absurdity of predica- ment brought on by himself): He had been pestered, he alleged, by one of the owners, Mr. Zinz, who continually looked askance at everything Pop did (alas, his inveterate chafing at any kind of subordination). He gave Pop "arguments" about his work. In vain, Moe counseled: "He's the boss, he's paying you, and you're making a good collection from the tips of the five waiters in the place; you're making a living. Every waiter gets 'arguments,' if not from the boss, from a customer. Every waiter knows," Moe concluded, "when they give you an argument, you put it in your pocket."

To no avail. Pop hurled a water pitcher into the large plate- glass mirror on the wall. Someone, a customer, called a cop who arrived just as the tall, enraged Mr. Zinz was about to administer a thrashing to Pop, changing his clothes down in the restaurant cellar. "Look at him, and look at me," Pop appealed to the big Irish cop. "Can I do something to him? He was going to beat me up, so I threw the pitcher, somebody should call the police." And he had "squeezed out a few tears," Pop added by way of cynical parenthesis. The officer threatened to arrest Mr. Zinz.

Pop's violent act caused a rift between Mom and the rest of her family: Though Zaida censured, with characteristic acerbity, called Pop a lunatic, Mom sided with her wronged and persecuted husband—as she would for some while longer, until the truth of his nature finally became inescapable. Pop in turn dismissed the estrangement with typical contempt—and with typical ingratitude. "I don't need their help. I've mastered this learned calling," he said scornfully, "I've learned this complicated skill. I need my in-laws, you know where? In the rear! I'm a seasoned waiter."

He made good on his boast. With newly bought dickey and secondhand tuxedo, he succeeded in passing himself off as a waiter, and in a short time became a competent one. His income increased, but to what extent, he kept a secret—as always.

The pawned valuables were redeemed. And once again, Mom brought up the subject of Ira's attending *cheder*. It was now Ira who resisted: "I don't wanna go!"

"Go you must. What do you mean you don't want to go? You'll become entirely a *goy*. I have the twenty-five cents. There's no longer excuse for your not going. How will you prepare for your Bar Mitzvah? And what will Zaida say? I don't want to hear any more protests. I'll find out the nearest *malamut*."

"Anh!"

Whining was of no use. She hauled Ira to the Hebrew teacher who conducted his *cheder* in his living room on 117th Street east of Madison Avenue, and after concluding arrangements, she left Ira there. It was now late spring. Because of the ill-will between his own and his grandparents' family, months had passed since he had accompanied Zaida to the *shul*. And to Ira's chagrin—and bafflement as well—his rote reading of Hebrew, which he could babble with such facility only a short time ago, had deteriorated. Where once he had been warmly commended by his grandfather—and by his last *malamut*, who especially on Sunday mornings, when alone with his pupil in the bare cellar-store *cheder*, had often

rewarded Ira with a copper for his fluency—he was now the object
of frequent promptings, disapproving cluckings and head-waggings
and disciplinary ear-wringings. Nor did his old facility ever come
back—nor his eagerness to please. Heeding the text became oner-
ous. He seemed to retrogress rather than improve. Reproof by
word for his performance gave way more and more to reproof by
deed: ear-tweakings, arm-yankings, an impatient slap on the thigh.

"I don't wanna go!" Ira stormed at Mom after a few weeks.
"I'm not going!"

"You are going! I'll tell your father. He'll soon give you to
understand."

"I don't care. Let him hit me, that's all. I'm not going! The
rabbi stinks. His mouth stinks. It stinks from cigarettes and
onions!"

"Go tell it to your grandmother. He complained to me how
remiss you are. You heed nothing. At all admonition you cavil, you
shrug. What has happened to you? A year ago—more than a year
ago, the *malamut* on 9th Street told me himself you were ready to
begin *khumish*, to begin Torah. Woe is me! If he saw what a *goy* you
are today, darkness would shroud his eyes."

"I don't care."

"And what will you know at your Bar Mitzvah, if you don't go
to *cheder*? And Zaida, what will he say when he hears you *daven*
like a mute?"

"Who cares? I don't see him. I never go to Baba's house. I can
go to *cheder* just before Bar Mitzvah."

"*Oy, gewald!* Plague take you! I won't let you become a *goy!* In
this you won't prevail. We'll find another *malamut*."

She told Pop about what had taken place. "The way you bring
him up, that's what he's become," was Pop's brusque reply. "The
right kind of mother would slap his face roundly and make him
attend. So you save a twenty-five-cent piece of your allowance if
he doesn't go to *cheder*."

"*Geh mir in d'red!* I said we ought to find another *malamut*."
Mom flushed angrily. "What the man can contrive: I save a whole
quarter of a dollar if the scamp doesn't go to *cheder*. Is that a thing
to consider? I would gladly give twice that from my allowance if

he went to *cheder,* and went eagerly. What my father will say when he hears of it."

"Devout Jew. Let him hear of it. I'm not good enough for him. Let his grandson grow up a *goy.*"

"What has that to do with it?"

"Go relieve yourself. You want him to go, send him."

"And you not? You're his father."

"He's your pampered son."

Mom kept silent a few seconds, then sighed heavily. "I see, I already see. As you were, so is he. Did you care to go to *cheder?* Only your father's stick compelled you. You tormented your younger brother Jacob when he studied Talmud, no?"

"*Geh mir in kaiver!*" Pop snapped open the Yiddish newspaper. "I don't want to speak about it anymore."

"Go also into the dolorous year," Mom addressed Ira. "The grief you cause me."

"All right, I'll go," Ira conceded. "Jeezis!"

"Spare us so much Jeezising in the house, or I'll deal you one," Pop warned.

A few weeks more Ira attended, sullenly—until the exasperated *malamut* himself dismissed his pupil: "Go, tell your mother to seek another *malamut.* You need, you know what you need? To be whipped to shreds. You're nothing but a *goy.*"

"Then woe is me!" Mom mourned when Ira came home and told her. "You have a *goya* for a mother who doesn't believe; she has a *goy* for a son. But I tell you now: Once we become reconciled with your grandfather, you'll have to go."

VIII

So the weeks went by without his attending. . . . Summer passed . . . came the fall—November neared. Election Day floats rumbled through the street. Drawn by plodding horses, heavy drays bore prominent signs on them, signs leaning against each other like the walls of a tent, each wall proclaimed: DELANEY FOR ALDERMAN! HONEST AND EXPERIENCED! Or VOTE FOR O'HARE THE PEOPLE'S CHOICE. Or VOTE A STRAIGHT DEMOCRATIC TICKET! VOTE FOR THE PARTY OF THE PEOPLE! Election Day approached. Throughout the block, all available juveniles were marshaled—or volunteered jubilantly—to form teams foraging for wood, combustibles of every kind and condition, discarded furniture, mattresses, packing crates, planks, egg crates, milk boxes snitched from the front of grocery stores, barriers from street excavations. All of it was stored down the cellarways before tenements, piled almost to sidewalk level, the tolerant Irish janitors looking the other way— A fever of collection seized the juvenile and the half-grown. Ira too was infected: he who protested so vociferously when Mom pleaded with him to provide her with a little kindling from broken fruit boxes or other scraps of wood, the way other kids did on the street, so she could build a bed of fire to ignite the coal poured on top of the kindling in the cast-iron kitchen stove. No. He refused.

"*Shamevdick! Folentzer!*" Mom fumed: "Cowering shirker!"

Without effect. But now he was tireless in his enthusiasm to gather fuel, excelling his Irish peers. "They got a float! They got a float!" came the excited cry throughout the block—on the very afternoon of Election Day. "McIntyre an' Kelly an' dem—dey got an election float. Dey're pulling it under de Cut!"

Danny Heffernan and Vito and Eddie and Ira and Davey and Maxie, and a half-dozen more sped to Park Avenue under the Cut, the railroad overpass. And just around the corner, they saw it: approaching from 120th Street, an electioneering dray, with its VOTE FOR JAMES LEAHY still on its oilcloth tent, being tugged by a swarm of kids, and half-grown louts too, toward 119th Street. The newcomers threw themselves into the task of moving the vehicle along Park Avenue. "Steer it, O'Neill! Steer it, Madigan!" The wagon would make the biggest election night bonfire 119th Street had ever witnessed, the biggest in Harlem.

And then: "Cheese it! The cops!"

Bluecoats uptown, three of them, came charging down upon

the culprits. Dropping the shafts, letting go of the spokes of the wheels, everyone took flight. In an instant the slowly moving vehicle came to rest, abandoned and forlorn in the gray afternoon light in front of a pillar of the overpass. The cops pursued. Yelling, the juvenile pranksters scattered in all directions. The police hurled their truncheons after them; police clubs bounced on the pavement, rang on the asphalt, bounding after the scampering urchins in malevolent pursuit. Delirious with escapade, Ira raced into his hallway, and up the stairs. Panting, he sat down in the kitchen: "Ooh, the policemen threw their clubs!" he announced.

"At whom?" Mom was blanching cabbage leaves on the oilcloth-covered washtub work surface. "You're gasping for breath. What is it?"

"We were pulling one of those big wagons to burn in the street tonight. Election night."

"*Oy gewald!* To burn it? A whole wagon? This too I need for you to learn. *Oy vah is mir!* No wonder the police threw their clubs at you!"

"Yeh! Bong! Bong! Bong! The clubs jumped in the air after us." Ira giggled suddenly. "We ran. Everybody ran."

"They could have split your head. Your father is right: You'll be ruined by these wild Irish. They'll bring you upstairs with a broken head. You can't find good Jewish boys to play with?"

"Where'm I going to find them? There's Davey and there's Maxie, and all they like is gambling."

"If you'd go to *cheder,* you'd find them."

"And if they live on 114th Street, or on 115th Street? Or by Fifth Avenue?"

"Go there. Play there."

"So why don't you live there!"

"I'll show you why." She waved her hand, but her eyes were worried. "You do wrong; you sin: What can I do if he wants to live here? You mock at my sorrows."

"Yeah? You didn't want to live here? You didn't want to move to Harlem? To Baba, to Zaida? We don't even see them. Who wanted to live in the front? You."

"You're becoming like a stone," she said.

Even without the election float, the bonfire on election night was spectacular. The blaze raged in the middle of the block, and sparks flew as high as the six-story roofs, while at street level the flames luridly mirrored themselves in grocery-store and tailor-shop glass fronts. The heat was felt yards away, and most of the tenement occupants, Mom and Pop included, leaned out of their windows watching the display—until the firemen arrived. They scattered the blazing debris with a powerful stream from the hose which they had connected beforehand to the hydrant. And suddenly the street darkened. A Sanitation Department truck rolled into the street the next afternoon. Men shoveled up the charred and still-dripping litter into the vehicle. The odor of molten tar filled the street. Ira and the other kids watched the ruined area of asphalt being patched: the laborers tamping the macadam with their heavy implements, the jumbo steamroller traveling and returning. . . .

That was seventy years ago, Ira reflected: That was more than seventy years ago. My God! Who's alive? Yonnie True, Eddie, Mario, Vito, the barber's two sons, Petey Hunt? As if he had suddenly dislodged them, the images came tumbling into mind: The pipes, the copper-lined box over the flush toilet in the hall froze during a cold snap, and thawing again, torrents of water cascaded down. "A tub! A flood! The janitor!" Mom rushed from the kitchen to the hallway toilet and back. "Gewald! Run, Ira! The goya! The janitor!" . . .

Because of the falling-out between his parents and Mom's kin, he could no longer avail himself of the hot water and bathtub in Baba's house (for a short time Mamie too was included in Pop's blanket ill-will). How black grew the grime encrusting his feet, unwashed the whole winter long, so black, the crust that coated his ankles was something to admire, like a dark peel—to pare off, to part with almost regretfully, as he did in Baba's bathtub in the spring when reconciliation between families finally took place. "What were your happiest years in America?" he once asked Mom, fully expecting her answer would be the East Side, corresponding to his own sense of well-being, his sense of belonging.

But no: "Those first years in Harlem were my happiest years," Mom replied: "When Baba was still alive, and all my kinfolk lived close by."

"Those were?"

"Yes."

Sitting in the rocking chair in Baba's front room, he would croon mindless tunes to himself, as the Sabbath drew to an end, as the Sabbath twilight grew, before the turning on of lights, while the women chatted endlessly, Mom and her three sisters and Baba.

And again, because it was Saturday night, and Mom was loathe to tear herself away, and Pop was working an "extra," as he called his supernumerary waiting at tables at a banquet, Mom would send Ira out to the Hebrew National Delicatessen on 116th Street and Madison where he bought two kosher frankforts (though not kosher enough for Zaida, who still swallowed saliva, while eschewing), a quarter of slant-sliced, crisp white bread, a paper-twist of mustard. Swiftly returned upstairs, the Sabbath over, he waited impatiently for Mom to boil the frankforts. And so ravenously did Ira bolt down his food, a bit of frankfort with a mouthful of scarcely masticated bread, that more than once he heaved up the whole mess into Baba's flush toilet—and came out wailing at the loss of his most prized victuals. "What can I do," Mom laughed at him, "if you eat like a wild animal?"

That was Ira, the kid in midwinter, with the drear night coming on, swinging his tin can by a loop of wire, while the flames from slivers of wood, roasting the small spud inside that Mom had given him, spurted through the vents punched in the bottom. As through a dark medium, between stone stoop and curb, bundled-up figures hurried home from work, hurried past him through the winter night, and he, for once carefree, whirled his roasting spud in front of the house—until Mom called him in her contralto voice from the window that it was time he came upstairs for supper. . . . They were like strata, these new impressions, *goyish* impressions, strata built up by *goyish* ways and diversions drifting down over memories of 9th Street and the East Side: Halloween, when the Irish kids filled the feet of long black stockings with coal ashes (a few, a very few, with flour), stocking-slings that thudded cruelly against one's back, printing a dusty, pale stamp of impact on jacket or mackinaw (if one didn't wear them inside out, as some did to escape parental reproof). "Sliding ponds," long, icy ribbons slicked out of snow to glide on, but a hazard to steel-shod horses, suddenly skating in mid-stride. Snow-forts on opposite sides of the street, and the wild melee and abandon of snowball fights, snowballs often with chunks of ice embedded in them.

IX

Lightning, sulphurous as pebbles rubbed together, burned far off in sweltering summer. The nice Gentile neighbor—who wasn't Irish, and said wawtch for watch, and Wawrshington for Washington, lifted him up from the stoop stair to sit on the stone ledge that capped the sides of the stoop after the dented brass banister ended—was so surprised how wet and smelly his armpits were that she sniffed her hands twice with wrinkled nose, and exclaimed in dismay. And yes, that same stone ledge, where everyone did stunts by holding on while hanging upside down over the cellar a flight below—what a scare it gave him! The skinny ones could do it—safely—like Eddie, or like Weasel, after Eddie and his mother moved away.

But Ira weighed twenty pounds more than they did; and when he tried the stunt, the ledge tipped, the ledge tipped! Terrified, he flung his body back to the stoop. What would Mom have said had he and the ledge plunged down into the cellar? That might have been the end of him. Think of it: the end of him at nine years of age, plunging down into the cellar, holding onto the heavy stone ledge and screaming as he hurtled down. Benny Levinsky, whose big brother with the hook nose was a crook and was shot by a cop when he ran away after holding up a crap game, Benny fell off the roof of the *treife* butcher shop on Third Avenue, German butcher shop, where the beautiful fat sausages hung—the beautiful plump knockwursts and balonies. Oh, they made meat look so nice in a *goyish* butcher store—even Mom said so—with the bones of a roast raised like a crown and pot roast all neatly tied around with twine, and a turkey with breast pouting and enticing— not like a kosher butcher store where meat looked dead and a chicken hung from its hook in the show window as if it was sorry it looked so unappealing. Benny was trying to steal a salami, even though it was *treife*, but fell off the roof instead right on top of the butcher store awning. Wasn't he lucky? All he got was a kick in the ass. So at nine, if Ira had fallen down the cellar, he would have been extinct.

Ira's mind went blank. Ecclesias; never to have known seventy more years. Never to have known M. Whom would she have known, or loved? All would have been changed . . . as howling in terror he hurtled down into the cellar.

What a *dub* he was playing ball (and was struck in the eye once passing 117th Street, walking home from Baba's); sat on the curb sobbing, while the owner of the baseball crept up, grabbed it where it had rolled near Ira, and ran. The kindly Jewish housewife asking: "What is it?" And uttering curses at the players—who had by now disappeared. And Ira sobbing as he sat on the curbstone at the corner of 117th and Park Avenue.

Baseball. The very thing he was worst at: A *dub*, a ham, he couldn't catch, he couldn't hit, he couldn't run: He was the last man chosen in the toss-up—in baseball, in handball, in boxball—

chosen after everyone else, if another player was still needed. He was scarcely chosen; he was included with a reluctant groan. Apt at no sport, except touch football (the ball was so large, had to be caught so differently—with arms and body, not hands—and he learned to punt exceptionally well), and swimming—he was at home in the water. But at nothing else was he apt; neither at tops nor at marbles nor at flipping checkers. In the spring when he was in 4A in school, the teacher took him to the playground in Mt. Morris Park, and each one took hold of a long ribbon, and circled the Maypole, singing. The strangeness, the innocence would never wear off. And he rubbed plum pits on the rough granite curbstones in midsummer to make a whistle, after he dug out the seed, the bitter seed. But there was something not usual about the way Ira stayed close to Mom on the stoop in midsummer, even learned to tat on a handkerchief between wooden hoops, the way Mom did. She laughed at him before the neighbors, apologetically. What a marvelous green pool of light filled the western sky one evening after a shower. He would never see the like again, emerald, emerald rare to gaze at in wonder. Kids sneaked into the movies (he could still see the Levine kid caught and roundly cuffed by the movie-manager in front of the theater). Mom took him to a vaudeville show once, of which she understood only a little: the jugglers and the tap dancers. And the Jewish Hawaiians, their grass kilts swaying to the plink of ukuleles as they sang:

"Tocka hula, wickie doolah, Moishe, *lai mir finif toolah*. I'll give it beck to you in a day or two. I'll go to the benk; *Sollst khoppen a krenck. Uhmein!*"

Unfortunately, Ira was so regaled by the absurdity of the song—Moishe, *lai mir finif toolah*, meant, "Moses, lend me five dollars"—that he moved his head abruptly—and struck Mom in the nose. She slapped him involuntarily. . . .

If you went to the movies, alone and on Saturday, it was better to go there with three cents, and wait outside for a partner with two cents (that kind of ratio was more conducive to successful admission than the other way round); and ask an adult who was about to go in, "Mister, will you take us in?" Two for a nickel on

Saturday morning was kids' price . . . And once inside, you could see the roly-poly man—was his name Bunny?—Ira never thought him very funny (who some years later was convicted of involuntary homicide in the death of a female guest at some scandalous Hollywood orgy, rupturing her vagina into which he had crammed cracked ice). Nor that lugubrious, downtrodden character, Musty Suffer. But oh, when Chaplin came on the screen, what rib-cracking laughter in those early two-reel films! And how desolate one felt too, after coming out of a movie with Davey and Maxie, who had somehow scraped a nickel together (perhaps their father had won at cards, perhaps there was a little more to spare after the baby died), who insisted on watching the features and the shorts over and over again, to come out into the real world, the real afternoon sunlight filtering through the El on Third Avenue where the movie was, how forlorn one felt, jaded, wasted in spirit. He would never do that again.

They sneaked into the subway, again he and Davey and Maxie, and a couple of Irish kids, and because the others made such a nuisance of themselves, scurrying about and jumping up to hang on the straps, the trainman put them off at the last stop, Bronx Park at 180th Street. Far, far from home. The others giggled nervously, or sat sheepishly on the benches of the platform. Far away from home, from Mama, Mama. He began to blubber: "I wanna go home! I wanna go home! My mama's waiting!"

It was too much for one of the station guards. "Now, get on there, and see you behave yerselves."

"Thanks, Mister! Thanks! Thanks!" Ira was rapturous with gratitude.

And he did behave himself (as he had before, self-conscious and constrained), but not the others: they tore about the train as they had previously. And they teased him: "Crybaby. Crybaby. I want my mama."

"Yeah, but I—I was the one who made the man let you back on the train!" Ira defended himself. And for the remainder of the return trip, he separated himself from the rest, sat by himself, refused to recognize the others.

Mom gave him a nickel when he was promoted to 5A, and the Irish kid he had once fought and lost to that first time, McGowan, grown taller, but still with the same dripping front teeth, sat beside Ira in the backyard at 114 East, waiting for Ira to decide how the nickel was to be spent. Whether they should spend it in the untidy little candy store next to Biolov's, owned by the slow-moving, old, old Jewish couple, patiently attending to the Irish kids: "Gimme t'ree o' dese, two o' dem, four o' dem—no, gimme four more o' de udders." Ah, the euphoria of sitting in the shade of a wooden fence in the backyard at the end of school! He was promoted, with B B B on his report card, and Mom's blessing in heart. He was promoted, with a nickel in his pocket, and an Irish friend beside him, who said yes to whatever he said, but didn't understand, his mind elsewhere, maybe couldn't understand that delicacy of mood, the brief precious bliss of lounging in the backyard amid the golden fences at the beginning of summer.

It should have gone into a novel, several novels perhaps, written in early manhood, after his first—and only—work of fiction. There should have followed novels written in the maturity gained by that first novel.

—Well, salvage whatever you can, threadbare mementos glimmering in recollection.

In part for reasons of health (his lungs were affected, Mom hinted), in part because of his socialist convictions, Uncle Louie lived on a farm in Stelton, New Jersey. And he once took his adoring pretend-nephew there. After they got off the train, Ira rode on the handle-bars of Uncle Louie's bicycle the rest of the way to the small farm. And how wretchedly he had behaved there: He had fought with Uncle Louie's two sons, teased Rosie, Uncle Louie's daughter, mim-icked her when she was practicing on her cardboard dummy piano keyboard. And when Auntie Sarah scolded him for almost drown-ing a duckling in a pan of water—and ducking its head under, too—he had blubbered loudly: "I wanna go home!" (What a nasty brat he was; no wonder only Mom could abide him.)

He stole a nickel from Baba—he had noted that she kept her pocketbook in the second drawer of the bureau—which she kept locked. But above the second drawer, the top drawer was left un- locked. How clever of him to pull the top drawer all the way out and get at her pocketbook. Even Zaida acknowledged, after he had chastised his grandson, that he was an ingenious little rascal.

He threw dice in the shade under the Cut once, rolling the tiny dice to the concrete base of one of the urine-malodorous, cross-braced pillars that held up the railroad overpass. It was the only time he ever had any luck gambling, throwing six or seven— or eight!—consecutive passes. Had he been a seasoned gambler like Davey or Maxie, he would have cleaned up; instead, he kept drawing off his winnings after each pass—to the angry disgust of the Irish kids who faded him: What the hell was he afraid of, with a run of luck like that? But he was. So he won only a dozen pennies. (With five of which he bought a hot dog and sauerkraut on a roll from the itinerant Italian hot dog vendor. And conscious of Davey and Maxie, who had been too broke to play and were now watching him with their bright brown eyes, as alertly and mutely as two hungry dogs ready to snap up any morsel, Ira impulsively tendered Davey the last of the tidbit. It was marvelous to watch Davey take a nip of the tiny morsel, and without pause, but with the same sweep that he received the morsel, hand the even tinier remainder to his kid brother.)

Those were a few, a very few, of the strands out of which a child's life was woven in East Harlem in the teens of the twentieth century, Ecclesias. Futile to ask what his life would have been like among his own kind in the Jewish ghetto he had left.

—You say a child's life?

Well. His.

—When will you redress the omission, introduce the crucial factor?

In good time, Ecclesias, in good time . . .

X

It was late on a sunny morning when he climbed the rough granite steps leading to the summit of Mt. Morris Park hill. A trio of kids were playing tag about the bell tower. A solitary individual sat on one of the green park benches. Vacant otherwise, the benches bordered the inner circle of the iron-pipe barrier separating the summit from the hillside. Down below, Harlem streets and avenues stretched away in different directions. On Madison Avenue, at the base of the hill to the east, stretched the Fourth and Madison trolley tracks. At eye level, an irregular view revolved: the tops of brownstone roofs, the spire of a red-brick church on 121st Street, stodgy tenement facades, and bordering the west of the park, decorous and well-kept apartment houses. Smoke and shreds of cloud hovered in the sky to the pale horizon. And directly overhead—the thing he had come to see—hung the great bronze bell, motionless in the open belfry atop the massive wooden beams of the tower.

Breathing a little faster because of the climb, Ira walked about the tower, looking aloft, enjoying the sight of the huge bell among its equally huge timbers open to the sky—and wondering how the bell could have been used long ago as a fire alarm, which was what he once heard somebody say. How could anyone have climbed the hill and rung the bell in time to summon the firemen before the house burned down?

Unhurried and with little commotion, the trio of boys played their sporadic game of hide-and-go-seek, dodging behind the tower or trotting to the pipe railing about the summit. The lone adult sitting on the park bench watched them negligently—until Ira came close enough to speak to, and then to his surprise, the man greeted him. He engaged Ira in conversation. He said he could see that Ira liked hills and woods and country. Did he?

Ira did. He loved the country. So did the stranger. He knew some wonderful places too, not far away either, after a real nice trolley car ride. Did Ira like to ride in an open-air trolley car? Ira loved open-air trolleys. Then they could go out together—ride out and see a real wild place and ride back.

The man must be fooling. He wouldn't take Ira on a long trolley-car ride. A trolley-car ride cost five cents. Everybody knew that. No, the man was going to go out there himself anyway. Be nice to have company. He'd pay the carfare, if Ira wanted to go.

Ira hesitated. The stranger was smiling, but he was in earnest too. Ira stared at him, trying to make sure the other meant what he said: He was blue-eyed, loose-limbed and slender. He wore his brown felt hat crimped all around, "pork-pie" style, Ira had heard the other kids on the block call it. And there was a sort of rusti-ness about his clothes, as if weathered, but not mussed or wrinkled. No, he was serious. And he was so friendly, good-humored and relaxed.

"I have to go home first, and eat. My mama'll worry."

"That's all right. After you eat your dinner. We got plenty o' time."

"Yeh?"

"I'll be on 125th Street. When you finish your dinner, you just wait for me on the corner of Fifth Avenue. We'll take the trolley and have some fun."

"All right."

"My name's Joe. What's yours?"

"My name is Ira."

"O.K. I'll meet you on the corner, Ira: Fifth Avenue and 125th Street. Remember?"

"Yeh."

Ira said nothing to Mom. She might spoil his adventure. And lunch over, he hurried to 125th Street, early, and waited on the corner of Fifth Avenue, where the trolley ran west, just as Joe had directed him. And there he came, lanky, now that he was walking, and looking straight ahead as if he was about to saunter by non-chalantly, as if they hadn't made an appointment to meet there; so noncommittal, he would have gone on if Ira hadn't intercepted him, greeted his grown-up friend with, "Here I am, Joe!"

Oh, yes. He recognized Ira, indulgently. They would take the trolley here on the corner, an open-air trolley—and ride to the wonderful park he knew, Fort Tryon Park, at the end of the line, the last stop after a nice, sightseeing ride.

They rode and rode, on the open-air trolley, where the seats were like benches that went from one side to the other, and the conductor stood on the running board when he came to collect the carfare. After the trolley turned north on Broadway, and Ira could see the Hudson River, they rode uptown, uptown till street numbers went way up toward the 200's, and traffic grew less, and you could see real country, open fields and groves of trees, and isolated houses. They rode so far and so long that something began to stir within Ira: uneasiness.

Yes, it was a wonderful park, full of big shade trees. It was wild and secluded, like a forest. A narrow trail, overshadowed by leafy branches, slanted down a sharp declivity through ever thicker woods. But something wasn't right; no; to be so alone . . . with Mr. Joe. They should go back, now that Ira had seen the place, even though the Mister talked so kind, so cheerfully, as he went ahead, or stopped and looked around so good-naturedly.

"Here's a nice place." He led the way—from the path around a big boulder, stopped, surveyed the vicinity with a calm turn of the head. And then, gently, but with unmistakable insistence: "Take your pants down."

"Wha'?" The full import of his situation, his peril, his helplessness, toppled down on him with crushing force.

"Take your pants down." The voice was still easy, but more inflexible.

"I don't wanna."

"I said take your pants down."

"I don't wanna." Too frightened for tears, Ira began trying to force tears by whimpering: "Lea' me alone! I wanna go back."

"C'mon, kid. I ain't gonna hurt you. Get those pants down." Mr. Joe became all lanky arms, unsmiling face, strong fingers at Ira's belt, his other hand pushing Ira's hand away. "Let go, I told you I ain't gonna hurt you."

But worse than hurt lay in store, if he didn't submit, worse,

worse: terror. One hand strove with Ira's two. And in another moment the same hand was raised, impatiently. "C'mon, you little bastard." Mr. Joe's palm poised to slap—

When out of the thicket, up above from the covert that secluded Mr. Joe and Ira, the undergrowth swished, sounds approached, a woman's blithe giggle, a man's quick chuckle, mingling, and near and nearer, blessedly, angelically descending the inclined way, and now at hand: The young couple appeared, brightly out of shade, apotheosis, never again so blooming, shining-eyed, blushing Irish as she, nor as husky Irish as he, white shirt open at neck, laughter on lips, strong and eager. Barely surprised at seeing Ira and Mr. Joe, the two lovers glanced in momentary self-conscious check of amorous intent. They smiled, in friendly apology, veered away, and brushing away undergrowth as they proceeded downhill disappeared among the bushes.

It was enough, their passing, their grazing so close to the shameful, nameless knot that bound the victimizer and his victim together, Mr. Joe a hairsbreadth from discovery of his guilt, and Ira so bound to him, he couldn't even run to the passing lovers, the young man and woman, to say: "He, Joe—the Mister—him, he wants me—" Ira felt he himself shared in the shame and the guilt to have accompanied Mr. Joe out here.

It was enough to end the impasse. And both knew it. "Let's go back," said Mr. Joe.

Ira followed him with alacrity, uphill along the path. But then Joe stopped. Just before they came out into the open, and could already hear the automobiles on the street, the trolley cars, voices calling out, reassuring, Joe stopped. He led Ira behind a clump of trees, and reassured by the proximity of other beings to him, his own to them, close enough to be heard, could almost run to, Ira followed. Unbuttoning his own fly, Joe began a tranced pumping of the swollen thing he had in his hand—until—his breath became animal audible—he suddenly grabbed Ira's buttock, and began squirting a pale, glairy substance against the bark of the tree.

Mr. Joe buttoned his fly. The two walked the short distance to the street, to the trolley tracks, boarded a car when it came.

*   *   *

Mr. Joe paid the fare, and they rode back, street after street, their numbers so happily, happily diminishing. Ira didn't care if all this time Mr. Joe kept his hand on his young friend's thigh. To overjoyed eyes, the trolley reached and rounded familiar West 125th Street, and then traveled east: Seventh Avenue, the Hotel Theresa— Oh, he could walk happily home from here, but he stayed: Lenox and Fifth and Madison, and the welcome, welcome gray-painted trestle of the railway overpass with the station bustle and ticket office below: Park Avenue! He was home! "I have to get off here," Ira stood up. "My mama's waiting."

"Sure. See you later." Smiling amiably, Joe reached up and pulled the bell cord.

Ira alighted from the trolley; turned immediately downtown around the beer-parlor corner, downtown to face home. Hurrying along Park Avenue, past the plumbing-supply corner on 124th Street, he glimpsed the edge of Mt. Morris Park a block to the west. Seen now, as he would see it, at the end of each street he passed, the park—and the hill above and the bell tower—seemed fixed within a harrowing nimbus—as everything was: houses, people, store windows, pillars of the overpass, everything was steeped in something sinister, sinister, diluted by deliverance, but ineradicable, an inescapable smut.

Don't say anything to Mom. Pop'll murder you.

XI

He too, Ira thought, ironically, he too could date his writing A.C. and B.C.: After Computer and Before Computer. Because what he wrote now (today, this 4th of February, '85) was in essence — largely — of what he had typewritten, beginning almost exactly six years ago, in February of 1979. So he faced himself, and would face himself from time to time with asides of another period, a period when he was typing—when he was still able to type, his hands still able to stand the impact of the keys of his Olivetti manual typewriter.

Such was the case today: The yellow second-copy page waiting for him to transcribe it to disk began: This is Tuesday, April 3, 1979. The morning is clear, temperature a bit chillier than seasonable. I passed the night in considerable pain. M, my selfless spouse, will again have to drive me to the Presbyterian Hospital this afternoon for the blood and urine tests that determine how well the body has been tolerating the "gold" injections, remedy of last resort, or almost, of arresting the depredations of this pernicious disorder, hight in medical language rheumatoid arthritis, abbreviated hereafter as RA (Joyce would be happy at the correspondence, being batty on the subject that RA in Hebrew meant anything bad, the whole spectrum of bad). Outside my study window at the moment, the first transitory bronze buds blur the cottonwood boughs.

Menachem Begin is in Cairo. He is reported to be enjoying the cool, though correct, reception accorded him by the Egyptians (and refrained from mentioning that part of the labor that went into constructing the Pyramids he viewed was that of Hebrew slaves). To me the man is without appeal, both in presence and address, something like our own Cal Coolidge of long ago mapped into a fiercely partisan Israeli context. But all that's irrelevant, dubiously whimsical, I tell myself. El Arish is to be returned to Egypt on May 27, 1979. Most of the Arab world is focusing its hatred on Sadat; and yet, even his Arab enemies are divided—as always, praise be to Allah.

Is it genuine, durable, I ask myself: Will the peace between the two countries hold? Or should one regard the whole business as a piece (peace) of consummate trickery on the part of Anwar Sadat, a genius at machination and trickery, who apparently succeeded in lulling the Israeli government, the Israeli high command, into complacency—and then with Syria for ally, attacked on Yom Kippur. As usual, the minor detail tends to attain undue prominence in memory because human and dramatic: the debate between the two allies whether the attack should be launched at dawn or dusk, when the sun would be behind the one, and in the other's eyes. Truly, the man is a genius of trickery, and with the help of portly

German-Jewish Henry Kissinger—"Vee biliefe . . . und dun't preempt"—
regained oil fields captured by Israel and so vital to her economy without
firing another shot; and now, with the blessings of Prexy Jolly Jimmy, is
about to recover the entire Sinai.

And yet, what other alternative than to do so? Not whether Begin is
personally, or politically, attractive to me is the important thing; but
whether his agreements and concessions have placed Israel in mortal
danger—or brought a real peace a step closer. . . .

It was more than he could hope to disentangle at the moment. He frowned
at the ensuing pages, yellow, slippery, tissue-thin second-copy he had
saved money in purchasing—like Pop with his ineffable, inveterate buying
by price alone, inferior merchandise. "Doesn't the merchant know the
cost of his goods?" Mom would try to reason with Pop. It did no good:
He would still buy the printed piece of floor covering rather than genuine
linoleum of some quality; and in a short time his purchase was scuffed to
dead brown underlay, the painted floral design flaked off. Mom's practical
common-sense importunings did no good.

Had the pages slithered about? The narrative on the ensuing page
began in the middle—and he knew, he knew that events of that year—
or was it the year before?—were of great significance to him personally,
to him as narrator. It would be best—he looked at his watch: 3:20 P.M.—
it would be best to take time out, save the working copy on the screen,
and try to impose some order on what followed. He could hear his tongue
click in annoyance at the unpleasant prospect of making a little sense of
the disarray before him. But there was no help for it. Somehow he would
have to assemble it, account for it, dispose of it—clear it out of his way.
Like Plato's infinite mind (was the thought worth recording, as he poised
mentally to terminate, to "save"; no, it was silly: the notion of infinite
mind existing on an infinite floppy disk).

XII

Kids who owned the new steering-sleds, as the latest models were called, sleds with iron runners, scooted down the snowy slope on the west side of Mt. Morris Park. How few were the times of joyous abandon: when the kids who owned steering-sleds allowed you to fling yourself on top of them as they belly-whopped down the slope in full career. Uncle Max built his impoverished nephew a sled out of a wooden box and scrap-wood runners—and stood to one side, sheepish and noncommittal at the ridicule that greeted his nephew when he joined the others with his crude homemade sled. With their steel runners, they could even belly-whop down the snow-covered stone stairs of the Mt. Morris Park hill. Ira's flimsy sled came apart after a few tries on just a gentle incline. Yes, spraddled out into a silly apple-box with the label still on it, and pieces of board with nails sticking out of the erstwhile runners, a sorry cripple, a caricature of a sled, abandoned in the snow . . .

And with Harry, the ordeal of his elementary schooling over, the two tried hawking Yiddish newspapers after school, crying the headlines through the darkening streets of Jewish Harlem, but with little success. They had no great "Wuxtra" to peddle like the great extra in August a few months ago, and passersby knew it. . . . So their cry was in vain, and most of their papers went unsold, and in a day or two they gave up the venture.

But for over seventy years there would remain in Ira's mind the projection of a kid in knee-pants and long black stockings hustling, panicky and shrill through a Harlem street into the twilight of the past. . . .

And ever and again in idleness, he would experience a harking back to a time — or forward to a time — not haphazard as the present had become, but seamless again, as it once had been; a harking back, an inarticulate yearning that somewhere, somehow, the scattered pieces of his random world would coalesce into unity once more. Else, why did he stand here on this street corner, in his solitary rambling, familiar street corner in bustling Jewish Harlem, suddenly transfigured, full of aureate promise, a redemption beyond the big dope he was, the "big ham," the kids on the block called him, beyond Pop's exasperated cry in Yiddish: "*Lemakh!* What a lame Turk you've turned out to be!"

—Oh, yes, you did have little jobs, didn't you? You tried to earn something.

Before school. He got up early in the morning, in the slum-bleary winter morning, and delivered fresh rolls and butter or cream cheese to homes on 119th Street, between Park and Madison, where the houses were a little better—and more Jewish. Yes, the grocer in the same block hired him. Shadowy, the kid running up and down stairs with fresh "bulkies." Though Pop was always pleased when Ira earned a dollar or two, and his attitude during the time of his son's earning would change—he would become friendly; he would tease Mom that Ira's earnings should be deducted from her allowance. "*Geh mir in d'red!*" she would flush, and cry out, "*Geh mir in d'red!*"—it was Mom who objected to her son's before-school delivery route, his early-morning exploitation, poor child. "I don't need the few *shmoolyaris,*" she said, calling the despised dollar a *shmoolyareh,* as was her wont. And he worked after school in a small, frowsy storefront shop where the owner and his wife, who lived in the rear, made fancy buttons; and Ira was taught how to make fancy buttons too: by spreading a patch of cloth on top of the bare metal button, and with a lever-operated press, force the cloth to unite with the metal. Working, as was his wont, lackadaisically, he caught his thumb between punch and button, and howled with pain.

He was sent on errands: once to deliver buttons to a tailor shop on east "A hundert und taiteent stritt." Of course, Ira duly went to east a hundred and eighteenth street, found no tailor shop there, and reported back, with the buttons undelivered.

"I said a hundert und taiteent stritt," the boss repeated in a dudgeon.

"I went there!" Ira clamored: "A hundred and eighteenth street."

"No! *Oy, gewald!* Vot's wrunk vit you? Taiteen, taiteen, not eighteen!"

And: at age eleven (How brief the age of innocence: The troll is on the bridge, Billygoat Gruff.). At age eleven, he worked in Biolov's drugstore. Every day after school, and Saturdays all day. Doing all kinds of things, from chores to running errands: mopping the tiled floor, polishing the showcases—with a sheet of newspaper. "A little more elbow grease," said the short, bald, affable Mr. Biolov. Elbow grease. It was the first time Ira had heard the expression, and for a moment he thought such a substance really existed. Delivering prescriptions, running errands. And all this for $2.50 per week. And when he lost, or his pocket was picked of a five-dollar bill Mr. Biolov had given him with which to buy drugs at the wholesale drug depot on Third Avenue, Ira had to work two weeks to make up for the loss. Mortars and pestles, yes, yes, in which drugs were ground, mixed in the back room of the drugstore. Syrup simple was sugar-water, wasn't it? Sarsaparilla went with castor oil. Mr. Biolov was a "*shtickel duckter,*" Mom said, meaning he was a "bit of a doctor." He gave first aid to accident victims who were brought into the drugstore, until the ambulance arrived. He took cinders out of eyes; he knew when to prescribe Seidlitz Powder and when to prescribe the dried berries that Mom brewed into a tea and were so pleasantly laxative; and when to prescribe citrate of magnesia—which was kept on ice, was cold and bubbly and lemony, and sent you to the toilet just as fast almost as castor oil. Sarsaparilla. Spirits of ammonia. Oil of peppermint. There were jars and jars of every sort of compound on the shelves, not ordinary jars, but all uniform in shape, made of pretty enamel, with wide mouths and glass stoppers.

In the back of the drugstore were special boards with long grooves in them which Mr. Biolov filled with the paste he made by grinding drugs together, and then cut the long worms of paste into pills, rolling them afterward in powdered sugar. In each corner of the store window stood two glorious glass amphorae, each one full of liquid, one brilliant green in color, the other brilliant ruby. Between them, in the middle of the show window, a fake monkey performed his tedious, tireless trick of pouring the same fluid from one glass to another. And once, made curious by Mr. Biolov's secretive manner, Ira peeked into the little package he was given to deliver: a peculiar shallow rubber cup around a ring: puzzling; it wasn't a condom; he had already seen those; he knew about them: scumbags they were called in the street. He too retrieved a package of them that were thrown into the waste basket, and tried blowing them up, but the rubber had deteriorated, and they popped. Best of all, he liked fetching people to the telephone booth in the store; they almost always gave him a nickel tip for the service; and more than once, when he called an Irish girl to the phone, a pretty Irish girl, with pink cheeks and eyes glistening, hurrying down the stairs after him through a cabbagey-permeated tenement, the deeply-breathing, far-away-looking girl gave him a dime. He could guess why, though he couldn't understand why. Rankling over Mr. Biolov's callousness in making him work two weeks for nothing, Ira worked a few weeks longer, and then quit.

And now it was summer again; random, rambling summer. There were certain trees on Madison Avenue that grew between the sidewalk and Mt. Morris Park, which shed a small green seed-pod that came twirling down. "Polly-noses," the kids named them; they could be split and were sticky and stuck to the bridge of one's nose. It was on a summer night that Ira licked the only kid he ever licked in Harlem, Jewish Morty Nussbaum who lived on the top floor of 108 East. Morty had wanted to show Ira how to "pull off"—when the two were sitting in warm weather up on the roof, and both had gotten their peckers out. And then suddenly Ira refused to go on. Memory seemed to scramble into separate ugly clots: of a lanky individual in a pork-pie hat and rusty-neat clothes, of what he wanted to do to Ira, and of what he did afterward against a tree trunk. Despite Morty's urgings that it was good, Ira balked; instead he rebuttoned his fly. How could anything be good that was as loathsome as that? Later, over some trifling dispute, he beat Morty in a fistfight, beat him easily. And even as Ira knew he was winning, he was conscious at the same time of the Irish kids egging the two on, two Jewish kids. And though exultant at winning, when

Morty all at once admitted defeat, Ira disregarded the Irish kids' injunction that he pound Morty on the back while yelling in traditional boast of triumph: two, four, six, eight, nine, I can beat you any old time. Soon after, Morty and his family moved away.

In the summer, you could walk and walk and walk all the way to the Museum of Natural History. You had read in the 6A Current Events news-sheet that several large meteorites that fell from out of the sky now rested in front of the museum doors. You didn't have to go inside—maybe they wouldn't let you—but it didn't matter, because it was the meteorites you wanted to see, and they were outside. You wanted to see them, because it said in small print down at the bottom of the *Book of Norse Mythology* that the reason why Siegfried's sword was so sharp might have been that it was made from a meteorite, and meteorites often contained special steel, so hard that after the sword was forged and sharpened, it could be dipped in a brook, and would shear tiny bits of lint and fleece floating against it. Imagine how sharp that was! Something to marvel at while walking and walking along the paved paths inside Central Park in the green, green of summer—past stylish people sporting silver-headed canes, past the nursemaids and the fancy baby carriages, fancier even than Mrs. Biolov's, the fanciest on the block—until the long, long walk brought you to the immense museum building whose entrance was at the bottom of a short flight of stairs. And down the stairs you went timidly, to stand in awe before the stark, pitted boulders: those were meteorites fallen from heaven to earth.

"*Siz a manseh mit a bear,*" Mom twitted him fondly, when he had trudged home at last, and told her what he had discovered.

"It's not a *manseh mit a bear!*" he flared up. "It's about the Norse gods: Odin and Thor and Loki. And about Siegfried and Brunhild. You don't know what a wonderful sword he had."

"*Azoi?*" she placated. "My clever son. A *bulkie* and fresh farmer's cheese would go well after such a long journey, no?"

Stories with a bear, Mom called them. But he liked them much better than he did those by Horatio Alger, the kind of stories that Davey Baer liked: *Tom the Bootblack* or *Pluck and Luck,* the kind the other kids liked: Tom Swift and his motorcycle, and how

resourcefully he could fix it with a piece of fence wire; or the Rover
Boys who were so honest, and played baseball so well; or Young
Wild West in fringed buckskin fighting treacherous "Injuns,"
though Ira couldn't tell why. And some of the fairy tales, and stories
about witches and hobgoblins scared him so, he was afraid of the
dark, afraid to go down into the cellar alone and fetch a pail of
coal out of the padlocked crib; fearful even when he had to take
the garbage can down to the big trash cans in front of the house
at night—how he shirked, how he fought doing that chore! The
closed cellar door at the foot of the feebly lit stairs before he turned
to enter the hallway to the street filled him with panic.

Still, those were the stories he prized above all others, stories
he loved: of enchantment and delicacy, of princelings and fair
princesses. So often the princesses were not only fair, but they were
the fairest in Christendom. You couldn't help that. Maybe they
wouldn't mind if he was Jewish. And King Arthur's knights, they
sought the Holy Grail, the radiant vessel like a loving cup out of
which Jesus had drunk wine. So everything beautiful was Christian,
wasn't it? All that was flawless and pure and bold and courtly and
chivalric was *goyish*. He didn't know what to feel some times: sadness; he was left out; it was a relief when Jews weren't mentioned;
he was thankful: he could fight the Saracens with Roland. Or he
could appreciate seeing Mr. Toil everywhere, when the boy in the
Grimm fairy tale ran away from his teacher, Mr. Toil, even leading
the band of musicians—as long as he wasn't Jewish. . . .

XIII

M came into his study. She had two skeins of wool she wanted to show
him, one jet-black, one oxford-gray. "I don't know why I didn't think of
weaving the worn places in the *chaleco* again," she said.

"The one on your back?" he asked: M was wearing the salt-and-
pepper woven *chaleco* she had bought in Mexico — where was it? Not

Tlaqui-paqui, or however it was spelled, where the young weaver worked in dim light at a loom (and Ira also bought a *chaleco*). That was in the late '60s.

"Yes. It's true it doesn't owe me anything," she said. "But I like it."

"And where will you get such a rarity again," he agreed.

Such a rarity again — he thought afterward, after she left for the piano in the living room. My love, it would take a Taj Mahal in *belles lettres* to do you justice, tall, spare woman grown old, your once tawny hair, gray. Wrinkled, your lovely countenance, but still noble. Where did the millions of moments go, the million millions of moments spent together? She had just returned from shopping, and she said: "Do you think the cold weather kept the shoppers away? They were out in droves today. Of course the last two days weren't very conducive for shopping. No one wanted to brave the cold."

"No, that's right."

"And I brought you a present for your birthday: a turkey pastrami loaf." She displayed it, a small brick of meat, tightly sealed in plastic.

He thought of an electric slicer, of getting one, but she wouldn't approve: One more thing in the house, she would say in her equable, sensible fashion. He settled for, "Oh, great! Thanks."

"I guess we'll have to throw away those two coupons for Hardee's two-for-the-price-of-one roast beef sandwiches. Tomorrow is the last day, and we're having Margaret for company."

"Do you know McDonald's is now advertising a thirty-nine-cent hamburger?"

"The competition must be fierce."

"There's another thirty-nine-cent hamburger chain that's just opened in town. You saw it with me the other day."

"Oh, yes."

"I wonder what a thirty-nine-cent hamburger looks like?"

"Let's buy a half-dozen — " he suggested. "Since the McDonald's place is so near."

"I'll probably put all three meat patties in one bun."

That was why she remained so thin and distinguished in figure: three patties in one bun. And he, plebeian: "Oh, I like my tissue-paper buns. I'm used to eating that way."

And all this, he reflected — after she was well launched rehearsing a piece at the piano, a familiar piece whose name he would be ashamed to admit he didn't know — he would find out another time — all this, because he had asked her if she knew where one of his short stories was kept, or stored: She was so methodical, so efficient, all the enviable things he wasn't. She knew, and faithfully brought him the carton, requiring only that she would have to sit down while she rummaged for the one he wanted: It was a sketch he had done for *The New Yorker,* and been lucky enough to have it accepted. Done in 1940, and what would he think of it now; would it fit into what he was doing, fit into the structure, or the mood? Forty-five years ago, forty-five years closer to the self-involved, self-indulgent, ill-at-ease, lonesome, moody, aimless scapegrace he was then . . . tailored, to be sure, for *The New Yorker.* Would the piece still contain enough truth in it, fidelity to something he once was, to warrant the work of retyping, of inclusion here?

SOMEBODY ALWAYS GRABS THE PURPLE

Up a flight of stairs, past the vases and the clock outside the adult reading room, past cream walls, oak moldings, oak bookcases, and the Cellini statue of Perseus was the children's room of the 123rd Street Branch Library. Young Sammy Farber drew a battered library card out of his pocket and went in. He was a thick-set, alert boy, eleven or twelve years old. He flattened his card on the desk and, while he waited for the librarian, gazed about. There were only a few youngsters in the reading room. Two boys in colored jerseys stood whispering at one of the bookcases. On the wall above their heads was a frieze of Grecian urchins blowing trumpets. The librarian approached.

"Teacher," Sammy began, "I just moved, Teacher. You want to change it—the address?"

The librarian, a spare woman, graying and impassive, with a pince-nez, glanced at this card. "Let me see your hands, Samuel," she said.

He lifted his hands. She nodded approvingly and turned his

card over. It was well stamped. "You'd better have a new one," she said.

"Can I get it next time, Teacher? I'm in a hurry like."

"Yes. Where do you live now, Samuel?"

"On 520 East 120th Street." He watched her cross out the Orchard Street address and begin writing the new one. "Teacher," he said in a voice so low it was barely audible, "you got here the *Purple Fairy Book?*"

"The what?"

"The *Purple Fairy Book.*" He knuckled his nose sheepishly. "Everybody says I'm too big to read fairy books. My mother calls 'em stories with a bear."

"Stories with a bear?"

"Yeah, she don't know English good. You got it?"

"Why, yes. I think it's on the shelves."

"Where, Teacher?" He moved instantly toward the aisle.

"Just a moment, Samuel. Here's your card." He seized it. "Now I'll show you where it is."

Together they crossed the room to a bookcase with a brass plate which said "Fairy Tales." Sammy knelt down so that he could read the titles more easily. There were not a great many books in the case—a few legends for boys about Arthur and Roland on the top shelf, then a short row of fairy tales arranged according to countries, and finally, on the bottom shelf, a few fairy books arranged by colors: Blue, Blue, Green. Her finger on the titles wavered. Red . . . Yellow . . . "I'm sorry."

"Ah!" he said, relaxing. "They grabbed it again."

"Have you read the others? Have you read the Blue?"

"Yeah, I read the Blue." He stood up slowly. "I read the Blue and the Green and the Yellow. All the colors. And colors that ain't even here. I read the Lilac. But somebody always grabs the Purple."

"I'm pretty sure the *Purple Fairy Book* hasn't been borrowed," the librarian said. "Why don't you look on the tables? It may be there."

"I'll look," he said. "But I know. Once they grab it, it's goodbye."

Nevertheless he went from table to table, picking up abandoned books, scanning their titles, and putting them down again.

His round face was the image of forlorn hope. As he neared one of the last tables, he stopped. A boy was sitting there with a stack of books at his elbow, reading with enormous concentration. Sammy walked behind the boy and peered over his shoulder. On one page there was print, on the other a colored illustration, a serene princeling, hand on the hilt of his sword, regarding a gnarled and glowering gnome. The book was bound in purple. Sammy sighed and returned to the librarian.

"I found it, Teacher. It's over there," he said, pointing. "He's got it."

"I'm sorry, Samuel. That's the only copy we have."

"His hands ain't as clean as mine," Sammy suggested.

"Oh, I'm sure they are. Why don't you try something else?" she urged. "Adventure books are very popular with boys."

"They ain't popular with him." Sammy gazed gloomily at the boy. "That's what they always told me on the East Side—popular, I don't see what's so popular about them. If a man finds a treasure in an adventure book, so right away it's with dollars and cents. Who cares from dollars and cents? I get enough of that in my house."

"There's fiction," she reminded him. "Perhaps you're the kind of boy who likes reading about grown-ups."

"Aw, them too!" He tossed his head. "I once read a fiction book, it had in it a hero with eyeglasses? Hih!" His laugh was brief and pitying. "How could heroes be with eyeglasses? That's like my father."

The librarian placed her pince-nez a little more securely on her nose. "He may leave it, of course, if you wait," she said.

"Can I ask him?"

"No. Don't disturb him."

"I just want to ask him if he gonna take it or ain't he. What's the use I should hang around all day?"

"Very well. But that's all."

Sammy walked over to the boy again and said, "Hey, you're gonna take it, aintcha?"

Like one jarred out of sleep, the boy started, his eyes blank and wide.

"What d'you want to read from that stuff?" Sammy asked. "Fairy tales!" His lips, his eyes, his whole face expressed distaste. "There's an adventure book here," he said, picking up the one nearest his hand. "Don't you like adventure books?"

The boy drew himself up in his seat. "What're you botherin' me for?" he said.

"I ain't botherin' you. Did you ever read the *Blue Fairy Book?* That's the best. That's a hard one to get."

"Hey, I'll tell the teacher on you!" The boy looked around. "I'm reading this!" he said angrily. "And I don't want no other one! Read 'em yourself!"

Sammy waited a moment and then tried again. "You know you shouldn't read fairy books in the library."

The boy clutched the book to himself protectively and rose. "You want to fight?"

"Don't get excited," Sammy waved him back into the chair and retreated a step. "I was just sayin' fairy tales is better to read in the house, ain't it—like when you're sittin' in the front room and your mother's cookin' in the kitchen? Ain't that nicer?"

"Well, what about it?"

"So in the liberry you can read from other things. From King Arthur or from other mitts."

The boy saw through that ruse also. He waved Sammy away. "I'm gonna read it here and I'm gonna read it home too, wise guy."

"All right, that's all I wanted to ask you," said Sammy. "You're gonna take it, aintcha?"

"Sure I'm gonna take it."

"I thought you was gonna take it."

Sammy retreated to one of the central pillars of the reading room and stood there, watching. The same play of wonder and beguilement that animated the boy's thin features while he read also animated Sammy's pudgy ones, as though the enjoyment were being relayed. After a time the boy got up and went to the desk with the book still in his hand. The librarian took the card out of the book and stamped the boy's own card. Then she handed him the book. Sammy's round face dimmed. He waited, however, until the boy had had the time to get out of the reading room and down the stairs before he put his worn library card in his pocket and made for the exit.

"Somebody Always Grabs the Purple"
The New Yorker, March 23, 1940

Well . . . it was touching, but not too touching. It was *The New Yorker* after all, of that period, with its aim, as it was perhaps today, though he scarcely read the magazine, with its aim of diverting the reader, presumably the fairly discriminating, well-to-do reader. It had been written according to the directives his literary agent at the time impressed on him: that he was never to get the reader to identify with the central character of a story, but to feel slightly superior to him. And so the kid in the sketch was himself and not himself. Ira thought ironically of the Hamlet alternative of being or not being. It was both always, it could only be a unity when both were together. It was strange though, and more than a little retarding — was that the right word? — arresting, inhibiting, to view this evidence of the writer he was, he once was, the preserved specimen of the writer he had been: the arrogant, egotistic, self-assured author of his first novel. Rereading his product of forty-five years ago drained him of what he was today . . . something better than he *had* been, he thought, he hoped. Ah, how could you have let that life, all that life and configuration and trenchancy and conflict escape you? when it was still accessible, still at hand, retrievable, still close.

God, fourteen years spent in that slum of Harlem, with its changing composition and context, its squalid designs — let it get away from you, a mountain of copy, as the journalist would say, local color, novelty, from the moment you stepped into the street, stepped in or out the hallway. You blew it, that was the current expression; he would think of it a million times more, after M had lifted him up in bed, because his rheumatoid arthritis all but immobilized him after a night's immobility. He took his hot shower, to limber him up a little, and came out of it, mourning rather than reflecting: Ah, the lost riches — what was it? The Joycean, sordid riches?

Perhaps because his view of it had changed: He couldn't accept *only* a surface perception of it anymore. Was that the effect of Marxism? Of the Party's influence? He had to consider, to recognize, somehow to indicate implicitly in his writing the cruel social relations beneath, the cruel class relations, the havoc inflicted by deprivation concealed under the overtly ludicrous. No more the Olympian mix of Anatole France's irony and pity. And that was why he rebelled against Joyce with such animosity today. Anyway, something had barred the way, at the same time, as it undermined the way. That something they would call today loss of identity. And with loss of identity came loss of affirmation. And without either identity or affirmation, the great panorama of fourteen years of life in and out of 119th Street in Harlem was denied him — in fact, if one wanted to amplify it, ramify it, even adulthood was interdicted, adequate adulthood.

So he felt gloomy, pensive. . . . You know why I can't delineate it now, Ecclesias.

—I know you know why.

What summer day was it he went striding in the freshness of morning, in the happiness of a newborn school vacation, to the Metropolitan Museum, solitary? (Set it down, set it down: No one else on 119th Street wanted to go.) Hiking between the dark, weathered, low stone wall that girded up the embankment of the park inside, separated it from the avenue and the row after row of mansions, the immeasurably opulent mansions across the avenue. Under the trees, in leaf, on Fifth Avenue, sturdily striding Ira, admiring, reveling in the lordly bay windows of imposing edifices pouting in pride, with each shade drawn down to the same distance. And the marble lintels, the organ-clusters of chimney pots rising from slate roofs with verdigris copper trim. While on the avenue, the double-decker buses ran, the ten-cent-fare buses that only the rich could afford.

"Where are you off to, young man?" asked the stout gentleman with the straw-colored mustache who was standing beside the lady with eyeglasses who was also waiting for the bus at the curb.

"Me? I'm goin' to the museum."

"Really? So early in the morning?"

"Yeh. It's far away." Had he by now learned to be wary of gentle strangers? Or did the presence of a woman give him a sense of security? "And after I go there and see, I have to come back all the way too."

"Of course."

The two waiting for the bus turned toward each other, a faint smile on each face, and he was on his way again. The moment would abide in memory like a fine stanza of a poem, or a few bars of fine melody that consoled in later years. In these hollow, later years, Ecclesias, when the silver cord is loosed, and the bearings burned, the threads stripped off the screw, or the contact lens blown away by the breeze.

XIV

The Great War had come much closer—he would have to make his way as best he could among roughly typed sheets in disorder, and his memory a farrago. Much closer. Already Ira had seen and heard elderly Jews in Mt. Morris Park rise angrily from benches and brandish canes at each other, while they exchanged insults in Yiddish: "Pompous German! Coarse Litvack!" . . .

Waylaid en route to the floating East River swimming pool by a scowling little gang of Italian kids, he was menaced with: "Which side you on? What're you? A German? You from Austria?"

Ira surmised what might be in store. "Nah. Not me."

"What're you then?"

"I'm a Hungarian. Hungarians don't like Austrians."

His accosters were nonplussed. "Talk Hungarian," their leader challenged.

"Sure. *Choig iggid bolligid.* That means I like you."

"How do we know?" a henchman demanded.

"I can say it again," Ira offered.

"Say that you're on the 'Tollian side in Hungarian," the leader probed.

"*Choig iligid bolligid Tollyanis.*"

"Let him go," the leader decreed.

And go Ira did . . .

The Great War came closer. The Huns impaled babies on their

bayonets—though Mom ridiculed stories of German atrocities. "What, the Russ is better? Czar *Kolki* [*kolki* meant bullet] *iz a feiner mensh?* Who in all the world is more benighted than the Russian *mujik?* Who doesn't remember their *pogroms,* the Kishinev *pogroms,* in 1903? *Pogroms* led by seminary students, especially on Easter— Kishinev when I was still a maid. And after they lost to the *Ya-ponchikis* when I met your father, immediately they take it out on the Jews. Go! More likely the Russ impaled the infant on his bayonet."

And for once, Pop agreed wholeheartedly. "Don't you remember Mendel Beiliss when we still lived on the East Side?" Pop prodded Ira. "Where is your head? You don't remember the turmoil there was when the Russ tried and sentenced him? And why? The Jew butchered a *goyish* child for his blood to make *matzahs* for Passover. And the *mujik* believed it."

"Maybe a *goy* saw us eating *borsht* on Passover." Ira suggested. "That's red."

"Go, you're a fool." said Pop. "A *mujik* is a *mujik* and he'll die a *mujik.* Who doesn't know a *mujik?*"

"I'll tell you, child," said Mom. "It's thus with Jews: When two monarchs are at war, and one scourges the other's Jews, the second one says, 'Since you scourge my Jews, I'll scourge your Jews.' " Mom laughed mirthlessly. "You understand?"

The Great War drew closer. Oh, the confusions in a child's mind! Uncle Louis, still wearing his postman's uniform, came to the house with the Socialist *Call* in his pocket, and unfolding the newspaper on the green oilcloth-covered kitchen table, read from it what Eugene Debs said about the war—and always drew Mom into the orbit of conversation: "You hear, Leah? Debs said it was a capitalist war in which the workers paid with their lives for capitalists of one country to become more powerful than the capitalists of another country, to take over their trade, their colonies—which were seized by force from the simple people who lived there, stolen, you might say. But no matter who won, the workers would still be wage-slaves."

Pop listened intently, his whole face taking on a new appearance, as if illuminated; Mom more distantly. "Woodrow Wilson talks about defending democracy. You have no idea of how much the anti-Semitism in the Post Office has grown."

"Where is a Jew liked?" Mom asked rhetorically. "Nowhere. He makes good cannon fodder. That's the way it is in Russia, in all of Europe. Even in Austria where Franz Josef tolerates the Jew. He won't allow Black Hundreds to instigate *pogroms,* as they do in Russia under the Czar. So the Jew is a little safer, he can breathe a little freer. Still is the Jew liked? Need I ask? One thing they like him for: Give me your Jew to be a soldier. He at least has learned to read and write."

Uncle Louie regarded her admiringly, looked away, his lips spreading as he swallowed. And to Pop: "You almost became a soldier yourself."

Pop beamed; he loved to reminisce: "When I returned to Austria where I was inveigled into marrying her."

It was joke Mom didn't appreciate. "Naturally, you quarreled first with Gabe," she reminded him. Gabe was Pop's oldest brother, and lived now in St. Louis. There was a whole web of relatives on Pop's side of the family, almost all of whom had immigrated to Chicago or St. Louis, relatives too numerous and too remote to hope to keep track of. As disclosed by Mom, it was mostly their scandalous behavior in America or Galitzia that provided Ira with the meager sense of kinship with them he possessed.

What if they had settled in New York, as Pop eventually did? Then there would have been two clans, the long-established Americanized first generation, the "yellow-ripe" Americans, as the Jews termed the acculturated immigrant, and the "green" Americans, Mom's family. What a web that would have made as he shuttled back and forth between Zaida's orthodoxy and traits, and Uncle Gabe and Sam in St. Louis, and Uncle Jacob in Chicago. It was safe to say there would have been an affinity, or similarity, between Uncle Jacob and Zaida, but not much, or much less, with the other two uncles on his father's side. Though they were close to Zaida in age, temperamentally, Ira gathered from Mom's report, their outlook and behavior were much closer to that of his more recently arrived uncles.

Oh, it would have been some web—Ira paused to thank his lucky stars he didn't have that to struggle with. The merest outline of what he recalled would suffice—if it wasn't already superfluous:

Sam, Pop's next older brother, strong and strapping, had been a soldier, and had fallen in love with someone else's wife—to the great disapproval of his father, the stern, bearded Jew with earlocks, next to the portrait of his equally severe-looking wife on the front-room wall. And they quarreled, Sam and his father, who had lifted his cane to strike his son only to have it snatched from his hand by his son and be struck with it himself. Sam fled to America with the other man's wife. So Mom, the source of all these stories, related, and that Gabe had married a woman considerably older than himself, Clara by name, and a termagant. "*Oy*, is that a Clara," said Mom. "And jealous. And a shrew. Fearful!" Pop's nearest brother in age, Jacob, the one in Chicago, the one who had irruptions on his skin, was a weakling, and often when studying Talmud was baited by his younger brother, Pop, until the two came to blows. And once Jacob was so badly beaten by Pop that he had to hide out from his father's retribution. He slept in an outbuilding, was fed surreptitiously by his mother late at night. There was an older sister, Khatche, who married a dandy by the name of Schnapper, an extremely handsome man and a libertine. They too lived in the Middle West, though not in St. Louis or Chicago. And so tortured was she by the knowledge of her philandering husband's ill-concealed and continual *amours*, that one day she poured kerosene over herself and set herself on fire (Mom lowered her voice in the telling). And Ira would note, yes, years and years later, when visiting Fannie, a very pretty, regular-featured woman—no mistaking she was Schnapper's daughter—Ira would note how the old man, Schnapper himself, now in his nineties, sitting by the window on the ground floor, would appraise every female that went by: It was like a reflex, the way he would twitch at the sight of a skirt. And since Pop was the *youngest* of his parents' children, while Uncle Louis was the first-born of Pop's older sister, that was how it came about that the nephew was older than the uncle.

And Pop's father—though Mom said that the night before she and her child were to leave for America, Ira, a tot of two years and a half, had danced so fetchingly before his grandsire that tears had sprung to the old man's eyes as he leaned on his cane watching—Pop's father Ira never remembered. Out of another age, truly, Ira would feel—as he did about some of his very old grammar school teachers—this grandfather in his eighties who died in 1914, soon after the outbreak of the War. Seized as a rich Jew by Czarist soldiery, when they invaded Galitzia he was held for ransom. He was thrown from the wagon into the ditch when the Russian troops fled in disorder before the counterattacking Austrian army. The weather had already turned cold; he suffered frostbite, and was only rescued because some peasant passing by heard the old man's groans and recognized him as Saul, superintendent of the baron's distillery, and known far and wide for his skill as a veterinarian. The peasant took the octogenarian to his hut, cared for him until relatives were notified and came for him and brought him back under their own roof. But the exposure and shock were too much for his aged constitution, and Saul, the superintendent, Shaul Shaffer, as he was known, died soon after— in the fall of 1914, the fall of the same year Baba and Zaida and their offspring came to America. Pop hadn't quarreled with his in-laws yet. He went to their home, when Ira was there, and squatted on a footstool close to the floor. It was the first time Ira had ever seen anyone sit *shivah,* as the seven days of mourning were called. . . .

"Yes," Pop resumed, addressing Uncle Louie. "They threw me into jail, into the *sraimoolyeh* (wasn't that a comical word for jail?). Pop laughed. "Because I came back to Austria, and I hadn't reported for conscription. So they threw me into jail. They didn't know I was an American citizen already—or they didn't want to know. Gabe made me a citizen before I was of age, so I could vote a straight Republican ticket. In 1900 I became a citizen. I was born in 1882. I was only eighteen, and a birth certificate I didn't have. So Gabe said, say you're twenty-one; Gabe was my witness I was twenty-one."

"And why did the Austrians let you out of jail?" asked Uncle Louis.

"Whether because they found out I was an American citizen,

or because I didn't pass the examination—big and strong I'm not—
the warden came in, and 'Out! Out!' he said." Pop laughed, and
laughed again: "There was somebody else there—we were three,
four in the cell—you should *anshuldig mir,* he could make a *fartz*
whenever he wanted. Say to him, '*Fartz,* Stanislas.' Hup! A *Fartz.*
Kheh, kheh, kheh!"

XV

The war came closer. Confused by strange stirrings within him,
strange rumors without, the Great War would always remain
cloudy, a nebulous complex of memory without regard for time
or relevance. Mamie, mother of two daughters now, always bought
Ira a flannel shirt for his birthday, a new gray flannel shirt. Of
what relevance to the Great War was that? The question made him
feel as if he were answering some kind of catechism: In the impoverished life in that taken-for-granted, dreary cold-water flat,
gas-mantle-lit still, the kitchen alone was heated in winter—by the
twinkling row of blue beads of the single long burner of the gas
oven. The kitchen alone was warm, fetid sometimes, while the other
three rooms on the other side of the closed door to the rest of the
flat were ice cold. And so he went to bed under the frigid goose-
feather-stuffed ticking. Unquilted, the feathers in it shifted and
bunched from one end to the other, and one had to pedal an
imaginary bicycle the first few minutes after getting into bed in
order to generate a pod of warmth. Yes, they came from Europe:
The featherbeds were heirlooms made of goosedown.

"In the winter when we had nothing to do," said Pop, remi-
niscing nostalgically, "everybody sat around the big table in my
father's house, and we took the big feathers from the goose, the
big wing feathers, and the tail feathers, and we stripped off the
feather from the quill. Even those we saved, the little feathers from
the quill." And the ticking also had two or three coins enclosed in

it—Ira could feel the coins sometimes when they collected in a corner, but the ticking was sewn so tightly, you couldn't get them out. (They were charms, he learned later, included with the feathers to bring fecundity and good fortune.) And kind-hearted Mamie gave her nephew a pair of high-laced boots, not new, but oh, how treasured! High boots to wear in snow of any depth.

"On your soil they didn't grow," Mom said ironically. "Well, may you mirror yourself in them."

Unaccountable stirrings and compulsions: He was in 6A or 6B, the last year of his attendance in P.S. 103, the "elementary school," as it was called. What prompted him to skulk across the street that afternoon, after dismissal, opposite the big oak doors of the main entrance? And to wait until Miss Driscoll came out, his teacher. Tall, slender, unsmiling, aloof Miss Driscoll, of the refined, delicate features. With guilty, nameless excitement, he stalked her, block after block, to 125th Street, keeping her just barely in sight ahead of him. To what mysterious abode was she bound? What mysterious rites would be performed there, or what languors would she surrender to, or to what secret lover?

Miss Driscoll sauntered west along busy 125th Street, alone and dignified, while Ira, in her wake, wove in and out among pedestrians. Now north along mundane trolley-traveled Amsterdam Avenue, flanked by nondescript five-flight brick walk-ups whose roofs and stoops each rose a jog higher up the hill than the last. But Ira was sure that at the end was an inkling of breathless revelation, a rare insight, a discovery. North to the 130s, and still north. Miss Driscoll turned east again, downhill, between the walls of a huge stadium and gray and white buildings, like churches he had seen in pictures in fairy tales, or formidable castles, gray and white. And then—she turned a corner around one of the castles at the bottom of the hill, and as if by magic, disappeared. . . . But there was a door open at the corner where she had turned, at sidewalk level, where the buildings enclosed a big square, with flagpole and trees and a lofty clock in a turret of gray and white stone. So that was where she went? There were other people about, some women, like Miss Driscoll, but most of them young men, and many of them carrying books or briefcases. So it was just another school. Was that all? Disappointed and chagrined, he turned to retrace his steps in the hour before dusk, leaving behind the gray and white buildings that looked like churches or castles. . . .

How many times would he pass that same door on his way to class, pass it so many times he all but forgot it was the same door. One could brood, one could brood, that the fecklessness, nay, the folly of the youth was even greater than the simple fecklessness of the kid he had been. But what the hell good was it to be aware of the fact?

Came those first intimations as well—signals whose significance he would recognize later, he would be able to name later when he strove to realize them—intimations of a calling. Something innate burgeoned inside you, identifiable, and yet mostly wordless, an urge that was yours alone. The kid in his mackinaw on the way home from the library on 124th Street, at 6:00 P.M. at closing time in the upstairs reading room. Tucked under his arm are the volumes of myths and legends he loved so well. And he passes below the hill on Mt. Morris Park in autumn twilight, with the evening star in the west in limpid sky above the wooden bell tower. And so beautiful it was: a rapture to behold. It set him a problem he never dreamed anyone set himself. How do you say it? Before the pale blue twilight left your eyes you had to say it, use words that said it: blue, indigo, blue, indigo. Words that matched, matched that swimming star above the hill and the tower; what words matched it? Lonely and swimming star above the hill. Not twinkling, nah, twinkle, twinkle, little star—those words belonged to someone else. You had to match it yourself: swimming in the blue tide, you could say . . . maybe. Like that bluing Mom rinses white shirts in. Nah, you couldn't say that. . . . How clear it is. One star shines over Mt. Morris Park hill. And it's getting dark, and it's getting cold— Gee, if instead of cold, I said chill. A star shines over Mt. Morris Park hill. And it's getting dark, and it's getting chill. . . .

P A R T   T W O

I

The time draws near. . . . Logy, and still under the spell of the mad dreams of last night, feverish and despairing, and affected by the influence of the drug he had taken in the early morning to ease the extreme pain of RA, he was loathe to proceed. But more than all that, because the time drew near.

Oh, it was not only the War — what was the War to a kid turned twelve? A surface comprehension, a sporadic awareness: the collection of peach pits for gas masks — in school — a patriotic speech, a comic strip, a poster, a song, a few words now and then, addressing the subject at home and in the street. He joined the Boy Scouts briefly, on a summer evening sitting on the curb with Davey Baer in front of the 124th Street Library opposite the north end of Mt. Morris Park — and he was soon diffidently selling Liberty Bonds in the evening to crowds gathered about a patriotic rally staged by his troop on Seventh Avenue and 116th Street. Heterogeneous fragmentary aspects that made few lasting and deep impressions — until that April day when America was already at war.

— But that was a year later. You were twelve.
Indeed. That was in 1918.
— And you're speaking of the year before, 1917.
Just before the United States entered the war. Yes.
— But the critical point, or moment, was 1918.
Yes.

—Then why not let it wait?

Why not indeed.

—You'll sooner or later have to get over that hurdle.

Yes.

—I told you at the outset, when you deliberately omitted that most crucial element in your account, that you would not be able to avoid reckoning with it.

You did, Ecclesias. Perhaps I wasn't ready for it.

—And are you now?

Yes. I became so.

—When you had to. It finally became inescapable.

Yes. Face-to-face with it as a consequence of continuing. Which is something, you notice, Ecclesias, I managed to evade in the only novel I ever wrote: coming to grips with it.

—It was adroit. You made a climax of evasion, an apocalypse out of your refusal to go on, an apocalyptic tour de force at the price of renouncing a literary future. As pyrotechnics, it was commendable, it found favor, at any rate. Proceed.

Pop suddenly decided he wanted to go to St. Louis; he yearned to revisit his brothers there; or was it some nostalgia too for those very first months in 1899 when he came to America? And interwoven with this, the usual illusion that in some way he might make a fresh start with the help of his brother Gabe, who by steady devotion to the Republican Party (and also by his allegiance to Freemasonry) had risen to a position of some importance within the ranks of the Republican Party: It was through Gabe's good offices that his brother Sam had secured the position of Inspector of Sanitation in the St. Louis Street Cleaning Department. In the same way, Gabe had secured for his nephew, also named Gabe, a position in the Comptroller's office. Uncle Gabe, Pop's brother, had become a power in the Republican Party not only because of his long and unswerving devotion to it, but even more because he had chosen to live in a largely "colored" neighborhood, and served the interests of his district with great sympathy and such exceptional dedication, he could be counted on eventually "to deliver the colored vote." "Maybe, maybe," said Pop, "I'll have luck this time." Success or failure was almost always a matter of luck with Pop—*mazel*—almost never a matter of good or bad judgment. "Maybe, maybe I'll have luck. Gabe could help me. He's got a lot of pull. You understand what pull means?" He interrogated Mom, and translated the word into Yiddish for her benefit: "Pull means he has the ear of the mayor and the assemblyman, and other *g'vir* among the politicians. He knows maybe where is a good luncheon-ette to open in City Hall. With pull and a few hundred dollars to help me out, I could also became a *makher*."

"You quarreled with him last time," Mom reminded him.

"Last time was last time. What has that to do with this?"

Mom grimaced.

"Then if nothing comes of it, still I would see my brothers. *You* have a whole tribe here in New York. Whom have I to turn to? Nobody."

"And when you were there, in St. Louis, much good it did you."

"Go, you speak like a fool. How can you compare the youth of eighteen I was then to the man I am now? I have a trade. I'm a waiter. I understand the restaurant business. A luncheonette, if I opened one with Gabe's advice, I wager would be a success. Let him only intercede for me among the politicians. Look what he did for my brother Sam, for my nephew Gabe S. And for young Sam, I hear he's helping him open a cigar store on a busy avenue."

"Let it be so," Mom acquiesced. "As long as you leave me my allowance to run the household."

"I'll leave you, I'll leave you. What, I'll depart without leaving you your eight dollars a week? The rent is paid, the gas bill is paid," Pop lapsed into *davening* singsong. "Two weeks' allowance I'll leave you. And the rest we'll see."

"*Nu,*" Mom raised resigned eyebrows, adding wryly: "I'll be without a husband—abandoned, like Mrs. Greenspan across the street. And when the family hears, what they'll say." She rocked her head.

"Let them gabble," said Pop. "Much good they've done me. Let me only have a little luck, I'd show them."

It was a relief for Ira to know that his father would be gone—for days on end—a relief, and yet also a little disquieting. The respite of Pop's absence, gladness of the new freedom he would enjoy meanwhile, was overlaid with Mom's anxiety over the absence of the family breadwinner.

In a week, Pop was packed to go, the clasps of his second-hand satchel on the kitchen floor reinforced with washline. Tense, his face pinched, his nervousness manifest in every movement, tiny red and blue capillaries webbed the end of his nose, conspicuous despite their minuteness, like the threads on a bank note. "*Nu*, Leah," he said, brusque with nervousness, "let us bid farewell and embrace."

"Let us bid farewell," said Mom.

They embraced, the thin, slight man with eyeglasses, the heavy, buxom woman, full-lipped, almost stolid. Like two strangers, embarrassed by the formality, they separated. "Go in good health," said Mom.

"I don't want to hear any bad report of you," Pop said to Ira.

He stooped, kissed Ira with strangely soft, tender lips, and picked up his satchel.

"You'll write," said Mom.

"What else? Of course." His face darkened with apprehension, he opened the door. "Goodbye." Closed it behind him.

"May he go in a happy hour," Mom said, but without conviction . . . sighed, "Ai, how he runs. Runs. God help him. Strange man. What can one do?" And after a troubled pause, "I'll go to Baba's for a little while. And shop on the way home. Do you want to come along?"

"No, I'll read."

"You'll read your eyes out. Shall I light the gas mantle now? It will soon be dark."

"No, it won't be," he said sulkily. "I can still see by the window."

She was gone an hour or two, returned just as dusk began to settle on the washpole and washlines in the backyard. She seemed not so much forlorn as resentful, angrily cheerless. Frowning, she prepared supper—one of Ira's favorite dishes, breaded veal cutlet—and then tried to restrain his voracity. "Now twice left behind. The first time in Tysmenitz with that stern, unbending mother-in-law, now here. Well, let him go—in a good year," she added, vexed at herself for being upset. "It's not Tysmenitz, where I waited on sufferance of my in-laws, months, till passage arrived, and with an infant. I can see by your face you don't care to hear these things."

"No, I don't. That's Europe."

"Much difference that made— No, indeed," she corrected herself. "You're right. That's what I ought to say: That was Tysmenitz, and I was alone, half among strangers. This is New York, America. My family is here. I have relatives. Still, where is he running? Will he find better reception with the brother he quarreled with years ago? They need him? As I need a plague. He hunts for rusty horseshoes. A settled man would long ago have found a suitable livelihood: If not in ladies' wear, like Mamie's Joe, then in other things. He's a waiter, then remain a waiter. My brother Moe is now a head waiter in the same restaurant where he began as a waiter. My Chaim has become known in half the dairy restaurants on the East Side, and without doubt, half the vegetarian restaurants as well. What to do?"

"All right!" Ira countered impatiently.

"Indeed all right. I made some compote."

"All right."

She got up from the table to serve him. "Upstairs lives a Mrs. Karp. The man goes to work day in day out. At what? He's a curtain maker. He doesn't seek to become a boss overnight. I'm sure they're saving money. Because she told me when the time is ripe, and they have the money, with God's help they hope to buy out a small curtain-making factory. The boss himself might accept part payment. His children shun curtain making. Their minds are set only on going to college. So prudent people plan. She will help; her youngsters will help. They're practical. They trust each other. They devise the future together. With him, everything is a secret, his earnings, his schemes."

"All right!" Ira interrupted.

"In truth, why do I trouble you with this." She set the compote before him. "The heart speaks of its own accord."

He did homework until bedtime. He disliked arithmetic drill; most arithmetic that had to do with dollars and cents: interest on money in the bank, commission on sales, profit in trade. He hated long division. Only when there was a figure to deal with did he like doing the example: an oblong, a square, a triangle that gave you a formula to apply. He disliked geography, he tolerated history. But reading, ah! That was the trouble; he spent too much time reading, at the expense of everything else. He hadn't read so much on 9th Street; he couldn't even recall where the library was on the East Side. He knew where the *cheder* was, but not the library. Now it was almost the other way round. He knew the location of at least four different libraries. And he could read English so much better; he could guess words in a fairy tale or legend, even if he couldn't say the word right. Ira smiled at himself. Once when he was reading aloud in 3B, he said "kircle" for circle. Even the teacher laughed.

II

Squat, dumpy Mrs. Shapiro visited them in the evening (would Ira ever forget her kindness and her courage in the face of Pop's fury). Alerting them by a knock on the door, Mrs. Shapiro would announce herself on the other side of the portal. She had begun dropping in during the evening the last few weeks because Pop was working as a "sopper": Pop was waiting at tables for all three meals lately, for dinner—in addition to his regular stint of breakfast and lunch—in order to accumulate all the finances he could in readiness for opportunities in St. Louis. Because she dearly loved to hear the *roman*, the serial romance that was printed daily in *Der Tag*, Mrs. Shapiro had been taking advantage of Pop's absence. Ira insulated himself from Mom's flow of Yiddish, grinning sarcastically now and then, when he heard Mom say, "Kha! Kha! Kha! *hat er gelakht.*" What a way to say, "Ha, ha, ha, he laughed."

Mom said nothing at first of Pop's departure, since Pop hadn't been home evenings anyway, but after a while she confided in her neighbor that Pop was in St. Louis. They talked about his absence a great deal, and Mom read a long letter from Pop in Yiddish all about his St. Louis. He was very favorably impressed. He was hopeful of prospects there, of achieving success in the easier pace of life there—not like New York, snappish and full of *khukhims.* And he got along fine with the *shvartze.* Gabe thought a luncheonette or a café would do well in the precinct where he himself lived, mostly surrounded by *shvartze.* They preferred to patronize establishments owned by whites, rather than those owned by people of their own race. Besides, they hardly knew the first thing about running a restaurant.

"He sounds very much as if he would like to go live there in this St. Louis," said Mrs. Shapiro. "And you?"

"I? If he thinks I would go live in St. Louis, then he's truly demented. I would go live there with those cold relatives of his?"

"*Azoi?* And what would you do?"

"We haven't reached that point yet," Mom rejoined shortly, but resolutely.

"Pop says it's a big city," Ira chimed in. "Maybe there wouldn't be so many Irishers there. I could have friends."

"If not Irishers, then blacks. Would that suit you better?"

"It would be different."

"Such an ungifted people," said Mrs. Shapiro. "And homely. *Oy gewald.*"

"And *shleppen* with the furniture. You would have to go to a different school too. You complain about Irishers—*goyim,* rabid anti-Semites. How do you know what you'll have to suffer there?"

"Pop says they're friends. There's more Irishers in P.S. 24 than in P.S. 103," Ira countered. "Next year I'm going to go to P.S. 24. So I have to change schools anyway. How do you know you wouldn't like it better in St. Louis?"

"You hear the child?" Mom turned to Mrs. Shapiro. "Childish wits are childish wits. When we moved here to Harlem, he wept to go back to the East Side. Now that he's accustomed to living here, he wants to move to St. Louis."

"You have here grandmother and grandfather," Mrs. Shapiro reminded Ira. "And aunts and uncles—"

"I'll have aunts and uncles there too," Ira interrupted.

"But so few blocks away: on 115th Street."

"Go," Mom dismissed him. "Here I have sisters and a mother. Here I have learned my way around. I know where to shop for clothes, for a bedspread, where to buy horseradish and fresh pike and cracked eggs. A Jewish bank teller greets me in the savings bank. What will I know, a new *goyish* city? So far away into the wilderness. Immediately they'll be mimicking my every step and tread. There'll be havoc if he takes it into his head to move there. I won't go! At least I have my kin here; I can endure this penury. What will it be like among his folk? They're alien. Aloof. And you don't think he'll be embroiled with them in a short time? Then where will I turn? I'll stay here. Let him send me my weekly allowance. No, Mrs. Shapiro?"

"Indeed. Indeed," said Mrs. Shapiro.

"All right." Ira looked worriedly at Mom's vexed, obdurate face. And yet, infringing on the uneasiness that her disquiet awoke in him, odd contrarieties beckoned: shapeless notions of life in St. Louis, a distant world, a more spacious one, a fresh and better one than here in Harlem. Which did he want? Here without Pop, there, with him in St. Louis? Here without Pop, beyond the danger ever of another terrible beating like the one after Mrs. True came in to complain—and Mrs. Shapiro—here she was this evening, so expressionlessly had saved him from who knew how much worse. No, he had never told anyone—and whom was there to tell?—that he had dreamt that night of trying to pick up a knife with which to stab Pop, but it was stuck fast to the table, as if a magnet held it. And he had dreamt it another time too, so bright the sharp blade! No, he would like it better without Pop, or with Pop in a new world, with new relatives, relatives who spoke English. He couldn't say.

After Mrs. Shapiro left, Mom seemed to reverse herself; she became annoyed at her own agitation: "What am I babbling about?

They already haven't had to do with him, his brothers? They don't know Chaim and his giddiness and his antics? I babble. It's nothing. You'll have a father—give him a week or two." She nodded in abrupt confirmation. "What? They'll bear with him as I do? They'll pity him as I do? As yesterday is today. Are you ready for bed?"

"Yeh."

"You'll sleep in my bed."

"Where will you—" He didn't know how to finish. "I'll sleep in yours and Pop's bed?"

"Indeed. To have you close by me, should anything happen."

"What's gonna happen?"

"Who knows. I'm alone. That I know. Go, pee."

He still wet his bed sometimes, humiliating him, but he couldn't help it: He dreamt he was peeing in the gutter often, or down at the foot of the outdoor cellar steps. He left the kitchen, went out into the passageway, dark because the janitor always turned out the skimpy fish-tail burner in the stair hallway on the odd flights— after nine o'clock. From the passageway to the toilet door; even in the dark, you could still see the glimmering white of the toilet bowl—it was near the window was the reason why—past the long, long tin bathtub in its wooden coffer; he urinated. Be awful if he wet—nah, he wouldn't, not tonight. He found, grabbed the chain in the dark, yanked, held for the usual length of gush. Returned, undressed to his underwear, looked at Mom questioningly, before asking her. "Where do you want?"

"You sleep next to the wall," she said. . . .

III

Two or three evenings later, early, supper scarcely over, too early for Mrs. Shapiro to knock, the voice on the other side of the door replied to Mom's "Whozit?" with, "It's Louie, Louie S." Mom flushed, opened the kitchen door, and tall and thin in his postman's uniform, in came Uncle Louie.

"Uncle Louie!" Ira leaped up in rapturous greeting. "Uncle Louie!"

"Yingle," he smiled his broad, square, gold-dentured smile. "He's growing to a big *yingotch, kein ein n'horreh,"* he said to Mom. That was the other wonderful thing about Uncle Louie: He could speak Yiddish like any other Jew, and yet speak English like a real American, a Yankee. *"Nu,* Chaim is in St. Louis, Leah. I got a postcard from him. When did he leave?"

"This Monday. He wrote you? Come sit down," Mom invited. "How is your family? How is Sarah? And the children?"

"Everyone is well, praise God. Sarah is busy with the house and children. We bought a piano for Rose." He turned his gold-toothed smile toward Ira.

"Yeah?" Ira dropped his eyes and grinned sheepishly.

"Nu, mazel tov," said Mom. "A little *zjabba,"* she joked. *Zjabba* meant a frog, and could also mean coffee: java, kava.

"No," he declined. *"A scheinem dank.* Chaim wrote you."

"He wrote me," said Mom. "A long letter. He's staying with Gabe and Clara."

"So he wrote me. And how long?"

"That is"—Mom smiled speculatively—"that is something only Chaim knows."

"He wrote me that he felt as if he had just come to America. To a new land. Indeed," Uncle Louis meditated. "His words sounded to me as if he sought more than to visit Gabe and Sam, and the rest of the *mishpokha.* Is that so?"

"Me he told—what can I say? A visit and more. I know Chaim. Nothing that happens to him can happen to him by itself—if you understand me: Everything draws after it another notion, an opportunity. Perhaps Gabe will help him in business. Gabe is a politician; perhaps he will use his influence, he will guide him where best to open a luncheonette, a cafeteria, among the *shvartze,* such things. Will Gabe help him? He doesn't know Chaim? It's foolishness. And I don't say this to belittle him. He doesn't have that kind of head. And me he doesn't take either into account nor into his confidence. Not that I have that kind of head either."

"But calm. But reasonable." Uncle Louis shook his head in demurral. "You know what you endure without help. And the chronic catarrh?"

"Today it's to be borne. A mere piping in the ear."

"A mere piping," Uncle Louie repeated sympathetically, and nodded. "Does it seem so, or can it be heard?"

"Only misfortune knows."

Louie stood up, bent his head toward Mom's, so close their cheeks almost touched. She flushed. It was the only thing Ira was sure he wasn't imagining, that Mom's features suffused, not that Uncle Louie's eyes were fixed on Mom's bosom or hers moved quickly away from his mailman's blue thigh. It was the strangest thing what you could imagine if you wanted to. And you wanted to, and nearly knew why.

Louie straightened up, his glance compassionate. "No, I hear nothing, Leah."

"It's a malady, and no more. I'm happy when it whines so faintly. An affliction, *nu.*"

"I fear so." Louie sat down. "A few more joys in your life would do no harm, I'm sure. Companionship, change, another climate, to learn English, to see a little of the world—"

"Passion and Kholyorado," Mom laughed.

"Indeed passion and Colorado," Louie reiterated. "Who knows? High in the mountains, in thin, clear air, the whistling might vanish altogether."

"In the other world. Ben Zion, my father, inflicted many a blow on me because I was so stubborn. If she says no, he would cry, you can slay her."

Louie shook his head ever so slightly, turned his attention to Ira. "Well. *Yingle,* you remember that flock of chickens your father and I raised in East New York."

"I remember!" Ira said eagerly.

"East New York? *Azoi.* You couldn't have been more than three years old."

"A big, big red rooster," said Ira. "And Aunt Sarah scolded me from the window. Maybe I was gonna hit him with a stick."

Uncle Louie laughed his wide, gold-toothed laugh. "A *yin-gotch*," he said admiringly to Mom.

"Ah, was that ever a handsome rooster," said Mom. "And they were all stolen one night, every chicken."

"I like Chaim," Uncle Louie said earnestly. "He sees so much to laugh at, when he isn't nervous. And good-hearted he is. But a settled judgment, that he lacks, no? It's sad, what else is to say? And Gabe knows that too."

"At present it's better for me that way. I know he'll come home. I won't have to journey—" she gesticulated. "St. Louis I need to add to my sorrows. And you, you're in New York tonight."

"A mail sorter is sick—perhaps the whole week. I'm staying with Fannie in Brooklyn. Leah, why don't we go for a short walk. It's pleasant out. Almost like summer. A short walk to that park you have nearby."

"Mt. Morris Park," Ira offered eagerly. "I like it there."

"I wear only my postman's jacket," said Louie. "It's so much like summer."

"Mom, come on with Uncle Louie!"

Uncle Louie helped Mom get into a light coat, and they left the house, the gas mantle-light still burning. Ira was overjoyed. To be near Uncle Louie, walk with him, while he talked about the farm in Stelton and about the crisis in the world, the certainty of war, to Mom's "Thank God, I have no son to be a soldier. Now almost three years," she added: "A curse fallen on the world. And how is Sarah?"

"Sarah is Sarah," Uncle Louis said, and made a regretful sound with his tongue. "It's not enough for her to be a housewife and mother of three. And I earn a good salary; I don't have to tell you—"

"This way," Ira directed as they reached Madison Avenue. "Here's my school."

"Yes." Uncle Louie took Mom's hand to guide her.

"What does she wish?" asked Mom.

"That we should move from Stelton, from among the socialists, somewhere else, somewhere in New York. Buy a larger house there, and take in a few paying guests."

"*Yiddisher* business," said Mom.

"Indeed."

"Well, if she wishes. All the work will fall on her."

"I know. And we would have more money, perhaps. But I'm not a businessman, Leah. She doesn't understand that. To me to speak to other socialists, to other free-thinkers, to hear a good speaker enlightens one. And afterward a discussion—" Louie's lean face became animate, his long arm blurred the space it swept through. "About the future, about how different people will be, when religion no longer divides us, and *geldt,* as we say, when women will have equality, in politics, in marriage, in love. Sometimes I even have an urge to write about it, especially about how changed the life of women will be. Free love I'm sure will come in the future. We can talk for hours on that. And we get angry and excited, and we'll still be friends. Sarah doesn't understand that."

"*Azoi?*"

IV

The early spring evening was truly balmy. The street lights shone softly from the dark interior of Mt. Morris Park, along whose perimeter the three walked, shone wistfully on the few lampposts climbing the hill to the summit. The night sky bent overhead benignly, accommodating Mt. Morris Park hill and its dark tower on top that thrust its belfry among the misty, wavering stars strewn to the west. Strollers passed at a tranquil pace. Autos too, and infrequent trolleys, seemed to roll by more quietly than usual. Madison Avenue had never seemed so calm and reassuring. Why didn't Pop ever do this? Ira wondeed. He never did, never. Too nervous always, always on edge. He walked just to get there, to get there as soon as he could, to get there and get it over with—not the way Uncle Louis did, enjoying the walk itself, talking as he sauntered, lean and tall in his postman's uniform. Gee. And talking about things Pop never brought up, interesting things, things full of promise, not about the relatives or the rent or the gas bill or Mom's allowance—

"When I hear Debs speak," Louis was telling Mom in Yiddish, "I feel as if my own heart were speaking."

"So eloquent is he?" There was a trace of formality in Mom's tone—and in her bearing too, as she walked along beside Louis, something guarded or self-consciously distant. "I've read about him in *Der Tag*. He's not Jewish. But a truly fine person he appears to be."

"He's a socialist," said Louis. "And among socialists, Jew or Gentile doesn't matter. He has fought against oppression and persecution of all people. Not only Jews, the downtrodden, Southern colored man as well."

"*Azoi?*"

"Show me another person, show me a Jew, who has done as much for the poor and the working man as Debs has. He's spent time in prison for them."

"I know."

"It's his dream that the workers should rule," Louis continued enthusiastically. "The writer Jack London wrote about it—the Dream of Debs: The workers need only unite and hold firm. They could bring all the factories to a stop. They could bring the bloated capitalist to his knees. Nothing would move, not a train wheel, not a sewing machine in a sweatshop. All would have to go to the workers."

"It's a worthy dream," Mom said, and then laughed shortly. "But indeed a dream. Does the common worker understand that? What common worker in America doesn't seek to be a businessman? Why did he come here? Like my Chaim today: He yearns to own a restaurant, a cafeteria. Even I have learned that word 'luncheonette.' I say it right, don't I? And so it is with most Jews. It's America, the golden realm. In Europe the steamship companies showed us pictures of ordinary laborers carrying sacks of gold coins on their backs. What will the socialists do with the storekeeper, with the vegetable peddler, with the *Galitzianer* herring peddler on Park Avenue—he owns only two or three barrels of herring? Still, he's a proprietor. Why else has my Chaim gone to St. Louis? To be a proprietor, a boss, as they say in English."

"But some of us, and not a few, have ideals," Louis countered earnestly. "Some see further than the *Galitzianer* herring peddler. He came here to get ahead, and why? Because he lived under a benign tyrant, Franz Josef. But those who lived under the Czar came here seeking freedom. Many were Bundists, Jewish socialists. And socialists seek freedom for all mankind, and first and foremost freedom from wage slavery." Louis lifted his head. "If not for idealists, if not for those who strive for the good of all mankind, the whole human race would be lost. And I'll tell you, Leah, with these small people, like that *Galitzianer* herring peddler, the socialist isn't concerned. They hardly count. It's the big industrialists that count, Mr. Schwab of the steel company, Mr. Ford, that anti-Semite, the railroad magnates, the shipping companies; in Massachusetts, the cloth manufacturers. They together with the banks and the Wall Streetniks, they're the ones who count. But on whom do they depend? On whose backs have they built their fortunes? On the backs of the workers. In the steel mills, in the mines, in the factories. Without him where are they? Where is even the banker, where is J. P. Morgan? Once the toilers in their millions, the steel mill worker, the railroad worker, the miner, get together, the owner, the magnate, the capitalist is finished. Do you realize it was a Jew who thought of this first? Karl Marx."

"I've read of his name in the Jewish newspaper," said Mom. "His father converted, that I know, a rabbi's son and an apostate. My father, Zaida, says he was a bitter enemy of the children of Israel, like all apostates. How terrible, a Jew himself."

"And because of that, you don't believe his words?"

"*Oy, gewald,* Louis, what do I know? What shall I say? I admire your ideals, but to me it doesn't seem practical. You're a mailman. You've told us yourself how anti-Semitic the *goyim* are there. These are people with some education, no? And you expect them to unite?

You don't see how everyone tries to rip the skin off everyone else. Even I, from my Chaim, for my paltry allowance. What can I do? I must do as the rest."

"Chaim will drag you down to his level. You deserve better than Chaim."

"That's something else." Mom nodded sideways. "What I deserve depends on who is the judge. To Ben Zion Farb anyone willing to marry me was the husband I deserved—I was already a lumpish maid of twenty-two years. I don't have to tell you that by eighteen in Galitzia a girl was already looked on as—"

"Don't say that. I'm a free-thinker. And we're not in Galitzia."

"True, but I speak of what was. Attainments I had none. And with four sisters all pining for their turn to marry. *Freg nisht*. My father Ben Zion was frantic. And all of us stuck in forlorn little Veljish, with only a marriage broker to depend on for escape. And didn't I weep when my father took me on a visit to my aunt Rebecca in Lemberg. 'Let me be a servant girl here,' I begged him. 'Father, let me stay.' He had to threaten me with his cane before I would leave."

"I know. I know the whole story. It's a tragedy."

"*Nu.*"

"You have such a fine nature."

"It helps to have a fine nature," Mom said dryly.

"Ah, Leah, you shouldn't talk that way," Louis shook his head. "Your heart, your goodness will never change. It is what draws me to you. Sarah," he raised a finger to stress his words, "Sarah is truly the one without tenderness. Sarah is cold. Not you."

"For me it's too late, Louis, all this you say and wish. The way I live is the way I shall die."

"You're a young woman still, Leah. And believe me, an attractive woman."

"Can one be affluent without means; so I'm young without youthful thoughts."

They walked on awhile without speaking. "*Nu, Yingle.*" Louis smiled his broad smile at Ira walking with springy step on the bare ground between the paved sidewalk and the palings about the park.

"I love to walk on the ground," Ira declared.

Uncle Louis laughed. "You see, Leah, how much he loves natural life, the earth itself."

"He longs to be a *khunter,*" Mom said with peculiar emphasis, the kind Ira had long ago recognized was meant to conceal meaning from him. The word sounded almost like hunter, but not quite. He could guess he wasn't supposed to understand more than that. Still, the word had a familiar sound in English. Could it be? Mom's features looked mischievous in the lamplight, amused and prim at the same time.

"I didn't say *khunter,*" Ira explained to Uncle Louie. "I said *hunter.* Sometimes I like to read that kind of a book, a book about a hunter."

They both laughed, Mom's laughter high-pitched.

"Your socialism believes in free love, no? As I've heard others say in English."

"Many of us believe it. Yes."

"And to me that's something to laugh at. *Freia lokh.*"

She was punning on the sound of the English word *love* in Yiddish, and Ira understood the pun: *Lokh* in Yiddish meant *hole.*

"Leah, no." Louie took a deep breath. "*S' ganz andrish.* It means the woman has the same right as the man if she loves another—"

"Even if she's already married?"

"Even if she's already married."

"Azoy?"

They had walked a single length of the park, to 124th Street and now, walking back, they reached 120th Street again. In silence, they turned east to Park Avenue, Uncle Louie holding Mom's arm across the street. Back at the house once more, he lingered tentatively before the empty stoop. Mom too hesitated.

"Do you want to come upstairs?" she asked.

"Do you want me to?"

"It's immaterial to me. My neighbor calls on me every evening since Chaim is gone. If you don't mind, she'll probably join us."

"Oh, your neighbor may call on you?" Louie asked.

"I read her the *roman* in *Der Tag* every evening," Mom replied, and went on to explain that she read the romance in the paper for Mrs. Shapiro because she was illiterate.

"I see. And her husband, doesn't he read it to her? Or is it only in *Der Tag?*"

"He treats her like dirt," said Mom. "A gross, ugly little cap-maker. And skimps at everything, even more than Chaim. A dog. Compared to her spouse, my Chaim is a paragon."

"Aha," said Louie. "Well, then I won't come upstairs. Stay in the best of health, Leah."

"And you also, go in the best of health," said Mom.

"Good night. Good night, *yingle.*" Louie smiled his broad gold-dentured smile, slipped his hand into his pocket—

"He doesn't need it," Mom tried to dissuade but couldn't. Despite her protest, a jingle of small change passed from Uncle Louis's hand to Ira's.

"Thanks, Uncle. Thanks!"

Even in the dim light of street lamp and hall, Ira could see Uncle Louis's expression under the visor of his postman's cap change from a smile to something intent as he looked at Mom. Then he turned away, strode off, lean and tall, his postman's uniform growing a lighter blue with every step he took toward the corner street light.

Alone again with Mom, Ira counted his riches as the two climbed up the stoop. "He gave me twenty-two cents, Mama."

"You shouldn't have taken it. *Shnorer,*" Mom chided.

Ira mumbled in demurral. "He wanted to give it to me. I didn't ask."

"The only thing you failed to do was to ask." Mom said ironically over her shoulder, as they climbed the murky gas-lit stairs. "I don't need him, and I don't need his gifts."

"Huh?"

"You're a poor man's child indeed. Why should I scold you? It's a pity." They turned at the first flight landing and entered the gloomy hall. "Don't leave the house if he comes to visit again. You hear? You stay with me while your father is gone."

"Yeh?"

"How soon he came calling. How soon." Mom unlocked the door. "It's a good thing I thought of Mrs. Shapiro. It shows that sometimes kindness has its rewards." She turned up the gas mantle-light, which had been left barely on, and as her uplifted features grew more luminous, "*Lyupka*," she grimaced wryly, and uttered a peculiarly mocking sigh.

It was a Polish word, or a Russian word, or a Slavic word from Galitzia, but anybody could guess: *lyupka*. She didn't like it, she didn't approve. What was *lyupka*? Like the movies? Kissing and hugging. Why did she twist her lip that way? It made him so avid to understand. Why had her face turned so red and scornful? *Lyupka*. That must be what the big kids meant when they said those words in the street: fucking, screwing, laying, all those words: piece of hide, piece of ass, pussy, cunt—*khunter*, the word Mom had made fun of; was that it? And what those rubbers were for that Biolov threw in the garbage can, and the kids fished out? Scumbags, the big kids called them. You shoot into them when you come. Shoot what? Come what? That lousy bum that wanted him to take his pants down in the way-far-away park, and squirted like egg-white against the tree . . . Oh! Then was that *lyupka*? When that Irish couple came down just in time, all excited, was that a different kind, or what? Was Uncle Louis's like that kind of *lyupka* . . . ?

He got under the featherbed, too warm with the advent of spring; he slid to the outer edge of the ticking, slid close to the wall, as he had been doing since Pop left. He never slept close to Mom. Wasn't supposed to. Why? That had something to do with *lyupka*. Even as his hearing distinguished the sounds of Mom un-dressing in the kitchen, behind his shut eyelids appeared Mom's image when he had come rushing into the house that time—when was it?—when they didn't want to have anything to do with Baba and her family, "*Oy, gewald*, I didn't lock the door!" Mom had cried. She was standing in the round iron washtub, feet in the water, bathing, her great big everythings naked. She grabbed a towel, and shielded herself with it. "Shut the door. Go in the front room!" she bade. He did as he was told. You weren't allowed to see. That was *lyupka*. That was why Pop had given him that awful licking with the butt of the horsewhip because he and the other kids had played bad with the little girls on Henry Street where they lived, because their mother complained they played bad. *"Genuk! Shoyn genuk!"* Enough! Like Mrs. Shapiro, Mom wouldn't let Pop push her away. But what blue stripes Ira had on his back afterward. So . . . that was it, *lyupka.* He could see Mom still on the screen of closed eyelids, but he was falling asleep . . .

And awoke—to his horror! He was playing bad against Mom's naked legs, lying on his side and pushing, rubbing, squeezing his stiff peg between Mom's thighs. She woke up.

"I didn't mean it!" Ira wailed in his shame. "I was dream-ing—"

She laughed indulgently. "Go back to sleep."

He rolled quickly away, and still panting, lay with his back to her as far away as he could. What was that bliss that seemed about to well over? That drove him, made him do that to Mom in a dream . . . just a little more it would have, it wanted to: *lyupka.*

He slept in his own bed thereafter.

—I foresaw you'd have difficulties.

It wasn't difficult to foresee.

—Shall I waft you into the future a quarter century hence aboard a freight train bound east?

I cry you mercy, Ecclesias.

—What will you do?

Do without.

—Chugga. Chugga. Chugga. Whe-e-e! The whistle at the crossing. Dark is the night over Texas. And cold. And stars thick as traprock come tumbling out of the moonless heaven.

Yeah. But *Procul O, procul este, por favor.*

V

It was a Saturday evening when Uncle Louis called again, this time out of uniform. He looked even leaner, sinewy and tall, flat-chested. Something about the way he watched Mom, with unwavering eyes behind his gold-rimmed spectacles, something about his voice made Ira try to keep his gaze fixed on his book, *Boys' Book of King Arthur*. But something, that same something, charged the air of the kitchen, and despite himself, impelled Ira to raise his eyes from the page and steal a greedy glance at the two, while they sat about the green oilcloth-covered table, conversing. He could sense their matter-of-fact tones were dissembled; he was almost sure of it, though he wasn't sure why. They were talking about the War, a capitalist's war, Uncle Louis described it; working men fought and bled for the advantage of capitalists. Thank God their children were still young, and were spared that charnel house, said Mom. Would Pop be exempt from the draft? "My stalwart," Mom laughed. "He wrote me that Gabe had a new proposal: a concession for a cafeteria in City Hall. A businessman, owner of a business, married and a father, he would be safe from the military service, no?"

"But you would have to go to St. Louis."

"I am to write him forthwith."

"Are you going?"

"Never."

"And if he stayed? If he insisted on staying in St. Louis?"

"Let him send me my stipend here."

"Leah," Louis began—Foreign words, Polish or Slavic, suddenly occluded the rest of what he said.

"I know," Mom answered in Yiddish. She shook her head. "I'm considering writing him this very evening."

"Leah, don't torment me!"

"*S' narrishkeit*," Mom said. "It's foolishness."

Ira knew the word, knew for certain that his surmise was right: It was all about *lyupka*.

"You have a wife," Mom continued, clearly, firmly in Yiddish: "A wife and three children. You're asking for grief."

"But if I'm consumed?"

Mom shrugged slightly. "You have a wife—if you're consumed."

"It's not the same thing. You know it's not the same thing. You have a husband."

"Indeed. You've spoken truly."

"You love him? Speak truly yourself."

"It no longer matters. Years ago, on the East Side, I already knew: Love is denied me. Where Love should be, there is a hollow, a vacancy." She lapsed into Polish, glanced at Ira—who anticipated her by a moment, and dropped his eyes to the book. "The *yeled*," she warned.

"Then tell Chaim to stay. Why not tell Chaim to stay?" Louis pleaded. "He craves success, a business of his own. He may find both, he may find himself in St. Louis among his brothers—in the place he first came to in his youth. You would give him happiness, respect, all the things he craves. And us, you would give us life. I don't have a vacancy too in my life? You would fill the vacancy in my life. You would fill the vacancy in both our lives. You would give us both love! Leah, only think what happiness that would mean!"

"No, Louis, once it would have mattered: When I stood in the kitchen, on 9th Street, and the hollow thought would come over me: something, a folly: *lyupka*. But now—it's truly a folly. I'll tell you one thing more, and then let's make an end—"

"No, Leah! I throw myself at your feet. Leah!"

"That would look seemly indeed. I beheld my brother Morris in his nakedness once, and I became consumed. I confess it. It's shameful to—" Mom reverted to Polish or Slavic, and then into Yiddish again. "But the truth. Consumed. And so I am now—" the fingers of her two hands spread wide. "And so I am now: *ausgebrendt*. I made up my mind then and there—"

"Leah, what are you saying? I'm not your brother. I'm Louis S. Give me what I yearn for: Your love. Satisfy me!"

"In vain, Louis. I won't submit."

"You care for me not at all?"

"Louis, for the last time, I have no more to do with love. *Ich bin ganz ausgebrendt.* Believe me."

Louis sat still a few seconds, then stood up, dark, brooding, regarding Mom. "*Nu,*" he said with bitterly ironic intonation. "When does your neighbor come in to hear the latest installment of the *roman,* Leah?"

"Today the Sabbath is over," Mom rejoined. "*Der Tag* isn't published on the Sabbath."

"No. Naturally." He sighed deeply, remained standing, bony hand against his lips. "You need not write Chaim about me. You won't see me again—alone."

"I'll say nothing about you," Mom replied. She looked in Ira's direction. "Where do you go now?" she asked matter-of-factly.

"To Fannie and Will's home. They always have an extra bed."

"Greet them for me."

He nodded almost curtly, grim, opening the kitchen door at the same time as he said, "Good night, Leah," closing it behind him before Mom could answer.

And no gift of small change either. The print swam under Ira's gaze: unseeing eyes followed Mom from sink to china closet, where she got out the wooden penholder with the steel pen in it, and the bottle of blue ink. Why couldn't he have Uncle Louis for a father? Even though he had misbehaved in Stelton, at Uncle Louis's farm, still he would rather live on a farm like Uncle Louis's. But Mom, she was the one who hated farms; she hated *dorfs,* little hamlets, she said. She had seen all she wanted of them. But even if Uncle Louis didn't live in a village, on a farm, she didn't want him anyway. What a shame: He was lean and dried out, as Mom said, yes, and he had a "touch" on his lungs, which was why he became a soldier. But he knew all about the Wild West, he knew about America, he knew about Debs, he knew about socialism, about a better world where they wouldn't always say, Jew, Jew-boy, mocky, sheeny-bastard.

Mom sat down, and began scratching away with her pen on a sheet of lined paper of the pad Pop had bought. So what would a father like Uncle Louis have meant? It would have meant speakers on platforms under the electric lights in Stelton at night. Drowsy, humid night and mosquitoes. His name was Cornell, Ira still remembered. It would have meant warm sunshine and open country, and gardens where vegetables grew, and cows and chickens, and long dirt roads he could explore.

He shouldn't have teased Rosy when she practiced on the cardboard piano. He was supposed to marry Rosy—because long ago, when they all lived in East New York where goats were tied in empty lots and snow was deep in the winter, long ago she had shown him her red crack, and he had shown her his *petzel,* and he had told everyone afterward that he was going to marry her. Oh, how different it would be if you loved your father: The Irish kids ran to meet theirs when they came home from work, still daylight in the summer, and hung on to their fathers' hands: "Hey, Dad, how about a nickel? What d'ye say, Dad?" And their fathers smiling, trying not to, but fishing a coin out of their pockets. If *he* tried that, he'd get such a cuff alongside the head, he'd go reeling.

Mom paused in her writing. "You won't say anything."

"What?" Ira asked.

"That Louis was here— Once. He was here once. That much you can say."

"He was here once?" Ira repeated dutifully. "Did we go to the park?"

"Very well. We promenaded." And then on the impulse of afterthought: "I'll tell him myself. I'll let him know. At least something." She resumed writing.

So that was how it went: from the little red crack and the *petzel,* it grew up to be *lyupka:* Louis pleading with Mom, "Satisfy me." And how would it be done? The way he dreamt with that strange welling up when he rubbed against Mom. That was how it went. That rusty, lanky bum didn't need ladies—and then he did it himself against a tree. And if Mom had said, yes, instead of "I won't submit." If Mom had said, yes, would Louis have become his father? Pretend you were sleepy, then what would they do? "Look what I have, Leah," said Morris. Oh, if she would only go to St. Louis—

"I'll have to go into Biolov's tomorrow and buy a two-cent stamp," Mom said. "I wrote him in Yiddish. You think you can write on the envelope in English?"

"I think so. What do I write?"

"The address he left on this slip of paper."

"I can write that." Ira studied Pop's handwriting. "The first is Hyman Stigman."

"Then write." Mom moved the envelope toward him. "Put aside the book a minute."

"You're not going?"

"Who listens to him?" she transferred pen and ink. "Here. Be careful."

VI

He had no choice, Ira thought. He recalled nothing of the momentous declarations that Woodrow Wilson made as the United States was drawn ever closer to entering the Great War. The declarations, charges, countercharges. 1917 was almost seventy years ago. (He sat gazing at years so jammed together they seemed opaque.) What could be said, said that was genuinely remembered? Surely he must have heard mention over and over again of how vast was the slaughter in Europe, of the growing crisis in U.S.-German relations, of the sinking of the *Lusitania,* the death of Franz Josef of Austria-Hungary — "Franz Yussel," the Jews humorously dubbed him. Once again Ira felt course through him that pang of lost opportunity: Ah, in 1934, when he had finished his first novel, when he was only twenty-eight years old, when he was a full half-century closer in memory to those events and still could turn to people who remembered them, who could refresh his own memory of those critical days leading up to America's entry into the Great War. Alas, a kid's memory, that was all he had, the battle of Verdun reenacted on a vaudeville stage, a spectacle that perhaps his Uncle Max had taken him to: Sparks flew from gutted buildings, burning walls toppled, distant artillery thudded . . .

He had long passed his three score and ten. Who had time now to research the historic events of his eleventh year, to recreate 1917 in 1980? Still, something, however brief, was needed to provide a bygone setting. What? At the moment, he had no other alternative than to consult the nearest thing at hand, the microscopically compressed synopsis of the most important events of 1917, according to *The World Almanac* of 1972. 1917, the year Pop went to St. Louis, and Uncle Louie tried to woo Mom. Fateful year for Ira, when he rubbed against Mom in dream, and felt that strange welling up — and shame. Fateful year for Ira, when he was beginning to get a glimmering of what Uncle Louie desired, and Mom wouldn't grant. And his own ambivalence afterward, fantasizing: What if Mom had said yes to Louie — lean Uncle Louie and plump Mom. Pretend to sleep and listen . . . and imagine . . . sanction what never happened.

Why? Ira asked himself: Why was he so crazy? Interlarding the bomb blast at the San Francisco Preparedness Day parade of the year before, and the death sentence imposed on the innocent labor leaders, Mooney and Billings, with Louie's furor and Mom's rapture. Why? Abnormally, precociously attuned to Mom's deprivation, probably. That was it, his deprived mother consumed at the sight of Moe's phallus, *Ai, vot my mannikin gevesen zoi vie, Moishe:* "One needs a horse for you. A horse for you." *Verbrent,* from two in the morning, when he left for his milk-wagon, alone I flamed, with a stout brother snoring in the next room. *"Oy, gewald."* Fateful year for Ira: Even if she had said yes to Pop, and they would have moved to St. Louis, how different life would have been.

1917—U.S. ENTERS WAR

When Germany began unrestricted submarine war, the U.S. Feb. 3, broke relations, refused negotiations until the (German) order was rescinded. Wilson Feb. 26, asked Congress to order arming of merchant ships; when Senate refused, Wilson armed them by executive order Mar. 12. An intercepted note of German Foreign Sec. Zimmerman to German minister in Mexico suggested Mexico be asked to enter war to recover U.S. Southwest Feb. 28. U.S. declared

war on Germany Apr. 6, adopted selective conscription May
18, registered men 21–30 June 5 . . .

Soon after he returned from his trip to St. Louis, as Mom foresaw
he would, Pop was notified he had to go into war-essential work—
otherwise he faced imprisonment or draft into the armed services. "You are required to present evidence of employment to
your local draft board before the 30th instant," Ira helped Pop
translate the document into Yiddish for Mom's benefit. The document had come in a large, daunting envelope, and bore the bold
black heading: WAR LABOR RESOURCES BOARD. "Below you
will find a partial listing of essential work. If you have any questions
with regard to whether the work you are presently engaged in is
essential to the war effort, inquire at your local draft board in
person or by telephone. You are hereby advised to do so at once."

"*Nu,* read. Let us hear what is needful labor," said Pop.

Ira ran his eye over the columns of occupations listed below:
"Cons—Construction. That means they build," Ira read aloud and
translated each category as best he could. "Dock worker, Farmer,
Food Processor, Fisherman, Highway Maintenance, Machinist,
Welder, Transport Worker, i.e., Trainman, Conductor, Motorman,
Track Maintenance, et cetera—"

"*Vus heist 'tsetra'?*" asked Mom.

"You don't understand?" Pop said patronizingly. "Ten years in
America, and she knows nothing!"

"Then you're the clever one," Mom retorted. "Where am I to
learn? Over the pots and pans, or among the Yiddish pushcart
peddlers?"

"Then learn now. 'Tsetra' means other things."

"Can't you say so without making a ceremony of it?"

"Shah!" Pop stalled her indignation. And to Ira: "Food Prot-
zess, what does that mean again?"

"Like salami," Ira ventured. "Or all kinds of *goyish* things to
eat. You know: like ketchup in the restaurant. I think."

"Then perhaps they defer cooks?" Mom suggested.

"Go," Pop scoffed. "Cooks! If they defer cooks, they'll defer
noodle-porters too."

"Then what?"

"I've found a remedy."

"Indeed? So soon?"

"A trolley-car conductor. Read again, Ira, from that tsetra."

Ira reread the list of transport workers.

"That would stop their mouths—a trolley-car conductor," said Pop.

"Do you know how? What do you know about trolley cars?" Mom asked.

"What is there to learn? If a thick Irisher can learn, I can learn. They drop a nickel in the glass *pishkeh*. You grind it until it falls into a little tray at the bottom. You pull a cord. You give out a transfer. They'll teach me the other things. I'll go find out where to apply."

"But the streets," Mom reminded. "Such a frightful myriad of streets! You'll have to learn them too. *Gewald!*"

"The woman gabbles!" Pop dismissed her fears with a practiced gesture. "In New York I have nothing to worry about. How did I learn the streets as a milkman? I learned. *Shoyn.* And I had to drive a horse and wagon through them too."

"That was the East Side," Mom reminded him. "There are—" she clutched her cheek—"Brooklyn, the Bronx, and who knows where else?"

"What? Is it better to molder in a stockade than to learn a route in—ah!—anywhere: In Brooklyn, in the Bronx. *Nu.*"

So Pop became a trolley-car conductor. The route assigned to him could not have been more conveniently located: the Fourth and Madison Avenue line that crossed 119th Street only a block away. His was the "relief shift," as it was called: from midmorning to well into the evening. Reporting for work or returning home, he wore the uniform of the trolley-car conductor, a navy-blue jacket and a visored cap with badge. Ira caught sight of him once or twice when school let out—he still attended P.S. 103 on Madison Avenue and 119th Street—saw his father on the rear platform of the passing trolley, cranking coins down the transparent chute into the till below.

All would have gone well. Pop's job met the official criterion that the work be essential. It was essential. But after awhile, the constant lurching of the trolley—so he complained, though it may have been his nervous tension—began to affect him. He suffered more and more from diarrhea. Finally it became chronic. Diarrhea on a trolley car! Sometimes his bowel spasms were so severe, he was unable to contain himself long enough until the trolley reached its terminal, in whose offices were toilets. Instead he had to signal the motorman to halt the trolley in midroute, while he ran into one or another of the lunchrooms along the avenue and relieved himself.

"*Mein oormeh mann,*" Mom commiserated (in a way that Pop both welcomed and rebuffed). "My poor husband. Perhaps if you eat only wholesome food, hard-boiled eggs, a little chicken broth, coffee with scalded milk, such things as prevent diarrhea. Or strong tea with lemon. But best of all, scalded milk with a thick skim— that will stem the wild flux."

"How? Where? To keep scalded milk with a thick skim in a trolley car? Had you come to St. Louis as I asked, I wouldn't be suffering these pangs. But you refused. So I'm twice a poor man, poor in money, poor in health."

"And what if you had gone to St. Louis and opened a cafeteria and failed, then what? How would you be any better off? A bankrupt, the military would surely have seized you."

"Uh, she has me bankrupt already!"

"No? You become so bewildered in transactions."

"Go whistle, and not talk," said Pop. "I have brothers there in St. Louis, no? Even if I failed in business, Gabe is a political fixer. He would have interceded for me. He wangled a garbage collection inspector's job for my brother Sam; he could have found some safe crevice for me to escape the military."

"Who could know things would come to this bitter pass," Mom continued her self-restrained exoneration. "You needed only to send me my allowance, you could have stayed in St. Louis until the Messiah came."

"*Azoi?* Without a wife? Two separate abodes. I might as well have landed in the military, stout soldier that I would have made. And a fatherless household. It's clear what you wished."

"To you it's clear," Mom said stonily.

"No? And if I didn't send you your allowance?"

"Then I would accompany Mrs. Shapiro to the synagogue that sends them to homes to wash floors."

"And you think I would live alone? All by myself."

"My paragon. Blessed be the day you found another." Mom leveled her sarcasm evenly. "Chaim, it was you yourself who chose to be a trolley-car conductor."

"Much I could do about it."

"You could have chosen to be a milkman again. Milk all people with children must have."

"Go, you don't know what you're talking about! Milkman. Do you see milk-wagons today? Milk-wagons drawn by a horse?"

Mom was silent, then tilted her head in acknowledgement— and sighed. "Indeed. Were my griefs as rare."

"Aha. Today the milk companies want only drivers who can operate those little hand-organs, with a crank in front that you spin, and the whole cart shudders. That's the sort of drivers they want today."

"Perhaps they would have taught you if you hadn't fallen out with Sheffield and with Borden's."

"You speak like a fool."

"Then I don't know. *Oy*, it's a dire affliction." Mom swayed from side to side—stopped: "Do you want to hear a panacea? Don't laugh at me."

"I'm in a good mood to laugh," Pop retorted with a grim jerk of his head.

"You go past 119th Street every day. One way, the other way. Again and again. Let the *kaddish* wait for you there. I'll give him a bag with food you can eat. You'll tell us a time—when you pass. He leaves school. He runs home. I have the food ready. He runs back to the corner with it."

Pop meditated in harassed uncertainty.

"Cornmeal mush is also good for this kind of spasm. With a pat of butter on it. Your favorite dish," Mom urged. "I'll have it hot. And on Fridays a little broth in a jar, a bit of boiled fowl in a clean napkin. Ira will wait with it on the corner. He knows where."

"*A shlock auf iss!*" Pop snapped furiously. "They and their accursed war. May they be destroyed with it one by one and soon!"

"Amen, *selah*," said Mom.

So day after day, a few minutes after he came home from school, Ira was dispatched with a brown paper bag containing Pop's midafternoon meal. Always Ira waited on the corner on the uptown side because the terminal was only a dozen or so blocks away in uptown Harlem, and in the few minutes while allowing the preceding trolley a little more lead time, Pop managed to consume most of his meal. Ira stationed himself at the newly opened variety store opposite the gray school building and waited for Pop's trolley to arrive . . . and waited . . . and invariably daydreamed, woolgathered—

Until suddenly out of the haze of reverie, there was Pop in his blue conductor's uniform leaning out of the rear platform of the trolley, calling irately in Yiddish: "*Dumkopf!* Bring it here! The smallest task you bungle!" And almost at the point of leaping off the trolley step to fetch the paper bag himself—and probably fetch Ira a blow for his laggardliness as well.

Poor Pop! The home-cooked meals helped at first, but only for a while, and then he relapsed again into chronic diarrhea. It was no use. The cause of his disorder, he maintained, his *shrotchkee,* as he called it (the very sound of the Yiddish word suggested gastric turmoil), was the lurching and jouncing of the trolley car, nothing else. And coffee with scalded milk, and strong tea with lemon, or hard-boiled eggs wouldn't help and didn't help. The constant motion caused a commotion of his bowels. He cursed the "jop," he cursed his luck—and time and again, he reminded Mom how much she was to blame for his plight because she refused to move to St. Louis. "Had you granted me a few weeks, abided here a few weeks," he fumed, "till I accumulated enough money to send you passage by train and have the furniture moved, we would have been reunited as in a new land. What am I saying? For you it would have been better than in a new land. It would have been easier. It's the same land. And a little you've learned—true, it's a smattering— but a greenhorn you're not anymore: You've learned to ask where and how much, and to say yes and no."

"Indeed."

"We would have quit this accursed New York." Pop rubbed his abdomen. "Who would have needed your hard-boiled eggs and your scalded milk with skim? Perhaps in time we might have bought our own home on the outskirts of the city, as my brothers have, lived decently, with a tree in front and grass in the yard."

"Another Veljish," said Mom. "Here in New York, here in Harlem are my relatives. I made my choice. Here I remain."

"You'll pay for remaining here, just as you'll pay for my suffering," Pop warned ominously. "A ruinous choice you've made. You'll see."

"And you didn't want to come here with your pitiful milk-wagon?"

"I but followed after you. Who knows what I would have done otherwise? I could have driven a horse for other kinds of deliveries. Like your cousin Yussel with the red beard. I could have delivered bread from the bakers to the grocers."

Mom maintained her grave composure: "Chaim, tell me: How do these *goyim* stand it, the rocking of the trolley car?"

"Because they're *goyim*," said Pop.

"It's not because they're always on edge like you? It's not because they have a skittish stomach?"

"Why should they have a skittish stomach?" Pop echoed in nugatory denial. "Did they have to skimp as I did until I saved enough money for your passage to America?"

"Who told you you had to starve? To live on a sweet potato the peddler baked in his street oven, or a boiled ear of corn, or a duck dinner for fifteen cents, and who knows how the duck met his end. So it would have taken another month or two to buy my passage."

"Another two months, then I surely would have had to pay full fare for him. Who would have believed he was only a year and a half." Pop's retort was quick in coming. "In Galitzia you were reasonable when it came to waiting; you were patient. Why not when I would have been in St. Louis?"

"A good reason."

"What?"

"Chaim, to talk about it further is in vain."

VII

Where could he try it out, when a *petzel* stiffened into a peg? Dora Bahr, Davey's scrawny sister. Their tenement cellar-door opened on the yard. You could hide behind it. Or Meyer Shapiro's younger sister, if you could get her alone and if she wanted—or one of the little Irish *shiksas*—"Mary, Mary, what a pain I got," the Mick kids singsang. "Let's go over to the empty lot. You lay bottom. I lay top. Mary, Mary, what a pain I got." Pop should never have left for St. Louis. You wanted that feeling again that came with rubbing against Mom—that's what Uncle Louie must have wanted. Uncle Moe too, exhibiting his great tower of red flesh—and that rusty bum who wanted Ira to take his pants down. And then pumped his big thing against a tree. And most startling of all, Mom too, even if no longer—she said—*ausgebrendt* in Yiddish. "Burned out." So girls too. And for her own brother Moe, more, more than for Pop, but not allowed. All for that feeling. Where could you get it? With whom? The Hoffman kid on the roof; that was lousy, sitting down pulling your own peg, like that rusty bum. It had to be somebody to pry into: living, warm, like Mom's thighs, a girl it had to be, like Rosy S, Louie's daughter, who showed him she was a girl, with a fire-red slit instead of a *petzel*. Who liked it, who wanted it the same way he did, who got the same wonderful feeling between her thighs he almost got with Mom, when she woke up and laughed. What girl? Where?

And then one evening, long before his shift was up, Pop came home with both eyes blackened, nose bruised, blood still adhering to his nostrils. He had tried to eject a drunken sailor from the trolley car and been badly beaten, badly enough so that the dispatcher had sent him home.

Mom wept; so did Ira. And Pop too at his malign fate.

"*Oy, gewald!*" Mom cried out. "What woe is mine! Did you have to wrangle with a drunken sailor?"

"I with him? He attacked me. He wouldn't pay his fare when I told him to. I merely said he would have to get off."

"Then let him be. And let him be slain," Mom lamented. "May the war take its toll of him!"

"It's my jop," said Pop. "And if there was an inspector aboard the car, and I was a fare short, I would be fired."

"*Ai,* my poor husband!" Mom clasped her slightly built spouse to her large bosom. "Would I could take your place! Would I were there to defend you. I have shoulders. I have strength!"

"Now you comfort me!" Pop extricated himself from Mom's arms. "I thought that with America in the accursed war, it would last two months, three months. When so many men were soldiers, businessmen too, I could easily establish myself in a luncheonette in St. Louis. Or with Gabe's finagling—I'm his brother—*ai,* fortune, fortune. Such good fortune betide Woodrow Wilson and his advisers. Gabe said: Have nothing to do with the stinking Democrats. How right he was. How right, how right! Ten days longer I'll suffer there on that *verflukhteh* trolley car—until my black eyes recover—fortunately I took off my glasses when I went to put him off."

"*Oy, gewald!*" Mom grieved. "I thought so."

"*Nu,* what else?"

"And then?" Mom asked.

"And then let them be destroyed with their jop. Ten days, two weeks more. The most. I'll sneak to the employment office: not to the union hall full of patriots, but to a plain employment office *goniff.* Where is there a jop for a waiter, I'll ask. They must be jops in the unheard-of thousands."

"And if they come after you? Those who seek the shirkers, the dreft-dodgers, as one hears on all sides the hue and cry?"

"*Luzn seh mir gehn in d'red.* I'll tell them: Go be a conductor on a trolley car yourself, when you have to discharge every half-hour. Let us see what you'll do. I'm like an invalid, no? Cremps. Cremps. Cremps. You want a soldier with cremps in the *militaire?*"

"Indeed," said Mom. "*Oy,* that they may not seize you!"

"Seize me!" Pop scouted. "I've already been seized."

"And I would ask them a general doesn't need a waiter? An

officer doesn't need a waiter? He doesn't have to be a stalwart, a hero—"

"As long as he knows how to set a table, how to serve, that's enough." Encouraged, Pop interrupted. "Better to be a waiter to a general, a colonel, than a trolley-car conductor. *Allevai*," he added fervently after a moment. "Wages they would have to pay me to support my family. Even if they never gave me a tip, it would still be better than spasms of the bowels on the back of a trolley car." His fingers stroked his discolored cheekbones. "And black eyes when you try to collect a fare. Such an ugly fate may my friend, President Wilson, have to endure!"

VIII

Pop worked for another two weeks, reported to the personnel office that he no longer could work on the trolley line because of the disorder of his bowels. He requested a release so that he could seek other essential work. He was accorded a release, and he handed in his badge (visored hat and navy-blue jacket were his by-purchase, and Mom sold them in the same secondhand store on 114th Street where she so often and with such tenacity— to Ira's intense embarrassment—haggled for his secondhand clothes).

The day following his separation from the trolley line, Pop was already working. So scarce were experienced waiters, the employment agency sent him to one of the most exclusive restaurants in the city: the Wall Street Stock Exchange Club dining room. No tips—the diners were enjoined from paying them and he from accepting them. He received a fixed salary and a percentage of the bill, and that was all—not as much as he might have received otherwise in as high-toned a restaurant but he was free weekends, and could seek, and easily find, "extra jops by a benket." But at least he was over that trolley-car plague, he congratulated himself, adding. "Anything is better than that. A living I make. My bowels are at peace. And seek me out I'm sure they won't."

"No? Would it were so. Why?" Mom asked.

"I work among magnates. Not only magnates? Magnates of magnates."

"*Azoi?* So rich?"

"Yesterday I waited on J. P. Morgan."

"*Azoi!*"

"And Bernard Baruch the day before."

"*Gottinyoo!* And they allow a plebeian like you to approach them?"

"Who else will set a salad in front of them? Naturally, the headwaiter takes charge. He takes the orders. He oversees all that I do. I take the plate of food from the cart, place it on the table. Everything is done according to rule. But I hear them talk, one to the other."

"And what do they say, such powers as these?" Mom marveled.

"What they wish. Morgan will say to Baruch: 'What do you think of such and such a stock, Bernie?' And he will answer: 'I'll tell you, John, such and such a *gesheft* has a great future.' They talk about the war, about Wilson, his kebinet, about great transactions."

"Hear, only hear!" said Mom. "And none of these mighty asks whether you are—" She hesitated. "I have such a clogged head I've forgotten the word. You're not needed for the War?"

"The headwaiter is only too happy to have an experienced waiter on the floor," said Pop. "And a lively one, not some broken down *alter kocker* from a private club. He's as quiet as a mouse, the headwaiter, whether I'm essential, whether I'm not essential, as they call it." Pop used the English word. "*There* I'm essential. Sometimes Morgan or some other of the mighty brings in a guest, an admiral, a high state official. Believe me, they look the other way. Had I only known before. I would have heeded them with their essential like the cat."

"*Gott sei dank,*" said Mom.

What Pop said was true. He worked in the Stock Exchange restaurant throughout the entire War. He was completely ignored or deliberately overlooked. Not so Uncle Moe, now a headwaiter in Radsky's famous dairy restaurant on Rivington Street.

Husky, sanguine Uncle Moe was drafted.

"*Mein Moishe*," Baba lamented, wept, rocked back and forth with anguish. "*Vah is mir, oy, vah is mir.* My good child, my devoted, happy son, my Moishe. *Ai! Ai! Ai!* They're sending him into that charnel house. God give me strength to endure it."

Grieving continually, from the day that Moe received his induction notice, she shrank visibly—she withered. Neither would she be distracted nor humored, refusing all solace. "May I not live to see the day that anything happens to him."

Nor would she respond to Zaida's chidings: "You must eat! You must live! How will you help him by starving to death? You'll make a widower of me with your mourning, that's what you'll accomplish."

Morris was sent away to camp. She pined; she scarcely spoke. Her face became brown, shriveled and wrinkled. Fortunately Tanta Mamie lived across the street. She did most of the shopping for the household, and much of the cooking too. Listlessly Baba sat beside the window under the summer awning, sat for hours with two fingers on her cheek and one across her lips, gazing, gazing out on the street. A physician was called in, and he tried to reason with her. "She wants to die before she lives to see her son dead," he told an exasperated Zaida. "See that she drinks enough. If she won't eat, force her to drink. Otherwise, she may have to go to a hospital."

"*A shvartz yur!*" Zaida clawed frantically under his *yarmulka*. "Such a punishment to befall me. If she won't eat, she won't eat. But at least cook. I die of hunger here. If not for Mamie, I would wane away to a stalk, a dry reed. *Oy.*"

But it was Baba, not Zaida, who became more and more wasted as the weeks of Moe's training went by. She would surely have been taken to the Mt. Sinai Hospital—Mom told Ira—if Moe hadn't come home on furlough when he did. Together with others of the family, Ira was at Baba's to greet him. They had refrained from writing him about Baba's unhappy condition while he was at camp, and now they waited grimly for him to see for himself. Under his broad khaki campaign hat, Moe looked at his repining mother with the strict stare of one accustomed to command. "What's wrong with you, *Mamaleh?*"

"They're sending you to the slaughter. I don't want to live." Her tears lingered in the wasted furrows of her cheeks.

"*Azoi?* You already know I'm going to be sent into the slaughter?" Moe's voice was ironic, and his strong hands quiet on his khaki-clad thighs, but he never took his eyes off Baba. "A Yiddish soldier truly carries a heavy load. He has two commanders. One, his mother, the other, his colonel. Fortunately he is exempt from the Torah, or God knows how he could stand it all."

"Tell her, tell her!" Zaida urged. "Such madness has seized her that she will hear nothing. God commanded the remnant of Israel to live. Talk to a stone."

"*Mamaleh,*" Moe said. "None of my friends should be worse off than I am. I live like a count. As I live. Like a lord."

"Go, with your idle talk. Don't torture me."

"I swear to you, *Mamaleh.* You see this?" Moe turned his arm sideways the better for her to view the insignia on the sleeve of his uniform: three chevrons with a quarter-moon under them. "*S'heist* mess sergeant," he explained the meaning of the stripes. "The Almighty blessed me when he made me a headwaiter. Not one in the entire camp knew how to order food for so many men: how to feed so many men, how to tell the cooks what to do. And who and how was to arrange the service for such a horde of men. It's called mess, *Mamaleh.* Your Moishe is in charge. *Zoi vie an offizier bin ich.*"

Baba looked from the sleeve to her son's broad, light-skinned face, with the scar on the brow; she searched with sad skepticism his blue eyes.

"Believe me, *Maminyoo,*" said Moe earnestly: "With these stripes I will never be sent into carnage. I could even become rich— The suppliers prod me on every side with money. If I only dared accept."

"Moishe, child. *Ai,*" Baba moaned in disbelief.

"No? Ask, ask whom you wish, a total stranger. Ask, what is a mess sergeant. *Treife* I must eat. But to be sent into carnage, never.

Who will buy for the whole regiment? It takes a Yiddisher *kupf*."
Moe spoke as though he were commanding Baba to understand.
"I have authority, I alone. Would I buy from this dealer, and not
from the other, he nudges me with fifty dollars. Believe me. But
I refuse. Not that it's worth my life to be honest, but I do it for
your sake. Not to risk my 'rank,' as it's called in English. These,"
he pointed to his chevrons. "You understand? You have nothing
to pine about."

Perhaps Baba wanted to believe. As long as Moe was home,
her appetite perked up. She even went shopping, hovered over
her firstborn son with the freshest *bulkies*, lox and smoked white
fish, every delicacy she could think of; she baked *kishka*, stuffed
dermer; she cooked *borsht* and *kreplach*, *blintzes* and *lotkehs* and carrot
pudding, *gefilte* fish and chicken. Moe took precedence before
Zaida, who was glad enough to yield: At last his wife was active
again, dressed herself in her best black satin on the Sabbath, wore
her pearls, served dinner and dined—ate, because Moe refused
to eat unless she did. Her cheeks filled out, almost visibly absorbing
nourishment; her blue eyes seemed to emerge from their caverns,
like iris, her color returned. She wanted to believe. And again and
again, her gaze rested on his Moe's mess sergeant's insignia, as on
a talisman. Her son would be spared.

And then came the dread last hours of Moe's furlough, the
dread time when everyone except Baba knew, even Ira, and everyone had been enjoined not to betray, not to hint, that in a matter
of days Moe's division would be sent overseas—across the Atlantic
where the U-boats lurked—to France, to the battlefield. The secret
was well kept, the conspiracy of silence remained intact, even till
the last moment: Cheerfully, Moe embraced everyone, once more
hugged his weeping, clinging mother, her eyes squeezed shut, her
hands groping for his chevrons. He told Max and Harry to look
after her, and with Zaida and Saul, left the house. The whole family
was crammed into the two front windows, waving and calling; and
Moe, with upraised arm, kept returning their farewells, until at
Madison Avenue, the trio rounded the corner and were out of
view. A few feet behind them, scarcely noticed, the eleven-year-
old Ira trailed.

A clear, temperate summer day. 1917. Pedestrians seemed more numerous on Madison Avenue, lolling at the fronts of houses or sauntering unconcernedly along. Ahead of Ira, Moe and his two escorts, Saul and Zaida, reached the corner of 116th Street and Madison, crossed to the northwest corner, and wheeled west toward Fifth Avenue. They crossed Fifth Avenue. Ahead of them in the middle of the very long block between Fifth Avenue and Lenox was the marshaling yard, the open court of P.S. 86, the very large gray-stone public school building. Buses were already parked in front of it, buses full or part full of uniformed men. An empty bus, another and still another lumbered up beside the others and double-parked. At the sight of them, Zaida and Saul, who hadn't said a word all this time but walked as in a daze, suddenly burst out into frenzied lamentations. Howling in despair, each one hung onto Moe's arm. And Moe, stalwart, the more so with his weeks of training, his countenance under his khaki campaign hat ruddy with effort, dragged them along like a tug between two barges. When they saw it was futile to try and hinder him, each let go. Each abandoned himself to extremity of grief: Zaida tore at his beard, tore out bunches of whiskers, wailing at the top of his voice. Saul snatched at his hair, flung himself about, screaming hysterically. Passersby stopped to watch, automobiles slowed down, people leaned out of windows.

At the very edge of the curb, Moe halted. And still filial and forebearing, "I pray you, Father, spare me," he said. "Let me be. If not, and you too, Saul, go no further. It's bad enough I'm a soldier. I wear a uniform. Don't add to my trials."

They quieted down, lapsed into suppressed groans. Scared, cringing with embarrassment, near tears, Ira watched them near the marshaling yard mingle with other servicemen and their kin walking toward the buses.

"Will yez look at them Jews," said the cop on duty to a hanger-on beside him in front of a store, a beefy, blue-coated cop talking to a lean civilian: "Didjez ever see the loik? Ye'd think the guy was dead already."

IX

So Moe went off to the war across the ocean. For awhile, Baba believed her family's reiterated fabrication that Moe was still in Camp Yaphank in New Jersey; but then, as the weeks passed, and she saw no sign of him, and though the letters were full of good cheer, she recognized the letter paper was European and asked to see the envelopes. They were never shown her and she saw through the deception. " 'How long will you cajole me with falsehoods?' " Mom told Ira that Baba chided her. " 'You are all frauds. As if I didn't know where the fighting and the killing were taking place.' " Finally Zaida told her the truth: Moe was in France.

To everyone's surprise, Baba took the news with strange fortitude. "With God's help and those stripes on his arms, my Moishe will live," she said. Nevertheless she brooded a great deal, grew gaunt and worn. She shopped, she went about her household tasks, and though it no longer took a tirade on Zaida's part to make her eat, she seemed to fade; she seemed to fade waiting . . . waiting from letter to letter from her son, but always as if vitality were slowly draining away. Thus the weeks and months of a distant war went by. Aunt Mamie, so buxom, so brash, offered the doughboys who did guard duty under the Grand Central overpass fresh Jewish pastry and hot, sugary *café au lait* in her enameled milk-bucket with the narrow neck. And Mom, unreticent and frank in her immense pity, would say in barely intelligible English to some young soldier patrolling the viaduct: "You heff such beautiful, strung lecks now. Gott shuld helf you'll heff them when you come beck."

And the young American lad would laugh: "Aw, don't worry, Mom. We'll be O.K."

Oh, the terrible years, who can bear them, Ecclesias?

That August afternoon in 1914, when he had been sent into the heat-shimmering street to buy the "Wuxtra" the two vendors cried, Ira was now old enough to connect in his own mind as links, the one with the other, two isolated events, no longer isolated, but as if one was precursor to the other, even if the other came so late you almost forgot the first: a warm Yiddish newspaper bought in the street, and Moe in khaki off to war, off to France—and Saul howling and Zaida pulling out handfuls of beard . . . And the cop on the corner sneering to a bystander, "Will yez look at them Jews? Ye'd think the guy was dead already." Ira had the meaning within him, brooding on it, though he couldn't tell what it was. He could only think of it just so far: that he contained both episodes in feeling, and they were fused together in his mind but that was all. Other things were fringes to that same indelible fusion: Moe sent letters from France, letters and souvenirs to the nephew he was so fond of, so much more fond of than was Pop—fond of him like Mom almost: brass artillery shell casings, engraved and stippled, a pair of French opera glasses, three German iron crosses . . .

Winter came on, and after the return to school from the Christmas holidays, winter brought a new date to write on top of composition papers: 1918. 1918. History swirled about him in little spindrifts. Debs was in jail. IWW meant "I Won't Work." Draft dodgers were cowards. Cartoons in the newspapers showed that mosquitoes had bigger souls than profiteers. Bolsheviks wore bristling whiskers and carried round bombs with ignited fuses.

Ira brought the three iron crosses to school to his 6B teacher, Miss Ackley. Miss Ackley was known as the most formidable teacher in the whole school. She was large of body and raucous of voice: "Oh, the audacity! The audacity of this boy!" she would exclaim, while she administered punishment by gripping the culprit's cheeks between thumb and strong fingers until he yelped with pain. (*Audacity*, Ira took note, in the midst of chastisement: What a beautiful new word!) Miss Ackley screamed in horror when Ira inventively misinformed her that his uncle had taken the iron crosses from the cadavers of German soldiers on the battlefields of France.

"Take them away!" She seemed close to fainting. "Take them away!"

He was getting even with her, the sudden, expanding buoyancy of his mind told him. Intuitively, he had lied just right, just where it would have the most effect. She had gripped his jaws at least a half-dozen times. Mostly because he had been guilty of disorderly conduct, giggling during penmanship exercises. He couldn't make Palmer ovals. He tried, but they always changed shape and course and jumped wildly outside their boundaries of blue lines until they looked like smoke blowing in the wind; and he dipped his penpoint too deeply into the inkwell on the desk, so the up-and-down line exercises merged into blotted walls. *Shlemiel,* as Pop said: A *shlemiel* in everything. And *shlemiels* were punished. So Ira grinned to himself, when Miss Ackley nearly fainted at the sight of the iron crosses, because of a lie he made up about dead German soldiers stretched out on the battlefield, and Moe plucking iron crosses off their chests. Maybe he did. . . .

Entrusted into each pupil's safekeeping when he (or she) "graduated" from P.S. 103, the elementary school on 119th Street and Madison Avenue, was his "blue record card." On it was recorded his scholastic performance up to and including the completion of his sixth year of school. After that, he no longer attended elementary school; he attended grammar school. Ira was directed to take his blue record card to P.S. 84, the grammar school that extended from 127th to 128th Street near Madison Avenue, and there present himself, together with his blue record card, to one of the teachers in charge of admitting the new pupils. It was an all-boys school, and each boy, his blue record card in hand, stood in one of several lines before the stout oak lunch tables at which sat a teacher registering the newcomers.

It was a February day, the first week in February, 1918. In another few days he would be twelve years of age. And farewell to childhood . . .

X

You keep a battery of such pretty signs on the top of your keyboard, Ecclesias. Or should I say, array? ! @ # $ % ^ & ( ) — + . . . I am seventy-nine years old. In one way, I look forward to dying; in another I am filled with too great a sense of gratitude to M to yield, even in the mind, to the wish of having my life come to an end. Other than that, what's the use of living? Or what's the difference? I ring changes on the same theme, the same old theme. I wonder if "the branch that might have grown full straight," of which Kit Marlowe speaks, retains forever within it a sense of that lost straightness, lost rectitude. Let's imagine my father, a Zionist. In a few months, the Balfour Declaration will be published. Let's away to Israel, let's away to a kibbutz. I would know chiefly hard work, rigor, danger, but also kinship, precious kinship, dignity. But alas, I wouldn't have known M —

— You're back on the same treadmill, my friend, or the same roller-bearing race — call it what you will: ball-race. Fate or history devised it. But more to the point, it was only because you could compel yourself beyond it, and thanks to M, you attained a measure of growth, something approaching maturity, an approximate maturity, a passable facsimile. Or to put it another way, for almost five decades you were well-nigh immobilized by your inability to go beyond childhood. Isn't that true?

Well, my liege . . .

The multipurpose lunchroom, drab, indoor-playground-basement where everyone waited his turn to be registered was steamy and rank that winter's day, a brumous day —

— Proceed. That isn't the crisis.

And what shall I do when I come to it?

— Do you remember the shaft that Siegfried threw, the unseen Brunhilde aiding? And that leap?

That quantum leap? Yes.

— Have faith in an existential universe, in the dialectic of five decades.

I'd rather, Ecclesias, my friend, have taken that blue record card and hidden or destroyed it. Never attended P.S. 84 at all. Who would have known? Mom and Pop. But otherwise? What primitive trust institutions had those days. Give the juvenile his blue record card to convey from school to school. What control was there? Or what verifying that the pupil had really presented himself and been enrolled in the school to which he had been transferred? Oh, probably there was a list of pupils, their names separately transmitted. But if not, then to hell with the damned card. Chuck it in a trash can in front of a tenement and disappear. Do you remember Kelsey who ran away from home at the age of twelve?

—Yes, good Jewish boys don't run away from home at twelve. And Mama's good Jewish boy at that. You would never have known M, and never have striven for and achieved, if only partially, redemption—

Oh, that sounds so jeezly Miltonic—

—Rebirth then, renewal, rehabilitation.

I might not have needed it.

Steamy and rank, the stagnant air of the dreary basement playground was fraught with the exhalation of the slate urinals in the toilets at one end. In the low ceiling, wire cages protected nests of electric lights. Underfoot, muddy slush splotched the dark concrete floors. The small, barred windows looked out on a narrow play-yard on one side, and the street on the other. Against the darkly wainscoted walls stretched rows of heavy, scarred wooden benches. On one of these benches, adjacent to the line in which Ira stood waiting his turn, sat a trio of Irish kids, bigger than kids, adolescents; their size, their air of assurance marked them as eighth graders. "Let's see your record card," said one—in a tone that brooked no refusal.

Docile, though hesitant, Ira handed over his blue record card. They examined it a moment, looked around, then all three spat on it. One threw it on the floor, and the others ground the card underfoot. In another second, with an eye on the teacher at the desk, they darted out of the side door into the street.

. . . Once again it came to Ira, as he sat recording the incident: how sad. How sad he hadn't fought every step of the way — like Greeny, even if he lost a tooth, an eye, was stabbed, even if he lost his life — like that kid in the slums whom the toughs in the block called a sissy for wearing a wristwatch: Soldiers had begun to wear them in the trenches. If he *had* to be wrested from the East Side, if it was his fate to have been pried out of protective homogeneity, then to have fought, and the very attitude, the toughening and belligerence, would have been manifest, would have deterred further abuse, victimization— Oh, hell, he told himself, paused to reflect: Probably that was the reason why he had chosen Bill Loem for the central character of his second and aborted novel: Bill fought. And he, the novelist, had gone overboard because of that, romanticized his fictional character, glorified his belligerence, interpreting it as socialist militance. Everything interwove, as better minds than his had discovered long, long ago. But to try to follow them was vain: One could not follow into the past; one could only be edified, and seek to apply the principle. And had he been able to, he wouldn't be sitting here writing about his failure to do so. Alas. Docile dolt, already wearing steel-framed eyeglasses.

"What's this?" The teacher at the table frowned when Ira presented his blue record card. The teacher was Mr. Lennard, Ira was to learn later, a history teacher, a man with lips full to puffiness, whose blue eyes stared up at Ira through a pince-nez.

"Some big boys grabbed it and spit on it and stood on it," Ira quailed.

"Which ones?"

"They ran away."

His frown mingled resignation with annoyance. "You'll have to help me out then. Is that Tysmen where it's smeared—what? Austria-Hungary."

"Tysmenitz," Ira said. "That's how my father says it. With a 'z' near the end."

"With a 'z' near the end." Mr. Lennard's gold-nibbed fountain pen formed new letters on top of the smudged-over ones. "And you were born—what day?"

"I was born February eighth, 1906."

"It distinctly says January here." Mr. Danroe said sharply. "January tenth. Is that a six at the end or a five? Nineteen-oh-five."

"Oh, I forgot!" Ira pleaded. "I forgot!"

"You forgot what? What did you forget?"

"My mother made a mistake. She thought they meant when she was married." Ira knew better: Mom had deliberately lied in order to enroll him in school a term earlier. "She didn't talk English good."

"You're in 7A-2. Here's your homeroom number, 219." Mr. Lennard handed Ira a slip of paper with the numerals he had just written on it. "Report there tomorrow morning before eight-thirty. Next boy," he terminated Ira's admission process. And as an afterthought: "You'll have to straighten out that other thing at the office."

Such was Ira's induction into P.S. 24, the school in which he was destined to spend, not the next two years, as he had expected, before going on to high school, but three: two years to earn his public school diploma, and a third, when with typical flabbiness of purpose, he allowed himself to be cajoled into swelling the attendance of the newly instituted educational excrescence known as a junior high school. It was a commercial junior high school at that: offering courses he detested, bookkeeping, typing, stenography. Was there ever such a *shlemiel?* Was there ever such a *shlemazl?* But of that later. To speak of it now made Ira feel as if he were shifting so abruptly he was grinding the gears of time. Of that later. More pertinent was the D D D he received on his first report card; D D D his first month's grades: D in deportment, D in effort, D in proficiency. He had fetched bottom, a dismal, total failure.

Both Mom and Pop had had enough acquaintance with report cards to know what the marks meant. "It's worth sod over it," Pop signed the report card with hasty flourish. "Send him to school. A *golem* made of lime; he'll go to high school and college, yeh, yeh, as I will go." Disapproval cleared the way for vindication. "You enjoy deceiving yourself? Then deceive yourself," Pop mocked his wife. "He's fated for the life of toiler, and be fortunate if he succeeds in that."

"All at once he's become a toiler, a turf layer," Mom retorted sarcastically, but with tears forming in her eyes. "I'll not allow it. I'll wash floors, but to high school he'll go."

"I know, I know," said Pop. "She already has him in high school. Listen to me: Better you took two stones and pounded loose the foolish notion in your head."

"Never!" Mom declared. "When the midwife laid him on my breast, I blessed him: 'May you achieve noble renown,' I said. And he will yet. My blessing will not be denied. Let his report card read D D D, let it—What!" she suddenly recollected: "His *malamut* didn't come to the house to praise him? Your son is a rabbi in the making. He can *daven* like a grown-up already. He retains like marble— What has happened to you?"

"I don't know," Ira answered sullenly.

"Try to expound with him," Pop flipped the report card along the green linoleum-covered table back to Ira. "And heed what a *malamut* says— You know what: a heave with a spade and a toss on the dunghill."

"My clever spouse," Mom retorted.

XI

The more he recounted, the more dreamlike it all became. He heard his wife return from her weekly shopping expedition, tall, slender in her gray coat. "Do you want some help?" he asked, knowing only too well how slight his help could be in the present state of his capability.

"Yes, in a minute," she smiled her ladylike smile of forty-five years of intimacy, and made for the bathroom. . . .

The grocery bags had been weighty, taxing him to the utmost, his carrying them through the long corridor of the mobile home, through the living room with its Baldwin piano and into the large kitchen-dinette, where Bizet's symphony greeted him from the small radio on top of the refrigerator. No negligible burden. Breathing heavily, he had set the bags down on the chairs, rather than lifting them to the table, he who had once lugged hundred-pound sacks of grain and scratch and pellets for the waterfowl he raised, not as if the sacks were light, but nothing formidable either: Without strain he regularly emptied five or six sacks into the three sugar barrels in the barn where he stored the poultry feed. And he had even carried M on his shoulder and set her down in the car those months that she suffered from an "undiagnosable" form of Guillaume-Barre syndrome, paralyzed, in a Maine farmhouse, when the boys were young.

Well . . . Today especially, though he regarded himself as largely inured to the pain, it seemed excessive. This morning he had felt as if he would break in half when M lifted him to a sitting position in bed.

"It's all a dream, hain't it?" the old farmer, senile psychotic committed to the Augusta State Hospital, had looked at Ira with innocent, faraway blue eyes, after Ira had humored the doddering geriatric away from his intention of getting his "overholts" on to do chores: "It's all a dream, hain't it?" Ira had dwelled on that word: "hain't," *haint*, old dialect for "haunt," meaning the same thing: a dream haunted. If only mankind knew it. But one got nowhere, got nowhere with that; it was only at the end of life, it might seem that way: a dream haunted. Until then it was anything but dream, anything but haunted. It was Longfellow's earnest reality. Even these twinges, pangs, aches, alas, were real. His eyes moved away from the keyboard to the daunting pile of mss. in separate manila envelopes. Not quite a foot high. Would he live long enough to retrieve all this prose from paper to disks? It was doubtful.

Ira did better the following month: C C C; his improvement noted in a comment to that effect on the back of the report card. It was the beginning of Easter Week, the beginning of the Easter holidays, overlapping with those of *Pesach*, the Passover. Sunny, warm weather had begun, the blithe days of the spring of 1918, two months after his twelfth year. Mom housecleaned for the Passover, laid bedding out of the window to sun, sprinkled corners under the sink with roach powder, doused bedsprings with arrant-rank kerosene, and who knew what else. She would soon be unwrapping the Passover dishes on the top shelf of the china closet; Pop would be polishing the engraved silver wine cups, the silver salt cellar on its three little feet—and the silverware too, all brought over from Europe, wedding gifts: with benchmarks in the handles whose dates could still be distinguished: 1898. Oh, there would be *matzah* soon, of course, *kharoses* soon, of course, horseradish on *matzah* chips and homemade red wine, maybe not too sour this time. And the Four Questions to ask, beginning, *Mah nishtanoo haleila hazeh:* Wherefore is this night different from all other nights? And hard-boiled eggs in salt water, of course; and the thing Ira was especially fond of, the pictures in the *Haggadah:* Moses smiting the Egyptian, bam! with a long staff. And the Red Sea opening—and closing again to engulf Egyptian horse and rider. That was fun. *Gefilte* fish, and chicken soup with *matzah* balls were delectable. But the chicken, well, all boiled out and no flavor. But that was the only indifferent part; afterwards, Mom always served compote made from dried fruit: pears and prunes and raisins.

—Yes?

Two big pots of water were simmering on the gas stove; they were meant to temper the cold water that came out of the bathtub faucets. The pair of brass faucets in sink and bathtub both ran cold water. Why have two faucets in sink and bathtub, and both running cold water? Ira never understood. But so they did. And to mitigate the keen chill still lingering in the water from winter, it had to be mixed with water heated on the gas stove. Oh, the water from the brass faucets made a good cold glass of water to drink, but not to bathe in. Br-r! And you had to let some cold water gush into the bathtub first, the long, tin bathtub in its wooden coffin-box of brown-stained matched boards. Because if you didn't, the hot water softened the green paint on it—when that Irish, *goyish* anti-Semite of a landlord finally, after many pleas, consented to have the bathroom daubed: green paint that came off on your *tochis,* yeah, smeared green on your ass. He should live so, that landlord, as Mom said, with his green bile that he daubed the kitchen and the bathtub with: Such a long bathtub was never seen, long enough, and deep too, you could float full-length on your fingertips if there was enough water in it—in the summer, for sure, when you filled it up with lukewarm water from the tap.

But this time of the year, there would be just enough water in it to bathe in, to be clean for the Passover, Passover of 1918 during the Great War.

What else can I tell you?

— *Mucho mas.* You are the painter who painted himself into the corner of childhood.

It isn't that, I still insist, though very likely it helped. Undoubtedly it helped. All right? Enough conceded? It was those awful thrashings, atrocious thrashings Pop perpetrated made all the difference—

— You were thrashed as heinously on the East Side. Oh, I know what you're going to say: Would God you knew about—or there existed—institutions protective of abused children. Probably, had you taken the black-and-blue emblazonings on your back to any cop on the beat, you would have been given shelter, protection. But granted you knew nothing about such things, feared them more than the scourgings you received, screwball though your father was, how often were you the nasty, sneaky little scamp?

Yes, but I didn't make my point.

— I already know it.

Then why accuse me? As long as I had, at least, an external milieu that was supportive, the homogeneous, the orthodox East Side, estrangement from an unstable and violent father might be borne. But here in Harlem, both home life and the street had an element of insecurity, were disparaging when not hostile (except for Mom, who out of her indulgence probably contributed most to the disastrous impairment of the psyche).

— I am well apprised of it. *Verfallen is Yeroshulaim.*

Indeed. The audacity! As Miss Ackley screamed at me that somnolent September afternoon, at the beginning of school, when I built a sail of a blotter pierced through by the inclined pencil; and zephyr billowed through the open window and wafted my boat along the desk.

— You can't stay there.

No.

Mr. O'Reilly stopped Ira in the hall, singled him out from a file of pupils passing by during departmental change. "I want to see you in my office," he said. Mr. O'Reilly was the principal of P.S. 24— His office was the principal's office!

Quaking, Ira entered, sat down and waited. In a few minutes, Mr. O'Reilly came in. White-haired, clerical-looking, wearing a wing collar, his lean cheek twitched with a severe tic. "That grin on your face is going to get you into trouble, young man," Mr. O'Reilly said.

"I didn't know I was grinning, Mr. O'Reilly," Ira faltered.

"I know it. You're Jewish, aren't you?"

"Yes, sir."

"I don't have to tell you your people have a hard enough time in this world, without your making things worse for yourself."

Worriedly, Ira tried to smooth his cheek.

"I happen to understand that you don't mean anything by it," Mr. O'Reilly continued, clipping his words. "You don't mean anything bad or mean. But not everybody will understand that. They'll think you're sneering at them. Do you know what a sneer is? It's making fun of people. Nobody likes that."

"I'm sorry, Mr. O'Reilly."

"Try to get the better of it," Mr. O'Reilly's face twitched. "Just make up your mind you will."

"I'll try, Mr. O'Reilly."

"Before you get into trouble."

"Yes, sir."

"You're excused. Just a minute, I'll give you a note for your teacher."

XII

Home and school, home and school, and the walk in all weather connecting the two. With textbooks strapped together, with varying gait, chance meetings with schoolmates, he passed and repassed the rocky hill and bell tower of Mt. Morris Park on the one hand, and on the other, across the trolley tracks of Madison Avenue, the deteriorating brownstones, a few carved out by a grubby store at the bottom, across the street the abandoned red-brick church that changed denominations (to Ira's naive surprise: How could a church consecrated to one denomination unconsecrate itself, draw out the hallowness from its interior to make room for another faith?). A new and imposing Eye and Ear Hospital was built on Madison Avenue, along his route. And he passed and repassed 125th Street, shopping mart of show windows in low buildings a story or two high. How many times? Two years, and then a third. He made the trip at least 500 days, often as many as four times a day, going and coming, when he hurried home for lunch, unless Mom gave him a couple of *bulkies* with chopped tomato-herring or a Muenster-cheese filler, and a nickel to buy two slabs of ginger-bread in the bakery at the corner of the school, which stuffed him but he didn't like them; or a napoleon, that miracle of custard and flaky pastry.

Like a riffled deck of cards, scarce seen, the compacted days of the past sped by; but now and then a pause, when a card was glimpsed: Once on the way home for lunch, he found a dollar bill on the sidewalk, so conspicuous, so verdant, he couldn't believe everyone else had overlooked it except himself. . . . He pounced on it, pocketed it, and in high glee sprang over the corner hydrant no-hands—and struck his shin so cruel a blow on the iron breast of the cap protruding midway from the hydrant that ever since, superstitiously, like Pop, he braced for calamity after windfall. And again hurrying home for lunch, he hitched a ride, as he had seen so many kids do, at the rear end of a Madison Avenue trolley car;

and when it went past 119th Street, fearful it would take him too far out of his way, he jumped off, couldn't maintain his footing over the cobblestones between tracks and fell, bruising his knee so badly, a great crimson blotch glowed where his long black stocking met his knee-pants.

How Mom fumed when she spied the damage he had done: "The evil year take you! Twenty cents thrown out! New stockings! Cholera take you!"

"I still got one left," he whined.

"Indeed. *Veh, veh, veh!* I nurture a dolt! Out of the miserable pittance he doles out to me, buy your shoes, your clothes, the food on the table!" Angry scarlet mounted from throat to brow. "May the sod cover you. Eat, eat. You'll be late for school. *Oy, gewald!*" She stripped his stocking down. "Unbutton your shoe. What an oaf is capable of. Only look at that!" She soaked a cloth under the faucet, wrung it out. "You could have been killed."

"I didn't mean it," he wept. "I tried to get home fast."

"Fest," she repeated the English word while he winced under the pressure of the wet cloth. *"Sollst mir fest gehen in d'red!"*

The school janitor slapped him for posturing on a bench in the indoor playground–lunch room, something the other kids did hundreds of times, but always Ira seemed more conspicuous, more provocative. The shop teacher slapped him on the ear, but so hard that it rang all afternoon and still rang that evening when Pop came home from work. Mom reported it, and to Ira's surprise, Pop wrote an indignant postcard to the principal, Mr. O'Reilly. What he wrote, Ira never knew, but it had its effect on Mr. Ewin, the shop teacher, because he came up to Ira, deprecating and smiling, jollied Ira about the incident. That time only *one* of his ears rang—Ira couldn't help snicker at his everlasting improvidence—only *one* ear rang, and he had reported it. The next time both ears rang, and went unreported: He had expended ten cents for a fat, crimson firecracker (the kids in the school had disclosed the location of the store that bootlegged the illegal jumbos). What a firecracker! Mom was out when he got home after school. Who could resist lighting a match and touching the flame to the fuse? Now to throw the firecracker down the bedroom airshaft, filthy airshaft, where the sun only penetrated, magically, once a year, and the rats ranged freely over the garbage, the moldering newspapers, wrecked furniture, smashed bottles, and even a bashed-in pisspot, all compacted into the refuse below. What a scare that would give everybody, but especially the rats, when the red tube, fuse sputtering spitefully, exploded. He ran to the bedroom window to hurl the firecracker out but—the window was closed! Never closed in summer, but closed this time! An instant of indecision, and barely was it out of his hand when the firecracker exploded. His hand throbbed; his ears rang. He told nobody.

— So little left of the once-teeming density of living.

It's because of the evasion, Ecclesias.

— Even so. But not only for that reason.

The ports are closed, closed to verbatim and the desiccated diurnal out there. Oh, once in awhile, through some rift or aperture, Louis, the *Luksh,* as Leo Dugonitz called him (Hungarian Leo Dugonitz), *luksh* meaning noodle because Louis was so elongated in height . . . as we walked along the side of Mt. Morris Park after school, Louis introduced us to the new hit song: Jada, jada, jada, jada, jing, jing, jing. Bizarre but funny, a moment rescued from oblivion, three eighth-graders wending their way home from school. Well, I'll tell you, given everything else against me, I was about to say, or as it probably would have proved to be the case, a mediocre, ordinary personality, now slowly underwent the disfiguring change that imposed a certain distorted distinction, enforced a brooding isolation, a complex uniqueness. Isn't that strange?

—Yes.

I think so anyway. . . . To be sure, I have no evidence and alas, there is no way of doing the same thing twice, choosing the alternate for comparison.

— Except mentally, imaginatively, not materially.

Strange though, for awhile it seemed forgotten, during youth and manhood; most of the time, it seemed surmounted.

— But not truly, not in the psyche.

No, that's right, Ecclesias.

—Then why do you exhume it all so often?

I hadn't meant to tell you until this instant, Ecclesias: to make dying easier, more welcome, for myself and my fellow man, perhaps.

Jada, jada, jada, jada, jing, jing, jing. Sometimes he played touch football when impromptu sides were chosen on the playground, the dirt playground in Mt. Morris Park. He was generally a welcome candidate when it came to touch football. Not that he was very fleet of foot, but punting the ball came naturally to him—his passing was poor, again because of his inept hands—but he could punt: Somehow he had learned the knack of sending the ball up with just the right spin off the instep of his foot, with a high follow-through afterward that sent the ball forty or fifty yards. His punting won acclaim. Also he had a certain confidence about catching a football that he didn't have about catching a baseball or a handball, even though he now wore eyeglasses: The ball was larger, softer than a baseball and not caught by hands usually, but caught in a basket formed of abdomen and arms. Only trouble was, punting tore the right toe away from the rest of the shoe, which brought down upon him Mom's standard execrations, because the shoemaker charged ten cents to repair the break. Ira dreamed of the day he could earn enough, save up enough, to buy football shoes—with leather cleats—and a football too, so he wouldn't have to stand around waiting to be chosen, though he usually was—but only after the friends of the kid who owned the ball were all duly included. And what if Ira was the odd man?

Like the blades of a condenser in which time is stored: Geography, History, English, Arithmetic, Physical Training, Manual Training, the weekly school assemblies, pledges of allegiance to the flag, reading of the Scriptures by Mr. O'Reilly. Once, because he had recited the poem so eloquently in class, his English teacher, henna-haired Miss Delany, asked him to recite it in the assembly: Walter Scott's "Breathes there a man with soul so dead who never to

himself hath said: this is mine own, my native land. . . ." But the
words which he had spoken with such feeling in the classroom
became stiff and mechanical in the assembly. Ira knew his teacher
was disappointed with his performance. Why couldn't he do the
same thing well a second time, or time after time, regularly, uni-
formly, the way some people could? The way an actor did, the way
that a certain soldier did who went to every school and gave en-
thralling imitations of the noises made by different pieces of ord-
nance, different shells and machine-gun fire: Whiz-bang! Whoosh!
Whe-e-e Pom-pom! Ticaticatica . . . And he sang:

> Chief Bugaboo was a Redman who
> Heard the cry of War.
> Swift to the tent of his bride he went,
> The beautiful Indianola:
> "Oh, me wanna go where the cannon roar.
> Oh, me help the white Yank win this war.
> Oh, me tararara gore,"
> Blankety blankety blank blank blank.

"Over There," and "Johnny Get Your Gun," and "Keep the
Homefires Burning" had quite crowded out "I Didn't Raise My
Boy to Be a Soldier." At home Mom still opposed the War, to Ira's
irate, patriotic protests. The names of Lenin and Trotsky were in
the air, grotesque demons in the Hearst newspapers, demons to
everybody, it seemed to Ira, except to Jews. Bolsheviks were Reds.
All Reds were wild-eyed; all Reds had bristly, unkempt whiskers in
the cartoons, and carried round bombs with fuses graphically sputtering. So did anarchists. What a horrible word, anarchist! But Mom,
and Pop too, paid no attention to what the American newspapers
said; Baba and Zaida especially: All they wanted was for Moishe
to be safe, for Moishe to come home again safe and sound. They
had no patriotism, no "Breathes there the man with soul so dead
who never to himself hath said" . . . Souls of rattlesnakes and mosquitoes were shown in the cartoons in the newspapers Pop brought
home from the Stock Exchange restaurant. The greatly magnified
souls of cooties and ticks and other detestable insects were shown,

and lastly the souls of Slackers and Profiteers: They were invisible under a thousandfold magnification. Kaiser Bill—everybody knew Kaiser Bill—with his spiky mustache and spike helmet. And Charlie Chaplin too capturing the Kaiser. Oh, how funny that was! Who else was a hero? And there were aces who shot down five enemy planes. And everywhere Montgomery Flagg's red-white-and-blue Uncle Sam in top hat trailed the pedestrian with stern gaze: *I Want You!* "Ashcan" depth charges were dropped on submarines. Baron von Richthofen flew a red Fokker; the "Big Bertha" shelled Paris. Marshal Joffre, Marshal Foch and General Pershing, and all the people in President Wilson's cabinet—one of Ira's classmates, some kids were just naturally bright that way, made up a whole sentence with everyone in President Wilson's cabinet punned into place.

In 1918 you read "The Lady of the Lake" in grammar school, in 1918 you read the "Lay of the Last Minstrel" (Who was she? Yee-hee-hee!). But how pretty some of the words were: " 'Tis merry, 'tis merry in the good greenwood where the mavis and merle are singing." And you had to bring Mom to school because of your grin—at which your singing teacher took offense—for nothing, as Mr. O'Reilly had warned you, and you were humiliated, standing in front of the class saying you were sorry, and blubbering: Hatchet-faced, bespectacled Miss Bergman. Ira hated her forever, hated her to this very day.

How he hated Miss Bergman! He would hate her all his life, hatchet face in eyeglasses, hate her for the gratuitous humiliation she had inflicted on him, punishing him so inordinately for a grin that somehow twisted his face into a mask that people didn't like. And even now, as he typed, old man as he was, his resentment at the injustice done him returned. Sixty-five years later! Who else of her music class would remember all through life, as he remembered—and appreciated—and could still sing—the songs she had taught them:

> *A tinker I am. My name's natty Dan.*
> *From morn till night I trudge it . . .*

Of course, everyone whispered, a "stinker I am" (and perhaps his grin over that had gotten him into trouble). Still, how he enjoyed the song, relished that double entendre about being a lad of mettle.

He had departed from his text, the yellow second sheet beside him, wandered from himself abroad, as Tom O'Bedlam said, included all sorts of unforeseen, extraneous material. It was the prevalence of the war undoubtedly, the ubiquitousness of the war in everyone's life that swerved him off course. Lame excuse, but (he heard himself sigh): Again and again, what bitterness welled up in him over the accident, at the terrible deformation that was its consequence. Bootless his grudge against fate, and yet he couldn't help it: indicative of the depth to which the inner life had been scarred, a whole life long, mutilated, a whole life long. Fortunately, fortunately, and more than fortunately, there was M.

Well . . .

The first image that always occurred to Ira, the teacher whose face Ira always saw first when he thought of P.S. 24 (perhaps after that of Mr. O'Reilly), was his General Science teacher, Jewish and tired-looking—he, too, like Mr. Sullivan and some of the others, may have had second jobs after school—Mr. Steifen: looking over his shoulder at the class with worn, weary face, as he demonstrated how to find the center of gravity of the cardboard triangle hanging in front of the blackboard . . . or as he showed the awesome weight of the earth's atmosphere, when he turned off the heat of the Bunsen burner under the sheet-steel gallon can, screwed the top on tightly, and while he spoke, so patiently, sadly, a mysterious force suddenly crumpled the can; it fell in upon itself before the awed, incredulous eyes of his pupils, as if by wizardry.

Next, in no definite order, Mr. Kilcoyne. He taught Civics or Government, or something of the sort. A big man, in his early forties, not too tidy, an oyster of mucus might adhere to his fibrous mustache—which some of the kids said was foam off the beer he drank in the café on 125th Street where he had his lunch. He commuted to work from the small dairy farm he owned in Yonkers. His familiarity with every aspect of dairy farming, and his willingness to impart his knowledge, made him easy prey for the tough, case-hardened gamins in his class: who, choosing the right moment, perhaps after a talk on the order of succession to the presidency, might pop up with: "How d'you milk a cow, Mr. Kilcoyne" (usually not so blatantly irrelevant as that, but something close).

Mr. Kilcoyne hesitated.

"We never seen a farm," Victor Pellini pleaded.

"No. Well, the first thing you've got to do is wipe the udder clean, with a cloth and good sudsy warm water—"

"De udder?" Hands were raised, those of harriers in wait, accomplished accomplices—like Vito or Guido Spompali. "De udder what?"

"No, no. I didn't say other. Udder. That's the bag under the cow. That's where the teats hang from."

"Is dat what you grab?"

"One in each hand, yes." Mr. Kilcoyne milked the air. "And after you strip 'em . . ."

But the kids had heard enough. Heads ducked under desks whose owners sought figment property on the floor, while faces contorted in glee. Tits. A teacher talking about tits. What could be funnier? Gone for that period at least was the succession to the presidency of the United States.

Dickensian, Ira thought. Not altogether: It happened often enough so that it survived a half-century in memory; more than that, it survived three score and seven, as Lincoln might have said. The predominant farm-type individual with his normal-school teaching degree, the once-average American faced by sly little first-generation urban rapscallions: "So you grab 'em by de tits, Mr. Kilcoyne?"

"Teats. An udder has teats."

Mr. Kilcoyne might have been duped. But Mr. Sullivan was not to be fooled with. The first day of class he brought out his shillelagh, a massive cudgel, which he slammed twice or thrice on the desk, and invited anybody to get funny. Nobody did. He was a badly crippled man, stunted, grotesquely stooped, and compelled to get about with two canes. A gentle, long-suffering man underneath his pose of cantankerousness, with a disproportionately large head on whose temples blue veins crinkled like miniature lightning, Mr. Sullivan never touched a pupil, relying instead on his bitter, sarcastic comments that stung the most mischievous into behaving, and very few ever misbehaved in Mr. Sullivan's class. He had a vestige of a brogue, and something that was worse, a speech defect that in any other teacher would have destroyed all possibility of his controlling a class of Harlem slum toughies, shillelagh or not. Perhaps it was merely an attribute of his brogue: he "shushed" every "s." "Shtand up," Mr. Sullivan would say. "Shit down."

Behind his back they called him "Shitdown Shullivan," but nobody dared smile when ordered to "Shit down" in his class. He taught English—he was a C.P.A. and moonlighted after school hours as an accountant for several small firms.

"Yoursh truly, Johnny Dooley," Mr. Sullivan taught his class how to conclude a business letter. "Bad, worsh, wursht," Mr. Sullivan mocked the scholar faltering over the comparison of an adjective. Or he might vary reproach with "Shick, shicker, dead." And for the poor, stumbling reader's benefit: "Vosh von haben gaben schlobben, gaben schlobben haben." And one day, to Ira's zany-pretending, shame-faced chagrin, when he was called on to read and explain the passage from James Russell Lowell's "The Vision of Sir Launfall" that went "Daily with souls that cringe and plot, we Sinai's climb and know it not." Ira *did* explain; but with so much protective, self-disparaging antic of demeanor that Mr. Sullivan snapped in waspish rebuke, "Thatsh right. Make 'em laugh. You know more than any of 'em. But make a boob o'yourshelf. Shit down!"

Flustered, ears burning, Ira sat down. Mr. Sullivan had found him out, had seen through him. Mr. Sullivan knew who he was.

Mr. O'Reilly, the principal, was gaunt and gray, with a tic ever creasing his lean, severe face. In his sober vestments, unvarying dark clothes, he looked more like a priest than a school principal. Perhaps it had once been his aim to be a priest. He must have worn the wing collar and tie of conservative attire of those days, or perhaps even more conservative, more old-fashioned, the high, stiff collar and cravat that Pop wore in his wedding portrait of 1905. Whenever Ira tried to visualize him, Mr. O'Reilly always wore a high, stiff collar—but turned backwards, like a priest's. Energetic, though surely in his early seventies, he was wont to enter an English class with startling quickness, shut the door behind him, and stand listening a minute, his probing blue eyes scanning the faces before him. Then, with rapid, decisive nod and movement of hand, he would take over the class. First, he would detach his starched cuffs and placing them like upright cylinders on the desk, take a piece of chalk in his hand, and face twitching, write on the blackboard: "Time flies we cannot their speed is too great." And he would ask for a volunteer who thought he could punctuate the string of words correctly? No one could. He had an endless store of these devices; he seemed to come with a fresh supply for every grade: "What do you think we shave you for nothing and give you a drink." How should the barber punctuate this sign so it would be free of ambiguity? These and so many more.

They gave Ira an insight—dimly—of a world he never knew, and never would know: an insight into the traditional Catholic parochial school world with its rigid, fixed, age-old accretion of subject matter, often ingenious, but always invariant, and reassuring because it was invariant—like the whole gamut of correct usage: shall and will: They shall not pass! "My right is crushed," Marshal Foch wired Clemenceau, the French premier, "My left is in retreat. I will attack with my center." The whole gamut: the difference between lay and lie, may and can, who and whom, like and as, drilled over and over again, as if, Ira reflected afterward, life depended on their correct usage, the life of street urchins, slum adolescents like himself. Obviously, the seeds fell on fertile ground sometimes. But one couldn't help ponder on the vast gap between the septuagenarian and juveniles in his charge. It was more than mere age, the span of years—superfluous to say so. It was a qualitatively different age, qualitatively different in traditions—different in prospects, perspectives, in the midst of a war that would mark the rending of Western attitudes, perceptions, would mark the repudiation, the rejection of the precepts Mr. O'Reilly tried to instill, so earnestly and for the most part vainly.

Ira wished he could recall verbatim that strange, anomalous moment when Mr. O'Reilly suddenly seemed to depart from himself and began expounding for the class some elementary ideas—as he interpreted them—of Nietzsche. Nietzsche, of all people! Strength is the main thing, said Mr. O'Reilly: You can do anything in the world you want, bad or good, commit any sin (and lowering his voice, as if he knew how greatly he was violating propriety), behave badly with women. But strength was what people admired and respected: power. What a strange disquisition from an aged Victorian, confessing to a class of adolescents who barely understood—who he knew would barely understand—this almost furtive disclosure of the repudiation of his straitlaced nineteenth-century respectability: "I became a school teacher, and not a businessman," he told the class, "because those marbles or tops I didn't lose, the other boys stole from me." And years later—how many? a mere fifteen—when Ira visited Mr. O'Reilly to present him with a copy of the novel his pupil of P.S. 24 had written, the once taut, strenuous, commanding presence was now only a tremulous, frail, lonely old man in a bathrobe, who remembered not at all the kid he had counseled once, wisely, but to as little avail to overcome his provocative grin as Mr. O'Reilly his tic.

And there was an elderly woman who also taught English, Miss Delany, even older than Mr. O'Reilly—frail and decrepit and slow, her white hair a foggy yellow with age. They said she kept a peepot in her closet. She was the one who made everybody in the class memorize Cardinal Wolsey's farewell speech in Shakespeare's *Henry VIII:* "Farewell! a long farewell to all my greatness!" Why? again why? What was the relevance, the timeliness, the usefulness that would justify trying to inculcate such lofty sentences in the mind of slum juveniles like himself, kids of immigrant parents or rambunctious offspring of uncouth Irish?

He himself bore the memorized speech within him all his life, like some kind of noble monument of the spirit. But did anyone else? Not to flatter himself, did anyone else? Why should they? Relevance was important; timeliness and usefulness played important roles in retention. Why was he so sure that only he retained the great speech after so many years, and no one else did? And if he did, why did he? If it were true that he alone did, why was it? Was that a sign he was already showing an inclination toward literature, a susceptibility, something that Mr. O'Sullivan had discerned and no one else had? Ira didn't know. He had lived with the quotation so long that he even thought he detected a certain ambiguity about it, as if the Bard had forgotten the initial figure of speech or the initial thrust of the metaphor. The little wanton boys that swam on bladders in a sea of glory were finally swept away by a rude stream that would forever hide them. But he was maundering.

Mr. Lennard was a homosexual, a flagrant fag. What were they called today? Deviants, fairies, gays? (A pox on 'em for besmirching such a pretty word as gay.) Well, deviants, fags, fairies, they would have to wait—

Listen. Ira was sure he heard the continuous cry of cranes or geese over-head. How early for them to return: the 17th of February. That meant an early spring, or was that an old wives' tale, an Indian sign? *E come i gru van cantando lor lai, facendo in aer di se lunga riga,* Dante wrote, if the words were rightly remembered. . . . Knock off, go outdoors and see if you can locate their long arrowhead formation, not always easy, they were so diaphanous when high, melting into azure space.

—Press the red Escape button, and save.

I thank you, Ecclesias. . . .

XIII

In 1918 also, it seemed to him in retrospect that his reading preferences underwent a change. Whether the change occurred because he attended grammar school now and was entitled to a library card that gave him the privilege of drawing books from the downstairs, or adult, reading room; or whether, like an apparition inseparable from his recollection of that distant period, the change from the mythic to the actual took place accidentally—and drastically—he was no longer sure. It made a good story, he told himself. There it was: the evening in spring when he thought he had at last found the treasure he had so long sought—the *Purple Fairy Book*—and checked it out with other books he was borrowing, sliding the pile of three or four volumes along the oak counter where the thin, spinsterlike librarian in the pince-nez stamped one's library card. So far so good, except for one thing: There was something awry with the time frame of the picture, with the ambience of the moment of his borrowing the books. He was on the downstairs, the adult floor of the library—that was his distinct impression—and the lady with the pince-nez was the head-librarian: As befitted her rank, she was the one who always stamped books downstairs. The chances of the *Purple Fairy Book,* or of any fairy book, being downstairs were very slight. Hence it was something he had concocted in his own imagination, a sheer figment: When he got home, and opened his treasure to revel in new variants of the exquisite and chivalrous, the book turned out to be Mark Twain's *Huckleberry Finn.* Outrage at misfortune changed into absorption; as he read, he became engrossed; vociferous disappointment changed into enjoyment, into mirth, into complete ravishment. Oh, this was wonderful, wonderful, the real world, the homey, though real world. Though not *his* in the asphalt grids of Harlem, but by the side of that faraway Mississippi River, still the story dealt with the plain and everyday, funny and real and wonderful. Were there others like it? There must be.

So he would envisage his initiation into realistic fiction to himself, so he would account for the transition. From then on, anything that first caught his fancy after a few pages read in the library was taken home to peruse at leisure on the kitchen table, under bluish gas mantle-light. Sometimes just the title alone was enough to base a judgment on, whether to take the volume home or leave it. And sometimes something heard about the book, that it was recommended as classic, that it was a necessary ornament of the cultivated person and ought to be read.

He once took home Marx's *Das Kapital,* which brought a trace of polite amusement to the face of the librarian. . . . And so he came to read Victor Hugo's *Les Misérables*—Less Miserables—because he had somewhere seen reference made to it as being a great book, a great work of fiction, a classic; that it was his duty to read it. He had to try to like classics; he had to try to find out why they were classics, why those who were learned, those in authority, said a certain book was a classic, so that somehow, even if he didn't fully comprehend, he would be exposed to the aura, humbly submit to sublimity. The other kids might say, nah, the book was no good. They were far more independent-minded—and smarter—than he was. He was submissive, he knew, uncertain, just trying to learn certainty, find a path to it, lacking the aggressiveness of his mates, who were so sure of the rightness of their preferences. He was dumb, and he had to hide it. So it was, in that muzzy state, with muzzy motivation, he brought home *Les Misérables*. And for days and days, he lived with Jean Valjean, the escaped convict who purloined the abbot's silverware and candlesticks, the lime-streaked workmen plodding through the streets of Paris impenetrable in lowly disguise—until that act of simple heroism that saved the carter's life furnished the first clue of his identity to the relentless police inspector, who, caught between duty and humanity, flung himself from a promontory into the sea.

Ira wept, numberless times. And he grieved over the lessening pages that brought him nearer the end of his companionship with Jean Valjean—to the end of the book that he kept under his bed in the little dark bedroom, that he woke up to on Saturday and Sunday as to a precious gift waiting for him to reclaim it. He tarried and reread, dreamed. Hundreds of new words lurked within the pages, unfamiliar words within the hundreds of pages of narrative, and yet they offered no obstacle to understanding. He had no dictionary—even the thought of owning one never entered his mind. He scarcely needed one. It was as if feeling all by itself guided him through context, and once the word's meaning was surmised, it seemed to lodge in his mind ever after, dwell there for him to admire its luster and resonance.

And so at random he sampled books like objects of a haphazard and voracious whim: After *Huckleberry Finn, The Call of the Wild,* from *The Sea Wolf* to *Lorna Doone;* through *Riders of the Purple Sage* to *The Three Musketeers,* from *The Prisoner of Zenda* to *The Hunchback of Notre Dame* to *The Count of Monte Cristo,* and Poe's ghastly tales, and H. Rider Haggard's *She,* and Lew Wallace's *Ben-Hur,* and . . . how strange: In the world of print, the world between the covers of a book, in the world of "true" stories, as before in the world of myth, he submitted to being a Christian, just as the heroes of the book were—except for Ben-Hur, who was Jewish-Roman or a Roman Jew—it didn't matter. Ira submitted to being a Christian. What else could he do when he liked and esteemed the hero? All he asked of a book was not to remind him too much that he was a Jew; the more he was taken with a book, the more he prayed that Jews would be overlooked.

And there was something else that he could sense but couldn't define—it never occurred to him to try to define: Just as the mythic had held him before, the "true" held him now, even more strongly. But held him how? Or why? He couldn't tell. The story had to go a certain way, not the way of a history book, or—no!—geography, or Current Events, not that way. But the way that made you want to follow, because you cared, because you wanted to share in or maybe had to share in the trials and tribulations of the central character. Ira didn't know. He could feel the way the story had to go, without knowing just why, the way you learned to read Hebrew over and over again in *cheder* on the East Side, without knowing just what you read. . . .

There seemed no end in sight to the terrible World War that raged on in Europe. On the surface (the surface to which thus far Ira had committed his twelve-year-old character, a surface, Ira knew, could no longer be plausibly maintained), the war was a composite of Zaida's fantastic Yiddish execrations (fantastic, it occurred to Ira, because forced, helpless, forced, hypertrophied, as a chained goose might be force-fed through ages of captivity): May those who incited wars be flayed, burned, throttled, beheaded, crushed, mangled—His stock of futile imprecations appeared to be inexhaustible.

And Baba's repining. Her vigor returned sporadically, as if in spurts, only when accusing her kin of withholding the truth from her, that husband and children alike were lying to her: Moe was dead. "God will requite you for this—deluding me as you did when he was sent off to the slaughter." And rocking back and forth in woe: "Mocking me with my own heart plucked out of me. You'll see." She wept, so terrible in Ira's sight, her transparent tears welling up out of closed eyelids. In vain, the others tried to revive her faith that God and Moe's chevrons with the half-moon under them would preserve him from harm. She doubted the authenticity of Moe's letters home, disbelieved that the stippled shell casings and the iron crosses that Ira brought her as proof that Moe was alive were his.

The World War raged on. The *Boche*, the Hun, in hated spiked helmet stood on the edge of the trench, arms uplifted in surrender: *Kamerad!* he cried. But on the ground, between his bestriding legs, his fellow-Hun treacherously aimed his machine gun at the viewer. Liberty Bonds. Patriotic rallies. Ira was still a Boy Scout, had taken his oath of allegiance to observe the rules of the Boy Scouts in the basement of his beloved library on 124th Street. There also, or sometimes in the scoutmaster's home, he learned how to tie knots, timber hitches and bowlines and sheepshanks; which knots were suitable for what purpose, and always to eschew granny knots. He studied Dan Beard's books on the lore of the wild, how to set up a lean-to, build a campfire with only two matches, distinguish between different animal tracks in the snow; how to apply tourniquets and treat venomous snakebites; how to carry people out of a burning house and resuscitate them afterward.

He was inept at everything, even that simple role he played when the scouts staged an exhibition of their skills: The scoutmaster and his assistant sat on the edge of their chairs on the platform, while Ira clumsily demonstrated tying a bandanna into an arm-sling. But oh, he learned that sphagnum moss could filter turbid water into a clear and potable drink. He learned that the tips of pine trees pointed north, helping to orient those lost in the woods; and where to look for the Pole Star in the night sky, and why General O'Ryan's Division wore the peculiar constellation on their shoulder patches, the constellation Orion.

On the gravelly bank of the New Jersey side of the Hudson River, after a hike down a trail from the Palisades, the troop gathered around the campfire the assistant scoutmaster had built, over which was suspended, from a notched stick, in approved scout fashion, a kettle full of stewing vegetables to whose ingredients all the Boy Scouts had contributed. In the tonic chill of the advancing autumn afternoon, with the shadows of the Palisades already encroaching, the pockmarked, affable assistant scoutmaster ladled out the concoction into his mess-cup and tasted it, with care—the stuff was hot! And then, in order not to soil his scoutmaster's uniform, stooped over and consumed a whole mouthful. He ate it! Soup greens and all, with the very parsnip in it that Ira had contributed. Whoever ate that? And a boiled onion too! A celery stalk! At home Mom used those only to flavor the chicken soup. Nobody ate them. At home Mom strained all that out, and threw them into the garbage can: They were soup greens. But here, if you were a Boy Scout you ate them. And lo and behold, they were good.

—Obviously, the memory appeals to you.

Yes. Without nostalgia. Every precious memory now is tarnished. A mild way of saying it, Ecclesias. Tarnished, frayed, gnawed, blighted. Alas. No, not nostalgia, probably because usurped by overweening fear and anxiety . . . Fortunately, I have you to speak to, Ecclesias, or I doubt if I could manage to keep going, so hampered, burdened.

"Thank you for the tea," he had said to M, as he left the kitchen for his study. She had invited him to partake of a snack of lunch early, earlier than usual, because her cellist was due to arrive soon, within the half-hour. M was to perform with him this Sunday at Keller Hall at UNM, a piano-cello piece of her own composing. His beloved wife: saying this morning at breakfast, while a Hebrew melody was being broadcast: "It doesn't have the usual augmented seconds. It's technical. Someday I'll play it for you so you'll understand the difference."

From the ends of the world they came and met, Ira thought (again for the thousandth time); and she, despite his psychic deformity caused by woe and guilt, loved him enough to cleave to him, made their day-to-day life, their domestic quotidian, a means to his salvation. One could vary the statement a multitude of ways; it came down to the same thing: If life, his life, were worth living, it was she who made it so. And though she was quite aware (he was certain) of the vexations and trials that were the penalty of her love, well . . . obduracy was a trait to be thankful for sometimes — No, not obduracy, New England tenacity, Pilgrim steadfastness. There was something to be said for breeding, for lineage, for stock.

XIV

At last, at last, Kaiser Bill abdicated. At last, it was Armistice Day! At the eleventh hour of the eleventh day of the eleventh month. Fire engine sirens went berserk, church bells pealed and jangled from every belfry, factory whistles hooted and auto horns tooted. Anything capable of adding to the din did, whether it was only a penny whistle, a tin horn, a toy drum, a human throat. School was let out. Impromptu parades of antic mobs funneled through 125th Street. Doughboys were smothered with kisses; people danced and frolicked in the street. Hooray! Hooray! Hooray!

Moe had survived, miraculously survived, unscathed. "OK everything love and kisses Moe," his cablegram was read and reread. Zaida *davened* prayers of deliverance. *"Baruch ha Shem, baruch ha Shem, Moishe lebt!"* he repeated for the benefit of skeptical Baba. *"Er lebt!* Would I tell you he lived if he didn't? He comes home, no? You'll see him. Ira, child, read her the paper, the telegram. Say it in Yiddish."

"A hundred times," said Baba. "A hundred times until I believe."

"A hundred times!" Ira objected. "It says, OK everything—"

"Say it in Yiddish." Baba just sat and listened, sat and seemed barely to breathe, as if the bliss of her son's resurrection within her were sufficient to sustain her. Then she sighed, slumped and uttered a barely audible: "Woe is me that I rejoice. For everyone spared, a hundred others are mourned. Woe is me," she slapped her lips. "God forgive me my joy."

But Moe was not to come home at once. He wrote that he had been assigned to the Army of Occupation, and he wasn't sure when he would return to America again. Weeks, months were to pass before he did. In the meanwhile, to keep Baba from pining again, Mom and Mamie, but Mom especially, since Baba communed with Mom more than with any of her other children, spent much time there—usually during the early part of the afternoon, when Ira was still in school; although he frequently came home when Mom was away, lingering at Baba's house . . . and might not come home until four or later in the afternoon. Strange, perhaps not so strange, how well he remembered the lock on the kitchen door of the flat. Black, with a small brass nipple protruding that when pushed down released the tongue that locked the door, pushed up, would hold the tongue in check. Oh, yes, that and many other things about their domicile he remembered, some things because he couldn't forget. Then or now . . .

How ancient a device are these dots, this string of dots, Ecclesias?

— Not so very ancient, probably. Not before printing, certainly. It's a good question. I had thought at first that you would find yourself in straits for having omitted or excluded so key a witness, one that imposed thereby severe constraints upon yourself, but now I rather think it's—

Clever?

— No, not exactly, since you didn't plan it to begin with, but rather, shall I say, enabling.

It comes of being two beings, one a mere hull and moderately sage; while the other a chimney of the extinct volcano—we have such in the state—a flue, a memento of fiery throes, though today sans lava.

—No need to go to such graphic lengths of metaphor.

Not with you, of course. Is it too early to introduce here Fred Skelsy, whom I met years later in Los Angeles?

—Point is he ran away from home at the age of twelve, is that it?

Yes.

—In due course. You've a long way to go before then. There's something to be said for observing the actual order of events.

The timeline?

—Yes.

XV

It was 1919—February 8th. His Bar Mitzvah.

PLUMBER'S PROGRESS (an excerpt)—so ran the next line of his "script," his typescript guide on the yellow second sheet beside him. He had evidently written the piece on another occasion and meant to consider it for inclusion here. But where was it? Always when he filed something, some of his writing, always it seemed to him, the niche he chose for filing it was the most obvious one in the world, and always he couldn't remember where it was. So now. He had searched in all the "obvious" places. With him, filing was truly forgetting. Well, he had had his reservations about the piece anyway.

He wool-gathered, mulled. Last night, in a debate on professional boxing presented by the noncommercial Channel 5, he had seen the spindly young Welshman—bantamweight? featherweight?—knocked out by his Mexican opponent; knocked out, the young Welshman suffered a brain concussion from the blow and died: Such a polite, sterling young Briton, saying, yes, sir, no, sir, to the attending physician and the referee. (And, Jesus Christ, why did all those goddamn promoters have the unmistakable Semitic hook, despite their anglo names! They made him cringe, especially that wise guy in floppy felt hat, contemptuously refuting those who thought professional boxing ought to be outlawed: "The only place where that's true is in the Communist countries." What an unwitting boost for Communist sanity! Oh, God! O Popule me!) The shock he felt witnessing the fatal punch still lingered; and led his thoughts to the summer of the year 1919, when Jack Dempsey knocked out Jesse Willard — and where he, Ira, was at the time, and what his mind was fixed on and obsessed with. But that was later, only a short time later.

He thought he would introduce here, as preamble to that Bar Mitzvah of sixty-six years ago — preamble, ambience (preambience, Meister Joyce) — a description of their Harlem living quarters where his parents and he had lived these fourteen years, from 3A in P.S. 103 to a mangled B.S. degree at CCNY. All dark and comfortless, said the brutally blinded Gloucester in *King Lear.* Four "straight" rooms, as railroad flats were called then, comprised their living quarters; the rent at the outset was $12 per month. *All dark and comfortless.* The toilet, the "bad room," was the sound of the word in childhood, was entered via the narrow hallway separating opposite flats. Soon after the end of the World War, a doorway was cut through the partition separating kitchen from bathroom, a doorway between the kitchen window and the sink, thus giving direct access to the bathroom. At the same time, the gas lighting fixtures, the gas pipes, were removed, and electric ones installed in their place — and the rent raised $3 per month. He had thought he would take the reader on a tour of their quarters, a slumming tour: So he had written, realizing as he wrote what treacherous ground he had ventured on here, the ground between his original approach to his material and his changed attitude toward it. Did he mean a changed view of what might be called the Joycean allure of sordidness, surface allure Ira had repudiated?

Their cold-water flat was entered via the kitchen door from the darkness of the narrow corridor separating the two opposite flats. The corridor ran almost the entire length of the two opposite flats, ending at doors inset with frosted glass, token doors that provided seldom-used entry to the front rooms at the other end of the flat . . . It was a "dumbbell"-type tenement: One passed from

kitchen to Ira's dingy narrow bedroom, the crypt, Mom called it
"*kaiver*," or tomb, passed to his parents' wider bedroom that followed, both rooms sharing the same grimy, narrow airshaft; and
then, without benefit of door, through wide archway to the front
room, ending in windows on fire escape and street.

A large, round, green oilcloth-covered table stood in the center
of the kitchen, a built-in, glassed-in china closet covered one wall,
an illustrated calendar hung on the wall between the gas stove and
the icebox. At the foot of Ira's "single" bed, a small chest of drawers
accommodated both his scanty linen and the bed's. Tenpenny nails
driven into a wooden cleat nailed to the wall sufficed for clothes
hangers. In his parents' bedroom, a large built-in wardrobe with
drawers at the bottom provided them with storage space. Initially
the front room, the parlor of the home (weather permitting), had
displayed a black pier-glass between the two front-room windows,
as well as a long black horsehide couch. But these had been replaced by a secondhand glass-topped "set" bought from Broncheh
H, a prosperous relative renovating her own living room. The set
was quite attractive, the separate pieces of finely turned walnut,
but it crowded the room. Bric-a-brac, miniature Dresden sheep,
wolves and deer, ranged on the pseudo-mantelpiece above the
sheet-metal shield to the flue opening. On the opposite wall hung
portraits of Pop's dour and departed father and mother in sepia
orthodoxy of *peyoth* and *shehtl*, or wig. And most important feature
of all, most decisive in fact, were the two front windows. The one
on the right was masked by fire escape (on which, as slum-dwelling
kids still did, Ira slept many a sweltering night). The window on
the left was Mom's chief consolation, and often Ira's as well (Pop
was too retiring to avail himself of its prospects). Unobstructed by
fire escape, the window on the left was the one out of which to
lean, observe the street's changing aspects, or—Ira's special joy—
watch the trains go by, so smoothly, quietly, on the gray Grand
Central overpass . . . and read the names on the Pullman cars:
GRAND RAPIDS, TUCKAHOE, BRISTOL, and that most beautiful of all
names, so full of reverie, of intimations of solitude and distant
horizon: WYOMING.

There was another window where he spent much time, the vile

airshaft window outside his bedroom. Geologic strata of filth had settled at the bottom, headless dolls, assorted trash and an amalgam of garbage—over which the bloated brown rats foraged: He had bought a Daisy air rifle out of savings from his allowance when he worked in Biolov's drugstore, with which he aspired to exterminate the rodents down below. But he never even hit one—or scared one as far as he could tell: The BB's rolled out of the barrel when he pointed the gun down. So he had to content himself with firing matchsticks at the bleary opposing wall of the airshaft, into crannies where bricks had fallen out and spiders had built thick, dirty, velvety webs. Once or twice the head of the matchstick struck the wall before falling into the web, ignited and incinerated part of it. Two matchsticks would be more effective than one, he reasoned, and would annihilate the web in one fell swoop. To his dismay he plugged the bore of the air rifle. What to do?

Who to the rescue came but Uncle Max—Uncle Max, that great fixer. He came to the house and did what? He charred the matchsticks inside the air-rifle tube by heating the tube over the flame of the gas stove. How grateful Ira was, how speechless with admiration at his uncle's ingenuity—until he discovered that the air rifle when fired wouldn't propel a BB beyond the barrel. The solder that sealed the tube airtight had melted. Whimsically, whimsically.

Ha, yes (Ira returned from serving himself a cup of tea; M was away on manifold errands). Was it to ease the strain that made him break in upon himself this way, upon his narrative, such as it was? Undoubtedly. But life was in the making, while he remade his: Tomorrow, Jane would arrive from distant Toronto, at his and M's invitation, his son Jess's girlfriend, now curiously estranged, to talk about the affair with Jess's parents, with his father especially, also curiously estranged from the son he once doted on. He knew the moment of dramatic rupture, Ira thought; and he had written an account of it as well; but that would have to wait. Order—Ira supposed the formulation of the idea went back to Aristotle—the perception of order was inherent in beauty. Order. And the only ordering that he had ever achieved reposed in a single novel and was ever after lost; perhaps undone might be a better word. Still, disorder had its attraction too, or was it only when perceived as subordinate to a higher order . . . or was it a substitute for the unobtainable, a sop to his addiction to words, to prose, good, bad or indifferent, to narrative. Lord.

So the moony urchin without his air rifle sat quietly beside the airshaft window studying the ways of the rats, unmolested, traversing their province below. (He awoke one night as a rat scampered across his face.) Well, in a wry vein and easy.

But when he thought of his Bar Mitzvah, did he mean the festivities, the celebration? Everything turned bitter, turned dreary, scarifying. It was not only not funny; it was beyond him to be funny about it. Oh, well, perhaps, not altogether: The comic was ingrained in him, part of him, gift or antidote to plight, or the soul's immunity: from his halting, stumbling recital of a brief portion of the Sabbath reading from the Torah scroll in the synagogue, with an embarrassed Zaida at his side prompting, embarrassed and deprecating over his woefully ignorant grandson, he who had once been so glib and praiseworthy at producing the sound of the language—*lushen koidish*, it was called.

From synagogue to Pop's home-staged feast set before most of Ira's homely relatives—Zaida too, food and utensils kosher, of Mamie's providing—seated on rented chairs, at rented tables, stretching from parents' bedroom to front room, never-heated rooms in winter, where the frost seemed well-nigh impacted, in spite of reeking kerosene stove borrowed from Mrs. Shapiro for the occasion, and the fishtail gas burners flaring yellow overhead. The parental bedstead had been knocked down to make room for conviviality, and together with the mattress had been stowed in the rear of the long passageway. Nothing to be distressed by, nor even by Pop's nervous and high-strung hosting, nor by Yiddish din within *goyish* hearing, nor even by the oration Pop chose for his son, and under threat of the usual dire consequences, compelled him to memorize and deliver, which Ira did, in English, standing surly and glum between rooms, back to one doorpost, staring at the other, thanked God and his parents for having brought him up a Jew. He could have smirked at all that in his amorphous, chaotic mind, and even grinned tolerantly at the memory in later years.

But the Bar Mitzvah brought the realization he was only a Jew because he *had* to be a Jew; he hated being a Jew; he didn't want to be one, saw no virtue in being one, and realized he was caught, imprisoned in an identity from which there was no chance of his ever freeing himself. The kid who had once been like a drop of water in the pool of water that was the East Side, indistinguishable from the homogeneity about him, who had wept and wailed to be allowed to return and felt the tears of separation rise in his throat, during his brief return, wanted none of it now, chafed at his lot, fantasized obliteration of the imposition, feigned with burgeoning cynicism that he was not a good Jewish boy: "Thanks, Tanta Mamie" (who brought him his gray flannel shirt); "Thanks, Zaida and Baba" (who gave him a two-dollar bill); "Thanks, Tanta Ella" (who gave him a fountain pen); "Thanks, Uncle Max" (who gave him a retractable fountain pen); "Thanks, Uncle Nathan" (Zaida's brother, the jeweler, who gave Ira a slender gold watch-chain—but nobody gave him a watch! If only his uncle Moe were there, and not in Germany far away.). Dissembling stood him in good stead, for behind his happy, staple smile he knew he was already concealing vice that would have horrified them. He loathed the ceremony; he loathed himself in it. Becoming a Jew, becoming a man, a member of the community was a sick mockery, became a sick memory.

—But that wasn't it alone.

No, exactly. It was like a resonance, Ecclesias, if that's the right word, a reinforcement within the psyche. As you can see: a self overt, a self covert, a self candid, a self stealthy. Nothing uncommon.

—No, but with you supremely exacerbated, into a veritable virtuosity.

I agree.

XVI

Though the intimations had been many before, Bar Mitzvah brought realization into sharp focus, not of the parting of his ways from Jewishness, but of never wanting to return. Vitiated for him, repugnant virtually all aspects of what he was to learn in time bore the name Diaspora. He knew it then only as *Jewishness*, detested it, was held to it, to the extent that he was held by a single bond: his attachment to Mom, his love for her, for the artless eloquence that imbued so much of her speech, for her martyrdom on his behalf, and for her nobility in spite of her sentimentality, humble nobility again and again shining through the rifts of its sentimental husk: "I didn't know how noble you were, Leah," Mom told Ira that Zaida said to her once—and removed his *yarmulka* and bowed: "Forgive me, Leah. I abused you when you were young." (Almost too much to bear, the picture of that selfish, intolerant old Jew removing his *yarmulka* and doing obeisance to his daughter, his firstborn, plain and seemingly unfavored, as her Biblical namesake.)

Once more the school vacation had begun, once again it was summer, the early summer of 1919. Warm, but not so stifling as that August afternoon in 1914, when Zaida sent him downstairs, nickel in hand, to buy the Yiddish "Wuxtra." It was more like the afternoon—and time of year—when Mamie and Mom and he and blonde little Stella waited in the newly furnished Harlem apartment for the immigrants to arrive. Another child had been added to the family since then: carrot-topped Pola, Mamie's second daughter . . . But now it was Moe that everyone waited for, the former immigrants too, all waited for Moe, safely back from France. Saul and Max had gone to the mustering-out center to escort their brother home. Everyone kept leaping to the front windows at the sound of an approaching motor car, kept looking to the west for a sign of the glorious appearance of the taxicab that would bear the one in whom all their hopes were centered: Moe, son and brother and uncle, home from the World War.

It was just at that moment when Mamie was admonishing her seven-year-old daughter, Stella, not to lean out so far, and Ira, stealing glances at his cousin's plump legs, slumped further down in his chair so that he could see up further, and fantasizing with fierce intensity that Stella was older, when a car was heard slowing down, chugging to a stop with a squeal of tires against the curb. "He's here!" Stella shrilled. "Uncle Moe is here! I saw him first!"

Crying "Moishe! Moe!" everyone rushed to the windows. Down below, doors were opened on both sides of the yellow-and-black-checkered cab before the house. Nimble Max stepped out on the street side as Saul stepped out on the sidewalk. And after him, Moe, burly and radiant in khaki. At the same time, across the street, from the candy store with the placard in the window printed free-hand, WELCOME HOME MOE, out rushed Dave Eshkin, rolypoly, curly-haired proprietor, in his chocolate-flecked white apron: "Moe! Moe! Hallo, Moe!" he cried as he ran to greet Moe with outstretched arms. "The whole block is heppy you home! *Gott sei dank*, you home! Look, everybody, from the windows! He's here!" Dave shouted upward at the increasing number of spectators leaning out of windows: "It's Moe!" And was met by a medley of cries descending from all levels, "*Mazel tov*, Moe! Hooray, Moe!" Some came out of doorways to shake hands with him.

"Moe! Moishe! Uncle Moe!" Everyone in the front room who could crowd into a window or beside it, so many, Ira would think afterward with a shudder: What if the wall gave way with such a mass of relatives pressing against it. "Hallo, Soldier! Hooray, Moe! Here's Moe!" reverberated from houses on both sides of the street, as some shouted from windows, others beckoned to those behind them to join in the triumphal chorus. Smiling with peculiar composure, Moe looked up, his blue eyes steady in the shadow under his campaign hat. Saul paid the taxi driver, Max lifted the duffel bag out of the cab. The three brothers entered the house, leaving behind cheering, waving spectators from sidewalk to roof.

Harry rushed down the stairs to meet them. Everyone else rushed to the door—neighboring doors opened; the sound of other doors opening on the floors below and above was heard, other tenants shouted their greetings. And there he came—up the stairs—a golden khaki apparition. "Moe! Moishe! *Oy, mein kindt! Oy, baruch ha shem*, blessed be the name of the Lord!" Everyone in the apartment surrounded him, clung to him, clamored with joy.

Moe entered, with jaw set in his bronzed-fair countenance, his lips thickened to pouting. Campaign ribbons were bunched on his chest. Gone was the quarter-moon under the three chevrons on his arm; in its place nestled a castle above an additional black loop. He no longer spoke in his former good-natured way, but with a dry, grating voice—and with scarcely an intonation. He sat down heavily on a chair.

"*Oy, gewald,* what they have done to my merry little Moishe?" Dressed in some dark, satiny cloth, Baba sat motionless, staring at her son. "My precious, happy child, my good child, my first son, they've turned you into a stone."

"Not a stone, *Mamaleh.* A soldier. A staff sergeant beside. They wanted me to reenlist, *Mamaleh;* my colonel told me, 'Reenlist, Morris'—he called me Morris—'you're my regimental sergeant.' "

"But you're home now," Baba appealed. "My Moishe, my Yiddish child, come back to us." She raised both hands, imploring: "Moishe, hear!"

"A regimental sergeant, and I wished myself a hundred times dead."

"Leave him alone," Zaida commanded. "In time he'll come to himself. He's home. He'll become Moishe again— May they be slaughtered, all who stunned him in that charnel house he had to abide. *Ai, ai, ai,* will they ever come to their senses? *Ai!* What lies and rots under the earth because of their madness. *Kadish, v' yiskadaish, shmai raboh.*"

"I'll go to *shul* with you, this evening, Father, if I may. God knows what will help me."

"*Nu,* come to the *shul* with me this evening? What else?"

"Why is everyone so troubled?" Mamie interjected. "What's wrong with us? We stand about him as if, as if, God knows, as if the Almighty didn't return him to us unscathed. He's here! He lives! And nothing maimed. It will all be forgotten soon. What is it with us? He'll be a headwaiter again. Perhaps soon he'll go into business. He'll open a restaurant. He'll be a success. With life he'll be all this. Come, let's rejoice. *Gewald,* what is this? I know what

you need, brother!" Mamie shook her finger at Moe. "I know very
well. I'll bring it, and you'll be another man. At once!" She hurried
into the kitchen, came back in seconds with a glass tumbler and a
seltzer siphon. "You're still my little brother," she wheedled as she
proffered the glass. "Here. This will restore you. Like old times
when you were a busboy: a glass of seltzer. This will make you our
Moishe again. Here, quicken your heart!" She pressed the lever of
the cold-sweating siphon, squirted a tumblerful of bubbling water
into the tumbler he held, until it almost brimmed over— "Drink,
drink, dear brother. It's good and cold, the way you always liked
it. You'll belch heartily. See if that won't restore you."

Everyone stood or sat about watching him, avid for him to
imbibe, to enjoy. *"L'chaim,"* he raised the tumbler to his lips, swallowed—one mouthful: His teeth clamped the rim of the glass,
crunched, as if it were some kind of brittle food. He pitched back
in his chair. His campaign hat snapped away from his cropped,
blond head and fell behind him to the floor. The hand—holding
a broken glass—dropped to his lap, staining the khaki-covered
thigh. He had bitten a great piece out of the tumbler, and now its
jagged edge gleamed between clenched teeth.

"Gewald! Gewald! Moishe! You hear me? Wake up!" Zaida
fanned his son's face with his *yarmulka.* "Moishe! Moishe!" Zaida
lashed Moe's cheek with his *yarmulka. "Gewald!* Help, someone!
Don't let him swallow! Saul! Max! Before he's destroyed!"

Mamie screamed hysterically. So did Ella and Sadie. Ira wept,
Stella sobbed. Saul tore at his cheek, screaming, "Moe! Moe! Come
back!" Baba seemed about to faint, her eyes shut, and would have
pitched out of her chair were it not for Mom, who seized her
swaying mother and called hoarsely to Harry to run for a doctor.
Only Max kept silent. His face pale, the lobes of his nostrils dis-
tended and oily, he kept his brown eyes fixed on the edge of glass
between his brother's teeth. Moe's tongue arched, his jaw dropped.
Deftly, as if they were forceps, Max jabbed two fingers between
his brother's lips, and extracted the shard of glass.

"I'll give you ten seconds to get up that fuckin' hill, you son-
ofabitch." Snarling, Moe glared at his brother with glazed eyes, at
the same time drawing the broken tumbler as if it were an ima-

ginary weapon against his thigh. Then he dropped the glass and slumped.

"Oh, woe is me, out to perish before our very eyes," Baba moaned. "Oh, I die."

"No, no, he's coming to himself," Mom assured her. "Mama, listen to me. Open your eyes. See! See! He breathes. He moves. Your son is saved."

Moe revived. He looked at the spreading water stain on his khaki breeches—and smiled, his old smile, simple and stolidly arch, as if he were a youth on the East Side again, saying: *"Ich khom mikh bepisht?"*

"You didn't bepiss yourself, brother," Mamie brought her face almost against his. "It's only seltzer water. It's nothing."

"Nothing it isn't," Moe smiled. *"Seltzer cust geldt."* He laughed weakly. *"Nu, Mamaleh,* I'm home. I'm your Moishe."

"My poor child," Baba wept.

"Don't fall on his neck, all of you!" Zaida shouted. "Leave him alone!"

"I'm all right, Father," said Moe, and smiled at Baba: *"Mamaleh,* don't weep. I'm a soldier no longer: *Ich bin aus-soldat, aus-sergeant."* And to Mamie: *"Nu, Shwester,* where's the seltzer?"

"I'm afraid to give you any more," said Mamie. "Shall I give him more?" She asked for advice.

"No. Don't!" Everyone else concurred. "Wait. Wait till he's come to himself entirely."

Moe chuckled indulgently. "Try me with the siphon, sister. The spout—" he chuckled again, sought his campaign hat behind him. "I haven't teeth enough to break the spout. Ah, *azoi.*"

So, although the Great War had ended months ago, for Ira, watching his uncle in khaki uniform gulping seltzer water directly from the dull metal spigot of the siphon and belching afterward with beatific grin, it was only then the Great War ended.

P A R T   T H R E E

|

"I want to be a soldier, Uncle Louie," Ira said, when Louie in postman's uniform next gladdened the house with a visit. "I want to go to West Point and learn to be an officer."

Uncle Louie smiled his gold-crowned smile, and shook his head: "They don't like Jews at West Point."

"They don't?" His disappointment spread within him like some sort of mildew, vitiating his dreams irrevocably. Uncle Louie wouldn't lie; Uncle Louie knew; he had been a soldier himself. "They don't, Uncle?" Ira repeated. He seemed to look at something stricken within himself.

The shake of Uncle Louie's head was slight, his sympathetic smile full of consolation. "No."

"And where do they like Jews? Where?" Mom bantered.

"He can't wipe his butt properly, and he's going to be an officer," said Pop.

"No, Chaim, he's only a boy," Uncle Louie demurred. "A child. I was a soldier, too. It's natural for a child here in America to want to be a soldier. My two boys also want to be soldiers. It isn't Galitzia where they cut off a Jewish boy's toe so he won't be conscripted—"

"Didn't they do that to Ben Zion, my father?" said Mom.

"What else?" said Louie. "We Jews did that to a thousand,

thousand infant boys to keep them out of the military, that they won't have to eat pork, worst victuals, or, *treife* of all, to go into battle—and who knew? at times against other Jews, fellow-Jews in the opposing army. Why? We had no country, no?"

"And here we have?" Mom challenged.

"No, I mean only there was a time, in old times, when we did go into battle for a country that was ours: in Eretz Israel. We fought the Canaanites. We fought the Philistines. We fought the Romans. It wasn't always this way, cutting off a toe to avoid conscription. Before we were Jews, we were Hebrews. You know that yourself, Chaim."

"Oh, that was long ago."

"True, but we still celebrate Chanukah, no? I'm a free-thinker, but I celebrate it, too. And the Bundists in Russia? Jews who had the courage to oppose the Black Hundreds—with weapons. *Nu?*"

"Well, should I let him grow up to be a soldier?" Mom asked ironically.

"No. But it's America. Why did we come here? It's capitalist America—we know that—and we have our quota of anti-Semites here. But let it become socialist America and you would see: It would become the country of all creeds, all people. Jews as well—and those with no creeds at all, like myself. Such a land all would be willing and ready to defend."

Mom grimaced in skepticism, then wagged her head.

"Just wait," Louie emphasized. "It has already happened in Russia. And who leads the Red Army? Trotsky, a Jew."

"Do you know I waited on him more than once in a restaurant on Second Avenue. I still see him, with his little beard—"

"Uncle Moe was a soldier!" Ira burst out. "He was a sergeant. He had a stripe more than a sergeant. You were a soldier, Uncle Louie. So why can't I be an officer if I want to?"

"I told you, *Yingle*, they don't like Jews. A soldier—well. But not an officer, they want an officer to be like themselves, people they think they can trust."

"Go, stop nagging," said Pop.

"With Jews for cannon fodder they're satisfied," said Mom. "Czar Kolkie, may he rot, abhorred Jews too. But to be soldiers, ah, that delighted him. The Bolsheviki have my wholehearted support."

"Well, would you consent to his being an officer for the Bolsheviki?" Louie asked.

"Who knows?" said Mom. "In the meantime one thing pleases me. If they don't like to train Jews to be officers, I am obliged to them."

"Have no fear," Pop scoffed. "An officer. He's meant to be a *malamut.*"

"You never spoke to him about the Dreyfus case, Chaim?" Uncle Louie addressed Pop.

"Go, expound with him," said Pop.

"I told him about Dreyfus," said Mom. "He knows. The Jewish officer they disgraced. You don't remember?"

"I remember something," Ira admitted grudgingly.

"Nu?" said Mom.

"He was a captain," Uncle Louie explained. "And not only that. He was on the French General Staff, too. You understand what that means? It means that he could betray all the secret plans of the army. But so strong was the hatred of Jews that when it was discovered that somebody gave away these plans, he was found guilty. He gave them away to the *Deutscher,* they said, and sent him to Devil's Island. To Devil's Island *noch.*" Uncle Louis's bony, hairy hand stressed his words. "A Major Esterhazy, a Gentile, was guilty of giving away the secrets of the French army—"

"I would spit in his face, if I could but see him," Mom interrupted.

"They feel safe only with their own kind," said Uncle Louie. "Do you understand? That's why you don't have Jewish generals. *Bist doch geboyren in Galitzia,*" Uncle Louie reverted to Yiddish, and smiled his wide, golden smile. *"A Yeet.* Do you know the first words you learned to speak in English?" He lowered his voice: "Goddemnfuckenbestit."

If only Pop would talk to him like Uncle Louie, could show him the way, could have been there before, prepared the way. But there were only Mom and Pop—and those just ripened into America, his uncles and aunts. And it was always money, money, business,

business with them. Te de benk, te de benk, te de benk! The *goyish* kids chanted in drum-beat staccato: "Football, baseball, svimming in de tenk. Ve got money, but ve put it in de benk. . . ." It was no use. He might have sniffled maybe, if he were alone. America didn't want him. Even though he was willing not to be a Jew, to try to be different, to avoid business, profit, commission and interest—the things he hated about the arithmetic books: If a gross of penholders cost . . . If a ton cost . . . If a barrel cost . . .

What made him think all at once about H. S. M. Hutcheson's book, *The Happy Warrior,* which he had finished reading only a few days before. Why did that passage come back to tease his mind: about the hero being a gentleman on a modest income of fifty pounds a year from a legacy consisting of shares in an Indian textile mill. How did that faraway mill by itself make him a gentleman? Those funny, swarthy people he had seen in geography books, barefooted, in crazy white diapers. How could that make an Englishman a gentleman? They didn't count, that was why. So what did that have to do with him, with the Dreyfus Uncle Louie was talking about, with West Point that didn't like Jews? If only he had Uncle Louie to explain it. What to do when you couldn't find the way something went? Thoughts always ended in a . . . in a tangle.

Why did he have to think about those Indians in their big diapers when no one else did? Out of a whole book, a long book, why should that have come back to him? He wasn't an Indian. No, it was that he didn't count. So he noticed what he wasn't supposed to about what didn't count. So they didn't want him at West Point. He could never not notice what he wasn't supposed to. Even if he tried . . . He watched Pop listen avidly to Uncle Louie talking about the possibility of taking in a few guests for the summer in his new place in Spring Valley. . . . No, just because he thought about things that didn't count didn't mean *he* didn't count. Just because he thought about Indians in white diapers in spinning mills that made the hero a gentleman of leisure—and Ira himself was Jewish and the son of a waiter, and they lived in a Harlem dump, too—didn't mean he wasn't a different kind of "high degree," as the fairy tales used to say. He could put words to what he felt. If you could put words to what you felt, it was yours. You couldn't tell that to any-body, but it was true. You didn't have to have realms and estates to be a nobleman the way the book said. You could put words to the way life went, the way life felt, and be a nobleman too—even if nobody knew your title: maybe Mom, maybe Uncle Louis, maybe Mr. Sullivan. . . .

And finally came 1920, a newly minted decade, and with it, graduation from public school: It was a winter graduation, at the end of January. Schooling was over for the majority of Ira's class-mates; schooling was at an end forever. Petey O'Hearn had already been hired as a helper on an ice-wagon. Frankie Spompini (so adept at braiding raffia mats, so neat) was bound for his uncle's barber shop. Scrawny Davey Bayer, who lived in Ira's block, hoped to get a job as an office boy. Sid Deffer, who already worked after school in a photography studio, had his job there assured. Leo Dugonz, the Hungarian classmate of Ira's with whom he got along well, had applied for a job at a materials testing laboratory and been told to come in with his diploma and his working papers.

Almost the whole class was going to work, almost everyone had his working papers or was going to get them. A kind of euphoria was in the air: euphoria at the last of school, euphoria at the future. Only a small number of Ira's classmates were going to high school, or like himself, were persuaded to go to the new junior high school that had just been innovated in P.S. 24.

II

Question in his mind at the moment was whether to interlard his narrative with events of strong personal interest, or reserve the information for another, a separate vehicle (his handwriting, incidentally, was now re-duced to near illegibility). Events of strong personal or immediate interest in one vehicle, and the autobiographic narrative in another, or both to-gether, that was the question. It would simply be easier to do them together, or both on the same document. As a matter of fact, he had already begun to do so, or rather had already done so without preliminary statement, without preface. So . . . even if not of greatest literary style, but more or less spontaneously, why not continue? It was more convenient.

He had called Jane over the weekend to find out her condition, mood and circumstances since her return to Toronto. He found her, according to her report, in fluctuating mood, and he again brought up the subject of the feasibility of her coming to Albuquerque. M protested that he wasn't giving due consideration to the responsibility his apparent magnanimity incurred — and she had called to him sharply to terminate the long-distance conversation. He had answered that he had an ulterior motive in having Jane here, one that he thought could be of profit both to Jane and himself. In short, he thought he could guide her, with very little expenditure of time and effort since she was an experienced journalist, in the writing of something that, to put it bluntly, would sell. He saw a story with an unusual twist. And this, this hunch, if nothing else, because she was so intent on getting a copy of the one tape of their conversation that he had decided to retain (he promised to send it, and did).

Of further interest was her stating that listening to the other tapes made it clear to her that she had been repeating the same thing over again and been unable to understand what a rational solution of her plight required (something that M and Ira had also concluded).

So matters in barest outline ended, with Ira promising to find out more about immigration laws and chances of her obtaining residency here, and also — key question — what her own inclinations in this direction were. She still sounded uncertain.

In the meantime, two other matters of moment cropped up: one with his computer, old friend, Ecclesias, aggravatingly replicating the old saw: Abort. Ignore. Repeat. So that for the entire weekend he was without means of communicating — while the computer was being subject to diagnostic tests at Entre, the purchase place and, exasperation of exasperations, nought was found wrong with it or the software. Returning and reinstalling the device in his study, he changed surge suppressor, removed fluorescent lamp, tape recorder adapter, changed location of cordless phone — and, perhaps sole source of the malfunction perhaps not, closed the little gate before the drive port less gingerly, more aggressively. Fortunately (!), he was able to coerce his unwelcome idleness into filling out his income tax return, at least to within sight of completion.

In the meantime, on Tuesday, came a musician friend of M's and freelance writer for the *Albuquerque Journal,* an oboist, Leslie H, together with her escort, John O, a tuba player, for the purpose of obtaining an autograph of Ira's youthful novel (Leslie H having been discouraged from seeking an interview because of exaggerated rumors of Ira's reclusiveness). Ira used the occasion of their visit to inquire about rooms, locations and rents — with Jane in mind — likely places to advertise for roommates, such as the UNM bulletin board; and in addition, to enlist Leslie H in assisting in Jane's settling in Albuquerque, if so inclined. . . .

III

With graduation assured, with discipline relaxed, Ira's class was left to its own devices, the individuals free to move around the classroom if they wished, free to talk. More than ever, the classroom seemed snug, sheltering them for a last time from the vicissitudes of a new stage in their lives, only hours away from beginning, the pragmatic and demanding outside world. Snow on the windowsills sealed up the cozy interiors of rows of wooden desks and slate blackboards, as if they were old dispensations, while the wooden clock above the blackboard ticked away the last minutes it would be in their view. No one misbehaved; misbehavior no longer seemed fitting, all but purposeless, when most of class would soon be on a par with the teacher in earning their own livelihood. Some read: reading material of their own choosing, books, magazines. As the genial homeroom teacher, Mr. Conway, suggested, some were engaged in writing a farewell letter of appreciation to Mr. O'Reilly; others sat in a circle around Mr. Conway discussing job opportunities and their ambitions. For some reason, when looking around the room, Ira's throat became choked with unshed tears.

Was it because he sensed the imminent, irreversible parting, not only of ways but of mind—of mind, of outlook? They were going to work, most of them; they were going to be shaped by concerns, by all kinds of aims and cares and activities from which he would be excluded, just as he was going to be shaped by those that would exclude them. Even though they and he might live on the same street, as some did right now, and see one another often, still they would be disparate forever. If they were different now, it was still only latent; they would differ soon, irrevocably. He made up his mind then and there not to attend the graduation exercises.

"Not even for me, for my sake?" Mom beseeched that evening. "That little crumb of comfort, my reward for these eight years of nurturing you, you would deny me? Why?"

"I don't wanna go," he said sullenly.

"You're ashamed of your Jewish parents, is that the reason?"

He blustered: "Don't bother me! There's lots of other Jewish kids gonna be there." (And yet he recognized that that, too, might be an unadmitted element of his refusal.) "I wanna go to work. Everybody else is going to work. Nearly everybody. They got jobs already."

"*Nu*, wouldn't that be better?" Pop looked up from *Der Tag*. "I ask you. The father may be a worker. The son not. Many and many a Jewish boy goes to work. How would it harm him? He could go nights to high school if he chose. That would be an upstanding son. He'd bring in his share of his keep. It would be easier for everyone. And you not? You're beginning to snuffle about a Persian lamb coat. A great deal sooner you could save for it; how your hoard would grow if he went to work, no?"

"Go deep under the sod, both of you!" Mom bridled. "Whether I want a Persian lamb coat or not, he goes to high school!"

"*Shoyn*," Pop baited. "She glowers."

"And why shouldn't I, when a father connives to have his son become a toiler, a turf-layer?" Mom retorted. And to Ira: "Becoming it would be, too, God forbid, that the earth close over you also for whom I wept and strove all these years."

"I'll get my diploma anyway!" Ira yelled. "I'm going back there next week to junior high."

"Go. True son of mine you are, indeed."

*   *   *

Cajoled by principal and teachers alike to enroll in the newly instituted commercial junior high school, those few of the class who did not go to work remained in P.S. 24, although the very few who insisted on attending a senior high school did so of their own choice. Graduates of other "grammar" schools in Harlem and its vicinity, lured by the prospect of learning shorthand, typing, bookkeeping by attending school only one more year, swelled the roster of the junior high. (For the first time, Ira saw black students in the classroom—subdued, self-effacing, but black!) He had always despised commercial courses, at least since becoming conscious, being made conscious by Gentiles and fellow Jews alike, that all Jews thought about was business: *beezness.*

But: "Knowing how to type and take shorthand, how to keep accounts and speak Spanish will be useful to you all the rest of your lives," Mr. O'Reilly induced. "You'll be repaid many times over for the time you spent taking these courses to learn these subjects. Remember what I told some of you about the marbles that those I didn't lose were stolen from me. Don't let the same thing happen to you. It won't, if you take these courses. They're true business courses. You'll learn to be alert in these matters. And in today's world you have got to be. And if you take them in P.S. 24, you'll be getting as good instruction right here as they get in the High School of Commerce downtown, right here in the school you've always gone to and with the teachers you know and who know you." Mr. O'Reilly's tic tocked away as he talked.

Mr. Housman, the Geography teacher, became instructor of typing and shorthand, teaching both subjects with all the assiduous care and neatness of one who had but recently learned the skills himself. He showed the class how to erase errors in typing by tucking a sheet of paper under the erasure like a dustpan to catch the crumbs of rubber before they lodged in the new machines—and cuffed Ira soundly when he was caught ignoring the practice.

Mr. Sullivan taught bookkeeping as well as first-year high school English, and found it impossible to understand how Ira could be so discerning in the one and so abysmally obtuse in the other. And he said so in no uncertain terms. But why in hell you debited when you debited, and credited when you credited, eluded Ira continually, though classmates not as bright as he was seemed to understand quite readily. And how to keep an asset from slipping with protean ease into a liability—and back—was beyond his power. It was beyond Mr. Sullivan's power also to explain the difference either—in any permanent way—so both teacher and pupil despaired. Mr. Kilcoyne, the dairyman from Yonkers, taught Civics, and Mr. Lennard, on the strength of numerous vacations spent in Puerto Rico, became transformed from an American History teacher to a Spanish teacher.

IV

Wracking arthritic nights, and the old man . . . In his excruciating rigidity he needed M to lift him to a sitting position in bed. No need dwelling on it. A peculiar insight this pain bestowed, hackneyed and vivid at the same time: He was no more than a suffering member of the animal kingdom. . . .

Last night he intended having a discussion with M about his son Jess, a discussion he hoped to tape; but conditions were inopportune, and he never brought the matter up. Now it swung in a dull, slow arc in his mind. After his return from Africa — from Tanzania, where he had taught school, from Johannesburg where he had operated a computer, from a long hitchhike to Dakar — Jess seemed by his estranged manner to have come to the decision no longer to communicate his innermost thoughts and problems with his parents, his father in particular. And with some brief interludes, he continued the practice — expanded it, until only the most surface topics were subject of discourse, those addressing the least personal concerns. He shunned, he guarded against any kind of serious interchange. And with Jane's revelation of Jess's actions, a complex of hypotheses emerged in Ira's mind: That had his son spoken of his "problems," had he and his father interchanged reflections, or better, he and *both* his parents, his behavior might have been modified to a point where he could not have treated Jane so shabbily, as was evidently the case, and with such appalling cruelty and callousness.

But then came the counterthought: It might very well be that his treatment of Jane *before* the point of crisis in their relations was reached was such that Jess already felt it needed concealing, and hence the cause of the prolonged lacuna in any meaningful communication between son and parent. Said M: "Is your solicitude about Jane based on your resentment of Jess?" And how could Ira deny that it *was* a component of his attitude: the sense of desolation at being rejected by the one he loved, rejected, excluded. He had never done that with Mom. To the extent possible, immigrant woman though she was, scarcely acquainted with American mores, to the extent that he could, he had told her of his activities, his experiences, and his reflections on his experiences (not so with Pop; he never had, being the spurned one himself from the outset). And yet—he had to admit to himself—his statement was not altogether true: What agonizing perpetrations he had withheld from Mom, what sordid troughs of deed. So there was an analogy here, a limited one, to be sure, between Jess's refusal to communicate with his father, and his own with Mom. What if he had said: "Mom, I—" What if he had confessed: "Yes, Mom, I—" No, it was impossible. . . .

He would never be sure, unless somehow the pertinent record could be uncovered or unless he was willing to go to the trouble of trying to locate it. (The public school record, he was reasonably certain, was still extant; but the record of Park & Tilford's employees, who knew? Was Park & Tilford still in existence?) He would have to make a stab at it, decide arbitrarily which preceded which, if they didn't take place more or less simultaneously. At any rate, one thing he could certainly count on: that for awhile the two things that played such important though different parts in shaping his life must have overlapped. Interesting, he reflected, this process of introspective delineation, introspective ordering of auto-biographical material; it was something in the nature of a chess game, though he knew very little about chess: a supposition in one direction was blocked by a contradictory recollection.

If he had obtained the after-school job with Park & Tilford before he met Farley H in junior high—and it was there Ira certainly met him—then he must have begun work at Park & Tilford when he was still only thirteen, for he was fourteen at almost the same time the new junior high school classes began, which was February. Were juveniles of that age, under the age of fourteen, allowed by law to be hired to do after-school work by well-established businesses? Ira wasn't sure. Some research, perhaps only a few phone calls could dispel the uncertainty (and he much preferred to work within well-defined contexts). But what the hell. Again, if he went hitchhiking with Farley of a summer's day, in his junior high school year, which was his fourteenth, why wasn't he busy at his duties at Park & Tilford? (On the other hand, the two might have gone hitchhiking on a Sunday, although the memory had the aura of a weekday.)

Amid the welter of conflicting impressions, probably his best assumption was that he had actually been hired by Park & Tilford when he was thirteen much to his present (as well as his past) surprise, had worked there during most of eighth grade, and into part of junior high, when he met Farley. If so, that would entail revising some of what he had previously dealt with—not that he would. So, to begin with, Park & Tilford—and there was one very definite bit of "evidence" to buttress his assumption, a bit of incontrovertible mental memorabilia: He recalled beyond all question that he reported for work that first day at Park & Tilford wearing his "new" blue serge Bar Mitzvah suit. That argued proximity to his thirteenth year, argued in favor of the year 1919 as the date he was hired, of his being in the eighth grade.

V

Pop's countenance was wreathed with cordiality when Ira came home that Friday afternoon. Pop even called him *Ira'leh,* the name he reserved for Ira when most pleased with his son—or wanted him to run an errand or do some other favor. Ira looked at Mom for explanation.

"The mailman brought you this after you left for school a second time."

"After lunch?" Ira reached out for the letter.

"May it augur well," said Mom.

And Pop in jolly mood: "One of your grandmothers awoke for your sake."

Ira extracted the letter from the already opened envelope: "Gee, I got a job! Park and Tilford! After school! Yea!"

"*Tocken* yea," said Pop. "Such a *goyish*, fancy store to admit a *Yiddle*. Something unheard of."

"Did they ask you?" said Mom.

"No. But I wrote on the application where it asked religion: Jewish."

"*Vunderbar!*"

"It must have been Mr. Sullivan then," Ira said. "He told me where to apply. He's a bookkeeper after school."

"Aha," said Mom. "You see: the *goy*. They say he's this, he's that. A *mensh* is a *mensh*, *goy* or Jew. He took pity on you."

Which made it all the more likely, Ira meditated, that he had gotten the job in his thirteenth year, while still in eighth grade where Mr. Sullivan was impressed with Ira's aptitude in English; for had it been the following year when he was in Mr. Sullivan's bookkeeping class, that crippled and cantankerous worthy, humane though he was, might very well have had his doubts about recommending so dense a scholar as Ira for any kind of job (and he did so again later).

He was to report for work Monday to the Park & Tilford store on 126th Street and Lenox Avenue. Weekdays, his regular hours of employment were from three-thirty in the afternoon until 6:00 P.M. Saturdays, all day, from 8:30 A.M. to closing time at 6:00 P.M. His pay would be five dollars per week.

Oh, it was long, long, long ago. . . . Mom cautioned him as he dressed with nervous haste in the morning before school, to show respect to everyone, do as he was told with cheerful mien—and try not to get his blue serge suit soiled before reporting for work that afternoon, to all of which he made irritable acknowledgment.

And in his best shirt and tie, with an extra nickel for lunch, and with Mom's blessings, off to Madison Avenue, explaining to school-mates he met along the route past Mt. Morris Park the reason he was "all dressed up." And to Mr. Conway, his homeroom teacher as well, just in case the class was kept for misbehavior. They weren't. And as soon as school was dismissed for the day, away Ira went.

And away he went toward Lenox Avenue, trying to restrain his gait, not break into a trot—and break into a sweat that would mar his holiday nattiness, spoil the impression he was about to make as someone suitable for the cloudy negotiations he would soon be engaged in, as the manager's right-hand man, or assigned to other financial duties requiring charm and tact and deference. He waited for a minute outside the richly arranged store windows for his excited panting to subside, took a fresh grip of his strap of books, and with the letter in the other hand, he entered the richly aro-matic, richly subdued mahogany demesne. The elderly, dignified gentleman in wing-collar and white boutonniere in his lapel, who was stationed behind the tobacco and mineral-water counter, di-rected Ira to the manager's desk.

It was in the center of the store, and Ira approached in a haze of anxiety and deference. On a podium, before a rolltop desk surrounded by a wrought-iron fence, sat Mr. Stiles, like a monarch reigning over a dozen clerks in tan jackets busily writing on yellow pads on a long dark counter, in front of which well-dressed patrons were seated on high revolving stools. They were ordering all man-ner of select comestibles, judging from the glistening array of glass jars on the counter, or the bags of aromatic coffee the clerks were busily removing from under the two showy red and gold electric grinders behind them.

Saturnine and thin, Mr. Stiles looked up from his desk. He had straight, mousy hair, combed back and parted on the side. His tongue nudged the quid of tobacco behind his cheek as Ira prof-fered the letter.

"So you're Ira Stigman?" he returned the letter.

"Yes, sir."

"Ever work for Park and Tilford before?"

"No, sir."

Mr. Stiles leaned over the side of his armchair, drooled a trickle of tobacco juice into the brass cuspidor just below, and stood up. "All right, Ira, come with me."

"Yes, sir." Ira felt as if his eagerness to please would burst through his skin.

He followed Mr. Stiles down a flight of stairs into the brightly lit cellar. Rows and rows of shelves filled with all manner of tins and glass jars stretched away toward the rear. In front, at the bottom of the stairs, two men in tan jackets were removing grocery items—canned goods, small fancy packages and string-tied paper bags—from the expanse of a wide zinc-sheathed table dominated by two tremendous spools of string. The two clerks fit the items neatly into a huge wicker hamper. Mr. Stiles introduced Ira to a short, sturdy, brisk man with curly brown hair, standing assertively on legs, not bowed but oddly concave, and speaking—with an unmistakable Jewish accent. He was Mr. Klein. He was the shipping clerk. He held a sheaf of small invoices in his hand. In the buttonhole on his jacket lapel, he wore the small bronze star that Ira had come to recognize as the badge of the World War veteran.

"Where's Harvey?" Mr. Stiles asked.

"Down here somewhere. Harvey!" Mr. Klein called.

"Rightchere."

"He's over at the sink."

Mr. Stiles crooked his finger at Ira to follow. Midway of the cellar, at one side, the sleek, muscular porter was churning soapy water in the deep, enameled utility sink, churning the water with a mop. "Right here, Mr. Stiles." He held the mop handle between powerful hands. His palm was pale against the mop-handle, his face gravely alert; on his tan jacket he too wore the same emblem as Mr. Klein.

"Harvey, that elevator sump is getting pretty bad, don't you think?"

"Yes, sir, Mr. Stiles."

"Will you show this young fellow—Ira?"

Ira bobbed with alacrity.

"Show him how to clean it out, would you?"

"Yes, sir!"

"When he finishes that, send him over to Mr. Klein. He'll tell you what to do next," Mr. Stiles instructed.

"Yes, sir."

At Harvey's suggestion, Ira hung up his jacket in the toilet next to the sink. Harvey wrung out the mop between the rollers of the big pail, emptied it into the sink, got a wide, flat shovel out of the sink closet, gave it to Ira, and carrying the pail himself, led Ira over to the elevator used to lift or lower freight to and from the sidewalk. The elevator platform had been raised out of the way to street level. Down below, a couple of feet lower than the cellar floor, the massive spindle around which the elevator cable was wound stretched like a bridge above the surface of a square pond of inky, malodorous water. "You just stand on that axle," said Harvey. "I'll hand you the bucket an' shovel."

That was his stint: to clean out the sump by scooping up the muck with the shovel and emptying it into the bucket. When he had filled the bucket as nearly full as he dared, because he had to hoist it to floor level while balancing himself on the motor housing, he clambered up, lugged the bucket to the utility sink and dumped it. So this was the nice job he had dressed up so neatly for, Ira thought sullenly. Lousy bastard manager, why didn't he let the porter do it? That's what the porter was for. Still—the presentiment kept recurring as he crouched to scoop up the foul sludge—maybe he was being tested. They were testing him, he bet. If only he weren't wearing his good Bar Mitzvah suit, his only good suit for weddings and special occasions, why did they have to do it just then? But that wasn't their fault; that was his fault for harboring such nutty illusions, for being so anxious to please. For all the care he took to keep clear of spatters, he already had a dozen spots on his knee pants. And look at his knees—smudges from the sump walls climbing out. Well, he couldn't help it. Whatever Mom said, he was earning money, five dollars per week.

He must have emptied the bucket a dozen times. Slowly the tarry water-level lowered. And each time he made the round trip to the sink and back, he used the occasion to make covert reconnaissance of the cellar. There, beyond the sink, was a very large icebox with glass doors. One side was locked, the other unlocked. Behind the glass doors of the locked side, he could see fruit he had never dreamed of: orange-colored smooth shapes, small and large, others chocolate-colored, others purple, all luscious-seeming and all choice. There were other fruits still that he recognized but had never tasted: grapes green and long, grapes round and ruddy, apples of unmistakable ripeness and succulence: pears, plums, peaches, apricots, cherries, tangerines. What a store! If he ever got his hands on them.

Behind the glass of the unlocked icebox were homelier, but still-tempting foods: cheeses, whole wheels of them, whole pineapple-shapes of them, and small crocks of cheese too—at least, the labels said so: cheddar cheese in wine. Whoever heard of cheddar cheese? Who ever heard of cheese in wine? Probably it wasn't kosher; that was why he had never heard of it. Packages of butter and cartons of eggs. Just wait, just wait till he knew his way around. And look at that aisle across the way: fancy cans of salmon. Cans of lobster and crab that weren't kosher, and what was that small jar? Beluga what? Caviar. Sardines he knew. But what were anchovies? Tiny little tins, he'd have to ask somebody. And that next aisle that he skirted about shiftily with empty bucket when no one was paying attention: Woo! Kumquats in syrup, what the hell were kumquats, chestnut glacé, figs he knew, but gooseberries, loganberries—maybe Mr. Kilcoyne could tell him. He knew all about fruit and vegetables. And that! Strangest of all: at the end of the cellar, double-padlocked, sealed, dusty, dirty, thick steel-bar lattice— Oh, he knew what that was, could see through to spider-webbed, dusty bottles: Inside was all that was against the law. Prohibition, that was why.

At length, after many pailfuls had been scooped up, miry patches of concrete began to show through the muck; then the damp floor of the sump itself, which he tried to scrape clean. He called Harvey for his verdict.

"You do it any better, you spoil it, kid."

"What?"

"Just go on and wash that bucket and shovel."

"Yes, sir."

"That's right. And the sink, who'll clean that?"

"You want me to clean it?"

"Ain't nobody else gonna do it."

"Yes, sir."

"Then see what Mr. Klein wants."

"Yes, sir."

Mr. Klein wanted him to wash his face and hands first. And when Ira returned from the sink, "How'd he do?" Mr. Klein asked Harvey, on his way to the stairs with pointed ladder, pail and squeegee.

"Oh, *comme çi, comme ça,*" Harvey twirled the squeegee easily.

Mr. Klein winked at his assistant, who stole up behind Harvey as he mounted the first step, and with tweety, clucking chirp, goosed him.

Harvey's whole frame convulsed: "Jesus, man, don't do that!" Water splashed out of his pail. "Man!" His eyes opened into a glare. "Jesus, man, I've told you. I almost jumped off a box car when someone did that to me while I was coming north!" He sidled warily up the stairs.

"Ever see anybody so goosy, Walt?" Mr. Klein grinned at his returning assistant.

"Me? Never." Walt, short and round, who also wore a veteran's emblem in the lapel of his tan jacket, reached for an item on the zinc-sheathed table. "I've seen goosy colored guys, but he's the goosiest. You know, Black Jack Pershing commanded a black regiment when he went after the greasers in Mexico. Can you imagine what those guys were like? All Pancho Villa woulda had to do was order his troops to goose 'em."

"Yeah. Pershine wouldn't hev no army left."

"The Mexicans woulda had a field day, Klein."

"Yeh."

"Jesus, you didn't git my gag. Did *you?*" he addressed Ira.

"I don't know. A field day?"

"Listen, Ira is your name?" Mr. Klein asked. "You see these small brown bags and this sugar in the barrel—did you ever weigh anything?"

"Lay anything?" asked the clerk named Walt.

"All right. You can go upstairs to the counter," said Mr. Klein. "I got a new assistant."

"Anything you say." And to Ira: "Look out for that guy. He's a slave driver."

"Okay, already." Mr. Klein dismissed his assistant, who walked from behind the counter and proceeded to climb up the stairs. And addressing Ira, he pointed to a barrel: "You see this? You know what it is?"

Ira looked. The barrel was half full of familiar white crystals. "It's sugar."

"Det's right." Mr. Klein pointed an accusing finger at Ira. "Can your mother get sugar?"

"Gee, no. She has to go all over."

"So now you understand. The sugar is scarce nowadays. We give only a half pound to a customer. We're Hooverizing. Other things don't make so much difference, but sugar I want you to weigh it out, not more and not less. But just!" The index finger of the threatening hand curled around to join the thumb in a threatening loop. "I'll show you the first one. You're Jewish?"

"Yeh."

"All right. So you got a Jewish *kupf*. Now watch me. This is a half-pound weight." He set the round half-pound counter on one of the white platforms of the scale, and rapidly at first and then more slowly, let the sugar dribble from the scoop in his hand into the paper bag, the weighted platform barely lifted. "*Ferstest?* Okay. Det's all. Try to be fest, but it should be right." He then showed Ira how to tie up the bag, yanking twine from a giant cone of it at the end of the table, whipping twine around the small paper package and forming a bight to snap the twine. "You'll get the heng of it," he watched Ira at his first awkward attempt, then went back to matching groceries to his invoices, stowing the items in one of the big hampers. Once in awhile, he would stop and consult a small red New York City street guide that he kept next to him on the zinc-sheathed table. "You know where 124th Street is?" he asked in peculiarly Jewish statement, when Ira had weighed out and tied about twenty or so bags.

"124th Street? That's where I go to the library."

Mr. Klein regarded Ira gravely a moment. "You go to the library. So, all right. Come with me."

"Now?"

"Of course now. *V'im lo akhsav, matai?* Do you know any Hebrew?"

"No." Ira followed him. "Yeah, maybe *baruch atoo adonoi.*"

"And you went to *cheder.*"

"Yeah. But I didn't like it there."

"What do you mean?"

"I liked it better on 9th Street."

"That's where you lived?"

"Yeah. 749 East 9th Street."

"So why did you like it better there?"

Ira shrugged. "Everybody in the block went to *cheder.*"

"Aha. So okay." Mr. Klein stopped before the locked glass door of the icebox, took the ring of keys off its clip on his belt. "You know what a steamer besket is?" He unlocked the glass door, stooped down, and as Ira was about to repeat wonderingly, "steamer basket," brought out from the bottom shelf the most breathtaking basket Ira had ever seen, beautiful in its wicker weaving, its high, graceful handle, and piled high with most of the glorious fruit with which that part of the icebox was stocked, a mound of diverse fruits interspersed with bonbons, mints and jellies and jars of mixed shelled nuts. The contents were all bounded by a stiff, transparent canopy of celluloid, made fast to the basket rim by several windings of cord.

"Gee!"

"Now, listen," said Mr. Klein severely. "I want you should deliver this to the party that's on the ticket here. To them and nobody else. *Ferstest?* It cost more *geldt* than I make week. So no—" He frowned, cocked his head, and once again shook a cautionary manual circle at Ira. "No mistakes. It says where and who. It's all right on the ticket here. Merrill. You should go to 27 West 124th Street. You ain't a kid. Just make sure."

"And when do I go?"

"When do you go?" Mr. Klein laughed shortly, hopelessly. "I told you. Tonight. This evening. Right now. You'll get your jecket and your kep, and you'll go this evening. You got the name and the address. It's dark already, so make sure you're in the right place."

"I know how the numbers go."

"*Sehr gut.* And after you deliver it, you go home. Thet's all. Now get your jecket and kep, and come to the table."

The gorgeous basket was waiting for Ira on the tabletop and beside it stood Mr. Klein: "It's all paid for. Just make sure you're in the right place. Merrill is the name. See the tag? 27 West 124th Street. Near Fifth Avenue—"

"I tell you, I know the place!"

"No becktalks, you hear?"

"All right."

"And *pavollyeh,* you know what that is?" he lowered his voice as he nodded his head. "Easy. Don't squeeze it. Hold it like that. It's Park and Tilford."

Ira curved his arm through the high handle and around the basket gingerly.

VI

A car bomb explodes beside a mosque, bringing Shiite reprisal against Israel, and distracting the writer from his narrative. In fact, the Syrians may be behind the provocation. When will the cold-blooded, pitiless slaughter end? Who knows — if in fact it will ever end? Scapegoat of the world, Israel. Equally gruesome, but naturally affecting me less, Vietnam warring against the Khmer Rouge, the Soviets in Afghanistan, Iran and Iraq mass-murdering each other's civilian populations. What does that amount to, as they were wont to say in Maine. The blood-libel still lives in many parts of the world. Dr. Maarouf al Dawalibi, advisor to the king and the Saudi Arabian delegate, said at a conference on religious tolerance held in Geneva last December: "The Talmud states that 'If a Jew does not drink every year the blood of a non-Jewish man, then he will be damned for eternity.' " . . .

As one broods on this piece of lunacy, there seems to be only one solution: Get rid of religion! If the human race is to be preserved, is to be prevented from annihilating itself, then Marxist-Socialist atheism offers the only salvation, Marxist-Socialist-atheist-cum-coercion. The Jews go, the Mea Shearim kinkies with their foot-long earlocks go, as do the rabid cuckoos of other persuasions, with their *purdahs* and *muezzins*. What other way out is there? They'll be destroying one another with fanatic frenzy till kingdom come. But no, but no, I'm wrong. That's not the decisive element in the peace-making process. Oh, hell, I'm wildly wrong. What religious difference enters into the warfare between Vietnam and the Khmer Rouge, between China and Vietnam, China and Russia, South Korea, North Korea, Iraq, Iran? Damn little, or none. So? Where am I? What is, or what are, the true reasons for strife between nations that generate this slaughter? The same "old" thing: material interests. Economic considerations, strategic advantage, expansion of territory, increased power . . . Alas.

My mood is further thickened by a long-distance call last night from Jane in Toronto. Most unsettling, most distressing. This time not about my son Jess and his behavior in the framework of my "theories." No, my theories are underlined. Jess begins to assume justification: His remark, which she produced, jotted down in red ballpoint on a slip of paper when he temporarily quit the premises, re his no longer being able to cope with her demons, now takes on validity in the light of fresh information. As M said, and that was the least or most favorable thing one could say, that she, Jane, was making no effort to cope. More, much more, could be added, could be brought to bear that would give the picture its grievous, disturbing chiaroscuro: She has been subject to a violent tirade (whose particulars she said were in a letter on the way) by her male roommate, who insulted her, inveighed against her on all sorts of grounds, which she construes as arising from his own frustrated love affair with some infidelitous woman. "Mapped," as it were, or translated into the temperament of the other individual, his tirade has a disquieting similarity to Jess's aspersions, figurative attribution of demons. In both cases the accusations seemed to arise from the same cause: Jane's aberrant state or eccentric behavior. To label her conduct eccentric would put the most charitable construction on her actions: Less charitably, they smack of paranoia.

Secondly, and probably of great import, her doctor has suggested that Jane enter a psychiatric hospital "for a rest, a bed and decent meals." One can make too much of this, or it may be no less than one makes of it: the girl needs psychiatric help. Her opposition to the doctor's suggestions, based on two counts, was adamant, almost irrationally inflexible: No, she was *not* going to leave the place she now lodges in, with her "batty" roommate, from whom it would seem any normal person would flee, no matter where (Is it that her cat keeps her there?). She is also disallowed unemployment support, or a dole, because presumably she is cohabiting with the room-owner, or partner.

The doctor's suggestion, to return to that, which was also accompanied by the explanation that she could not be admitted to a "normal" or general hospital because her physical condition didn't warrant ordinary medical care, the doctor's suggestion may have been a way of buffering the alarm, dissipating the stigma of staying in a mental institution. She resisted the suggestion, because she would then be segregated with mental cases — though I assured her as one who had spent four years as a psychiatric aide that she would be safe enough and need have no fear, less perhaps than sharing living quarters with somebody who raved dementedly at her.

No. She was not to be budged. Not an iota of consideration would she give the idea. Employed in the Augusta State Hospital thirty-five years ago, I invented the mnemonic, CIO, the initials of the words for the signs whose absence indicates psychosis in a patient: Contact. Insight. Orientation. And it begins to appear, say a strong hint anyway, that Jane lacks the second of the three mainstays of normalcy. What a shattering intimation!

VII

Harvey and Ira passed each other on the stairs, as Ira climbed up from cellar to store level. Lavishly electric-lit and yet mellowed by spreading stained-glass lampshades, the store looked rich and reserved. Though it was near closing time, a surprising number of customers still sat on the stools in front of the counters, mostly men. Perhaps they were businessmen picking up some article on the way home. Clerks in tan jackets behind the dark counters respectfully jotted down orders on pads, held up an item for a customer's approval. How dignified, polite— Ira tried not to stare. Or sniff too overtly. What was that square tin the clerk was displaying? Supreme Olive Oil. And the other clerk—that was Walt— saying, "Capers, yes, sir." What were those? Mr. Stiles was absent from his central podium. Mr. MacAlaney was the assistant manager, Mr. Klein had told Ira, and was the one who made up the steamer baskets. A bronze-blond, curly-haired man who wore gold-rimmed glasses looked up from his pad on the counter, saw what Ira was carrying, and squinted strictly.

"Only half a day today?" The dignified, white-haired clerk in the wing-collar inquired from his station behind the tobacco counter.

"Huh? I'm still workin'. I got this, this basket I gotta deliver."

"Oh, yes, that's right. Where to?"

"Here in Harlem. 124th Street."

"Mr. Klein let you off early?"

Ira looked at the large store clock on the wall above the shelves of obviously select tobacco in jars and cans. The time was twenty minutes to six. "I don't know."

"He's a good fellow that way, Mr. Klein. And sharp. You two ought to get along fine."

"I gotta go."

"That's right. You've got to go there still. Is the basket heavy?"

By now, Ira sensed something ulterior in the stately old clerk's queries, ulterior and unkind, quizzical. Meant to delay him? Make sport of him? *You two ought to get along fine.* Crafty ascendancy had to have its butt, especially if it was a Jewish one. "No, sir. It's not heavy." He made for the door.

"It's just a feather."

A smarting laugh followed him as he opened it. Fuckin' old bastard, what'd I do to him? He merged with the home-going crowd on Lenox Avenue, heaved into the street from the darkly

crammed subway kiosk at 125th Street. His first day on the job—
elation took the sting out of resentment: He did that dirty, lousy
work, cleaned out under the elevator—what'd he call it? Sump.
Some sump. And wait'll Mom saw his blue knee-pants. Ooh, ooh,
pants from his nearly new Bar Mitzvah suit. *Oy, yoy, yoy.* Wait till
he told her he weighed out sugar. Like gold, she'll say. And Mr.
Klein, gee, lucky he was Jewish. *You two ought to get along fine,* the
old bastard—but Mom would say, *Azoi?* She'd say, *Tocken gliklikh.*
Lucky. *Tocken.* And this basket. Wait till he told her about that.
What fruits and jellies. You should see. More than Mr. Klein's
wages.

Ira waited for the cop on his high pedestal at the intersection
of 125th and Lenox to pivot his Stop and Go signal-vanes, wave
white-gloved hands and whistle. "I'm big now," Ira told himself . . . crossed to the south side of 125th.

They are all dead, they are all dead — the thought cleaved to him as he was
about to press the "escape" key and "save" what he had done for the
day. You hear, Ecclesias, they are all dead. If I was thirteen at the time,
and the year was 1919, and am now seventy-nine, it is sixty-six years later.
Surely, not one was less than five years older than I was — who can be
alive? Not that pompous old roué of an ex-wine and fine liquor clerk, dust
and skeleton. Not Mr. Stiles, not Mr. MacAlaney — oh, perhaps the youngest of them: Tommy perhaps, Quinn's helper on the delivery truck. Still,
there are some World War I veterans alive, quavering, ailing, feeble. Who
knew them as World War I veterans then? They were just World War
veterans, or Great War veterans. There would be no other, Woodrow
Wilson promised, no other, no second Great War.

— And you?

Yes, and I. My stint is soon over, Ecclesias.

"It's four o'clock," says the dear and matter-of-fact voice of M, who
has borne with me and sustained me these many years. "Want me to ring
the curfew?"

"I'll have to think of that. Is that the right term? Curfew? Or knell?"

VIII

With basket still delicately perched on hip, he walked along Lenox Avenue to the next block, and turned east into 124th Street. Night and new responsibility altered the appearance of the otherwise familiar route. Halfway toward Fifth Avenue, the rows of brownstones on either side of the dark, quiet street faced each other. But not after the short avenue called Mt. Morris Park West; that was the west boundary of Mt. Morris Park. After that, there was only a single row of brownstone houses, and instead of facing other brownstones, they faced the lamp-lit park. The library's gray front still lay ahead. Anxiously he kept his eyes on the decreasing numbers above the transoms—what would he do if the number were wrong, if he couldn't find the place? That was the thing he dreaded most, dreaded above all else, that dogged him all the time: his bungling of errands. "A hundert un taiteent Street," the owner of the button shop had sent him to, and Ira had gone to 118th Street. And that time he waited for Pop on the wrong corner with his tuxedo-package for a banquet—never, never would he forget his joy at seeing a man approaching: Pop, at last! In every way it was Pop—Ira ran to meet him—and it wasn't! And waiting for the Madison Avenue trolley car with Pop's meal . . . and daydreaming, until Pop yelled at him from the trolley platform.

Oh, no! He'd have to hurry back to the store if he were wrong. Would it still be open? What a disgrace! Or horrible alternative: He'd have to carry the basket home to 119th Street—the beautiful basket through ugly 119th Street—and up the ugly stairs. And Mom saying, *Vus i' dis?* and Pop saying, Uhuh! *Er hut shoyn ufgeteen.* He did it again. And of course, the manager would fire him. The first day. No, maybe he could run back in the morning before school. Even if he was late: "I'll go, I'll go, Mr. Klein. Please tell me where." But maybe all the fruit wouldn't be fresh anymore— Ah! here it was: 27 in shining gold numbers, and with automobiles in front of it.

He climbed the outer flight of stairs—prayerfully. And just as he pressed the doorbell button, he felt a strong misgiving. Was he supposed to go upstairs? Wasn't he was supposed to go downstairs, where the steel door was? He turned to skip down, but too late: The front door was already opening, and the courtly gentleman, smiling cordially and expectantly, with head lifted to greet an adult guest, looked down—

"I made a mistake," Ira pleaded. "I— It's—" He pointed downstairs, "It's from Park and Tilford."

"Oh? Really? Is it for Merrill?" The gentleman inquired urbanely.

"Yes, sir. Yes, sir. Merrill. 27 West."

"Raymond, do let him in," a woman's voice called from the interior.

"Certainly, dear. Come in." The courtly man laughed delightedly as Ira entered the hall, and in utter confusion, was guided to a spacious drawing room, where someone said, a seated lady said: "Not a Prohibition agent, thank Heavens!" And the laughter of everyone rolled over him like a billow.

And now he saw what he had done: Under the brilliant facets of the chandelier hanging from the high ceiling, ladies, displaying long ropes of pearls and beads and wearing small, clinging hats, sat on contoured velvety chairs smoking cigarettes in long cigarette holders. And attending them stood gentlemen in dark suits and narrow trousers, with small neckties knotted in high, starched collars and gold watch-chains suspended before their vests. Two women in small aprons and frilly caps, bearing trays laden with curiously shaped morsels of food, moved about among the gathering, offering the delicacies, more often declined than accepted. And a man in striped trousers and a swallow-tail jacket replenished the shallow bowls of long-stemmed glasses out of a bottle with a napkin around it. A bubbly wine winked at the rim of the glass, and there was a scent of wine even through the cigarette smoke. He had butted into a party.

Awkwardly holding out the basket, Ira pulled off his cap. "This is the basket," he stammered.

Again laughter rolled toward him. With a kind smile, the gentleman who let him in relieved Ira of his burden with a "Thank you." And glancing at the tag: "You, Myrtle!" he accused one of the ladies lightly. "Only you could have thought of this!"

"Gorgeous! What delectable fruit. Oh, look at those cunning little pots of jam!" The guests chorused, as he set the basket down on a round, veined, marble-topped table.

"I think we'd better open it now, don't you, dear?" the courtly gentlemen asked one of the seated women in dark green dress with green involucres.

"I should think we'd better, while everyone's here. We'll never make an impression on it otherwise." Everyone laughed. "Jenny, would you open it please? Thank you," she spoke to one of the maids in the frilled caps. And to the other lady: "Myrtle, you have an absolute genius for creating an effect."

The lady who was addressed had heavily rouged lips, purple-shadowed eyes and rings on most of the fingers on both hands. "I didn't foresee I would have such a charming accomplice." How arch her voice. Her eyes rested on the abashed Ira.

"I'll show you out," said the courteous gentleman.

"Thanks, mister," Ira followed him only too eagerly.

"You can see your way down the stairs?"

"Yes, sir. Sure."

"Here's something for your trouble."

"I didn't—" Ira began to say, stopped when he felt the two coins in his hand, said fervently: "Thanks."

"Thank *you*. Good night." The door closed between the smiling gentleman and Ira.

He descended the steps to the street, with its line of automobiles at the curb, and as he turned east, noted that two or three of the vehicles had chauffeurs in them, black limousines with uniformed chauffeurs who eyed him as he passed. Rich. Gee. So high class. He examined the coins in the light of the library windows. Fifteen cents. Boy. Spending money.

Out of habit, he crossed the street, followed the course of the iron palings before the park until he reached the Fifth Avenue entrance, went in and skirted the base of the hill on the Madison Avenue side. Rich, so that was rich? That was being rich, that was— oh, he knew the word: taste. Taste. And manners. It made you dream: high ceiling and crystal chandelier and ladies with double ropes of pearls and holding bubbly wine glasses. And the mustached gentleman who lit the lady's cigarette. Dotted gold and chocolate wallpaper with little ribs in it. Checkered floors. Rich. Was it just a lot of money that made you that? Ira could feel a kind of sinking of spirit as he walked toward 120th. No. It was what Uncle Louie said . . . You had to be that way—not Jewish. Not just rich, but with that special luster, that style. Where was there a world like that for him? Where?

With the fifty-cent allowance each week that Mom accorded me out of my wage, I saved up enough to buy an Ingersoll dollar watch with a "radium" dial. You could hold the watch under the featherbed in the thickest gloom and the dial would cast a faint light within the tiny grotto, enough to illuminate it. What an enticement! Like the angler fish (See *Webster's Collegiate,* definition 2). Would I have walked home that evening thinking those thoughts, already in that particular rut I was avid to deepen, as if I knew nothing more than my surrogate knew? Or not plotting, machinating, wheedling toward oh, that Sunday morning, with what I could contrive with fifteen cents?

　　—Obviously not.

What a burden, Ecclesias. One sometimes sits back, and tries physically, yes, physically, to clear away the cloudy placenta that encloses one, and tries to sense, by an effort of will, perceive, if only for a moment, what life would have been like without it. Would I not have been buoyant to the skies? Fifteen cents, yippee! A chocolate éclair bought with my own nickel in the corner bakery next to P.S. 24, or a flaky, custardy napoleon. What else, what else could a kid buy with his fifteen cents in the year 1919? Admission to a movie. An ice-cream soda for a dime. My lambikin at the other end of the mobile home, what would she have bought in the glorious, strict innocence of her girlhood? An Eskimo Pie? When Uncle Bub came to visit them in Chicago, rich Uncle Bub, and took the family out to dinner: Oh, baked Alaska she always ordered. But I—

　　—You saved up your money, and bought an Ingersoll watch.

　　I went spelunking.

IX

The Park & Tilford branch where I worked was on 126th Street and Lenox Avenue, and P.S. 24 was on 127th–128th Street between Madison and Fifth. A distance of only about three city blocks separated the two places, an easy distance to cover in the half-hour between the closing of the school day and the beginning of my stint at the store.

On weekdays, when not running errands, fetching some item from another P & T store, getting the assistant manager's, Mr. MacAlaney's, Gillette blades rehoned at the shop that performed that kind of service on Third Avenue, or delivering a sumptuous basket of fruit to someone's home, I made myself useful about the store: I replenished the shelves down in the cellar, or refilled the coffee bins upstairs, or weighed out staples in brown paper bags on the scales on the expanse of the zinc-sheathed table downstairs. Most often, though, I spent my time assisting Mr. Klein, the shipping clerk. Stocky, spry and decisive, Mr. Klein was responsible for stowing grocery orders—with due regard to logistics—into the huge hampers that were loaded aboard the trucks every morning. Weekday afternoons I helped him pack the hampers to be ready for loading aboard the trucks the following morning. Saturdays, I was dispatched aboard one of the trucks myself.

The year was 1919, and in the larger and imposing apartment houses, goods were still delivered via dumbwaiter. Hence dumbwaiters became almost a way of life for me. This was true on Saturdays and frequently on weekdays too, a way of life and an ordeal: dumbwaiters in the dim basements of apartments on West End Avenue and Riverside Drive, dumbwaiters in Broadway apartment houses, dumbwaiters in the new concrete complexes in the Bronx. Unfamiliar with their location, especially at first, with a poor sense of direction and often too muddled by overanxiety to follow directions when given, I wandered at times in a veritable panic among square columns and labyrinthian cement partitions, seeking the dumbwaiter whose roster contained the name corresponding to the name on the list of groceries in my wooden box.

Ah, to locate at last the right name next to the right button, press it, and hear the door open overhead, see light slash across the dark shaftway, and announce, "Park and Tilford," place my box of groceries in the double-tiered conveyor, yank on the scratchy rope, until I had reached approximately the right altitude, and then try to satisfy instructions from above, "A little higher," or, "A little lower," and finally, "Wait. Hold it!" And at length, after being thanked, haul my box down at an accelerating clip that brought the dumbwaiter conveyor thudding to the bottom. Delivery accomplished, a fully successful mission meant being able to retrace my steps to the street on which the truck was parked, and doing so within a reasonable time. All three drivers, Shea, Quinn and Murphy—and Quinn's regular helper, Tommy Feeney, only a little older than myself—were vastly amused with me, when at last I came out of the maze, blinking at the daylight.

Once, after the Thanksgiving holidays, I found an extra dollar in my pay envelope, $6 instead of $5; and I went about bragging that I had been given a raise for exemplary services. Said the stately, wing-collared, old roué, once purveyor of fine wines and liquors, but now, with Prohibition, reduced to waiting behind the cigar and tobacco counter: "The P and T never gives raises."

I thought he was just being mean because I was Jewish, but it turned out he was right: I had earned the extra dollar because Quinn had claimed two hours' overtime for himself and crew—probably, at least in part, on account of my bemused, belated meanderings in quest of dumbwaiters in the cavernous, concrete basements in the Bronx, and then in quest of the correct egress. . . .

In the old-fashioned, smaller apartment houses and the sedate brownstones, especially those on the north and west side of Mt. Morris Park and others in the neighborhood of the store, deliveries were usually made without benefit of dumbwaiter. When Mr. Klein sent me out with Shea, who drove the Model-T truck that made only local stops, I would revert to an older and simpler form of delivering my groceries. I would climb up the stairs with the apple-box under my arm. I liked that way of delivering groceries much better than I did via dumbwaiter, because that way, there were no agonizing uncertainties and bewilderments, and beside, I might get a tip.

I also got a chance to see how a different class of people lived, refined Gentiles, not like those in the slum I lived in, the "dumps," as everyone called them: the cold-water flats on East 119th Street, but Gentile people in comfortable circumstances, whose homes didn't always have a picture of Jesus on the wall pointing to his exposed, crimson heart. Sometimes I would be rewarded by the sight of a dignified gentleman in leather house-slippers and velvet smoking jacket with satiny collar, puffing at a meerschaum pipe. Sometimes, I would be invited into the kitchen by the lady of the house, still wearing her lovely, figured, silk dressing gown. And more than once, while engrossed in my task of unloading the groceries on the kitchen table, I might feel the fingers of a hand run delicately through my hair, and look up at the roguish, dimpled face of a woman who seemed to wonder at herself for doing what she did: "You don't mind?"

"No, ma'am," I would assure her in worldly fashion. "Some other ladies did that already."

"Did they? I'm not surprised. What a woman wouldn't give for a curly head of hair like yours."

X

. . . He heard a thud in the living room, heard a thud, and couldn't identify it: "Are you all right?" he called.

"I was just being careless," M called back. "I'm all right."

"You fell. Poor kid. What'd you trip over?"

"I won't tell you." Her voice was girlish. She had already gotten to her feet and was walking toward the kitchen.

Girlish. The mind singled out the thought amid the welter of recollections of her previous falls, her all-too-frequent tumbles: that time in Florence when they were walking one evening with Mario M, the Italian translator of his novel, when she tripped over some unevenness in the sidewalk and fell before anyone could catch her. Her glasses were broken, her brow and nose lacerated. Foot-drop was the cause, the aftermath of her months' long immobilization, a quasi-paralysis brought on by an undiagnosable form of myelitis, akin to Guillaume-Barre syndrome. So much had to go before, so many episodes, so much "history" was needed to render with any justice the sketchiest of preambles to the subject of her girlishness, girlishness behind the wrinkled, dear exterior of the grandmother. It was within that girlishness he had achieved his regeneration, such as it was, attained an improved adulthood — what to say? — an image of a self more acceptable, a less repugnant identity.

. . . And reached that stage — ironically, always ironically — when he was already within the defunctive zone, the end zone, when again and again thoughts reverted to dead friends, vanished times, lost opportunities. Worst of all, they, those dead friends and vanished times, too, had left so little trace within him, so little enduring deposition of themselves, so that he could accurately recall, substantially recall, the topical contentions, the subject matter, the eddies of difference or agreement or opposition that formed and changed in those days, the chafings and chafferings, the diversions and discontents, the actual content of them, in their detail, with their particular formulations. Ah, he had not listened enough! Most often only simulated listening. He had not been involved, had not come to grips, profoundly, thoughtfully agreed, or passionately disagreed. He had been essentially unaffected.

He thought of Joyce: How many times it had been noted that, by abandoning Ireland in order to embrace the "great universal culture" of Europe, Ireland was nonetheless all he wrote about — confined, parochial Ireland. In short, he couldn't assimilate the great cosmopolitan "universal" Western culture that surrounded him on the European continent, to which he now had unlimited access. Why? Or why not? Another Irishman, Bernard Shaw, also of Dublin, though not a Catholic, had quit Ireland some twenty years before Joyce, without fanfare, posture or manifesto, but as a practical step, gone to live in England and had exploited easily, without let, Europe's foibles, mores, divertingly, successfully. In a word he had been able to "use" European culture as a writer, a playwright. Why? Quite simply, perhaps too simply, because he contended actively with current ideas and biases and issues.

Joyce had not, deliberately had not. He skipped Ireland precisely to dodge having to deal with ideology. "Silence, exile, cunning," borrowed from some religious order, had been his practice (he said). And why had he adopted that rule? He had made a virtue of necessity, in all likelihood. He had become locked into himself, for some reason, even as Ira had become locked into himself, locked into his "mind forged manacles," to quote Blake. To have striven with him, to have riven them, fought to emancipate himself from his vast ego, might indeed have brought him closer to his touted slogan than the course he took, might not indeed have taken its toll of desuetude. Whereas to accept his hermetic ego, exploit it, projecting his Freudian bonds on Bloom, the nominal Jew, promised him the foremost place in twentieth-century English letters, a promise that was fulfilled. He stored up creative static for one supreme discharge.

And to an incomparably lesser extent, so did he, Ira; he did likewise, who now was left with the realization that the good heart, the kind and affectionate, the discerning, loyal and understanding heart was far more precious than artistic acclaim. Here in this defunctive zone, where he felt himself verging ever closer to all that had vanished, at last came this wisdom, accrued from the woman who would not be deterred from loving him — and with the wisdom won from her came its minion: humility. Pity Joyce — Ira thought in passing — not only did the guy marry a functional illiterate, but unlike Blake, such was the man's monumental ego he made no effort to raise her to his level, as Blake did, which had *he* done, might have gone far to restore him to his folk, by her sweet discernment, her intelligent devotion: "In God's intention a meet and happy conversation is the chiefest and noblest end of marriage. . . ." So said John Milton. One might ponder here whether a meet and happy conversation might not in the end make all the difference between a fruitful and a sterile erudition, between a fruitful reunion with his people, and a sterile dallying with his medium . . .

XI

I became knowledgeable about the store, perhaps too knowledge-able—especially about the basement. I knew where every variety of viands was kept, what aisle, what shelf. Only the fresh fruit locked in the icebox, and that musty, spider-webbed wine and whis-key bunker, cross-barred and double-locked and sealed with stamped, leaden seals were beyond my prying—and my tasting. Left alone to replenish stock from newly arrived cartons, whenever possible I nibbled or savored any contents that were accessible, or wicked ingenuity could contrive to make so: a bright cherry or two from a jar of maraschinos, the ineffable briny delights in a wee tin of curly anchovies—which could be opened with its own key—tea biscuits and sea biscuits and dried fruit.

And I filched: a veritable gamut of dainties: a small can of fancy salmon in the pocket of my mackinaw, foil-coated wedges of Gruyère cheese, prudently distributed about my person. Eggs. During the era when the "Great Engineer," Herbert Hoover, ad-ministered the program of economic relief for Europe, and the "high cost of living" was on everyone's tongue, eggs were $1.20 per dozen. I brought an egg home in each pocket whenever I chose, at reasonable intervals. *"Oy gewald, goniff,* you'll be caught!" was Mom's permissive remonstrance. And sugar: The staple had become so scarce that Park & Tilford allowed only a half pound per order per customer. Not only did I purloin half-pound bags for domestic consumption, but I even made a deal with the Jewish ticket agent on the downtown side of the Lenox Avenue and 125th Street IRT subway station (which I used several times a week, and was given ten cents' carfare to do so): a half-pound of sugar in exchange for free admission to the subway platform. It's a wonder I wasn't caught. But I wasn't.

Luck held up marvelously until one afternoon when I suffered so painful an experience, it seemed to warn me of worse to come if I didn't mend my ways (I didn't; I just modified them slightly in the direction of greater caution). With Mr. Klein on the sidewalk, tallying incoming freight, and Harvey, the porter upstairs, attending to his duties, I sneaked over to the unlocked dairy icebox, where I had spotted earlier a freshly breached wheel of Swiss cheese. Beside it rested the broad cheese-knife. Stealthily, with eyes fixed on the stairs, ears cocked for an approaching tread, I proceeded to widen slightly the angle already cut out of the cheese. Unfortunately, I failed to notice which edge of the knife was against the cheese and which edge against my thumb, the thumb I was pressing so impetuously against the knife.

A moment later I knew only too acutely which edge was where. Blood was spurting profusely from the semisevered thumb. It was as if the cheese had reversed roles and sliced me! In panic, I dropped the knife and fled the scene—and then realized I had left the icebox shelf sprinkled with blood. And the Swiss cheese as well! And the knife too! I dashed back, dabbed frantically at the incriminating evidence but only succeeded in smearing it around. I rushed to the toilet, unreeled yards of toilet paper, and with handkerchief wrapped around my thumb to absorb if not staunch the bleeding, I soaked the toilet paper to a pulpy sponge under the faucet of the utility sink, wiped, mopped, wiped, got fresh sheets, wiped and blotted, expecting any second Mr. Klein or Harvey might come down, or worse still, Mr. MacAlaney, the assistant manager, to assemble a steamer basket. No one came down. Somehow I managed to remove all traces of telltale gore from everything, and doing all this with one hand, because the thumb of the other still dripped. I would bear the scar across my thumb for the rest of my life.

I rewound the handkerchief over sheets of toilet paper, tried to expose only the least bloody area, with not too much success, and secured the bulge of bandage with a dozen or more loops of twine from the big reel of twine on the zinc shipping table. The whole thing looked and felt like an idiot's prosthesis, about as inconspicuous as a small bedroll.

Mr. Klein and Harvey came down together, Harvey with a dustpan full of broken glass embedded in mayonnaise.

"What's with your hand?" Mr. Klein asked.

"I caught it on a broken— I mean a broken piece of glass."

"Where?"

"In the trashcan. I went to stuff some wrapping paper in it."

Harvey regarded me narrowly and walked off.

"You look like you got a hemorrhage," said Mr. Klein. "You better go upstairs to Mr. Stiles. He's got all that stuff for cuts in the cabinet. Maybe you need a couple of stitches. Maybe you should go to a doctor. Let's see it."

"Nah, it's nothing."

"Let's see it. It could be something you could get blood-poisoning from."

"Nah."

"The store'll pay for it. They're insured. What's the matter with you? They got doctors for that."

"Nah. I'm all right."

"Don't blame nobody but yourself then. Boy, *bist dee a yoldt*— you know what a *yoldt* is? How're you gonna peck a big besket of groceries with a hend like thet?"

"I can do it. I still got my other hand."

"If you start to bleed on the peckeges from groceries, I'm sending you up to Mr. Stiles. You're goin' home."

So . . . the old man writing . . . too imbued with literary irony to allow of self-pity, literary irony he loved so well; the old man scrivening to ward off time, while his wife in her turquoise bathrobe stands at the kitchen sink doing dishes. Recollections formed so long ago become discreet, immutable.

XII

I sit in Murphy's truck, parked in front of a drab six-story walk-up in the Bronx. An hour passes, an hour and a half. A shy young boy comes out of the doorway bearing a big wedge of coconut cream pie—for me. The boy goes back into the house; I gobble up the pie. After another interval, Murphy appears—curiously content in manner, curiously amiable. After the day's deliveries have all been done, my full day's work on Saturday is over. Murphy drives back to the garage, letting me off at West 119th Street. Sunday the store is closed. When I report for work the following Monday afternoon, I am interrogated by Mr. Klein: "Murphy keep you waiting outside that apartment house?" And at my vacant nod, he grins—so does Harvey; so does everyone else within hearing.

Why do Quinn and his helper, Tommy, watch me with such amusement when I sop up all the gravy around my roast beef sandwich with fresh slices of bread? They eat only one slice of bread throughout a meal; they use it as a backstop; their plates are piled high with corned beef and cabbage or baked Virginia ham and boiled potato. And the burly Irish waiter in his white apron, his shoes planted in the thick sawdust on the floor, smiles too. It is my first meal in a diner, my first conscious acceptance of a nonkosher meal. . . .

And now I stand emptying a burlap sack of fragrant coffee beans into the black, lacquered bin with the gold lettering that spells MOCHA; while on the other side of the counter, the well-bred lady and gentleman, seated there on the revolving stools, watch me. And in a self-conscious moment, my grip on the sack slackens; it slips from my grasp: Coffee beans patter on the floor. "Well, I got most of 'em in anyway," I remark extenuatingly. How merry and spontaneous their laughter.

And now with a steamer basket under my arm, I walk uncertainly on the deck of an ocean liner moored to her pier on the North River, a Cunarder, engines slowly, distantly throbbing, the deck agog with passengers, their friends and well-wishers. All are bundled in wool and fur against the cold, brisk wind blowing off the river. White jacketed stewards dart in and out of the doorways of lounge and salon. Directed by a crewman, I find my way to the Purser's Office and wait there, trying to make up my mind to knock on the door but hoping someone will come out and obviate the necessity of my doing so. Ship personnel pass me, entering and leaving. And finally, in his navy-blue uniform, the Purser (I am sure) charges out of the door with harried countenance and voice raised in irritation: "Who is this man? Where is he?" He speaks a different kind of English from that I'm accustomed to.

And I, flinching: "I got a steamer basket here for—for somebody here on the ship. Mr. and Mrs.—" I clutch at the tag.

"Oh, is it you they meant, sonny?" He nods, as if he's become aware of a prank. A smile displaces his irritation.

"Yes, sir. I got this basket—for this ship—Mr.—"

"All right, sonny," he looks at the tag. "We'll take care of it. You've come to the right place."

"Yes, sir." I hand over the elegantly heaped basket of fruit under their crinkly celluloid covering.

He seems to be laughing wickedly to himself as he takes the basket and disappears inside.

And relieved at having delivered the expensive burden in my care, I make my way back to the gangway. I move among clusters of fashionably dressed people, people jolly yet tense in leave-taking, in parting, their gestures and behavior quickened by the cold river wind sweeping over the deck. One group in particular becomes imprinted on my memory: two handsome, slender, tall young men in dark suits with narrow trousers bend in bright mirth at some witticism someone in the group has uttered. And one of the women sharing their mirth, polished in appearance, clad as befits her station in a rich fur, turns her face toward mine. She is middle-aged; her eyes glisten, yet her thoughts seem elsewhere; her eyes glisten, yet they seem remote from the laughter on her lips. The instant of our mutual survey dissolves—like the scanty smoke whipped into the taut, cold sky above the row of striped vertical stacks. I hear myself reciting the enchanting words recently read in our new textbook in English—the *Ancient Mariner*—which I couldn't help reading to the end, and rereading:

"The game is done! I've won! I've won!"
Quoth she, and whistles thrice.

XIII

P & T   Y U L E T I D E — a   s k e t c h

It was Christmas Eve. And we rode homeward, Tommy and I, in the back of Quinn's roomy panel truck, the new White. Save for a few undeliverables, all of the huge hampers were empty at last. Near midnight it was, and we lolled on the pads that were used to cover the hampers to protect the contents against the frost. The truck sped southward. And we in the back giggled in weariness at every inane remark. The truck turned east, bounded in and out of the crosstown trolley tracks of deserted 125th Street. Occasional oncoming headlights lit up Tommy's thin-lipped, gap-toothed Irish face. Tomorrow was Christmas. Tomorrow was everyone's day off.

"You know, you ain't like a Jew," said Tommy. "You're a regg'leh guy."

I shrugged involuntarily. "Well, I've been livin' with Irish and 'Tollians now five years. Five and a half."

"That the street we're goin' to?"

"Yeah, 119th Street."

"For Christ sake, don't say nothin' about me goin' way over east," Quinn said over his shoulder.

"All this is overtime. When we punch in at the garage, it's all overtime."

"Fer all of us," Tommy added.

"Yeah, I know. It's like Thanksgiving when I thought I got a raise."

"He went aroun' braggin', I'm gittin' six bucks a week. Did yuh hear about that, Quinn?"

"Yeah," Quinn replied. "You got a lot to learn, kid."

"I know it. I forgot, that's all."

Quinn chuckled. "You're lucky they didn't."

Tommy burst into laughter. "You forgot. That's what I mean. If you was like a real Jew, you'd never forget."

"Well, it was Wednesday we worked those two extra hours," Ira explained apologetically. "Then came Thanksgiving. And it was next week we got paid for it. So."

"Thanksgiving ain't a holiday fer Jews?"

"It don't matter," Ira shrugged.

"It don't? I know Christmas ain't."

"No. It's just like any day."

"So what the hell d'you do tomorrow?"

"It's like a Tuesday. Like a Wednesday. Only no school, that's all."

"You poor bastard."

"Well, don't rub it in. He can't help it," said Quinn.

"I ain't rubbin' it in. Honest, Quinn, I feel sorry for him because he's a regg'leh guy. Dey don't have no Christmas, dat's all. No toikey dinner, no eggnogs, no Christmas tree an' presents under it. You never believed in Santa Claus when you was a kid?"

"No."

"See what I mean?"

"Yeah, but they got their own holidays." Quinn kept his head fixed forward on the deserted highway, his hands moving in slight corrections of the wheel, as he spoke. "I had a buddy in the army, 'Shnitzel,' we called him, tall, skinny guy. He was a Jew. He told me all about their holidays. You know that guy fasted on Yom Kipper? Didn't eat a thing an' our unit was on leave too, way back o' the front lines. He was always tellin' me about Torah. That's your holy book, right?"

"Yeah."

"It's in the Torah, he'd say. Or what's that other thing? Talmud, yeah? It's in the Talmud. He was a helluva good scout, though. He was my buddy. I used to kid him: Does the Torah tell you how to fade the dice? I asked. No, he said. It's way too holy for that. Well, does the Talmud then? No, he said. Then what good is it? He knew I was kiddin' him. He said, no, but the Talmud'll tell yuh how much interest to charge. I thought that was a good one. I once asked him, What does the Talmud tell you to do if you're goin' over the top with fixed bayonets an' you meet another Jew? I say. What does a Christian do? he says to me. Yeah, but we're from different countries, I says to him. Well, so are we, he says. Yeah, but look at the fight you an' me got into wit' Craneby an' his corporal pal, when he said you ain't got no country—remember? He said your flag was the three balls over a pawnbroker's shop. Boy, what a battle. They'da beat the shit outa him if I wasn't there. I nearly slugged him myself once when he was gonna crawl out into no-man's-land an' get a bran' new Luger that was layin' there fer a souvenir. Fer Christ sake, I said, don't you know them goddamn Heinies ain't got a machine gun trained right on it. How the hell would a brand-new Luger git out there. His name was Abe, but we called him Shnitzel. Nearly everybody else in the fuckin' army was Al, but we called him Shnitzel. Because he was a Jew, I guess. We kidded him for bein' a Heinie. That was a hot one, him bein' a Heinie." Quinn fell silent, watched the road, steered into the open away from the tracks, yawned. "Ah, Jesus. We ain't got all the answers. I don't give a shit what anybody says, Father Mc-Gonnigle, or nobody else."

"Yeah? I wasn't rubbin' it in," Tommy reiterated. "We was just talkin'."

"So what d'*you* do tomorrow?" I asked him.

"Me? Sleep."

"Sleep!" I echoed. "Christmas?"

"Yeah. I wouldn't git outa bed for the Pope."

And suddenly the tension within me seemed to discharge. The awesome figure of the supreme Pontiff, seen in the rotogravure sections of the newspapers, loomed up solemnly in the darkness near the closed panel doors of the truck. In all his regalia, with crosier in hand and tiara on head, he sternly adjured Tommy to get out of bed—and was defied. It seemed so ludicrous, so gigantically ludicrous, that all at once I was convulsed with laughter; I squealed, I howled, I rolled on the pad. Tommy joined me without knowing why; and Quinn up front chortled wearily: "What the hell's got into yuh, kid?"

"I don't know. It's so funny!" I gasped. "He said he wouldn't get outa bed for the Pope."

"What d'you mean? I don't have to git outa bed fer nobody if I don't wanna on Christmas," said Tommy. "Right, Quinn?"

"Hell, you'll be up before anybody else gets up, time you get home," said Quinn. "The Pope won't have to get yuh up."

"Hey, that's right. I bet it's already Christmas," said Tommy. "God rest you merry gentlemen," he lifted his voice in song, "let nutt'n you dismay. For Jesus Christ, our Saviour, was born on Christmas day— you know that one, Quinn?"

"I've heard it." Quinn prolonged another yawn.

"We don't have to do everything the Pope tells us anyway, Irey," Tommy explained. "That's why we goes to Confession. Ketch on? If we done everything the Pope told us, we'd be a priest. We couldn't take a liddle floozie out or nothin'."

"Yeah?"

"Here's Park Avenue. I hate this goddamn avenue." Quinn braked the truck. The green glow through the glass of the New York Central ticket office door lapped against the pillars of the railway overpass. He rounded the corner steering south. "I wish the Pope'd git rid o' these—" Quinn nipped off his words. "Even when ye c'n see straight, when y' ain't been drivin' all day—and it ain't night, like now—them goddamn pillars look like they're everywhere. All I gotta do is pile up against one. Wouldn't they be askin', What the hell're you doin' way over there? A new White panel truck. The P an' T'd gimme a raise, wouldn't they? They'd gimme a roost in the tail."

"See that? Yer gittin' special service fer Christmas," said Tommy.

"What'd you say? 119th Street?" Quinn asked.

"Yeah."

In minutes we were at the little A & P grocery at the corner, the feeble blue light within the store barely visible. Quinn stopped the truck, came around the back and opened the panel doors. "Br-r!" he heaved his shoulders against the cold, stood waiting for me to get out, the fingers of his hands strangely locked together, knuckles upward, prayerfully.

"Thanks, Quinn." I scrambled out.

"Merry Christmas."

"Huh? Yeah. Merry Christmas, Quinn."

"Merry Christmas, Irey!" Tommy called from inside the vehicle, his hand waving a pale greeting in the gloom.

"Yeah, Merry Christmas."

Quinn slammed the panel doors shut, and returned to the driver's seat. The truck got underway. I watched it a moment: gather speed, become a red bead of taillight passing foreshortened pillars. By the time I trudged through the opaque shadow under the trestle, the red bead of taillight had risen up the hill on 116th Street. It disappeared west, as I reached Jake's somber mass of masonry on the corner.

119th Street. Past midnight, deserted in all directions, familiar yet unfamiliar. Heels clicking loudly, I plodded toward my stoop. Never saw so many, so many crowded stars, all shining together, studded thick as Mom's horseradish grater. Dark drugstore, dark candy store, dark stoop before me, dark windows overhead. Only in midblock, the street light sprouted above the short green lamppost. After the wild hilarity in the back of the truck, after so many hours together, I was now solitary. After so many dumbwaiters and basements and back stairs, and servants met and greetings heard, now silence, now weariness.

Maybe even sadness, despite the jingle of small change in my pocket: "There's something for you in the grocery box. Merry Christmas!" Was it that I felt left out, excluded again, with a kind of inbred exclusion. God save you, merry gentlemen. Was that how it went? Gentlemen. The hero of the book I had read by H. S. M. Hutcheson—what a lot of initials!—was a gentleman, the book said. A small legacy of fifty pounds from an investment in spinning mills in India made him a gentleman: those shiny black people in the crazy white diapers in the geography book made him a gentleman. Why did I have to think of everything? I mounted the stone stoop, passed the battered brass letter boxes, entered the long hallway, sealed in quiet, with the small, haggard electric light at the end, at the foot of the stairway.

A figment of fatigue, above me on the turn of the landing,

brandishing his crosier at me, the Pope stood in brocaded shadow. I shivered, mounted the stairs toward him. He vanished. I reached the sable window beside which the figure had stood, through which nothing could be seen. Jesus, the trouble was always the same: alone, alone. I found scant solace in jingling the small change in my pocket, as my fingers singled out the housekey. Christmas for the world, Christmas for Irish cops and Irish janitors, for Italian barbers and Italian ice men and white-wing street sweepers.

I could hear Merry Christmas unspoken booming in my head. Jesus, was I ever tired. And alone.

XIV

Scarcely had the first term of the pristine junior high school begun when Ira felt himself drawn to a newcomer in the class, a blond, trimly built youth, somewhat more mature than the rest, handsome, blue-eyed, with a rounded jaw, a light voice and a buoyant gait. He was taller than average, though not a great deal, and Ira noticed at once how fine the other's hands were—neither large nor small, but so neat and compact they seemed small for his size. How untroubled he seemed, frank and free. His name was Farley Hewins. He had come from St. Thomas Parochial School, adjoining the St. Thomas church on 130th Street, the red-brick church only two blocks away from P.S. 24 on Madison Avenue . . .

No, I don't think so—Ira became aware of the hum of the computer, like the hum of consciousness: No, your timing is wrong again, your timing and your sequence, your causality. Once again you can say, what difference will it make to another, your attributions and accuracy? This is a work of fiction. But the fact is it makes a difference to me, aye: Once again, perhaps at the beginning of the senior term, certainly before that senior grammar school term was over, Farley Hewins appeared — in Mr. Sullivan's class. And once again, or rather for the first time, I was to do what I repeated later: allow irrelevant or superficial considerations to influence a decision that was to have the most far-reaching effect on my life, that was to make all the difference. No, it was not inertia on my part, though that was certainly a factor, as were my passivity and gelatinous mentality (And to what extent did that dark and troubling, furtive enormity play a role? To a great extent, undoubtedly), my gelatinous mentality that made me vulnerable to Mr. O'Reilly's cajolings that we stay on in the newly formed junior high for our first year in high school.

No, it was the appearance of Farley Hewins before the last term in grammar school was over, when our friendship was formed. And before the term was over, our friendship had cemented. It was he, happy, easy, without definite goal, who elected to stay on in the newborn junior high, and I with him. Again — Ira looked moodily away from the monitor to the brown curtain behind it that blocked out the window's glare.

Some kind of sharp differences had arisen between Farley and the head of the parochial school, Father McGrath, differences over just what Ira paid too little attention to heed in his joy at finding an affinity, a companion. It had been because these sharp differences with Father McGrath had come to a head that caused Farley to prevail on his parents to consent to his leaving the St. Thomas Parochial School, leaving it even before he was graduated. Most likely it may have been the good Father's insistence that Farley enroll in St. Pius Academy, a parochial high school, after graduation from St. Thomas. All his classmates did so—those who were going on in school—Farley alone chose not to. (Ira was to hear an allusion to the friction between priest and pupil later—from remarks made by former schoolmates.) Farley preferred, nay, he was determined, to attend Stuyvesant High School, a technical school, after graduation from grammar school, and this undoubtedly was the cause of the sharp differences between himself and his Catholic mentor. And because of that too, Farley no longer felt at ease in the school. His discontent met sympathy at home. He left St.

Thomas's—quite abruptly—to enroll in P.S. 24, only a block away from his home. His appearance in Mr. Sullivan's class awoke in Ira the same kind of attraction Ira had felt years ago for Eddie Ferry, the Irish janitor's son.

It was the same kind of attraction, only much wider in scope: Here was someone who took life in stride (the metaphor was destined for literal realization in the coming months and years). Happy, untroubled as were his blue eyes, tranquil, at home in the world, Irish, Catholic, and yet compatible, without prejudice almost, blithe and cordial with his new Jewish acquaintance. The attraction was mutual. In a matter of days, the two became fast friends. Farley took to Ira's Jewishness as he did to everything else: casually. And he even went a step beyond: he mitigated Ira's Jewishness with unexpected tact and clemency, as if loyalty called for no less, called for the dispersion of religious differences. His reason for attending P.S. 24 Junior High instead of going on to Stuyvesant after graduation was carefree—and characteristic—"I just feel like mopin' around the old neighborhood for awhile longer."

As the weather grew warmer, they went hitchhiking, the first time Ira had ever done so. Because Ira worked at Park & Tilford, they hitchhiked on Sundays—to Tarrytown, to Dobbs Ferry, to New Rochelle. In each of these towns, Farley had an aunt or an uncle. They fed the wayfarers peanut butter and jelly sandwiches (again a new experience for Ira), or blueberry muffins and milk fresh from the cow, or redolent, cinnamon-savory apple pie. In the steadiness, in the tranquility of Farley's unassuming assurance, his good-humored poise, and the affectionate regard with which he was greeted and held by his kin, Americans all, part and parcel of America in their warm, tidy, suburban kitchens into which the breeze from the green outside seeped through the screen door, Ira could almost imagine that acceptance of himself was only a shadow away, no greater than the transient film of bemusement that covered their faces at first sight of Farley's choice of friend.

So the two, inseparable pals, on warm Saturday evenings, "moped" about Farley's haunts, in the environs of St. Thomas's Church, palavered, kidded with his former classmates at the parochial school, their moment of skew regard of Ira abating when he recounted asinine predicaments at Park & Tilford, thus reassuring them he was too foolish to be wary of. And he succeeded, for they soon lapsed into normal pinch-lipped, mock-solemn, Irish chaffering. They called one another hoople-head or satchel-back; they bragged gravely: "Where I come from, the canaries sing bass." And: "Where I come from, they play tiddlywinks with manhole covers." Sometimes, and in neutral silence, Ira heard mention of missions and novenas, masses, Holy Communion. And once or twice, he was given an intimation of the reason for the antagonism that had developed between Farley and Father McGrath, a strong hint of an issue Ira had never suspected before: "You'll be running for a bunch of black Protestants against Catholics, that's what you'll be doing," said Steve, in eyeglasses, impassive in his sobriety, the most owlish of Farley's friends.

"I'll be running for myself, and I'm a Catholic," Farley rejoined with uncommon heat. "That's what got me sore at Father McGrath. I don't have to go to St. Pius for my salvation. I go to church."

"Yeah, but if you're running for St. Pius, everybody'll know you're running for the glory o' Catholics, not Protestants."

"That doesn't make me any better runner. And going to Stuyvesant doesn't turn me into a Protestant either. That's what I told Father McGrath. And that's what I'm gonna do. Suppose I do go to St. Pius and don't turn out to be so hot? Then everyone'll say the same thing: He's a Catholic. He can't run. And I won't be in the school I want to be in either."

It took several minutes for the air of ill-will between Farley and his ex-schoolmates to dissipate.

It was Farley's running ability that had made the Father so importunate. From the very outset, Ira had been impressed, chagrined at first and then startled at the phenomenal bursts of speed with which Farley overtook a vehicle that had slowed down to pick them up when they were hitchhiking. Farley was already holding the door open while Ira was still laboring to catch up. Suddenly Farley's running ability took on a new and totally undreamed-of dimension.

Toward the end of the first term of junior high school, as the spring term neared summer, it brought fresh revelation of Farley's potential in track events. Three of the new junior high schools in the uptown area were to take part in a track meet. On the appointed day for the meet, 128th Street, the street fronting P.S. 24, was roped off, lanes were chalked off for the sixty-yard dash, thick pads laid down to cushion high jump and broad jump. Competition began. Ira was soon eliminated from all events; he trailed in the very first heat of the sixty-yard dash—and failed in everything else, just as he expected. Farley did creditably in both broad jump and high jump, placing second and third to black students from further uptown. But it was in the sixty-yard dash that he was nothing short of sensational: He won every heat easily and just as easily outstripped the pack in the finals. Easily. Running with knees high, and fists clenched. Easily. Drawing away to the finish line from all those straining in pursuit. Incredulously Ira watched; even though he knew how fleet of foot his friend was, Ira's chest still swelled with pride, with surrogate glory. Fleet, yes, that was one thing. But this kind of fleetness was no longer a matter of local repute, acknowledged by local praise. No, anyone could feel that Farley's fleetness of foot had an extraordinary latency about it, an inkling of universal acclaim, a destiny. . . .

XV

Aching, aching, hurting, hurting (this cursed rheumatoid arthritis), and loving, loving that darling aged spouse of mine. What a silly thing to say. But true. Silly as bald truth so often is. That she enabled a rebirth in me into something I can more nearly live with, you well know, Ecclesias; I have said it before (and likely will again). It is all in vanity, according to your dictum, yours and Omar Khayyám's: It comes to naught, to the same thing as if it hadn't happened. Had there been no sense of regeneration, but rather had I remained as I was, what I was, contemptible, despicable in my own eyes, it would still have come to naught, alas. But once again I can only say, at my unsubtle level of thought, that beyond life's limit, beyond death life is meaningless, as meaningless as the mark zero over zero, meaningless, that which an infinitely small instant before did have meaning. And so one has to speak of that, and to those still standing before the mortal instant when vanity is consummated. And therefore, my love, my love, I live, for whom I must live, who needs me. And for what little good my living may do the living.

The half tablet of Percocet works, Ecclesias, revives; perhaps until the combined agency of the daily dose of Cortisone and Imuran (whatever that is) exert their efficacy — "take a'holt," as my good, kind and gentle friend in Maine, old Gene Perry, was wont to say. So old age sums up life: with a sigh and shake of the head . . . But how soon these artificial highs flag, Ecclesias, these minimal stimulations of a spot of coffee and a half tablet of Percocet. But rather the Keatsian drowsy numbness than the pain.

Farley's father was an undertaker; perhaps he was the undertaker for the parish, little as the term meant to Ira. Little as the word "sexton" meant to him too, the word on a plaque next to the door of the front entrance of the brownstone house on Madison Avenue where the Hewin Funeral Parlor was located—and where the Hewins lived: on 129th Street, exactly midway between the parochial school Farley had left and the public school he now attended. . . .

Ah, yes, Ira reflected, reverting with new insight into the dispute between Farley and his Jesuit headmaster, the matter must have become intense, the pressure intense, with so much at stake, a runner of Farley's exceptional potential. Disagreement must have reached an extreme pitch of rancor to have warranted his parents' acquiescence in their son's quitting the parochial school before graduation, lopping off so abruptly the last months of attendance. The cleric must have exceeded all reasonable bounds in his importunings (probably spurred on by the track coach at St. Pius): threatened the boy with Hell's fire, for all Ira knew. Just a jot too much brimstone, Ira mused: the parents became indignant, and who could blame them? So the young schoolboy suddenly appeared on Ira's horizon.

Fate. Overtones of Inquisition, of Stephen Dedalus in the toils of sacerdotal authority. And lingering grudge though he bore against the Church — Ira nodded at his own words in amber on the monitor — "And with damn good historic reason too," he muttered. Would God, Joyce the necromancer himself and Ira's erstwhile literary liege, have succumbed to priestly persuasion, and taken holy orders himself? How old one had to become, one like himself, slow and phlegmatic, to begin to apprehend a little of institutionalized material interests, of the motivations of the seasoned manipulator, the casuist. . . .

It was queer at first, even a little dismaying, to have a friend who lived in a funeral parlor, the Hewin Funeral Parlor. But friendship had a way of quickly overcoming hesitations and misgivings, and making the friend's ambience a natural one. Ira soon became accustomed to seeing the ebony, glassed-in hearse beside the curb in front of the house, often with its retinue of two or three black limousines behind it. A little less frequently, when Ira arrived at Farley's home as his father, assisted by Farley's older brother, James, directed the movement of pallbearers down the flight of stairs from the funeral parlor to the hearse, it was a difficult matter to make a show of respectful detachment.

Upstairs, above the funeral parlor, were the sleeping quarters of the family, the parental bedroom and those of Farley's siblings, those still unmarried and living at home (James was married, so too was an even older sister, Margaret). Two younger sisters occupied a common bedroom, and Farley his own. It was there the two chums spent much of their time together when not traversing the streets; it was there that later, months later, when both attended Stuyvesant High School, they did their homework together. Below the funeral parlor, in the basement, were dining room and kitchen—and many a snack did Ira consume there, as Farley's guest, waited on by his mother, a low-spoken, nunlike woman with hirsute upper lip and gold-rimmed eyeglasses. Cold mutton sandwiches, fresh pork, and strange, un-Jewish, square slabs of corned beef between slices of Ward's Tip-Top packaged bread spread with salt butter.

It was then that Farley's father might come downstairs from mortuary duties in the parlor above to wash his hands at the kitchen sink. A robust, vigorous and serious man with a brushy brown mustache and blue eyes like Farley's, he was also a man of few words. He rarely wasted them on the two friends; he would march to the kitchen sink, wash his hands, dry them and leave, with scarcely a glance at those present, and without greeting. It was only when mourners or friends of the deceased gathered in the kitchen, that he might be drawn into conversation, become voluble, and once or twice, even vehement: When someone brought up the subject of Ireland, when talk veered to the subject of Irish freedom. "The Irish will never be free!" he declared emphatically as he dried his hands on a towel. "They haven't got brains enough to be free. Will you tell me how any people that keeps fightin' each other will ever be free?"

"Aw, come on, Tim. They've got the British lion on the run this time. He's tired o' bein' pelted with grenades. It's only a question o'time Ireland'll be free."

"Free to pelt each other with grenades, and that's what they're doin' now!"

Rich scent of liquor from somewhere among the bereaved, as Ira munched his cold sandwich—and marveled at his being so taken for granted in this Irish-Catholic milieu. Farley would wink at him, deprecatingly, which Ira interpreted as reassurance, his cue to act as Farley did: noncommittally, as one accustomed to this sort of disagreement, the way Farley's two younger sisters moved with total unconcern through the midst of it, from kitchen to backyard, their little iron jacks and ball and skipping rope in hand.

It was there in Farley's kitchen, at moments like these, that Ira for the first time glimpsed a certain similarity of condition, of oppression between the Irish and the Jews, something that had never occurred to him before on 119th Street, under the domination of the pugnacious and ascendent Irish: "He's Oirish," Mom would mimic them, her throat swelling up with extravagant pride. "The mayor is Oirish. Jack Dempsey is Oirish. Everyone of note is Oirish. Is it true?" she would ask. "Are they all Irish?" It seemed true; it seemed as if they had come from a long line of masters, of wielders of authority. But now for the first time, he realized, and not in words so much as in feeling, that they had come from a background of oppression and deprivation and subjection.

But once here, they menaced and Jew-baited Jews cruelly, who had also come from oppression and deprivation and subjection. Why? Wherein lay the difference? Because they already spoke English when they came here? Or because the Irish had come from a land of their own that held them together, in spite of everything, and the Jews had not, but came from Galitzia or Poland or Russia, where they were still Jews. If only Uncle Louie were around to ask. How different that made the two peoples, if that was where the difference lay. The one came from the "ould sod;" the word rolled off their tongues, "the ould counthry," said the people with black armbands down in the kitchen. Was that made them witty and scrappy and defiant, and so likeable? Whereas Jews came from everywhere, Rumania, Russia, Germany, Austria-Hungary, all laden with cares and anxieties, woebegone so often and commiserative in their woe—and scheming and scheming, against the other's carefree and resilient existence. If only Uncle Louie were around. Still, what did the Irish always jab you with when they wanted to mock you? "You got the map o' Jerusalem all over your puss." And no one he knew ever came from there.

The funeral parlor was sometimes unoccupied: No casket rested on the black-draped stand; not in use, that too had been removed. It was then that the funeral parlor reverted to a large, sandy-carpeted living room: a place for Farley and his chum to loll at ease among the crucifixes and the religious pictures—and wind up and play the phonograph, something that gave Ira the greatest pleasure. He fell in love with John McCormack's angelic tenor; it captivated Ira to the point of memorizing every song McCormack sang—and reproducing it with nearly impeccable brogue: "Oh, Mavourneen, Mavourneen, I still hear you callin' . . ." And, "There's a weddin' in the garden, dear, I can tell it by the flowers . . ." And, "A little bit of heaven fell from out the sky one day . . ." Farley grinned at his chum's rapturous infatuation.

One sits here musing, ruminating, Ecclesias, this 25th of March, '85, a warm Monday: the first day the thermometer has risen into the '70s. Rejected by father, long ago, and rejected by son, the one on whom (to repeat) I doted, to make it the more poignant. If not rejected then excluded, so self-enveloped he is, so occult his personal life, as I cheerlessly quipped, a mind-field. And the result? Antagonism. M cogently stated it: antagonism.

Without question, antagonism is what I feel, and in all likelihood, I manifest it too. . . .

Jane said Jess was a writer manqué; his prose gives that impression. But certainly — I think — there's no competition on that score. No, it is the sense of his condescension, his air of infallibility, and there's no denying, he is exceptionally gifted intellectually, though not apt manually. Still, he manages to surmount that particular shortcoming by dint of his quickness at perceiving the principle governing a device or the nature of its functioning. And undoubtedly, as I have more than intimated before, my sudden impulse to succor Jane in her abandonment by Jess, my strong affection for her, stems from that same antagonism, my sense of being wronged, and seeking an ally against the common miscreant.

So much for our shared emotional bonds. I do think, to reiterate, that if she could harness her feelings, her hurt, give them form, which implies both objectification and craftsmanship, she could produce a commendable piece of writing. . . .

XVI

1920. The summer drew near. It was the end of his first term of junior high school, and the summer drew near, summer of his fourteenth year. Green, green is the age of fourteen—or it should have been.

With what gloating Mr. Lennard, now become a Spanish teacher, in one of whose classes Ira was, and Farley in another— with what ceremony he would smooth the back of the pants, the cloth over the buttocks of a misbehaving pupil, after bending the offender over a front desk, and with greenish eyes behind his pince-nez ravished by the sight of the protruding posterior, administer a number of whacks with the "slappamaritis," a paddle with holes in it ("to let the air out," he jested). He had ordered it made for him in the woodworking shop. Everyone knew Mr. Lennard was a fairy, but no one ever reported him to the principal, Mr. O'Reilly. Or so it seemed. No one ever complained about him at home, as far as Ira knew; and why no one ever did, he could only guess: The others were like himself. Adolescents, perhaps they feared they wouldn't be believed; they feared to be branded squealers; or as in Ira's case, they feared they might have to confront an adult, a teacher, a person in authority, feared to get into trouble, if, for nothing else, than for knowing what they were not supposed to know.

No one ever reported Mr. Lennard, and yet everyone knew he was a fag, and an arrant fag. He would often sit in the lap of one or another of the bigger boys in the back row of the classroom, while class was in session. With his free hand slipped under his thigh, the hand not holding the textbook, Mr. Lennard would toy with the scholar's genitals. Incredible. And yet, how smoothly, composedly, Mr. Lennard would arise, if by chance the classroom door was opened, arise, adjust his pince-nez while looking up pleasantly over the open textbook at the visitor.

1920. Summer was near. (Ira had brought his aged, numb fingertips together for awhile.) Things were happening, simultaneously, integrally. One couldn't dwell too long on this or that aspect of the fourteen-year-old's existence, or else one ran the risk of excluding or forgetting the rest. The young adolescent still lived in the same home, but his role in it had changed. Once when Ira's fountain pen clogged while he was doing his homework, in a fit of temper he jammed the point against the paper, jammed the penpoint completely out of shape. Pop raised his hand to strike him, then seemed to remember that his son was now post–Bar Mitzvah; he counted as a man in the congregation; Pop desisted. Yes, Ira had the same home, and yes, he was fourteen. He was fourteen. Usually, Pop left quite early Sunday morning to wait at

table as an extra—an "extra jop," as he called it, a breakfast spon-
sored by some fraternal order in "Coonyailant." Less frequently,
his extra job might be a formal luncheon, and then he might linger
in the house until nine or ten in the morning. Those were the
exceptions. The rule was the fraternal breakfast, which meant a
very early departure. . . .

Soon after he left the house, Mom too would leave. Mom did
much of her shopping Sunday morning, when the produce displayed by the pushcart peddlers under the Park Avenue trestle was
freshest. She also brought dainties home for the late Sunday breakfast: bagels, lox at ten cents per quarter pound, cream cheese in
bulk, purchased in her favorite "dairy" store in the same area of
Park Avenue as the pushcart district. The same pot of coffee that
she had brewed for Pop in the morning would still be on the gas
stove for Ira to warm up, if he chanced to wake before she returned.

I told you all this before, Ecclesias.
   —So you have.
   No need to be impatient. Does anyone else, will anyone else see
through my motives?
   —I suspect many will. Most people, or let me say, most intelligent
people, are far more acute than you give them credit for being, in fact,
far more acute than you are.
   Yes, worse luck, but are they as canny intuitively as I am? As innately
endowed with a sense of form?
   —Well . . . there's little doubt you're only too well acquainted with
many of the signatures of the sordid. But that's little reason to preen.
   Agreed. Nevertheless, to keep the narrative from falling into separate
niches and vignettes, it is necessary to summon up, to present the various
aspects of his life at this time in their entirety, and as near to one another
as possible.
   —So you were fourteen, and your father ordinarily left early for an
extra job, and your mother brought home for your delectation bagels and
lox on a Sunday—
   Or *bulkies* and golden smoked whitefish. Or a chunk of smoked stur-

geon, believe it or not. Devoted Mama. If there were a crowbar that one could drive under a boulder of the psyche, and tumble the boulder out of the way, I would. But there is none — "Oh, there's none, there's none," as Gerard Manley Hopkins wrote, "No, no, there's none," and Time, T sub one equals a constant in Time, T sub one equals a date that is not to be eradicated. Ah, if the psyche were like this computer monitor, Ecclesias, where a change of word, a change of phrase, sends a ripple of change through the whole screen! A sort of spreadsheet of the soul. There can be no such ripples on the cuneiforms of the mind, once impressed. Or can there?

XVII

It was a time when Mom's chronic catarrh, without seeming to grow worse, began to impair her hearing—while continuing to produce noises of varying degrees of loudness in her head; tinnitus, it was called. Poor Mom. She learned to predict, and with considerable accuracy, the changes in the weather according to the loudness or softness of the noises in her ears. Meteorological turbulence conferred on her an auditory one. Mater, martyr, that was only another stage in her martyrdom. It was a time also when aunts and uncles were marrying or being given in marriage, or in Saul's case, driven into marriage: bestowing or receiving diamond engagement rings and then wedding rings and going under the *khupah*. And taxis would arrive each time at the curb before the Stigman tenement (sent there by ever-generous Moe); and Mom all corseted and dressed up in an ample new gown with loop-handle at the bottom, prepared to leave; and Pop, beside himself with nervous haste and frenzied apprehension, would rush wife and child out of the kitchen and down the flight of shabby steps into the dark street, pell-mell into the cab: *"Oy, vus yuksteh?"* Mom would complain. *"D'yukst aros de kishkas!"* And what was his irascible reply but: *"Klutz! D'yukst vie a klutz."* And away, away to the wedding hall on 110th Street and Fifth Avenue they would speed, festivity bound, nuptial merriment and *glatt kosher fressen.* . . .

But oh, Moishe, Moishe, Ira's dear Uncle Moe, long since out of uniform and now confident of his ability to confront his world as a full-fledged businessman; and oh, Ira, his nephew, pubescent and only too rapturous at being bound in the fateful concatenation of consequences. For it was Moe's opening of a restaurant, the Mt. Morris Restaurant, that year in partnership with his brother Saul, a partnership from which Pop, a waiter of six years' experience, was excluded, not because he lacked funds that invested would entitle him to a voice in the running of the business and a satisfactory share in its hoped-for profits. No, Pop was excluded because his business acumen was held in slight regard, and his temperament was felt to be incompatible with that of his two brothers-in-law. They even had their reservations about hiring him as a waiter.

It was the opening of the Mt. Morris Restaurant that inaugurated the train of fateful consequences. The Mt. Morris Restaurant, which all agreed was an appropriate name, being so near to Mt. Morris Park less than a half-dozen blocks away, was located on Fifth Avenue and between 115th and 116th Streets. The name was also seen as appropriate because it paid tribute to its director and senior partner, Moe, whom people had of late begun to call Morris. Set in the midst of a decidedly Jewish neighborhood, lower-middle-class in composition, thriving and sanguine in the thriving and sanguine 1920s, and skillfully managed, the servings generous, the place immediately appealed to a wide clientele. The cuisine was rich and thoroughly in accord with Jewish tastes; and though by no means strictly kosher, no meat was served, which made the meals "half-kosher," which provided further incentive to semi-assimilated Jews to patronize the place. Moe's warm personality, his large and expansive presence, and the widespread knowledge in the neighborhood of his recent service in his country's armed forces proved an additional attraction. The restaurant prospered.

Its immediate precincts became the locus of informal family gatherings. There, of a Sunday, as the weather waxed warm, Mom's sisters, pregnant, or with firstborn, and Baba, and Mamie with her offspring, would bring along small folding chairs, or borrowing one or two from the restaurant, would gather in a homey conclave across the avenue, directly opposite the restaurant, and seat themselves in a group before the tarnished, brown-brass railing that fronted the local savings bank. They would sit and *shmooz* away the hours, admonish kids, comment on the changing scene of promenaders and autos, on the ebb and flow of the clientele that entered and left the prosperous restaurant. Often, when the rush of business became very great, Moe or Saul would appear in the restaurant doorway and call to Mamie, or to both Mamie and Ira's other aunt, Ella, to come in and give the overburdened cook a hand. Mom they never called.

"Would that I too could work a shift in the kitchen to help the cook of a Sunday afternoon," Mom confided to Ira sadly. "And thus I might earn a dollar or two."

"So why don't they call you?" Ira asked.

"Don't you know? They rebuffed your father for a partner, so they're uneasy with his wife. You understand? With their sister, with me. Saul, sweet Saul, gives me to understand that Ella is thin, and that one gross bottom like Mamie's is enough in the kitchen. Beside that of the cook's. Another would block the kitchen passage. That's his reason, my fine brother. *Nu*. He knows how dearly I love mocha tarts; so to make amends, you've heard him invite me into the restaurant to have a piece of mocha tart and coffee. But I never go in, as you've seen."

"You never go in. But gee, I love that pineapple cake."

"It's different with you. You're a child. If they won't give my husband a chance to better himself in life, I won't accept their favors. I'm not a *shnorer*. Take away your false blandishments, and take him in as a partner— But, ah, what am I saying?" Mom reversed herself. "It is my curse. I don't know my Chaim'l? How long would he be a partner before he fell out with them? Before he would assault my brother Saul with the first weapon that came to hand. It's a punishment. I've been condemned."

Ah, the multimeshed events that impinged on Ira that year. How to deal with them? How to deal with them from a double perspective, and an impeded one?

It was during that same summer that Pop decided to embark on his own venture in food purveyance: He opened a small delicatessen on 116th Street between Lexington and Park Avenues. Both Moe and the expert Saul judged the choice of location unwise, pointing to the absence of "businesses" in the neighborhood, meaning other stores, and the relatively light pedestrian traffic passing through. But Pop counted on the 116th Street subway station of the new IRT line that had just been put into service to provide him with the necessary volume of passersby. He was wrong, alas. Temperamentally unsuited for running that kind of business, one that catered to the public; fitful, injudicious, vacillating, curt because of his misgivings, and often curt with customers, after the first flurry of the opening of the place, Pop saw his clientele soon fall away. He impressed Mom into service, preparing soups and *kishka,* stuffed *derma,* and other Jewish dainties that he thought might increase patronage, in addition to giving the place a homey atmosphere: She spent many hours of the day there, and weekend evenings, leaving Ira to shift for himself, which he did, in his way, avoiding the store, shunning the store for all he was worth.

Nothing new there; just more of the same to brood over.
 —Grimly.
 Yes, my golden opportunities.
 —Not golden. Gilt.
 Spell it any way you like.

The *gesheft* failed. Or rather, Pop through desperate connivance managed to unload it on another, a buyer from New Jersey, by having a string of Mom's relatives from near and far come into the place at sufficient intervals to give an appearance of sufficient patronage. The very next morning, early, Ira was given the buyer's check to certify it in Pop's name: The mopey kid was sent out to a bank in a New Jersey town, to linger about the bank's door until the place opened.

And did it open or didn't it? Was it a weekend or holiday? And did he come back, his mission a failure, as usual? Who could re-member now, who could retrieve the recollection of the actuality? Only the fair summer morning in the verdant square, like that of a commons of a small town, while he waited for the bank doors to open; only that afterward Pop exulted when the buyer had become *kharuseh*, when he thought better of the deal, and wished to withdraw, renege—but too late: Pop had cashed the check. "Khah! Khah! Khah!" Pop guffawed. Happy man, he hadn't quite lost his shirt. But the link had yet to be forged, the link had yet to be closed, as one good turn deserved another. And irony of ironies, her name was Link (though the name meant lung in Yiddish).

XVIII

Ida Link. She lived in the same house at the foot of which Pop had his delicatessen. A peroxide blonde in her early thirties, with a ruby wen on her chin, thoroughly city-wise, street-wise, native-born, stylish saleswoman of ladies' clothes on Delancey Street, Ida Link fawned on Pop. As soon as she learned he had unmarried brothers-in-law, she frequented the store and even lent a hand about the place. She dazzled Pop with her modish figure, her platinum hair, her glib, cheery address and Broadway spriteliness. It wasn't long before Pop's enthusiastic account of her charms brought Moe into her presence.

Poor Moe. The woman was as close to being a tart as it was possible to be without being an outright whore.

"Wouldn't you recognize my Chaim's contrivances," said Mom to Ira, and lowering her voice because the topic was shameful. "All Delancey Street knows her. Every saylissmon [as she pronounced the word for salesman] on Delancey Street knows her. Every say-lissmon of every sort. A common strumpet. Does she have innards? They're gone with yesterday. My poor brother, he loves children so. And he loved you. He'll have children in the other world."

Nobody told Morris, of course, or Zaida or Baba, hoping he or they would hear about Ida's flagrant promiscuity from other sources. They never did. And perhaps it might not have done much good if they had. For if Pop was dazzled, Moe was bewitched. Poor Moe, for all the rudiments of worldliness he had learned in the army, Ida's ways, her figure, her poise, her up-to-date breeziness, her lemon-ice hair were irresistible. The engagement went on apace, went on remorselessly to its consummation: the taxicab duly arrived at 108 East 119th Street; Morris stomped on the nuptial glass under the canopy; Pop probably got at least a token expediter's fee for his marriage broker's services.

And in the meantime, intertwined with all this, came the first hint of Park & Tilford's closing, of the closing of the Lenox Avenue store. Ira didn't believe it at first. Someone was just teasing, spoofing, the way they asked you to fetch a skyhook or some other implement that didn't exist. It was a joke. But the hint swelled to rumor, rumor to certainty. Ira was heartbroken. He had found such an enjoyable niche here. Everything he did was familiar, yet laced with enough variance to be interesting. The performance of his duties was almost effortless most of the time, or didn't require too much effort. And he was appreciated, and that was the thing he liked most: everyone's amused tolerance—well, maybe not the old cigar and tobacco clerk's, but everyone else's, including Mr. Stiles's, the manager. He felt at home here, that was it, accepted by outside the Jewish world, the way he felt with Farley: that precious element of confidence, of approval by those not his own, where it mattered, especially now, especially now.

"Wouldn't do you any good anyway, if you're going to Stuyvesant," said Mr. Klein. "You'd never get here in half an hour. They'd have to hire another boy anyway."

"Yeah," Ira agreed glumly.

"You could ask. There's a store downtown. Mr. Stiles'd recommend you."

"It wouldn't be the same."

"The same," Mr. Klein echoed. "What's the same, tell me? Nothing's the same. You work. You get used to the layout in a new store, the different clerks—or shipping clerks. You learn something new."

"Are *you* going?"

"With Park and Tilford? No. I'm getting a different job. A different company— What do you want to go to Stuyvesant for anyway? Stuyvesant is for engineers. You know what chance you have to be an engineer? Like you can fly. It's not for Jews."

"I don't wanna be an engineer."

"So what're you going there for?"

"My friend's going there."

"Oh! Now I understand," Mr. Klein nodded as if in fresh confirmation of Ira's fecklessness. "You know, you're a smart kid, a lot smarter than I thought when you came here. But it don't come out. Why do you hev to play dumb. Why? Tell me. Why do you hev to go to a school where your friend goes? You told me you wanted to be a teacher. There you stend a better chence. So what d'you wanna teach?"

"I don't know yet."

"So you go to a general high school. Then you go to City College, and you come out with a diploma, and you teach. Well?" Mr. Klein paused, regarded Ira with his unsmiling, unyielding demeanor. "You can make your whole life what it's gonna be by what you do now. If you do the right thing, and there's not gonna be another war, you could have a happy life. You grow up, you marry, you have kids, you're a teacher. This way, where are you?"

"I can still go to City College."

"And if your friend goes someplace else? He's Jewish?"

"No."

"I can see you're in for trouble."

"All right," Ira sulked.

"*Tsuris*, kid, you're askin' for *tsuris*. If you were my kid brother, I'd give you right away a few good smacks you should wake up. You remember what they used to sing in the army? What's become with hinky dinky, *parlez vous?* You're a little hinky dinky in the head, even smart like you are."

"OK."

"OK is right. Let's start peckin' the beskets."

"So what do they got to close the store for?" Ira burst out angrily.

"Ferstest nisht?" Mr. Klein picked up the sheaf of invoices and stepped back the better to survey Ira—who once again couldn't help note the man's peculiar, cocky stance: not bowlegged, but with rigidly locked knees: concave in front. "Can't you see the neighborhood is changing? It's getting *shvartze* uptown, more and more. It's getting Jewish downtown, high-tone Jewish Broadway, Riverside Drive. They don't buy Park and Tilford. But mostly, even if they did, there's no more whiskey, no more wine, no more brandy, no more cordials, no more beer. *Ferstest?* That's where the big profit used to come from. Ask the old *puritz* behind the tobacco counter, the duke from kacki-ack with his wing-collar. He had two helpers once, and that little percentage on sales the clerks get, he got the highest in the place. Ask the *alter kocker*. That was a nice bonus."

"I don't wanna ask him. I believe you." Ira's tone was hostile.

"Listen, don't get smart." Mr. Kline handed him the first batch of items to stow in the basket. "Put the gless between the cocoa and the split peas."

"They'll deliver from one place, from only one place. The big downtown store. And only in Manhattan. That's all. The other store, the one on Broadway on 103rd Street? Only with a kid with a box. Local. With kids like you. The cellarman sends you out."

Ira worked on, stowing goods away mechanically, resentfully. He felt bereaved, and as always when changes theatened, apprehensive. . . .

The school vacation began. To his great disappointment, Farley went to New Rochelle to stay with an aunt and be near the water. He came back once and sought out Ira: the immense, the ineffable delight of coming lonesomely home from the library—and finding Farley in the kitchen, in the homely, Jewish Stigman kitchen: Farley, tanned, hair sun-bleached, blue-eyed, in the kitchen where he had been talking to Pop.

"Farley!" Ira shouted at the sight of him. And Pop couldn't refrain from imitating his son's joyous cry: "Farley!" They spent a few hours together, hunted for snipes—they had both taken up cigarette smoking—puffed away at discarded butts, while seated on a bench below the bell tower on Mt. Morris Park hill. And then they separated a few minutes before three-thirty in the afternoon, when Ira went to work.

That was all he saw of Farley until the summer was over and school began again after Labor Day. But in the interim, when not working, Ira spent most of the day reading, at home in the morning, in the library after lunch, and going to the store directly from the library, as he did customarily from school to store. Books, books, books, the only solace now, without Farley, and the added unhappiness of knowing the store was soon to close. Books. Narrative after narrative, novels, short stories, tales of adventure. He knew, he was only too aware there were other things to read: The shelves were full of books marked History, Biography, Science, Philosophy, Poetry—no, that wasn't quite true: He took home a book of love poems once.

Otherwise, he cared nothing for a book if it wasn't a narrative, if it didn't appeal to his feeling and imagination, the way a story did. It didn't have to be prose; it could rhyme, it could be poetry, as long as it told a story: like the *Ancient Mariner*. And yes, once he found a book in the empty flat upstairs. It was called the *Prisoner of Chillon*—by somebody named Byron. That was wonderful. "My hair is white but not with years, nor grew it white in a single night as men's have grown through sudden fears." What a wonderful story! The prisoner made friends even with the spiders. But you had to read the prologue over and over again, the invocation it was called, before you understood it: "Immortal spirit of the chainless mind, brightest in dungeons, Liberty thou art . . ."

Maybe it would be that way with other poems if he wanted to spend the time figuring them out: But all he asked for was a story, that was all he craved; stories not only moved fancy, they held you, and while they did, they told you how people felt, what they saw and heard, and how they lived. That was the important thing:

They were part of a world, one that maybe didn't exist anymore, but that was the only way you could know it.

Oh, stories told you everything; you could guess what they often only barely suggested, you could daydream in their world, you could live in it; you could change what happened in your own mind, and then figure out the different kind of story that would have happened. And names, all kinds of names stayed in your head, like real people, not mythology, "characters" they were called, like Jean Valjean and Huck Finn and D'Artagnan, and David Copperfield and Martin Eden. They took you into their world, yes, the way Farley did. They took you into their world, even more than Farley did. You were more in their world than in the Jewish world, in their world where you wanted to be, and now that he was what he was and couldn't break away from their world and didn't want to, maybe some day he'd find a way out of his Jewish slum world into their world.

He knew more about their world than any Jewish kid in the block, any Jewish kid he knew, any kid he knew, Farley, anyone in the class. He knew, because he had to know, because it was his only hope, because he had nowhere else to go and only a rubble of what was left inside to dwell on: his Jewishness: Mom, *matzahs* on Passover, Zaida greedily pumping the fresh *bulkies* to test which was the tenderest. Jewishness, it would be like leaving nothing. Nearly . . .

XIX

Mr. Lennard arose a little more quickly than usual from big George Repke's lap in the back seat, arose, flushed and turned pale. Not because he had been caught in the act of sitting in a boy's lap by Mr. O'Reilly on his opening the door. No, but because Mr. O'Reilly was escorting a mild, white-haired gentleman with a white mustache and goatee into the classroom. Mr. O'Reilly introduced the distinguished-looking newcomer to Mr. Lennard. The two shook hands, and after a minute or two, Mr. O'Reilly left. Flushed again, and glowering at the class menacingly and uneasily—obvious warning signs against misbehavior—Mr. Lennard introduced Dr. Zamora: He was the supervisor of Spanish in the New York high schools, and he had dropped in to learn how "our junior high school was progressing in the study of Spanish." Did the class understand? Of course they did, and Mr. Lennard expected everyone to do his best.

"Naturally, Doctor Zamora," Mr. Lennard addressed the bland and quietly attentive supervisor, "the term has just begun, and I'm afraid you won't find us quite up to our best."

"I am prepared to make allowances," Dr. Zamora smiled. And to the class: *"Cómo están ustedes?"*

To which they answered in ragged variance, some, *"Muy bien, Señor."* And some, *"Buenos días, Señor."* Mr. Lennard bit his lip, frowned—in ominous displeasure.

And he continued to frown as the class fumbled every question or worse, gazed mutely at Dr. Zamora. For one thing, after Mr. Lennard's clear American-Spanish, Dr. Zamora's Spanish-Spanish was confusing. Behind Dr. Zamora's back, Mr. Lennard's glower deepened. Still, Dr. Zamora seemed unfazed, patient, undiscouraged. *"Quién es Don Zuixote?"* He asked. The question had an air of finality about it, as if he wished to leave on an optimistic note. "Don Quixote," his white mustache and beard transmitted to the mystified class. *"Si, Don Zuixote de la Mancha. En Inglés, si ustedes quieren contestar. Quién es el?* You may answer in English," Dr. Zamora encouraged. "Who is Don Quixote?"

And now Mr. Lennard came to Dr. Zamora's assistance, but tacitly. Behind Dr. Zamora, at his very shoulder, and so close to his periphery of vision no student would have had the impudence to do that to a teacher: With his round lips writhing eloquently, aided by fervent grimace, Mr. Lennard kept forming visual syllables: Don Quicksote! Don Quicksote!

At last Ira understood. "Don Quicksote!" he blurted. "I read about him. He had a fight with a windmill."

Mr. Lennard deflated with relief.

"*Sí, sí,*" said the kindly Doctor Zamora. "*Pero en Español decimos,* Don Quixote. In Spanish we say, Don Quixote. Repeat after me, please: Don Quixote de la Mancha. Everyone."

"Donkeyhotay de la Mancha," the class parroted with right good will.

"*Muy bien.* Once more: What is the name of the most famous character in Spanish literature?"

"Donkeyhotay," a few began and the rest swelled the chorus.

"*Muy bien.* And the author of Don Quixote was named?" Dr. Zamora scanned the class.

Ira raised his hand. "His name was Cervantes."

"*Se llama Cervantes. Muy bien.*"

Mr. Lennard exuded gratification.

XX

September neared its end; the hot weather moderating, the mens' straw hats disappearing . . .

It was the first fall of the new decade, decade of the '20s, that portentous and turbulent and innovative decade, probably to prove the most important decade of the century, decade of Einstein, decade of Bohr, decade of Eliot, decade of Joyce, Stein, Picasso, Stravinsky, Duncan, of Martha Graham, the Dadaists, of Spengler, of Hubble and Shockley, of island universes, innovations in cinema, Kellogg Pacts and Reparations, of Lenin and Trotsky's success in defeating the White Russians, of aborted revolutions elsewhere, assassinations of the German Communist leaders, Luxembourg and Liebknecht, of Lenin's death and Stalin's ascendancy, of the Leagues of Nations manqué, of the triumph of American Isolationism, the repudiation of Woodrow Wilson's dreams, of Republican Party sweeps at the polls, decade of Prosperity and Normalcy, epoch of Cal Coolidge, of cartoons of Germans trundling wheelbarrows full of devalued *deutsche marks* to buy a few groceries, of money-raising drives and benefit performances on behalf of starving Armenians cruelly massacred by the Turks, of wildly soaring stocks, and fortunes made overnight on Wall Street, and culminating at the end of the decade in the great Stock Market crash in 1929 when erstwhile millionaires hurled themselves from high windows . . .

Yes, but the kid was only fourteen, Ira brooded. And besides, he had already become so self-engrossed, become internalized by a veritable psychic implosion. Nay, he had become *tsemisht,* the stunned, dynamited fish, and consequently, less responsive than he might otherwise have been to the great changes and upheavals occurring in art, in science, in the economy, changes within nations and between them.

True. But why introduce that now? Perhaps he ought to reserve all, or some of it, till later, unfolding events parallel with young Ira's development. Well, perhaps he'd come back to it, to that and the hobble-skirts the women wore, to that and the stores that appeared on 125th Street selling army-navy surplus. The best thing to do, he thought: Best thing he could do—maybe—would be to excerpt sundry articles, dispatches, editorials from, say, the *New York Times,* and let it go at that, let the reader wade through the sociopolitical spate of happenings of the century's third decade in the appropriate studies of the period, and form his own impression. Lazy man's way, way of default and ineptitude.

From somewhere Farley's father had received a pair of tickets of admission to a new movie showing in a prestigious movie house on Broadway: Title of the movie was *The Golem.* The tickets had been given to Farley, and he and Ira rode the subway downtown to see the show.

They viewed a dark, frenetic movie, dark and frenetic as the makeup under the Cabalist rabbi's eyes, as he pronounced, with sound effects from the musicians in the pit, the awesome tetragrammaton that brought the image of clay to life. But unforgettable, the sorcerer-rabbi's swiftness in snatching from the newly animate figure the little plug in his bosom, where life resided, snatched it not a moment too soon against the ponderous defense of the lumpish, sentient giant, who toppled backward to the ground.

The plug became symbolic over the years, but of what, Ira was never sure: essence, crystal of life's principle, a vestige of 1920, of himself and Farley, hurrying full of anticipation out of the subway kiosk into Broadway's crowded sunshine and then toward the movie theater. No, there was something else, Ira leaned backward into the sway of office chair—something else: his Jewishness, wasn't it? That he had to deal with afterward, in a serious vein, not as humorous counters, something, the little he knew, the essential plug he had retained of his Jewishness, of Jewish tradition. Odd. And when he tried to pluck it out . . . creative inanition followed.

XXI

In packaging half-pound bags of sugar and other dried food, he had long ago learned how to turn the string back upon itself, and thereby form a little bight against which the string could be snapped. He was tying up the one-pound bags of lentils after he weighed them. "He'll give me permission if I tell him what it's for," Ira spoke to Mr. Klein.

"I don't want no mix-ups. I want you to come in Friday. Not at half-past-three. Twelve o'clock. I'm gonna be shorthanded for filling the beskets for Saturday," said Mr. Klein. "I'm gonna be shorthanded all day. Why do you have to ask him? Suppose he says no."

"He won't say no," Ira assured him. "He's let other fellers go. I know."

"Listen, if you're smart you wouldn't ask him. Do like I tell you. I know about school. I got nephews and nieces that go to school. You don't come back after lunch, *ferstest?* And then Monday you bring a note from home: Your mother was sick. Something like that. You have to mind the baby—"

"There's no baby in my house."

"Don't be a pain in the ess," said Mr. Klein. "So something else. She's gonna have a baby."

"I could say I got sick, and then I went home."

"All right. Say you got sick."

"So I'll have to bring a note Monday."

"So bring a note Monday."

"So he'll wanna know why I didn't tell him first."

"Listen," Mr. Klein smacked his tongue. *"Ich bin dir moichel.* You know what that means? Don't bother me. They'll have to get me somebody from another store. I was just trying to get you a little extra work on Friday; you'll make a little extra cash. *Az nisht is nisht.* Only trouble is you know where everything is. I'll hev to tell a new man where everything is."

"I tell you I don't need any notes," Ira urged vehemently. "I'll ask him two days before. All right? Then you'll know."

"Two days before, you'll spoil everything," Mr. Klein retorted. "Why?"

"Because you got such a head. Go on. Keep weighing the lentils. Once you tell him that, he'll know why you're taking off."

"All right. You wanna bet?"

"Yeah, I wanna bet," Mr. Klein said with clipped satire. "Finish. Finish. That's enough. Give me a hand here."

"All right." Ira carried the bags to the shelf marked LENTILS. "So when're they gonna close?" he asked, returning.

"By the end of the year. The lease is up. Maybe they'll give them an extension: January. But maybe P and T don't want it no more," he shrugged. "It's not like it once was in the store, with the champagne and the whiskey for New Year's. Here, take." He handed Ira a can.

"Kumquats," Ira read. "Something else I never tasted."

Mr. Klein laughed. "Boy, you're a—*bist a*—*bist a*— You know what a *yoldt* is?"

"Yeah."

"Harvey," Mr. Klein addressed the approaching porter, "we're gonna have a big time here Friday."

"Yessir, don't I know it. All that's gotta happen is for that elevator to break down."

"Thet's all. Thet's right." He looked fixedly at Harvey. "Thet's all we need."

"I ain't gonna stay here afterward," said Ira.

"After what? After they close the store? Nobody's gonna stay here."

"No. I mean after they move all that stuff."

"There's two more months. Maybe more. And then you can help move everything else."

"I don't wanna stay here."

"You didn't taste everything yet." Mr. Klein grinned provocatively, and handed Ira a paper-wrapped, odorous wedge, Parmigiano or Romano cheese, Ira would have guessed.

He flushed sullenly. "I don't taste everything."

"No? What didn't you taste?" His head wagged, encompassing in its motion the width and breadth of the cellar. "You hear that, Harvey? He don't taste everything. Only what ain't kosher."

"What ain't?" Harvey asked.

"Kosher? Everything ain't."

"Yee, hee, hee!" Harvey went off, snapping his polishing cloth.

XXII

Class was dismissed at the usual hour, at three. Ira waited until the classroom was empty and he was alone with Mr. Lennard. "I wanna ask you a favor, Mr. Lennard. For Friday."

"What is it?" Mr. Lennard removed his pince-nez, breathed on a lens, before delicately applying his silk handkerchief. Exposed, his green eyes appeared even more strict as they appraised Ira, strict yet peculiarly blurry. Lips so puffy, and deep, small craters on either side of the bridge of his nose. "I'll be glad to do you a favor if I can." He seemed to shade his face under the hand replacing his pince-nez.

"My shipping clerk where I work," Ira felt as if he had begun at the wrong place, but went on, "Mr. Klein. He asked me if I could come in Friday right after lunch. At Park and Tilford."

"Why?"

"They got a lotta extra work. They're moving all the—" Ira gesticulated. "All the stuff from the locked-up cellar: the wine, the whiskey. Beer. I don't know what. They don't sell it anymore."

"Oh, yes." Mr. Lennard permitted himself a smile. "They don't, do they? No, we're all prohibited from touching the stuff."

"No?" Ira misunderstood, disappointed. "I said I could. He wanted me to do him a favor, Mr. Klein, and come in early."

"Oh, it's all right with me," Mr. Lennard revived hope. "But it won't be all right with Mr. O'Reilly. Or with the Board of Education. I have to account for your attendance. Supposing something went wrong. You were hurt, and were supposed to be in school. And if I marked you present—you see where that leaves me?"

"Oh," Ira grimaced repentance. "Yeah. Mr. Klein said I should bring in a note afterward."

"Exactly, from your parents. That relieves me of responsibility. But the way you're going about it—" For some reason, Mr. Lennard relaxed in veiled cordiality. "Of course, only you and I need to know the real reason."

"Yes, sir. Thanks." Without knowing why, Ira felt cheated—by himself, or so he felt, as usual: dumb, placed himself at disadvantage. "I'll get a note."

Mr. Lennard looked up at the clock above the blackboard. "When do you begin work at the store? Three-thirty, isn't it?"

"Today? Yes, sir. The store is just on Lenox Avenue."

"You've got a few minutes." Mr. Lennard's voice was inviting and at the same time inflexible; it hinted at something Ira had heard before. It couldn't be. It was: echo of that trim, rusty tramp in wooded Fort Tryon Park. It couldn't be. It was: Mr. Lennard had gone to the door and given the knob that kind of twist that locked it. He returned, still composed, but emanating a darkness, relentless, unmistakable. "Let's sit down here." He indicated one of the spotted, gouged wooden surface-tops of a twin desk.

Ira sat down obediently, and Mr. Lennard sat beside him on the other desktop. He opened his fly, speaking casually: "You've grown a lot since that day your birthday was mixed up. I still remember it." He opened Ira's fly. "Do you pull off now?"

"No."

"Don't tell me you don't." He began a slow pumping on his own erection while he teased Ira's limp penis out. "With all that hair on your cock?"

"Somebody tried to show me on the roof," Ira shrank within himself. "I didn't like it."

"You didn't come, is that it?" Mr. Lennard increased the movement of both hands. "Ever screw anybody?" And at Ira's silence, "Come on, get a hard-on. Make believe you're trying to take somebody's ass."

Too numb even to be resistive, just too numb; become part of what was around him, not himself: slate blackboards, erasers in the channels, stumps of chalk, school clock, inkwells in the scarred desktops. Long window pole beside the big school windows gaping at blue sky. Mr. Lennard's hands bobbed up and down. "Come on, squeeze it, squeeze it, get a hard-on. See a nice big ass in front of you. Like your mother's or your sister's. You've seen it, haven't you? Bend 'em over. Nice and big—o-oh." His hands quickened to a flutter. "You get wet dreams. Nice wet dreams. Bring 'em out here in front of you. Come on. Get a hard-on."

Specter of that rusty, lanky tramp the Irish couple saved him from. "Mr. Lennard, I gotta go. I'm gonna be late."

"No, you won't. Let's go!" He hissed fiercely through his teeth. His features had become concentrated in hectic determination; his pince-nez vibrated so with the intensity of his pumping his own and Ira's limp penis, he removed his hand from his own, squeezed the clip that removed his glasses, placed them on the desk in the next aisle. "Come on, boy! Make it stiff."

"I can't, Mr. Lennard. I'm in school. I can't." Whining, shrinking, his instinct clung to the only available escape. "Please, Mr. Lennard. I have to go—Mr. Klein is waiting."

"Oh, hell!" Mr. Lennard terminated effort abruptly. "Button up." He got to his feet, snatched his pince-nez from the desk, fixed it on his nose, then angrily went to the door, buttoning his fly. "All right, you're excused." He turned the knob. "Don't forget to bring me a note tomorrow." He threw the door open, looked out into the hall, scowled at Ira quickly approaching, school-book strap in one hand, his free hand forcing the last button into place on the fly of his knee-pants.

Past his unforgiving teacher, out of the classroom door, into the hall, brass knobs of closed classrooms marking his frightened progress. Self-accused, befouled, bewildered, harried by sick nightmare, he scurried down the iron staircase, alone between thick glass partitions' dull translucence, the uriney basement. Why did it have to happen to him? Stupid. Mr. Klein told him what to do. Anh. The door, heavy oak school door. Out. Out. That lousy, rotten— bugger! Into the street, oh, better the street. Yell for everybody to hear, Mr. Lennard is a lousy, rotten bugger! Jesus, getting late.

He quickened his pace. He strode as fast as he could, feeling the bind of tightening calf muscles. Revulsion permeated his every fiber, an all-encompassing disgust. A teacher, no less. Like that morning in the gutter, soon after coming to live on 119th Street, the barber's son and Petey Hunt: "Goggle a weeny," they baited each other. "Gargle a weeny." Oh, God, it was all true, it was all true. Everything. They didn't imagine it. They didn't exaggerate. It was all true. Fags. Fairies. Fluters. Teachers or rusty bums in the park: What could they see, pulling, holding his dink, his ass, pulling? What? Mother's big ass, sister's ass. Oh, he knew what, he knew what. But he wouldn't say. Play dumb and get away. Play dumb and escape. Ira broke into a trot. Get to the store as fast as he could. Forget.

No, not necessary. Not necesssary.

   —What an odd way to put it.

I know. I know. So do you, Ecclesias.

   —It's still odd.

Odd or not, that's my dilemma.

   —You chose it.

As a precondition, yes. What are you going to do? Cut is the branch that might have grown full straight and burned is Apollo's laurel bough. . . . What can you do? What can you make? As Mom would say in her pathetic Yinglish. Old mole of Hamlet threading underground, or the Ancient Mariner's undersea sprite.

   —But then.

Yes, old mole. 'Tis called a bind. Did ever a literary wight get himself into such pickle?

XXIII

In a daze, he trotted by quiet yellow-brick and brownstone, and now and then a pedestrian, a girl on Fifth Avenue, curls and rosy cheeks, like a calendar girl, in a meadow, by a brook, not this, this loathesomeness of people inside. How? How could it be? Whom to ask? Not Farley, no, couldn't ask anyone. Only if Uncle Louie were Pop, ask how the everyday, the everyday prosaic proper waylaid . . .

To the side entrance of the store he loped, strap of books under arm. And reaching the door, he was startled out of his inner turbulence by the sight of all three P & T delivery trucks at the curb next to the side entrance of the store. He went inside, always like slipping into the store's shadows and aromas, skipped down the flight of steps to the basement—to meet Mr. Klein's disapproving glance from the other side of the zinc-lined table. But frowning or not, his face welcome, familiar and trusted those snapping brown eyes, reorienting him to the known, the dependable, the consistent.

"Always you're here ten minutes early, fifteen minutes early." Mr. Klein stabbed the small, red city guide book at Ira. "Today, when I need you," he wagged his head. "Nearly fifteen minutes late. What's the matter with you? You know I'm shorthended like hell. You can see." He threw the guidebook down on the table at the edge of the heap of groceries.

"It was my teacher," Ira extenuated, shoved strap of books under counter.

"That's the one who's giving you permission for tomorrow?"

"Yeah."

"So what'd he keep you so long? It took so long to say yes or no? And which is it?"

"He said yes."

"You're sure?"

"I'm sure. I'm sure."

"All right. Let's get to work," he grabbed his sheaf of invoices. "Wine vinegar, wine vinegar, wine vinegar. You see it?"

"Yeah. There."

"All right. So the sugar must be next, the box of thyme. Now, don't ask questions. I don't know how to say it myself—"

"I'm not askin' questions."

"What's the matter?" Mr. Klein's brow etched in long frets.

"Nothing."

"Nothin'? That's all? All right. So thyme, th-ime, *abee gesindt*. A big can crebmeat. Where? Artichokes— You hear what's goin' on?" He handed Ira the items.

"Yeah. What? I never heard that." Ira noted the thumping noise coming from the wine and liquor vault as he duly stowed the goods into the hamper. "They're fixing something? Hey, look. There's Murphy. There's Quinn. Everybody's in the basement. What're they doing over there? There's Tommy. Who's that guy?"

"Who's he?" Mr. Klein kept up a rapid handing over of staples and delicacies. "Who's *they* you mean. There's three of 'em."

"Oh," Ira's gaze followed the stalwart man in the gray fedora. "Where's three?"

"There. In there with the delivery men. You hear 'em? That's the boxes they're strapping. With iron straps. All the booze has got to go tomorrow; everything's got to be stamped and sealed and with a number. Where the hell is that vanilla?"

"So what're they gonna do?" Ira picked up the small flask of vanilla, fitted it into a niche in the hamper. "Are they gonna lock everything up again?"

"*Bist meshugge?* They *were* locked up. They're goin' to a bonded warehouse tomorrow."

"A bonded warehouse." Events of the past hour began to scatter before wholesome activity. "What's a bonded warehouse?"

"Don't stop," Mr. Klein handed over a package. "From everything right away you want to make a discovery: It's a place nobody can touch the alcohol, that's all. Volstead. The Volstead Act. That means Prohibition."

"Why didn't you— Why wasn't you—" Ira wrenched the words free. "My big brother?"

Mr. Klein showed genuine surprise: "Why do you need a big brother?" His sympathy was tentative, unsentimental, but honest. "I thought something was the matter."

"Yeah."

"So what's the matter?"

"I got a dirty, rotten, lousy teacher."

"That's all? So tell your father."

Ira fell silent, his throat too tight for utterance.

"All right, I'm your big brother," Mr. Klein plied his helper with comestibles. "Don't touch the beer and schnapps tomorrow. That's my advice."

"Me?"

"Yeah, it's a big fine for a minor like you. You're called a minor. You can't handle alcohol. You can't even go near it, you understand? Alcohol—it makes you *shicker*. Wine, beer. So stay away, whatever anybody else does, stay away— Here, take: watermelon preserves."

"Tommy too?"

"He's a *goy*. Nobody'll say— No, he's full-time workin'." Mr.

Klein contradicted himself. "I don't know how old he is. You, you're only a schoolboy."

"I don't like it anyway."

"No? All the *bekheles* wine you don't drink *Pesach?* And a *kiddush?* You know what is a *kiddush ha shem?* Here: Pettypoise peas. Three cans. Together. Mussels. Vichy. No, hell, what am I thinking? I was in France. I drank it. Vichy s-swah. Sugar."

"Kiddush, I know. What's the *ha shem?"*

Mr. Klein burst into a laugh. "What's the *ha shem! Oy, bist dee a Yeet."*

"Well, the wine anyway is like vinegar in my house. Sharp. My mother makes it in like a big pot in the front room."

"So that means *ha shem,"* Mr. Klein said ironically. "Listen, stay away from every kind of bottle tomorrow, you hear? I'm your big brother. There's gonna be *khoisakh* in this cellar tomorrow. I can tell already." He cocked an ear toward the hammering in the wine vault, nodded significantly. "Here: fruit salad. How is it today you're workin' like a—like a—like the way you should. Here: a box guava jelly. Next to it. Same order: package tea. Jazz-mine. Another sugar."

Ira knew he would have no trouble getting Pop to write a note of excuse from school as soon as he heard it would mean his son's earning a little extra cash. Ever querulous about anything that jeopardized her son's schooling, it was Mom who demurred, even this slight departure from regularity: "For a paltry *shmoolyareh,"* she denigrated, "to fall behind in school. I don't need it. First of all, I want to see you graduate."

"Yeah," Ira scoffed. "From bookkeeping and touch-system typing and stinking shorthand. And—" he brooded, surly a moment, "that rotten Spanish."

"So why did you take it? Who forced you? I don't know better, alas; I can't counsel." She thumped fleshy hand on bosom, "And he—" her fingers spread open toward Pop reading the Yiddish newspaper at the table, "—knows as much as I—"

"I know he seeks to become a *malamut*." Pop looked up.

"Then let him become a *malamut*. But always before it was Davit Clinton, Davit Clinton High School."

"Stuyvesant is as good as De Witt Clinton." Ira felt a recurring surge of resentment "I should never have gone to that lousy junior high."

"*Nu?*"

"Shah! *Yenta*." Pop had gotten writing material from the corner under the china closet. "What shall I tell him? First write me down his name."

"I got a pencil." Ira declined the proffered penholder. He spelled out the name as he wrote: "L-e-n-n-a-r-d. Mr. Lennard."

"*Azoi?*"

"Yeah. I told him Mom has chronic catarrh and doesn't speak English, so I have to take her to the clinic—"

"Aha. I don't need no chronic catarrh. I have to write yet chronic catarrh. Am I a doctor? You have to take her to the clinic. She's sick. You have to go with her. That's not enough?"

Sullen, Ira shrugged, the way he always smoothed over Pop's scorn of his son's suggestions, knit up his wounded pride. He watched Pop write the date. For so slight a man as Pop was, his script had the doughtiest of flourishes. "Dear is with an 'a,' no?"

"Yeh, d-e-a-r."

"Today a half-day, tomorrow a whole one," said Mom. "I won't stand for it."

"There won't be any again. I'm gonna quit soon."

"Aha!" Pop uttered brusque satire. "*Shoyn?* Enough. The task is ended? You're already spent?"

"I'm not spent. Everybody says they're gonna close anyhow. I told you."

"Then you have to lead the way. What else?"

"Let him be," Mom interceded. "Whatever he earned, he earned. That was all to the good."

"But his five dollars a week you grabbed at once."

"Then I'm the loser, not you."

"You lead him. Let us see if he ends where you hope." Pop

signed the slip with an inch-high Herman Stigman. "Here's your notel," he added in Yiddish diminutive.

Ira folded the paper silently. How could you breach Pop's contempt? How could you confide: Like yesterday, say, my teacher did this, my teacher did that. You know what he did? Right away it would be his fault, not Mr. Lennard's: Why did you let him do it? Why didn't you run out? No, maybe he was wrong. Maybe Pop would write a note, the way he did to Mr. O'Reilly when the shop-teacher cracked Ira on the ear. But then, Mom: Right away, *Oy, gewald!* The outcry that would ensue: *Gewald geshrigen!* Outlandish Jewish outcry. Nah.

—It was because you already felt guilty, wasn't that the chief reason?

Yes, because I might betray something even more heinous than Mr. Lennard's molestation.

—Isn't it time you cleared the air, exposed the clandestine burden? You can't go on indefinitely in this fashion, with an unaccountably eccentric orbit, like a visible astral body with an invisible satellite. Beside, the enigma is beginning to wear thin.

Very well. Soon.

XXIV

Eagerly, Ira greeted Farley, when the two met down in the school basement a few minutes before the bell rang. How much he needed Farley's cheerfulness, his laugh. If only he could tell Farley: Mr. Lennard tried to jerk me off. Then how do you know about jerking off? Mr. Lennard tried to pull me off. Then how do you know about pulling off? All right, Mr. Lennard played with my dink; he took his out and tried to make me get a hard-on—ah, then what, then what? Farley would say what to do. Maybe tell someone else. Then what? Ah, the hell with it. Mr. Lennard was excusing him from school this afternoon. That was all that mattered. Ira told Farley about the permission he had received from Mr. Lennard to skip school after lunch—and about the liquor to be moved from the cobwebby vault down in a corner of the cellar of the store:

"They're gettin' the hooch out," said Farley. "Hooch," what a funny word; they both laughed.

Ira's anxiety subsided a little; it was easier now to place Pop's note on Mr. Lennard's desk. He scarcely glanced at it. School was school—Ira went to his seat: Routines were routines, almost as if they were in a plaster cast—like that Golem in the movie. Gee, you'd never guess. The attendance roll was called. With noncommittal countenance, Mr. Lennard slipped Pop's note between the leaves of the wide attendance book and flattened the gray cover. A few minutes later, when the gong rang to summon the school to the Friday assembly, Mr. Lennard stepped out into the hallway, and with strict, impersonal mien oversaw the deportment of his class as they filed out of the classroom and marched through the hall toward the staircase. Everything tended toward the customary; the customary leveled out everything.

Still, a certain imprint showed through, like that of a lingering dream, as they pledged allegiance to the flag, sang "The Star Spangled Banner." And seated again, heard Mr. O'Reilly read the 23rd Psalm. How different that was now, different from what it was on the East Side, when he first heard the lady principal read it. Mr. Lennard stood so devotionally, so reverently near the window. Oh, to bring back those innocent days on the East Side, when he thought "my cup runneth over" meant my *kupf* runneth over. "He anointeth my head with oil," so of course your *kupf* runneth over— like Mom's cottonseed oil—from your head down your cheeks.

On the platform, Mr. O'Reilly was talking about the Russian Bolsheviks, and his face twitched with earnestness as he spoke: The Bolsheviks were evil people; they were dictators; they abolished free speech, free newspapers and meetings; they confiscated anything they wanted; they shot anyone who stood up for his rights; they closed churches and synagogues; they mocked at God.

Ira listened, but always with reservations, maybe Jewish reservations, maybe that was the trouble: Mom said the Bolshevicki killed Czar Kolkie, Czar Kolkie who detested Jews, Czar Kolkie who encouraged *pogroms,* Czar Kolkie, the Bullet. For that alone, she kissed the Bolshevicki. What was the use? It was best to forget everything—if you could—not think of who was right, not think of such matters. Like what? Like Civics? No. He hated Civics anyway. Not Geography either. He hated that too. History. Maybe sometimes: General Herkimer wounded and dying but still directing the battle, Captain André, the spy, with the map of the fortress in the heel of his shoe, General Wolfe, General Montcalm, dying in the same battle. That sort of history he liked, but not the Henry Clay and the great Missouri Compromise or anything of that kind. The Bolsheviks were one thing, according to Mr. O'Reilly. The Bolshevicki were another, according to Mom, saying of their execution of Czar Nicholas, *"Gut, gut, verfollen zoll er vie e likt."* Even Pop agreed; Uncle Louie was enthusiastic: A new world had opened up for the worker, Jew or Gentile. But not Zaida; he didn't believe Communist Russia would make much if any difference to the Jew. Would they let him trade, make a nice living? Everything the Bolshevicki took away from the prosperous Jew. Synagogues were closed. Then what good was it if you couldn't worship God? Kerensky, Kerensky and the Duma, that was the way the new regime should have gone. But did the Bolshevicki allow it? They drove him out as well as the people elected like those in the United States. So who knew how the Jews would fare?

But you had to think of something: If he could only turn his head and look at Farley, that would make you feel better, but he couldn't. Fix on the American flag hanging motionlessly over with its staff in its iron sleeve on the side of the platform, the Bible on its lectern, the partitions pushed back to open up the classrooms into an assembly hall, George Washington in profile high on the wall above and behind Mr. O'Reilly. . . . Sit still, sit at attention, and after awhile, see nothing, hear nothing, think nothing, like the three little brown monkeys in the Japanese store on 125th Street where they made those wonderful rice cakes. . . . Pop had wanted him to go to work; Mom wanted him to go to school. Pop wanted him to go to work because he was a *folentzer,* an idler, a sloth; Mom wanted him to go to school to become an *edel mensh,* a refined person. But look what had happened to him already. Mr. Lennard had gone to college; he was an *edel mensh.* But look what he did. Tried to pull both of them off right in the eighth-grade homeroom. You had to think about that. And why did it happen to you, that and so much else? It happened to you because of the one who cherished you so much and you clung to: Mom. She moved you to Irish Harlem, so she could live in the front, yes—and she acquiesced that day, that day, that day, that morning, that morning, she acquiesced: oh boy, oh, boy. O-o-oh! "That grin will get you into trouble," said Mr. O'Reilly. And if he knew what kind of trouble—never mind—and yesterday, Mr. Lennard. So who was right? Who was better? Even thinking about it made him—like he was double: as it did just now: self-despising—and at the same time, stuck to what made him self-despising. Wait till Sunday, oh, boy! Wait till Sunday. Bolshewitskies. Bolshewhiskeys. Who cared, one way or the other?

On assembly days, periods were shortened, made shorter still by little written quizzes, quizzes exchanged with classmates, who graded them according to the right answers to be found in the book or written on the blackboard by the teacher. The quizzes were graded, often grinned at in collusion, and returned. He was just no good in commercial studies, that was all. Even Farley was better than he was in Gregg shorthand, in touch-typing, in bookkeeping. Farley won commendation from Mr. Sullivan, who just couldn't find words harsh enough to give vent to his exasperation at Ira's sheer stupidity, his total incompetence at comprehending the rudiments of bookkeeping. Again, he didn't care. It was always money, money, money. Business, *beezeniss.* Oh, all the time.

The noon gong sounded at last. At the word "Dismissed," Ira seized his strap of books and tore down to the basement in the van of the class—then sped out into the street. He hadn't brought any lunch; no need to: He'd tear open one of those boxes of— what did they call them? Arrowroot—first chance he got. Oh. Tomorrow on the delivery truck, it would all wear off. And Sunday—his pace quickened—Sunday morning, there was Sunday morning. And after awhile, Mom returning with bagels and lox or smoked whitefish. Sunday morning delicacies. Yeh, yeh, yeh. Sunday morning delicacies— Wasn't he crazy? Wear it off and wear it on again. But then he could run away from it, could run afterward right over to Farley's house. The whole thing would wear off again, would be absorbed by Farley's cheeriness, Farley's buoyancy.

XXV

He turned into quiet 126th Street, westbound. Even from half a block away he could see Murphy's truck, the old White; but as he approached the side entrance to the store, he spied a forbidding-looking man, powerful, authoritative, posted beside the truck. Impassively, he watched Ira open the door, enter, waver at the sight of still another burly stranger inside. Ira scampered down the stairs: Mr. Klein was there—

"I got here on time, didn't I?"

"Nice, very nice," Mr. Klein spoke, munching a sandwich.

"Hey, who's those guys?" Ira thumbed upward.

"Never mind. You stay right here."

"You told me already ten times." Ira shoved his books under the counter.

"No becktalks!" Mr. Klein brought out his formidable rejoinder. "Those fellers are from the government. Prohibition agents. They work only by the wine and whiskey. Upstairs. Outside. Downstairs. The same thing. *Ferstest?* They got their work; we got to load these beskets. We're still going to be open two, three months. Let's see you be a whiz-beng, like yesterday." With sandwich in hand, he reached out for the sheaf of yellow invoices; then, with sandwich clamped between jaws, slid grocery items toward Ira—

Toward Ira—who grinned.

"So what's so funny?" Mr. Klein removed his sandwich. "Those four items go together. Here, these four—the box ladyfingers, the two pounds apricots, sticks cinnamon, kadota figs, that's all together with the bag sugar.

"So what's so funny?" Mr. Klein repeated.

"You and your sandwich."

"Why? It's good corned beef."

"It makes you talk like corned beef."

"Oh, a *kleege,* hey? On a day like this you eat like you can. You shoulda been in France. That's how we ate at the front. That's how we ate. That's how we kept from dying of hunger under fire. Out a' cans. They called them—what the hell'd they call them—you're gettin me sidetrecked. I forget already. You see? Something lousy you don't wanna remember. Now, wild rice—we scraped out the cans sometimes scraped 'em right out, crusted like gunk, *treife* like hell. Who cared? Anything to eat when you're in the trenches. Understand? So a sandwich maybe I hold like a dog a bone; it's funny—to you." Something harried closed momentarily like a shutter over his features. "What's gettin' into me? What did I give you just then?"

"I didn't look."

"You should always look. What're you here for?" He peered down into the hamper. "Two pounds walnuts."

"My uncle came home from the army—"

"Oh, you had an uncle in the army. Olives. Here's capers. That makes two jars. The eggs stay out separate. Heng on. It's a whole bacon—"

"My uncle came home. He was a mess sergeant first—"

"Oh, he was a mess sergeant *noch*—"

"Then he was a reggeleh sergeant. So my aunt gave him a glass of seltzer—" Ira stopped. The stalwart stranger in the fedora he had seen yesterday was accompanying Murphy, wheeling a noisy handcart to the street elevator. "Is Quinn here, too? And Tommy? I didn't see the new big White."

"They'll be here soon. And Shea too. Nobody took a full load today. That's why—" He used the last of his sandwich to point at the mountain of groceries on the zinc-sheathed table. "You saw somebody outside?"

"Yeah, and inside another one. Gee, big like an ox." Ira stole glances at Murphy and his escort, as the two ascended in the cellar-to-street elevator. In a few seconds their legs disappeared, but even before that, as the elevator platform rose, Ira caught whiffs of the sickly smell of whiskey. He could see the jagged edges of broken bottles lying on their side in the dark, shallow bilge in the elevator sump. "I can tell what I got to do tomorrow."

"What? Oh." Mr. Klein described the object of Ira's gaze. "Maybe it's gonna be done today. If Mr. Stiles sees it."

"So how'm I gonna stop an' do it today?"

"I didn't say you." Mr. Klein plied Ira with groceries. "They could highjeck the whole load. You know what we got here? For a bunch gengsters to highjeck is what we got here."

"What?"

"Bist tocken a yoldt. Go ahead. Peck. English marmalade. Uh! Look at that! Snails. A *mishigoss.* I saw them in France. I thought only a Frenchman—"

"I know. And we got frogs' legs too."

"Peck!" Mr. Klein raised his voice.

"All right, all right. So why was the guard standing by Murphy's truck?" Ira demanded. "And the guy inside?"

"Maybe now you'll begin to understand something. Here. Pay attention. This sugar goes with the other order, the one I just gave you."

"I'm the one paying attention. You're not."

"No becktalks I said! There's a guy up there with a pistol. He's a Prohibition agent, I told you. The other guys, too. They all got guns. That's enough. We'll talk from something else. We'll never get finished."

"Oh, boy." Ira sighed.

"You're enjoying yourself, or what?"

"I am?"

"Nu. Hustle. Hustle. This is curry. You got six things that go with it. English marmalade. Not too tight. Guerkins, jerkins. Almond paste. Buckwheat groats. You see why Jews don't buy from Park and Tilford. You know what buckwheat groats are? Plain *kasha.* And costs five times more."

"Yech!"

"What do you mean, yech? *Kasha?* With chicken *schmaltz.* What could be better? That's all they eat in the Russian army. Here's sugar. Did you fast on Yom Kippur?"

"Me? Never. I just take off from school. You?"

Mr. Klein's answer was a barely tolerant look. "Here's a big order: eight, nine items." His eyes traveled from invoice to hamper. "Put 'em all over here on this side. Coffee. Two cans pineapple. What's this?" He squeezed the small brown bag. "Ginger root. Peckage melba toast. Marrons glacés. Jar pâté de . . ."

Mr. MacAlaney, blond assistant manager, came down the stairs, sniffed with wry face, his sharp, blue eyes behind his glasses seeking the source of the odor of alcohol, located it. He stepped close to the elevator sump for confirmation, then getting his key ring out of his pocket, went to the icebox. He came back a minute later with a prim expression on his face, and a pink, sensuous globe of fruit in his hand.

"What's that?" Ira turned to Mr. Klein, as Mr. MacAlaney climbed up the stairs. "That fruit."

"Mengo. Mengo," said Mr. Klein.

"Mengo?" Ira tried to match the word with anything he had ever heard or read.

"Don't eat it. You can puke from it. Here: a bottle Lea and Perrins. Pimentos, a jar, George Washington coffee, a jar—"

Not only Murphy and his stalwart escort came down the stairs but Quinn and Tommy too. "Hey!" he and Ira greeted each other. Tommy winked broadly, and he and Quinn followed Murphy toward the vault.

"So far, it's not bad. One besket's nearly full." Mr. Klein stopped long enough from handing out groceries to look at his watch. "Only two o'clock. You'd still be in school yet."

"Yeah, my Spanish period. I nearly forgot."

"Forgot what? The Spanish? Here's the last item: asparagus tips."

Glowering, Ira tucked away the item, found subterfuge. "I forgot to bring my lunch."

"So whose fault is that?" And after a few seconds, "You stay here." Mr. Klein went into the aisles, brought back a box of Lorna

Doones, opened them and put them under the table. Ira stuffed two at a time into his mouth. They were grainy; they made him thirsty. "Can I get a drink?"

Mr. Klein indicated the utility sink with nod of brow. "Come right beck."

Ira opened the faucet wide to let the water rush cool, and as he reached for a paper cup, Quinn came out of the toilet next to the sink. He smelled strongly of liquor. "I gotta ask Klein somethin'," he said, and both returned to the counter.

"Hey, Klein," Quinn slouched, willowy. "You were in Belleau Wood, weren't you?"

"Château-Thierry. Argonne." Klein replied in clipped tone of voice. And to Ira: "All right. New besket."

"I thought you were in Belleau Wood."

"No. I had enough with Château-Thierry and Argonne." Unsmiling, Mr. Klein signaled for Ira to give him a hand; they dragged the full basket to one side.

Quinn kept talking: "I had a buddy—his name was Schein, Abe Schein. Like Klein. Tallest Jew I ever seen, taller than I am, lots. Jesus, he was lanky. We called him Shnitzel for the hell of it. Shnitz. He was always talkin' Torah, Torah. You remember Christmas Eve, remember? I told you somethin' about him." he addressed Ira. "It's in the Torah. Sometimes I'd kid him: Hey Shnitz, does the Torah tell you how to fade the dice?"

"You told me that already."

"I did, didn't I?" Once again, Quinn assumed the same strange posture he had taken when he waited for Ira to scramble off the rear end of the big White: He locked the fingers of both hands together, knuckles upward, his gray eyes fixed on remoteness: With locked hands so low in front of him, there was no telling whether he was praying or despairing.

"*Shoyn shicker,*" Mr. Klein muttered under his breath. "All right," he rustled the yellow sheaf aggressively. "We got first: lobster. Small ken. Jar, cheddar in wine, the one closed with the wire—"

"Wouldn't go to a whore. 'Why don't you git frenched,' I sez. 'You say it's against yer religion to lay 'em. Try that. That ain't layin 'em.' 'Go away,' he sez. 'Fer Christ sake, the Heinies might pick you off t'morrow. A guy tall as you. You stand out woise'n a second-louie in his Sam Brown belt— Git yer piece some way.' Nope. Torah. Torah. Jumpin' Jesus."

"Mint jelly, a gless." Mr. Klein kept his voice raised. "Coffee, a beg. Sugar. Cubes beef consommé—Where is it?"

"It's that tin box."

"You see? You're really smart already. I thought it was crystallized ginger. *Shicker auf toit*," he directed a subdued aside at the stooping Ira.

Quinn pressed his locked hands further down. "You know how you go up to the front. Klein, you an' your buddy, side by side— Yer in a long file. You oughta know."

"I know. I know already," Mr. Klein said abruptly.

"It pays to be a short guy like you," said Quinn. "You ain't no runt. But Shnitzel, he'd make anybody—"

"I know what you're goin' to tell me! All right?" Mr. Klein interrupted, all but snappish.

"Yeah, but he didn't make a sound, Klein," Quinn's voice burred harshly. "Not a fuckin' sound." Quinn suddenly sucked in his breath. "I never knew where he went. I never knew when he went. We wuz talkin' about different things. Not a goddamn tree in sight, blown to hell. What a pity he sez. Like they wuz innocent. An' me about the thirteen-, fourteen-year-old kids here gittin' free lays in gay Paree from married women with hot pants whose hubbies were at the front—"

"All right!" Mr. Klein said with explosive emphasis. "I gotta get these orders out. What's the use talkin' about it? We've been through it. We lived it. The mortar shells, the machine guns. So who needs more? Quinn, it's a big Saturday tomorrow. Like Thenksgiving nearly, and with no help. Some other time."

"Okay. But I been talkin' to Shnitzel ever since. A harp an' a Jew. But he was my buddy an' the way he went, it was like he was gone an' never left me. Been different if I'd seen him get his. But this way—"

"Okay. So what're you gonna do? It happened to everybody nearly."

"Not this way."

"All right, not this way. So a sniper got him. You tell yourself once and for all a sniper got him." Mr. Klein's vehemence turned on Ira. "Where were we on the orders?"

"Yeah, hey, Shnitz! Hey!" Quinn unclasped his hands. "Tell me about them thirty-six holy men that has to be here. Ah, Jesus." He made for the outside stairs.

Mr. Klein turned to Ira. "Where were we on the orders?"

"Nonpareils, you gave me a box of nonpareils."

"Nonpareils," Mr. Klein began, consulted the invoice, and looked up—looked up, and kept his eyes fixed in pained wonder. Above the noise of the rolling handtruck, while Murphy pushed the load of steel-strapped boxes, he and the stalwart agent escorting him were engaged in loud dispute.

"*Oy, gewald,*" Mr. Klein growled, all but inaudibly. "*Sit zan du khoisakh.* C'mon. Take! Here is a bottle maple syrup, Oregon prunes, two pounds—"

XXVI

It seemed that Murphy and the agent accompanying him behind the rolling handtruck were furious with each other. They weren't at all. Their loud voices were raised, but not in wrath—in uncompromising disagreement. "I'm tellin' youz, youz wuz." Murphy pressed the elevator button.

"How the hell could you tell it was me. It was night and a dark one, too," contended the Prohibition agent. "It was pitch dark. Only light we had was a starshell. We didn't light a match. We bummed lights off each other's smokes."

"That's right. Cigarette end, only light we had. That's why it took me so long to figure out it was you: your voice. An' your build, maybe. You wuz a captain, wuzn't you?"

"Maybe. I was a major at the end. What the hell's that got to do with it?"

"I'm tryin' to tell ye." Murphy watched the elevator platform descend. "All right, fergit it. You wuzn't there."

"Yes, but the whole goddamned Argonne. You know how many American troops were in that battle?"

"All right, I'm wrong." As the elevator platform settled at floor level, Murphy hunched to shove the handtruck aboard, stopped. "You wuz in the Boer War, right? You wuz a soldier o' fortune you said. You wuz a private. Remember tellin' us that big kick you got givin' the compliments o' General Kitchener to majors an' colonels, an' havin' 'em salutin' you?"

The stalwart Prohibition agent seemed to become rigid, motionless, his eyes never leaving Murphy's face. "Well, I'll be goddamned!"

"You fought that big Jew. When you were with the Rough Riders in Cuba." Murphy pressed on. "You said all the romance is gone out a' war. Wasn't that what you said?"

"Were you in that same big shellhole?" the stalwart man's face seemed gray under the cellar's unshaded incandescents, as if the burden of the coincidence taxed all his credulity. "There must have been a hundred of us pinned down that night."

"I'm tellin' ye." Murphy thrust the handtruck forward.

"Wait a minute. Get that box too," said the Prohibition agent.

"Yeah. Quinn, you comin'?"

Quinn left the side of the table, walked over, picked up the box Tommy had just brought, and joined the others on the elevator platform. Murphy tapped the elevator button on the side of the wall, and all three ascended out of sight. They left behind a strange kind of atmosphere in the cellar, something Ira had never felt before: an intrusion of danger, a peculiar imminence of past peril.

"Come on!" Mr. Klein cried angrily. "Wake up. Tonight is *Shabbes b'nakcht*. All right, so you don't have to be *erlikh*. But the candles your mother lights, no?— Listen, Tommy, do me a favor: go beck to strepping the rest of the boxes."

"All right. Don't git huffy," Tommy answered.

"Go beck! I wanna finish here by closing time. The whole day is one big headache already." Acrimony held Mr. Klein in its grip. *"Oy, a shvartz yur!* To get something done with these Irish *shickerim,"* he lamented as soon as Tommy turned his back. "Come! Two cans French-cut string beans. Grenadine syrup, a bottle. Van Camp's. Chicken à la king, three cans. Sugar. Move." Mr. Klein kept passing groceries. "Look what you're doin'!" he chided.

"Yeh, yeh, I am." Ira retorted, but he couldn't get the ominous feeling out of his mind.

"If they don't find them items in the beskets when they deliver tomorrow, you know who they'll blame?" Mr. Klein thrust his head forward in harassment. "Me, not you. So—"

"Yeah, but I'm putting 'em in right! You can see I am."

"All right," he conceded. "Those guys get me upset, it's terrible. I'm in that—in that *shlakht haus* again. Once, a shell hit so close, I didn't know my own name for two days. Did I give you the tarragon vinegar?"

"Yeah."

"So that finishes that slip." He put the invoice behind the others. "I'm gonna take a leak. I don't want you to move from the table, you hear? You're the shipping clerk." He gave Ira the sheaf of invoices. "Every clerk upstairs writes different. But you got a Jewish *kupf.* So figure out. I don't wanna lose no more time. This day should be over, *Oy!"* He left.

Was that the way war felt? Ira couldn't shake the sense of foreboding as he tried to decipher the scrawl on the invoice. Killing. Battle. What did he say? No romance—

"Hey, Irey! Hey, kid!" The cry came from the street: It was Murphy's voice.

"Yeah!" Ira yelled.

"Push the button, will ye? The down button."

Ira hurried to the elevator, pressed the lower button. "OK," he yelled.

The elevator descended, three men aboard it, Quinn, Murphy, the tall stalwart Prohibition agent, the one who had been at Argonne. But now their demeanor had changed. They were jovial, friendly.

"There's nothin' like a good slug o' booze to make you forget," said Quinn.

"Or remember, too," Murphy rejoined, barely humorous as was his wont. "By Jesus, I don't think I ever woulda remembered. Hey, I remember! Didn't you say, 'What's the use? You chew tobacco an' spit the juice.' "

"Yeah. Hard to believe. I thought that night never would pass," the agent puffed on his cigarette, offered the pack to the others. "Talk about steady machine-gun fire. They knew we were in there. If our mortars hadn't opened up in the morning, and that barrage—say, I recognize your voice now." He went into a gale of laughter, bent over, coughed cigarette smoke, wheezed with laughter again. "If that wasn't the funniest goddamn story I ever heard! It's still funny."

"That was me, all right." Murphy pushed the handtruck off the elevator. The others followed.

"What the hell was so funny I don't know," said the agent. "Every time somebody asked you what it felt like at the end of that rope, we'd go off." He laughed again, head back, laughter full and prolonged. "The Germans could hear us. We didn't give a damn." He laughed again.

Quinn laughed. Murphy began to laugh too. He was a short man but tough in mien, with a rocky jaw and long arms. He banged the handtruck. His normally fair skin suffused: "A rough sea, ye know, an' night, an' about ten guys over me yellin', 'Git goin'!' An' there ain't a goddamn lifeboat under me or nothin'. Black water, that's all. The whole fuckin' ocean."

The wooden boxes on the handtruck in his hands shook, as if in lieu of mirth—to which the roaring merriment of the other two men added dimension.

The laughter continued. Ira, too, was infected. It really was funny. He lifted his face, grinning appreciatively toward the laughing faces above him, saw the Prohibition agent's countenance turn sober, heard him say with quiet urgency: "Where is it, Murph?"

"Back o' the icebox. The big locked one."

"Hope it's good."

"Bushmill. Johnny Walker. Haig."

The agent whistled between his teeth: "You don't miss a trick."

"Not when it's all P and T."

"Any man deserves a sup o' poteen after bein' dipped in the drink," said Quinn. "There's more Lily cups at the sink."

"Right." The agent swallowed. "I'm McCrory." He took a few steps toward the stairs. "Craig, will you come down here?"

"Okay, Major." The beefy, short-necked man appeared.

"That's Murphy. That's Quinn. Remember the story I told you about standing in the mud in a helluva big shell crater all night? There's the soldier hanging from a rope when his troopship was torpedoed?" He pointed at Murphy. "Would you believe it?"

"No!" And once again a roar of laughter.

"Ira!" Mr. Klein's angry shout was loud enough to be heard through the swelling guffaw—and stern enough to frighten Ira.

"Here. I'm coming!"

"I told you not to leave the place, didn't I?" Mr. Klein's impatient glare tracked Ira returning. "You didn't peck a thing. Look, it's the same slip."

"You took so long," Ira countered.

"So you shoulda done more!"

"They called me to the elevator. To get it down," Ira answered.

Under fretful eyebrows lowered over the invoices, Mr. Klein seemed to be trying to block out the view of the group near the elevator. "*A shvartz gelekhter,*" he growled. "Here, take: three bottles Perrier water."

"They were in a shellhole together," Ira said.

"Six Knox gelatin."

"The one who's going in the back now is a major. I heard Murphy tell him—"

"Pay attention!" Mr. Klein scolded.

"Oh, Jesus!" Ira muttered rebelliously.

"Three cans pie cherries. Take. *Gib dikh a rick.* Salt water teffy. Another dozen eggs—beck on the counter. Extract cloves. Smoked kippers, six cans. Gluten bread. Coffee, cocktail onions, a jar—"

"You ain't givin' me a chance to pack," Ira complained.

"All right. No becktalks." Nevertheless, Mr. Klein slowed down—slightly. "If you knew what I feel, you'd do everything on the double. It's not enough once for them to be in that murder? Murder, and mud, and rats!"

One after the other, each of the four agents took turns walking around the opposite end of the cellar, even the agent supervising Tommy—and Tommy himself, and Murphy and Quinn. *"Shick-erim!"* said Mr. Klein. *"A brukh uf zeh!* Look! Look! Three on that elevator, and a double load whiskey." He scowled at the elevator creaking upward. "This is Prohibition? *S' toigt shoyn uf a kapura."* He slapped his own cheek with the sheaf of invoices: "What am I worrying about? Let Park and Tilford worry. Baker's chocolate. Hearts of palm. Butterscotch sauce. Coffee. Sugar. Yams, two cans. That's another besket."

Under Mr. Klein's forceful dispensing, they made good progress. The second hamper for the customers was full and pulled out of the way alongside the first: They would be Quinn's and Tommy's delivery stint for tomorrow. The summit of the mountain of groceries on the counter had subsided considerably, subsided to a widespread heap. Now to fill Murphy's big hamper for the east Bronx. That would leave only Shea's smaller basket to take care of. Shea's smaller basket was rarely filled all the way to the top, its contents destined for local stops.

"Oh, what has become o' hinky dinky, *parlez-vous?* Oh, what has become of all the Jewish soldiers, too?" Quinn sang as he came down the stairs from the street— "All the sons of Abraham are eatin' ham fer Uncle Sam, hinky dinky—" He passed in front of the table. "Them trucks're goddamn near down on their springs," he said out of the side of his mouth—and walked around toward the iceboxes. "Hinky, dinky, *parlez-vous."*

XXVII

"Ira," Mr. MacAlaney called down from the top of the stairs leading up to the store. "You down there?"

"Yes, sir."

"You know what the Camembert cheese looks like?"

"Yes, sir. It's in a round wooden box."

"Bring up a box."

Conscious of Mr. Klein's stern look following him, Ira left the table for the icebox. Quinn was there, and Tommy with a bottle of beer. At the sight of Ira, Quinn allowed himself a chuckle. Tommy proffered his bottle. "I can't," Ira grabbed one of the quaint wooden boxes of Camembert, "Mr. MacAlaney is waiting."

"Don't be a prick like Klein," Tommy's lips curled jaggedly, so Irish in crooked truculence. "Taste it. You ain't a Jew like them others. Remember what I told you Christmas when we were deliverin'?"

"Ye'll never git another chance," Quinn rubbed his eyelids. "Not after today. Imported lager like that. Home brew'll be all that's around. Shnitz used to say it's the only beer good enough for them thirty-six holy men that keeps the world goin'."

"Hebrew an' Homebrew," Tommy quipped.

"Try it, Irey," Quinn prodded.

Ira took a swallow, burbled lips in distaste, hurried off, their laughter trailing him. He climbed up the first steps, stopped short: on the top of the stairs, next to glinty-eyed Mr. MacAlaney waiting for his parcel, Mr. Stiles was talking to Harvey, who was leaning on the handle of his wide dry-mop. "No, I want you to do it this time," Mr. Stiles was saying to Harvey. "Get the glass outta there. What is there? Three or four bottles broken. You can smell it all the way up to the store. There's a law too about minors handling alcohol," he concluded impatiently. "And with that elevator going up and down, he'll forget to watch himself. You do it this time. I don't want any trouble."

"Yes, sir."

"I'll be glad when the stuff's out of here." Frowning, Mr. Stiles turned away.

Only too keenly aware of his own yeasty breath, Ira kept his head lowered, held up the box of Camembert, wished it smelled more, and as soon as Mr. MacAlaney relieved him of it, retreated down the steps. "Hoo!" he sighed noisily, returning to the table.

"*Oy, a shvartz yur!*" Mr. Klein exploded. "What have you been drinking? You stink like a *vershtinkeneh* zoo!"

"Tommy gave me some beer."

"You're a minor. You're a schoolboy. You could get everybody in trouble! I told you to stay away."

"It was only a taste."

"Mr. Stiles should catch you! He'd give you a taste. He'd fire you."

"Tommy's drinking. Everybody!" Ira flared up.

"It's none of your business. You're working with me. Eat another cracker. I should see this booze outta here already."

Quinn came around and headed for the elevator: "Take it easy, Klein," he grinned indulgently. "Don't git your bowels in an uproar. We'll be skidooin' outta here soon. Oh, mademoiselle from gay Paree, *parlez-vous.* Oh, mademoiselle from gay Paree, what a hell o' dose she gave to me, hinky, dinky, *parlez-vous.* Them fuckin' snipers. How come Shnitzel took a drink an' you don't, Klein?" He grinned, made for the elevator pit. And reaching the wall, he lifted his hand to the wall-button: "Hey, up der! Ready for me to bring her down?"

"Hold 'er a second till I git the truck on," came Murphy's answering cry.

"Say when," Quinn waited with upraised hand.

His displeasure smoldering on his dark features, Harvey came down the stairs, crossed in front of the table.

"You gonna go under the elevator?" Ira asked.

Harvey fixed Ira with an irritated glance, kept on his way.

"Gee, he's sore," Ira said under his breath. "He's gotta do my job, I bet."

"No, it's whiskey bottles on the bottom," Mr. Klein admonished sharply. "Pay attention. A peckage rusk. A peckage pralines. A whole Gouda—" he sniffed it. "It's all right. We can peck it with the rest. It's local. *Haguda.*" He handed the string-bound cheese to Ira. "You know from the *haguda? Mah nishtanu he laila hazeh?*"

Harvey reappeared carrying the familiar bucket and flat shovel—as the cry came from the street: "Let 'er go, Quinn."

"Ever see Senegalese troops, Major?" Murphy raised his voice above the creak of the elevator beginning its descent.

"Senegalese? You mean black Senegalese? I may have. I saw about every kind in France."

"They look like monkeys in frog uniforms."

Quinn tilted his head slowly in oblique look at Harvey.

"I don't think I ever saw 'em in action?" Two pairs of knees came into view.

"Action. That's a good one!" At hip-level, Murphy shifted the handtruck. His uproarious laugh crested the elevator's drone. "Weren't they corkers! We'd have 'em on our right, and as soon as the Heinies knew they had the Senegalese in front, they'd attack. You never heard such a squealin' an' scramblin'. They'd leave a hole big enough fer a regiment."

"Is that right?"

"Maybe they're runnin' yet." Murphy's rocky face came into view under the elevator lintel. "They could be all the way to Africa—" He spied Harvey waiting with bucket and shovel—and cleared his throat with a peculiar sound, as if he were warning the major—who was already aware. For a moment or two only the elevator's creak was heard in descent, and then when the platform was still inches from the cellar floor, Murphy shoved the handtruck forward. Steel wheels banged on concrete. "It's okay, Harv. I was just talkin'."

"You're talkin' about colored people. They just as brave as any white man." Already annoyed by the prospect of his task, Harvey's features became like basalt. The nails on his outspread fingers gleamed. "I've seen lots o' whites shit in their pants when they come under fire. Don't tell me about bein' brave. The enemy fired at us. We fired at them."

"All right," said the major. "Harvey is your name? It's all right, Harvey. It's just one of those misunderstandings. But no point getting worked up about it. He didn't mean to insult you. He didn't know you were around."

"I get sick of you white smart-asses like him." Harvey still trained his ivory eyes on Murphy. "Makin' fun of us, like we were yellow. I wore a U.S. uniform. I was infantry like you. Fourteenth Infantry Regiment. You never heard about us retreatin' 'thout orders."

"Who the hell wuz talkin' about you!"

"You wuz talkin' about colored."

"I wuz talkin' about Senegalese."

"That's colored!"

"The hell with you!" said Murphy. "What d'ye want me to do? Kiss yer ass?"

"The hell with you!" Harvey retorted.

Both men had raised their voices. "See? What'd I tell you?" Mr. Klein rasped. *Sit balt sein du a malkhumah.*

The two angry men could be heard throughout the cellar. The youthful, tow-haired agent in the vault with Tommy came forward, with Tommy trailing him, and the short-necked man on the stairs came partway down.

"Let's cut it out," the major said curtly. His voice was restrained, and his forefinger moved like a dial between the two adversaries. "Both of you. We'll all be in hot water in a minute. You better watch the noise. The store is still open."

"I don't want to get in no hot water, Major. I just came over to do what Mr. Stiles told me: clean out the broken bottles down in de pit."

"All right, it's all yours." The major put one foot on the elevator platform, raised his face to call up into the late-afternoon sky: "Everything okay up there, Ordwin?"

"Yes, sir," came the response from the street.

"When's that Model-T driver due back?" the Major spoke to Mr. Klein.

"Shea? He should be beck already. It's efter five."

"What's keeping the man?" The major stepped aside to allow Harvey to press one of the elevator buttons, and frowning, watched the ascending elevator platform block off all view of the outdoors.

"*Gott sei dank,* the trucks are upstairs in the street, not down here," Mr. Klein said in a dry undertone.

"Down here? The trucks?" Ira repeated, sure of his wonder at the absurdity.

"Why do you think there's a Prohibition man in beck of the door," Mr. Klein demanded—and without waiting for an answer: "He protects a flenk. *Sit a sakh helfin*," he added. "You know there's bottle goods up there in the trucks cost twice what I get a week, one bottle?" With the orders in Shea's hamper nearly all packed away, Mr. Klein allowed himself to relax. "Thet was before Prohibition. So what will it cost now?"

"You mean those dirty old bottles I used to see through that little window?" Ira hoped his ignorance would prolong the brief recess.

"Those dirty old bottles, yeh: chempagne. You know what is chempagne: Mouton and Lafite and Rothschild? Esk the *alter kocker* upstairs in the wing-collar. He'll tell you."

"So what?"

"*Oy, gewald!*" Mr. Klein arched backward in despair. "So what?"

"You mean somebody'll try t'take 'em?" Ira demanded, miffed at being so uncharitably found mystified.

"You never heard from hijeckers? *Shlemiel!*"

"Lorring," the major called toward the liquor vault. "I want all the rest stacked in front of the elevator ready to go. Get me?"

"Yes, sir."

"Would you two, and that young fellow in there, pull everything out here?" the major addressed Quinn and Murphy. "Set it right here, will you? Okay, Lorring," he called again. "You know what to do."

"Yes, sir."

"Where is that man?" Still frowning, the major turned to Mr. Klein.

"I don't know. The Model T sometimes—he has trouble."

"We should have been out of here by now." The major glanced down at Harvey in the elevator sump shoveling glass and murky water into the bucket, pursed his lips in a silent, reflective whistle. "We've been in the neighborhood too damned long. If he has trouble, we could have a lot of it." He strode over to the stairs, climbed up.

"Now there's three up there." Ira felt a not unpleasant vertigo of tension. "You don't think anything is goin' to happen?" He stopped to listen to the conversation.

"You know, Harv, I got nothin' against you. You're all right." Murphy didn't seem unsteady. He raised his arm and rested his hand against the wall, under the elevator switches. "But the trouble with some o' you boys is—I don't mean you—just because you had a little French pussy over there, you start struttin' aroun'. Them French floosies just thought youz wuz Yanks wit' a deep tan."

"Yeah. You're right, Murphy." Harvey's accommodating laugh belied the deeply sober eyes lifted up toward Murphy's arm. "Yee-hee-hee! That's right."

"You're damn right," said Murphy. "You know I don't git along good wit' people sometimes because I don't softsoap 'em. I don't give a fuck what color they are. I coulda made sergeant three times over if I'da brown-nosed."

"I know, Murphy. You don't have to tell me. I know that the first time I saw you." Placating in tone, Harvey kept his eyes rolled upward.

"Just because I'm short, some people think I'm a pushover. Shit, it wuz jist because I wuz a runt, everybody picked on me when I was a kid. I had to learn how to fight, you know what I mean?"

"Ain't that the truth?" said Harvey.

"So if I sez dem Senegalese wuz yeller, dem sons o' whores wuz yeller." He slapped the wall. "Dey couldn't fight der way into a crowded bar."

"Man, you're gettin' too close to them switches." Harvey no longer feigned negligence. The timbre of his voice became peculiarly rich—and vibrant. "You better get your hand away from that wall, and let me finish before I get outta here."

"Yeah?" Murphy tapped the down button. The elevator jarred in preliminary movement. He tapped the up button. "I'll tell ye somethin' else: Some bright colonel put some you guys in them same monkey uniforms them Senegals had on, thinkin' to give the Heinie a surprise. He attacked." Murphy thumped the elevator button, reversed it. "Those guys scrambled outta the trenches so fast, you couldn't see 'em fer the dust. Hell, they must be runnin' yet." He thumped the elevator buttons again.

The shovel left leaning against the ledge, Harvey clambered out to the cellar floor. He stood head and shoulders above Murphy. "I ain't looking for no trouble, Murphy. I ain't looking for no fight. But I tell you, man, I ain't running away from it. I'm ready any time you is. Any place."

"You better run upstairs," Mr. Klein nudged Ira. "No! No! Get that shavetail. Tell him there's trouble."

But they could already hear the major's voice on the stairs as he came hurrying down: "What the hell's happening to that elevator?" He took in the situation at a glance. "You men at it again? I'm really surprised. I'd think, by God, you two men would know better. You were soldiers. But you're acting like—like half-grown kids. Men who wore the same uniform. Who fought the same war. Who fought for the same cause, for the same ideals—and died for it, your own buddies: freedom and democracy. And remember we won it. We won it! You going to throw it all away down here in this damned cellar?"

"I wasn't looking for no fight, Major. I told the man."

"I know it, Harvey." The major's chin pressed down grimly on his chest. "Sometimes we say too damned much we don't mean. Come on, Murph, come on, both of you." He put his arms about both men's shoulders, and as all three walked in front of the table and around: "Let's hear that story again, Murph. Anybody doesn't get a laugh out of that's never been in a shellhole." They disappeared in the direction of the iceboxes.

"Put everything on top. All the rest," Mr. Klein ordered wearily. "He'll find it. Wait. Let me make sure. It's the lest one: cayenne pepper, yes?"

"It's here," said Ira.

"Knockbrod, Swedish, a peckage. White raisins, two pounds. Sage, a box. Onion flakes, a box. Mocha java, they want in the bean." He felt the bag. "Sugar. Turkish paste. Two cans button mushrooms. All right. What's this box coriander doing here?" He clucked in annoyance, "A day like this could heppen anything." He tossed the box into the hamper. "Coriander." He shuffled the invoices into a neat batch, slipped them under the open clip of the clipboard, and screwed up his face into a yawn—just as a burst of laughter came from the aisle where the iceboxes stood, where Murphy was retelling the story.

Tommy pushed the loaded handtruck up to the elevator pit; behind came the towheaded agent, Lorring, dragging an open crate of assorted straw-covered bottles. "Where's Murphy?" he called to Mr. Klein. "The elevator ain't down. Didn't I hear the major?"

Mr. Klein silently thumbed in the direction of the iceboxes.

"Okay, men, let's unload her. Pile 'em here."

There was a stir on the stairs. Shea came down. "I couldn't get that goddamn hunka tin started fer love or money. I blew out the fuel lines. I took out the plugs—"

"Oh, Major," the towheaded agent called toward the other end of the cellar. "That last driver's here!"

"Oh, is he? Okay." The major appeared, and with him, Harvey and Murphy, now grinning at each other.

"Where they keepin' it?" Shea sidled over to Mr. Klein.

"I know like my grendmother," Mr. Klein replied testily. "In beck from the icebox someplace. Esk Tommy."

"I'll find it," Shea moved toward the icebox aisle.

"Who's gonna drive those trucks to the warehouse?" asked Mr. Klein rhetorically. "The agents. Or who? Ever see such a *mishigoss*? Now all is needed is highjeckers."

"Thanks, Harvey." The major lifted his hand to the elevator button as Harvey pulled the shovel up from the ledge. "That bucket all right down there?"

"Yes, sir, Major. That bucket's too low to touch."

"Okay, Harold," the major called up. "We're bringing her down. Hit that button, will you—I almost said soldier."

"Right, Major."

"I'll tell ye somethin', Harvey," Murphy rocked slightly, spoke with muzzily contorted features. "When you climbed outta that hole, it all come back, you know what I mean? I was back there again, you know what I mean? An' there wuz McGrath, only guy

I could git along wit' follerin' me goin' over the top. Der was
McGrath. Big guy like you, only white."

"There's all kinds o' ways o' goin'," Harvey commented.

"Yeah. Right."

"Okay, men," said the major. "Let's pitch in while it's still light.
Everything okay up there, Harold?"

"Can't see a thing to worry about up here, Major," came the
voice from the street.

"I'm going to send Lorring up anyway. Okay, Lorring. Sentry.
Make it casual. Any car stops, take cover. Right? I'll take care of
the loading."

"Right, Major." Lorring left for the stairs.

With so many hands to transfer the load from cellar to elevator
platform, the shipment was loaded in a few minutes.

"First time I ever wished we were still on daylight saving time."
The major surveyed the load on the elevator. "Have we got the
last of it yet?"

"That's it, Major," said Murphy.

As Tommy got on the platform "Comin', Murphy?"

"Hold it," the major said. "Not this time. Last thing we want
is to get held up by a stuck elevator." He waited for Tommy to step
off. "Tell you the truth, Murphy," he raised his arm to press the
elevator button. "I'm beginning to feel like a Georgia nigger with
the sun going down on his back."

The men overhead laughed. The elevator ascending, the major
turned—to face Harvey—and was slightly taken aback. "I'm sorry,
Harvey, no harm meant. It's just a damned habit, and a bad one.
Damn!"

"That's all right, Major," said Harvey. "I understand."

"I'm glad you do." The major extended his hand.

They shook hands, parted. And just as he was about to join
the others climbing up the stairs, Quinn came down. "Where to?"
asked the major.

"The john, Major. I'm caught short."

"We're ready to go."

"Be right back." Winking at Mr. Klein's glum, averted face,
Quinn passed the counter.

The elevator platform overhead shook with the tread of those unloading it. Harvey knelt at the edge of the sump, pulled the bucket out, straightened up, and with bucket in one hand, shovel in the other, passed in front of the table. *"Comme çi, comme ça,* Miste' Klein."* His thick, limber wrist gleamed as he swung the shovel like a pendulum. Deliberately flat-footed, he shuffled a few steps: *"C'est la guerre."*

"You got a big cleanup job yet in that wine and whiskey corner. You know that?" Mr. Klein advised him, gratuitously.

"You're tellin' me? Mister Stiles got me a man-size hoe, a real he-hoe." Harvey looked at Ira. "I might need a helper too."

"Hey, Quinn, where the hell are ye!" came the cry from the street.

Quinn's voice preceded him as he rounded the corner: "Oh, the French, they are a funny race, *parlez-vous.* The French, they are a funny race—"

"Don't listen to him!" Mr. Klein swept his arm protectively toward Ira as if to brush him out of range.

"How am I gonna help it?"

"Oh, the French, they are a funny race," Quinn halted an instant as he came face-to-face with Harvey before the table: two countenances, almost at the same level, the one brown and solidly boned, the other by comparison pale and narrow.

"Quinn," Mr. Klein jerked his head toward the inner stairs leading down from the store. "Cut it out. Somebody's comin' down."

All eyes fixed on the stairs: In his tan jacket, holding the bannister, Walt skipped the last step to the cellar floor: "Boy, you can't smell the stink o' the booze for the cigarette smoke."

"They should know what's goin' on down here. It's busy upstairs."

"They're startin' to come in. Last-minute trade." Walt swung into an aisle.

"The French, they are a funny race—"

The honking of auto horns in the street almost drowned out his voice. "Hey, Quinn!"

"They'll be comin' down after you," Mr. Klein warned.

"Fuck 'em. You'd think I was hidin' in a fuckin bunker." Quinn teetered unsteadily. "The French, dey are a funny race. Dey fight wit' der feet an' fuck wit' der face—"

Against the raucous clamor of auto horns came down from the street: "Quinn!"

"Hinky dinky, *parlez-vous.*" Quinn licked the corners of his mouth, wobbled as he moved toward the stairs. "Well, the man's had a drop too much, y'know. I had to take an extra one for me Jew buddy, Shnitzel—" He mounted the stairs to the street. "Comin', comin'! Where the hell's the fire, you guys?" He climbed up out of sight.

Through the elevator shaft, from the street above, the din of racing motors peaked: to an explosion— All three ducked.

"Jesus, man!" Harvey exclaimed behind his lifted shoulder.

"O-o-h!" Ira cowered.

The two men stood rigid, motionless, eyes meeting in tense inquiry.

"Hear that?" Walt returned, hands gripping canned goods. He tossed a can on the counter; it was dented. "It's chicken à la king. I dropped it."

Another loud bang followed.

"It's nothing. It's nothing with nothing. It's a beckfire," Mr. Klein reassured.

All heads slightly tilted toward the din of racing engines above, heard gears engage, the sound of motor vehicles grinding into motion . . . The noise diminished, faded, ended.

"I told you it was nothing," said Mr. Klein.

"I bet a few of 'em musta jumped off the stools." Walt mounted the stairs.

"Only thing I ain't live through yet. I live through 'bout everything else." Harvey's face changed significantly. "What about you, Miste' Klein? What d'you take?"

Mr. Klein wagged in dour negation. "I don't take nothing. What should I take? I don't need it."

Harvey laughed suddenly, teeth gleaming in the dark height

of his features. "I don't either, Mister Klein. Just so not to lose democracy, like the major say." Swinging pail and shovel, he continued on his way.

"*A kleege shvartze,*" Mr. Klein admitted. "*Nu,*" he waved a hand in sweeping dismissal. "It's efter five o'clock. *Shabbes b'nakcht.* You know what I'm gung do?" He smacked his lips audibly. "Stay here." He stepped quickly into the aisle directly ahead, returned with a bottle. "Perrier water. It's French seltzer. It's a little warm," he brought out Lily cups and an opener from under the now bare, dented and gleaming table. "A little warm *shott nisht.* It's still good."

"It's funny seltzer," Ira expressed his reservations after a sip or two.

"Det's not seltzer, like you buy for two cents plain," Mr. Klein instructed. "This comes from the ground det way. Drink. It's like a *kiddush ha shem.*"

XXVIII

Oh, well—the loud thumping on the keys under the piano-tuner's hands, the turning of his tuning wrench, invaded Ira's consciousness: The piano-tuner had to bang them, M explained before leaving; he had to hear the beats. Oh, well, Ira listened to the notes increasing in pitch, becoming blue when visualized: He wasn't the first writer to have gone astray, gone off course, off the preplanned track. He wasn't the first, wouldn't be the last: he had written himself into a corner, exactly as cartoonists were given to depicting.

Why? Why had he departed from the script, from the first draft he had typewritten—in '79? Was that the reason? The first draft had been written five, no, it was now six years ago; had he changed that much? The first draft had stressed, crudely but more to the point, predictably, black-white confrontation, predictably, almost stereotypically. This latest, committed to the computer, had indicated reconciliation.

Why? To avoid the stereotype? Perhaps. But he didn't write that way as a rule, that consciously, cerebrally. He wrote subject to consonance with emotion, in phase with it, like the key and that piano-tuner's fork (it occurred to him). So why the departure? Was it any better? Who knew? Did it reflect an increased maturity, an increased understanding? Again who could say? Increased understanding, perhaps; but increased maturity at age seventy-nine sounded a little ludicrous. Gratifying to think so — if it was so. But if so, it was achieved at the cost of painting himself into a corner, a cul-de-sac, blind alley — you name it, Ecclesias. Things as they were changed upon the computer.

— Heaven and Wallace Stevens forgive you. My advice is: Proceed as if you hadn't departed from your original course, or not too much, and resume the track, the incidents you felt necessary to provide unity to your initial envisaging. The thing's a fake anyway; I don't mean in the sense that it's a deliberate deception. You spoke of painting yourself into a corner. You long ago painted yourself into a corner; your very premisses, not to pun, virtually hemmed you into a corner. So what is this you speak of, this present admission, recognition? A double encompassing: a circle within a corner. Nevertheless, round it out, round it out.

It's all so far away, Ecclesias. I hadn't dreamt when I began in '79, as late as '79, in the seventy-third year *de mon âge quand tous mes hontes j'ai bu,* long ago, how desiccated, to quote Baudelaire, it would all become in a few years, not unimportant, but not that important, shamefully, crushingly important. Is that the word I mean: un-important?

— It soon won't matter, these existential considerations will soon be consigned to dust.

I agree, and disagree, Ecclesias. Beyond the limit, nothing matters; the human condition no longer matters. But this side of the limit, everything matters: Israel, the sense of a folk; Mario, surrogate son, Italian — Florentine translator of my one novel — arriving in Albuquerque in a few days; poor Jane, who if anyone loved not wisely but too well, she did: my son. And pays for it now — I hope they are withdrawal symptoms — beyond all measure; has paid . . . I could sit back and dream. With that imagination with which I was endowed, churned up by or further churned up by — how the one thing ties into another! — I could conceive, I do conceive, the wildest, most erotic, wacky, and yet fully sustainable, plausible novelistic situations. I hope she herself can use her own traumas eventually in a literary way, without my, alas, dominating behest, use her woe to win plaudits, material rewards, other derivative consolations.

XXIX

A few minutes before six o'clock, Mr. Klein dismissed Ira, reminded him to get his books, and sent him on his way before the store closed: out the side entrance into the early autumn's near-sunset: Lying on curb, sidewalk, gutter, partly in the glow athwart the corner from the lights on humming Lenox Avenue, partly in ebbing twilight's lengthening shadows lay tufts and shreds of the day's activities, testimonies to Prohibition: chiefly antic stalks of straw in which the wine bottles had come wrapped that had somehow sifted through the boxes. He should have taken a leak before he left, he told himself, was on the point of going to the toilet but was distracted from his purpose by Mr. Klein's peremptory generosity in excusing him the last few minutes, perhaps to prevent him from going near the bottle still hidden there, Harvey's trove. Well, there was the park: Cut across from Fifth to Madison at the foot of the hill and duck into the Comfort Station.

So he thought. But when he reached the Comfort Station, hurriedly turned the knob of the GENTS door, it was locked. Six P.M. The need to urinate became more urgent, now that the way was barred and he kept thinking about it. He hadn't gone to the toilet since midafternoon, he realized, not since he had eaten the Lorna Doones, drunk water at the utility sink at around . . . when? Jesus, if it only were a little later: dark. He was too big to take a leak in the park. People passing, ladies—he couldn't see a cop, but maybe. Better make it snappy. Gee, that French seltzer, too. It was a big bottle, and Mr. Klein had finally persuaded him to take another swig. Cost so much. Get going. What did they say? Your teeth were floating, they said. His teeth were floating. Books tucked under arms, he began to jog. Jack and Jill climbed up the hill to fetch a pail of water—Oh, no!

Think of something else, he panted. As soon as he would get to 119th Street, duck down into a cellar, anybody's cellar: Take a leak. Between Madison and Park. Owoo. Jack and Jill went up the hill—No! Yes. That made it easier. Jill was Jack's sister. So up he got and home did trot. Yeah, yeah. He got into bed, he got into bed, he got into bed; my poor brother, she said, my poor brother, she said. . . . So . . . My poor brother, she said. Hurry up before . . . Where was their mother? Where was their father? So hurry up before: working in the delicatessen store. Puffing, he reached 119th Street. Get home. Just a little more. That holds it back. Get home before. Gee, a kid, when you could stand on the curb and pee. But now that sticking out; but even without. Hurry up! Park Avenue, yeah. Park Avenue, yeah. Under the Cut.

He was running full tilt when he reached Park Avenue, dashed under the trestle, past the cross-braced pillars: Right here; peed a hundred times here— But suddenly he had to dodge a car speeding toward him out of uptown shadows, a shadow itself without lights. He was duly cursed at by the driver—and afforded respite by his own start of fear, his own scare. Chest still heaving, he slowed his gait to a walk. All right. Nearly home.

Against the background of twilight to the east, indigo above the black band of the Third Avenue El, Weasel stood in front of the tenement stoop whirling a tin can on a loop of wire, flames spurting from vents in the bottom. Odor of woodsmoke conjured up sadly a lost state, past autumns when he'd done the same.

"I seen you runnin' in front o' the auto. You wanna look out," Weasel said. Weasel himself walked with a limp; he had tried jumping from the stoop stairs to the cellar floor, and broken his foot.

"Yeah, the bastid didn't have any lights till just before. I didn't even see him," Ira said.

"What wuz you runnin' for?"

"I had to take a leak." Ira raised his hand in parting.

"Go down the cellar," said Weasel. "Why don'tcha go down the cellar?"

"Nah, I'm nearly up to my house already."

"Go on down the cellar," said Weasel. "It's faster. Come on, I'm goin' down, too." He set his little improvised oven on the curb.

And suddenly the urgency returned—imperiously. Ira shoved the wrought-iron gate open before him, ran down the cellar steps, tore open his fly, and began urinating against the wooden, battered cellar door. Weasel followed.

XXX

I would like to finish that, Ecclesias. I have so much to do: puttering mostly: a new window fan to install; a knob to affix to the copper teakettle lid, which my darling M forgot and left empty on top of a high-gas flame (the copper looks as if it had smallpox now); and some sort of shelf beneath the stand on which I've set the printer, a shelf that would hold the box of fanfold paper. Such things. And I have already spent part of the morning—of April 17, '85, a Wednesday—at Entre, the shop where I bought the IBM PC jr., on which I learned to use the word processor. In another hour from now I leave, or rather, M will drive me in the car to Dr. David B, my rheumatologist, for a general checkup and the renewal of a few prescriptions, Percodan, mainly, a strong analgesic, which requires a new prescription each time renewed. So the day is and is about to be spent, and I shall scarcely have to get done with this disagreeable incident, alas, more than disagreeable: odious.

The damned things that happen to innocence, or ignorance, in the slums, that happen in alien slums, in heterogeneous ones, that probably might not have happened in homogeneous ones, at least, so I fancy, in ones dominated by orthodoxy, like the East Side, or by folkways, like Little Italy. And of course, they wreak havoc with the personality. That does not exclude similar traumatic episodes that may affect scions of the middle-class or the wealthy; given the terrible vulnerability, impressionableness of pubescence that exempts no one from irreparable damage at that period in life. I wonder how such things are dealt with in China, the Soviet Union, in other socialist states?

I am grateful for this electronic device. My gratitude should be extended or generalized into gratitude for modern science or technology (I write this the following day), despite the detractors of modern science and technology, such as one whose pronouncements I read recently, whose name I have forgotten for the moment but it is well known, who seems able to solve the Joycean three-dimensional crossword puzzle with relative ease, but referred to the personal computer as so much expensive junk cluttering up the house — or words to that effect. The gentleman doesn't know what he's talking about. The short period of discipline necessary to gain sufficient control over the device has repaid itself immeasurably (nor do I believe I speak for myself only); it has made possible a new — or renewed — bond between the one who would express his feelings and thoughts and the vehicle for that expression.

Even the preliminary fussing, sometimes less, sometimes more, required to set the "machinery" in motion: the slightly disconcerting message of "BOOT FAILURE," or even when all goes well, the routine requests for time and date and the need to answer them, the ascertaining of the number of "bytes" still available on the disk, provide a warming-up process for the mind as well, for the incomparably more subtle organic computer in front of the electronic one. What is man's future? One cannot help asking oneself, coming away from radio dispatches of battles between two Moslem sects in Lebanon, leaving some fifty dead and three times that number wounded — at the same time as men in space dramatically attempt, though they fail, to reactivate a nonfunctioning satellite. Will man's cortex prevail over his hypothalamus?

And so many other notions, considerations, come up between the writer and his narrative, beginning in the morning, notions drifting through the mind, as M helps her rheumatically wracked husband sit up in bed, plants a morning kiss of affirmation on a brow, grotesque, I'm sure, in its graphic signals of pain: What to do about all those people, all those "characters" I have introduced here, dealt with, whose ends I know, and others to come, whom I have survived in the flesh and won't in the narrative; and of the years I shall never live to deal with, nor care to, for that matter, years following my marriage to M, years in machine shops and tool rooms during the Second World War, years, vicissitudes in Maine, and the four-year tenure of employment in a psychiatric hospital in Augusta, the years spent raising waterfowl, the years of M's and my ludicrous, bitter summer seasons with our pathetic, feckless, impossible tenant: Pop, my father . . . years that I shall not have time for, that I shall not have time to attempt to render into literary form. M (who is at her desk this moment writing music—to meet a deadline: that of submitting it to her coach this coming Saturday)—M is all about me, M is part and parcel of my consciousness. She is part and parcel of the trials and tribulations of my attaining to my present consciousness. She, more than anyone, confers the kind of purpose that holds me to my task as a writer; she imbues me with a sense of worth, and above all, unity, a mighty fortress that defends the present from the past.

XXXI

Two streams of urine flowed in an intertwining chain down obscure door and jamb, dripped to gritty threshold. "You got a piss hard-on, ain't ye?" Weasel observed.

"Yeah, ye can see? I couldn't help it."

"You pull off a lot?"

"No."

"You don't?"

"No," with slight affront. "What d'ye mean?" Ira was sure he knew what Weasel meant: the same thing last year, on the roof, that Bernie Hausman had tried to show him, the only kid he had ever beaten in a fistfight in Harlem. The same thing Mr. Lennard had tried to make him do. He knew, of course, he knew: that lanky, rusty bum in Fort Tyron Park—against a tree. Oh, he knew.

He knew, Ecclesias, of course he knew.

—But never connected the two, associated the two?

I can vouch that he never did.

—Is it possible?

In his case, yes. We're dealing with someone almost completely autodidactic.

— He wasn't ready for this next phase.

He was and wasn't. It was he who had to provide the inferences that bridged boyhood to puberty, inferences sufficient to support his precocious sensibility. His timbers of mentality and judgment, inference, in a word, were much too slight to sustain so heavy a load of grossly misinformed and disinformed fancy.

"Pull off. Like this." Weasel's demonstration conformed to pattern. "You wanna pull off now?"

"No."

"Me an' Tierny pulls off."

"Yeah?"

"You oughta see him. What a handmade prick he's got. All right?"

"No."

"No. Why? You Jews don't have to go to Confession— Oh, I know: You're fuckin' somebody, aintcha?" Weasel persisted through Ira's silence. "Hanh? Who you fuckin'?"

"You left that fire burning in the tin can up by the sidewalk."

"Dat's nutt'n," Weasel hesitated, became confused by Ira's irrelevance; and when Ira backed away to button his fly, Weasel did the same. "You want one o' my spuds? I got two bakin' in der."

"No. I'm goin' upstairs right away."

"Oh, the navies old and oaken, oh, the Temerairie no more." Random quote, Ira ruminated: epigraph taken from Melville of a poem by Hart Crane. Why did he think of it? The appeal of the rhythm, the mood, the nostalgic purity of ocean and wind? Oh, the ambiguities, ambivalences the writer contended with and had to find his way through to some semblance of coherence. The contradictions, the subterfuges, the concealments — that had to be resorted to: He had refined the sensitivity he had been born with into an instrument capable of noting the weakest ephemerid within his mind, the permissible, the impermissible: Had he been a nineteenth-century novelist, or in fact, a true novelist mirroring the society about him, then so much that pertained to himself he could have projected onto a fictive character, into a fable about others. But alas, trapped in this mode of his own devising, albeit the divorce between present personality and a prior one was unforeseen, he had no alternative but to acknowledge the actuality: his own surge of curiosity to assay the experiment—and its failure.

You see, the whole "evolution" was reversed in my case, Ecclesias. It should have been the other way round, was, if I'm not mistaken, for most adolescents—
    —Very likely.
    I can envisage its development, even given the same set of characters, the same scenario—eliminating improbable fantasy, such as running away from home, an act which this, by now, totally Mama-dependent kid was incapable of. Given his thirteen, fourteen years of age, again all other things being equal, given the same heterogeneous Harlem slum setting, in a word, given the rule, not the devastating exception, then some similitude or "normal" development might still have been possible. You follow me, Ecclesias?
    —I'm afraid I do.
    Yes? Even if all that had happened were eventually to happen, given this cunning, wily, devious—and wholly unscrupulous, treacherous and relentlessly scheming entity—and now without, one must remember, for whatever it was worth, any boundaries in orthodox Judaism, any shorings, stays, restraints, the trauma could not possibly have become so single-minded nor gone so deep, so profoundly determined his behavior . . . so vitiated his character, undermined integrity and decisiveness in deed and opinion.
    And once again, M comes to mind, through that inveterate, nay, chronic fog of my own configuring, sitting there in a navy-blue uniform shirt—a park ranger's perhaps or a game warden's I bought at the flea market for myself, but it proved too small—sitting at her desk immersed in the unaccompanied cello sonata she has been working on, and she speaks now and then of unaccustomed fatigue, she, who, when young,

would often not begin practicing at the piano for hours before eight P.M., speaks of fatigue, good reason for selfish anxiety on my part, that one so fine, so good, of such esteemed American "stock" and first and foremost so sound, should have chosen to join her life with mine, and not without fair insight into the nature of her choice, is—I throw up my hands, Ecclesias.

— You might as well. It's a miracle.

YIDDISH GLOSSARY

Note to the reader: Any item in Yiddish that is explained in the text is not included in the glossary. Hebrew religious terms that are general knowledge—Torah, Talmud, or yarmulka, for example—are also not included.

a brukh uf zeh   a curse on them

a kleege shvartze   a clever black man

a scheinem dank   a handsome thanks

a schlock auf iss   damn them

a shvartz gelekhter   black humor

a shvartz yur   a black year

abee gesindt   as long as you're well

allevai   would that

alter kocker   (vulgarism) old turd

anshuldig mir   pardon me

ausgebrendt, "Ich bin ganz ausgebrendt"   burned out, "I am burned out"

az nisht is nisht   if not, then not

azoi   Is that so?, thus

baruch atoo adonoi   blessed are thou, Lord

baruch ha shem   blessed be the lord

bekheles   cups

bist doch geboyren in Galitzia   nevertheless you were born in Galitzia

bist meshugge   are you crazy

bist tocken a yoldt   you are indeed a fool

blintzes   rolled up pancake with filling

borsht   beet soup

cheder   Hebrew school for boys of pre–Bar Mitzvah age

d'yukst vie a klutz   you move like a log

d'yukst aros de kishkas   you're rushing my guts out

daven   to pray

derma   cow's intestine prepared into a special dish

dreck   trash

dumkopf   dumb head

erlikh   pious

ess   eat

fartz, fortz   fart

feiner   better

ferstest   understand

folentzer   lazy person

freg nisht   don't ask

g'vir   man of great strength

ganz   wholly

geh mir in d'red   "go get buried," or "go to hell"

geh mir in kaiver   go into your tomb

geldt   money, gold

genuk   enough

gerara   Yinglish for "get out of here"

gesheft   business

geshrigen   cried

gib dikh a rick   move

glatt kosher fressen   eating kosher

gliklikh   lucky

golem   dolt, monster

goniff   thief

gott sei dank   thank god

gottinyoo   dear god

goy   gentile

goyim   gentiles

Haggadah   the text of the Passover ceremony

havdallah   end of the sabbath

Ich bin dir moichel   spare me

Ich khom mikh bepisht   I wet my pants

iz a feiner mensh   he's a fine person

Kadish v'yiskadaish, shmai raboh   The first line of the prayer for the dead

kaiver   tomb

kamerad   surrender (German—"friend")

kein ein n'horreh   avert the evil eye

kharoses   bitter herbs used at Passover

kharuseh   repented

khukhim   wise person

khumish   study of Hebrew

khunter   (vulgarism) "cunt," whore

khupah   the marriage canopy

kiddush ha shem   in honor of the lord

kindt "mein kindt"   son, "my child"

kishka   stomach

kleege   clever

kolkie   bullet

kupf   head

kreplach   a stuffed pasta-like dish like ravioli

l'chaim   to life

lemakh   clumsy person

lotkehs   pancakes

lushen koidish   holy tongue

lyupka   love (Polish)

makher   big wheel

malamut   Hebrew teacher

malkhumah   war

mamaleh   dear mother

matzah(s)   unleavened bread

mazel tov   luck

mein oormeh mann   my poor husband

mensh   man

mishigoss   madness

mishpokha family
mominyoo dear mother
mujik Russian peasant
nu well
oy gewald cry havoc
pavollyeh slow
Pesach Passover
peyoth earlocks
pishkeh alms-box
pogrom an organized assault on Jews
s' toigt shoyn uf a kapura it is worth a sacrifice; not worth much
schmaltz fat
sehr gut very good
selah be it so
seltzer cust geldt seltzer costs money
shabbes b'nakcht sabbath eve
shamevdick bashful
shehtl wig
shicker drunk
shicker auf toit he's dead drunk
shiksas Gentile girls
shlakht haus slaughter-house
shlemiel an ill-fated person; a bungler
shlep, shleppen carry, pull
shlemazl a person with continued bad luck, an unfortunate
shmoolyaris, shmoolyareh dollars
shnorer moocher
shoyn already
shrotchkee diarrhea
shtickel a bit

shul synagogue
shvartze black; African-American
sit a sakh helfin that will help a lot
sit balt sein du a malkhumah there'll be a war here soon
siz a manseh mit a bear it's a story with a bear (fairy tale)
sollst khoppen a krenck catch the plague
tata, tateh father
tocken indeed
tov good
treife non-kosher food
tsuris troubles
uhmein amen
verbrent burned out
verflukhteh damned
verfollen zoll er vie e likt may he rot where he lies
vershtinkeneh foul
v'im lo akhsav, matai? if not now, when?
vunderbar wonderful
vus i'dis what's that
vus heist what does it mean
vus yuksteh why are you rushing
Yaponchikis Japanese
yeled boy
Yeet Jew
yiddishkeit the world of the Jews, Jewry
yingotch overgrown youth
yingle little youth
yoldt fool
yuksteh to rush
zvicker pince-nez glasses

ABOUT THE AUTHOR

Henry Roth was born in the village of Tysmenitz, in the then Austro-Hungarian province of Galitzia in 1906. Although his parents never agreed on the exact date of his arrival in the United States, it is most likely that he landed at Ellis Island in 1909 and began his life in New York. He first lived on the Lower East Side, in the slums where his best-selling novel *Call It Sleep* is set. In 1914, the family moved to Harlem, first to the Jewish section on 114th Street east of Park Avenue; but because the three rooms there were "in the back" and the isolation reminded his mother of the sleepy hamlet of Veljish where she grew up, she became depressed and the family moved to the non-Jewish 119th Street. Roth lived there until 1927, when as a junior at City College of New York, he moved in with the New York University professor and poet Eda Lou Walton. With Walton's support, he began *Call It Sleep*, which he completed in the spring of 1934, and which was published in December of 1934 to mixed reviews. He contracted for a second novel with the editor Maxwell Perkins, of Scribners, the first section of which appeared as a work in progress. But Roth's growing ideological frustration and confusion with the character of his second novel, a Communist proletarian, created a profound writer's block, which lasted until 1979 when he began *Mercy of a Rude Stream.*

In 1938, during a unproductive sojourn at the artists' colony
Yaddo in Saratoga Springs, New York, Roth met Muriel Parker, a
pianist and composer. They soon fell in love; Roth severed his
relationship with Walton, and married Parker in 1939. With the
onset of the war, Roth became a tool and gauge maker. The couple
moved first to Boston with their young sons, and then in 1946
moved to Maine. There Roth worked as a woodsman, a school-
teacher, a psychiatric attendant in the state mental hospital, a waterfowl farmer, and a sometime Latin and math tutor. With the
paperback reprinting of *Call It Sleep* in 1964, the block slowly began
to break. In 1968, the couple moved to Albuquerque, New Mexico,
after a short stay at the D. H. Lawrence ranch, where Roth was
writer-in-residence. Muriel began composing music again, mostly
for individual instruments, for which she received ample recognition. After her death in 1990, from congestive heart failure, Roth
has occupied himself with revising the final volumes of the monumental *Mercy of a Rude Stream.* In the spring of 1994, Henry Roth
received two honorary doctorates, one from the University of New
Mexico and one from the Hebrew Theological Institute in
Cincinnati.